Dr. Lesh

POWER HOUSE
WREN LEE

*Self published
in Grade 8
WPGA.*

Power House

Arranged by Carl Lemer and edited by Annushka Agarwal and Shae Wakabayashi

Library and Archives Canada Cataloguing in Publication

Lee, Wren
Power House / Wren Lee.

Issued in print and electronic formats.
ISBN 978-1-7750210-3-2

I. Title

Cover art by Helene Åsén
stormyscrapbox.tumblr.com

Published in Canada

Andrew

"Topaz."

I'm so happy! I feel like I haven't seen her in forever. I hold her tightly in my arms.

"Andrew." She's smiling, or at least I think she is behind the mask she usually wears.

"Tonnerre, are we friends?"

"O-of course."

"Then... why?" she whispers.

"W-what?"

"Why didn't you save me?" I can feel tears trickle down from her eyes. She pushes me away and looks at me sadly.

"Why didn't you protect me?" She's turning red, there's blood on her costume and she looks weak, limp. Her head hangs like she's ashamed of me.

"We were friends, maybe even more. Why didn't you save me?"

"I... I... I-"

"I. Died. Because. Of. You." She looks at me harshly, the yellow eyes of her mask boring into my heart.

"N-no, wait!" I stammer.

"Don't you even try to deny it!" She falls backwards limply. I can't catch her.

I wake up screaming and in tears. I'm used to it, but my family is worried. They try to send me to a therapist at least once a week. I still go out on patrol but it's not the same without her. It's like there's no point, like swimming without water. The news calls me brutal, but I can't help it.

I've already graduated from high school, but I lost contact with everyone, and I'm sure Aaron hates me. I can't blame anyone. She changed me for the somewhat better, and then she died. Right. In. Front. Of. Me. Imagine the person you love most in the world, in your arms, lifeless and cold.

***

I can't go back to sleep, not after a dream like that. It's only one o'clock, so I can head out on patrol for a while before the sun comes up. Over the past year, I changed my costume. The new one is all black with a white X on the chest and back. The old one reminded me too much of her.

There's no crime. No muggers, no arsonists, nothing. I guess I scared them all off. You accidentally break one guy's leg, and suddenly everyone is scared of you. She would understand, but she can't anymore.

It's started to rain lightly; her favourite weather. The roofs are becoming wet and slick. I should probably head back. But not before I pay my respects. I do it every night after patrol.

I land in front of the bronze statue the city commissioned of Topaz and me. They put it in the park I used to hang out with the guys in. But I never go near it during daylight.

"Hey, Topaz." I look into her bronze eyes, destroyed by the crude slices on the statue. That makes two of us.

"It's been really hard without you. It's like there's no point," I sigh. I miss her so, so much.

"I'd do anything to get you back," I whisper, and step forward, my boots clunking against the cemented ground.

"If you'd just give me a sign or something..." I wait patiently, staring at the statue like I have every day since she died. I stand there for hours. As usual, nothing happens. Just rain.

"How could you do this to me? To your best friend?" I say quietly, looking away from the statue.

"To the guy who loves you?" I say, a bit louder. I can feel tears streaming down my face, hot and angry, mixing with the rain. It's strangely satisfying.

"You must think I'm pretty pathetic, right? One bad thing happens and I just break?" I look back into the eyes of the statue.

"You would be so strong, you'd move right on and shrug it off. You wouldn't hold onto the past." I lean against the statue.

2

"I can only say 'I love you' to your statue. I shouldn't have even wasted time. I should've told you as soon as I felt that way. Would have, could have, should have..." I start walking away.

I sigh. "I think this will be the last night, so goodbye. Thanks for everything." But deep down, I know I'll be back.

Rikki

Hi. I'm French (yay!), I'm sixteen (yay!), and I'm pretty awesome (yay!). Of course, there are some drawbacks to being this fabulous. They mostly revolve around the giant the giant target I've got on my back. And the few dozen people who are thirsty for my awesome blood.

I used to live in the American city of San Francisco (I can still almost taste the American cheeseburgers and smell the patriotism in the air). But I've moved back to the crazy prices of Paris. Mainly because I 'died' in San Francisco (Not so yay).

A lot of stuff has happened since I was last in San Francisco. I read some of the online news. The good guy is gone, and some other guy called Tonnerre took his place. He's an idiot. He isn't French at all. Just his name, Tonnerre, which is French for thunder. Pure idiot, am I right?

He's brutal. He broke a guy's legs. But I'm not going back, there are too many bad memories. I was stabbed in the heart. I was what most medical professionals would call 'dead'. But I've decided not to dwell on that since the first day of my last year of high school is today.

"Rikki, is that what you're wearing?" Willow says, pointing at my loose pants, untucked button-up, oversized sweater, and blue sneakers.

"Yes?" I say, smiling innocently at her.

"No, no, no!" She snaps her fingers and takes a step towards me.

I book it out the door, down the stairs, through the lobby, into the street.

English isn't my native language, so Willow really helps me out with that. I do still try as hard as I can to fit in with any other English-speakers though.

Willow's a year older than me and we go to different schools. I go to a French speaking school, she goes to a bilingual one.

She cut her hair to annoy her brother, Andrew (who is two years older). I've met him once. He's okay, though he pushed me into a fountain and ruined all my drawings when I was in grade nine. Technically he's our landlord. Originally, Willow wanted it for herself but since she's only seventeen, she can't. Her brother officially owns it for the next year and a half. Her family wanted her to have a job so she told them she did real estate. I give her five hundred euros a month to prove it.

I walk briskly through the park that separates me from my school. I pat the bag bouncing at my hip, where I packed my books and outdated laptop. I just make it to the lobby before a piercing bell rings through the corridors.

As the bell rings, I launch into a full sprint to reach my class. It's like M.C. Escher designed the school. After failing twice to burst into class A-12, I finally rush into the correct class.

"Rikki Dubois?" my advisor asks in French.

"Here!" I yell, tripping on the door frame but quickly recovering. A bunch of people snicker. Oh well, let them laugh. I take a seat at the back of the class.

Did I mention the rather large prophecy to occur in which when I turn seventeen I'm supposed to become 'the ultimate evil'? Yeah, there's that too.

***

School's going pretty great. It turns out being chased by bullies is a great way to lose calories. They're really persistent.

I take a sharp turn down a hallway, and another and another. I reach a dead end covered with doors. It's like that door scene that's in old cartoons. I pick the one on my right. I slide in as quickly as I can, slam it shut and sit inside the room beside the doors. I let my breath out. The doors slam open again centimetres from my face. My body completely freezes.

"Hey, science dweebs, seen a short scholarship wimp around here? She owes us lunch." I may have tripped over their bags and spilt their lunches. On purpose.

I look around the room. There are actually people in it, looking about as confused as I am.

"No, we haven't seen any leprechauns," a tallish, raven haired boy wearing safety goggles says. "Also, we're in STEM club, not science club. There's a difference, you know, even if you're too stupid to know it, so why don't you leave?" he says and points to the door. They grunt and walk out.

"Are they gone?" I whisper.

"No, they're right behind you," he says, his voice filled with sarcasm. "What do you think? Of course, they're gone." He slides the safety glasses up on to his forehead.

"Well, sorry for intruding in on your little club," I say, matching his tone, I pick up my bag and get ready to leave. "By the way, that equation-" I point at their whiteboard on wheels, "won't work with that amount of salt. Just a forewarning. The results can be a little... explosive." Chemistry mic drop. Bam. I walk out of the room with a little hop in my step.

"Wait, sorry, maybe we could use your expertise in chemistry," I turn to the new person speaking. He's blonde and tall.

"Science, technology, engineering, mathematics club? I'd love to join, but I don't think your club members would approve." I glare at the original boy.

"No, you can-"

"Baron, wait, she needs to pass our test!"

"Oh god, guys, please, no!"

"What test?" I ask. Classic me. Of course I would ask.

"Hi." A second boy shows up. He looks identical to the first one

"What?" I blurt out, accidentally in English. I curse myself. When I try to fit in with my own people, I should use our language.

"What was that?"

"Oh, I speak a little English." I smile at them awkwardly, switching back to French.

"Anyway, I'm sure the twins would let you join if the rest of the STEM club is okay with it," Baron continues, glaring at the twins. Twins, right. That makes sense.

"Nah, it's okay, I just need a few more materials anyway," I say and flap my hand through the air. "What are you making, anyway?"

"A growth acceleration formula. Bye!" The original raven-haired twin smirks. I smile widely at him and walk out. No harm in being 'friendly'.

***

I sit at my desk. The room's empty since most people go home for lunch break. I don't have anything to eat. I can't run out to the nearest café before school and my apartment's too far away to take the subway there and back in time for class. I take out my phone and earbuds. I'll listen to some music until class begins again.

The door creaks open. One of the raven-haired twins steps through with a sorry look on his face.

"What do you want?" I glare at him sourly.

"They wanted me to apologise, so, sorry."

"Idiot." I mumble as I watch the clock on the front of the dark classroom.

"What was that?"

"I was just complimenting you on your brilliance."

"You don't need to be so rude."

"Really? I'm not trying to be rude." I paint my face into an earnest expression. He scowls at me, but I just smile in response.

"Listen, would you just join STEM club?" he says, exasperated.

"Why should I?"

"If you're not lying about that growth acceleration formula, you could save lives!"

"I know I could." Literally, I saved lives at night. I was a superhero. One of the best.

"Then... why don't you join?"

"You didn't want me to."

"Okay, I want you to join, is that enough for you?" He's getting a little agitated.

"If you wanted me to join, it's not as fun. Plus, you don't even know my name." I smirk.

"So?"

"You can't invite me to join your club formally." I stand up, turn on my heel and walk out. I turn that little conversation around in

7

my mind. Though my comeback sounded really snarky then, it's now sounding more and more stupid. Maybe I was a bit brash. Or not.

***

Marianne is going to fire me if I'm late again! Why am I so slow?

I work as a waitress for a French food company and it's pretty similar to when I worked at the Capricorn Café. It caters and serves like they do.

I pass the Eiffel Tower on my commute to my job. I smile at all the tourists snapping pictures and even wave at some of them, though none of them notice. I'm used to it. Sometimes it feels as though I never came back at all, like I'm just a ghost.

***

I burst through the door of the crumbling black bricked café.

"Am I late?"

"Rikki?" Marianne, my mentor, sits up, startled.

"Hi, sorry!" I let out my breath.

"Honey, there's an event tomorrow night, can you make it?"

"Um, yeah, I don't have anything to wear though. Will they supply the clothes?" I have no pretty clothes.

"Yes, just show up here at six, got it?"

"Yes, ma'am!"

"Good, you can go do your homework or whatever,"

"Thanks! See you later, Mrs. Moreau!"

"No problem, just don't be late."

"Have I ever been?" I walk backwards through the door. She just sighs.

I go straight from the Sèvres subway station and turn left at Barthélémy Road and then I'm home.

I trudge into the lobby, press the key combination, and walk up the stairs. I stuff my key into the hole and shove it open.

"Rikki!" Willow wraps me in a hug.

"Hey, Will," My English is a little squeaky after speaking French the whole day. I usually only speak English with Willow.

"Are you alright?"

8

"I am fine," I fake a yawn, "but a little tired, so I think I will go and hit the hay, or whatever stupid metaphors you Americans have for sleep."

I walk up the stairs into my room and lean against the inside of the door, I drop to a seat and relax.

I notice a wrapped item on my desk. My feet tap excitedly as I walk over to it, there's no note, so it couldn't be Willow, who leaves ridiculous notes for me. I tear open the plain brown paper cautiously. I cannot tell you how many times I've opened a package to have it explode in my face.

A black fabric slips out onto my wood floor easily, like silk. I bend down to pick it up and a note hits me square in the face.

> Embrace who you truly are,
> Make choices while you can,
> Love only those you trust,
> Trust only those you love.

I hesitate, then pick up the fabric. It's a suit, kind of similar to the one I used to wear, except that it's smaller and has built in mask. But I *liked* looking like a horror movie reject. I wonder how well it works. Only one way to find out.

***

"Woo-hoo!" I scream as I jump through the air. A light breeze hits my face as I soar through air. A lump of nostalgia builds in my throat with the feeling of slicing through the air.

I land on a lamppost and swing on it like a fire pole. The costume fits perfectly, maybe even a little loosely. It's a little creepy. Whoever sent it knew my size.

I leap back up a building and stop just short of an alley. The horizon is a little more difficult to grapple over, but it's worth it.

To my surprise, I notice a guy pointing a gun at a rather well-dressed man. I jump down just in front of the guy and fall down in front of him with a stupid grin. Everything feels the same but so different at the same time.

9

My landing was not as good as it could have been. "Aie! That hurt a *lot* more than I thought it would!" I breathe and mutter a few swears. I stand up quickly, grab my leg quickly and wince from the pain.

"What the hell?" he yells as he shakes the gun at me.

"Didn't your mother ever tell you how rude it is to point things at people?" I tease him in French.

He pushes the gun closer to my eyes and continues to shake it. "I'll shoot you if you don't tell me who you are!"

I look at the victim, and he's holding a phone and is shakily filming me then I look back at the guy with the gun.

"No! I'm deadly allergic to steel coated lead! Mercy! Please, don't take them out of the gun!" I fall to my knees and hold my hands together in front of the man with the gun. He looks at the man with the phone then back at me.

"Are you being serious?"

"Oh, of course not," I laugh as I spring up and kick his hand. The gun falls to the ground slides to the feet of the victim.

"Sorry! I meant to kick the gun! I'm kind of new to this." I say apologetically. I look at the now gunless man, who is really more of a boy.

"You should probably put some ice on that," I nod from underneath my scarf.

"What are you?" He asks and holds his hand tightly.

"That's easy," I snap my fingers and look back at him like they do on TV. "I think I'm a superhero. Unless I got things terribly wrong and in fact you were actually defending yourself and- "

"I'm fine, thank you!" the guy with the phone says in my ear.

"Well that's *wonderful*." I swivel over to face him on my heel. "Mr. Mugger, why don't you apologise to the man?"

"Sorry," he stammers, probably in awe of my awesome, practical, and slightly creepy suit complete with the standard grey scarf.

"N-no problem," stutters the victim as he looks down at the gun at his feet. I reach down and pick it up.

"Wait a minute, there aren't even any bullets in this! I put on that 'I'm allergic to bullets' act for nothing!" I yell and glare at the mugger.

"Sorry?"

"Go and walk yourself to the police station." I frown and point out of the alley towards the Luxor Obelisk where they used to have the guillotine (I don't mean that he has to be executed!) and where the nearest police station is.

"Do I have to?"

"Yes!" the man with the phone screams in my ear.

I let the mugger go, he walks quickly out of the alley and hopefully to the nearest police headquarters.

"Was that it? I think it was. Okay, then, uh, bye?" I climb up the building's fire escape, then turn back to the man. "Try not to die."

I wait till the man wobbles out of the dark alley with his phone before I start celebrating.

"Hell, yeah!" I shout. "That was awesome!" I pump my fists through the air. Rikki Dubois is back and better than ever, world!

Andrew

"C'est un superhero! Elle est Corbelle!"

"To translate, the man filming the video announces 'She's Corbelle!' Does this mean Paris has a new superhero? Tell us what you think at 1-800-XRADIO!"

I turn the TV off. So what if Paris has a new hero? It's not like she's going to come here, so what does it matter? She's getting more attention than Topaz got when she died. This 'Corbelle' is just an attention-seeking kid.

My phone rings. I pick it up hesitantly.

"Hey, Andrew! How's my favourite brother?" It's Willow, my younger sister.

"He's tired." I rub my forehead and eyes. I pulled another allnighter last night.

"Well, you need to stop by for a visit."

"Why?"

"I turn eighteen in a few months so I want all the papers in order to take over this place, and Rikki's working hard so she can get into Ivy League." She sounds impatient.

"Okay, when do you need me to be there?"

"Tonight."

"What? I'll have to be at the airport in half an hour. I'll have to leave right now."

"Okay. Then go. Just be here by ten o'clock, tonight." She hangs up abruptly.

I grab my keys. I don't need anything else, I can buy the things I need in Paris.

Actually... I'll bring my costume. I'll check on this kid Corbelle, give her some 'advice' and make her stop.

Rikki

I step out of bed. Last night was fun. All I need now is a dumb blonde partner. I smile to myself.

The smell of food drifts up from downstairs. Is Willow awake already?

I walk down the stairs.

"Willow?" I rub my bleary eyes and comb a hand through my loose hair.

"Oh, sorry Rikki, did I wake you?" she coos, hovering over a pan full of bacon and eggs.

"No, what were you doing?"

"Just talking to Andrew. He's coming over tonight."

"Oh, what time?" I ask, clearly not processing her words.

"Ten." She says, still not moving from her popping and sizzling pan.

"Tonight?"

"Yeah. Is that a problem?"

"Maybe. I am working tonight."

"Ooh, are you doing the charity ball?"

"Maybe. Marianne just told me, in her usual gruff style, to just be here by six."

"In that case, I think I'll go. I want to see you in a cute dress!"

I look at the clock. "I need to get going if I do not want to be late for school."

"You work really hard, you know, Rikki. You need a break." Her concern breaks out from her façade of makeup. Hesitantly, she asks, "How are you in the man market? Anyone you like?"

I roll my eyes at her. She knows I've had literally one date in my life.

"No," I say, and lurch for the door, but she counters.

"Ooh, you do! Who? Who?" She cackles excitedly. I look at my feet and roll my eyes.

"I do not! I honestly do not like anyone!"

"Then go on a date with my brother! He's also single."

"I am going to be late for school. I have to get going."

"Nice try! We're talking about this later," she says laughing.

I sigh. There's no way I'm avoiding this.

***

Rumours of Paris's new superhero have been sprinting up throughout the morning. But Corbelle? What kind of name is Corbelle? Why couldn't it have been something like 'The Shadow' or 'Phantom'? Something cool, not Corbelle. I'm not some bird. Birds are stupid little things that fly into windows (though I've totally done that before). They're like miniature versions of Tonnerre.

I smile in spite of myself as I take out my books for science. The twins walk in, and my smile fades just as theirs do. They take seats as far away from me as possible. I set my bag down beside my chair.

"Hey, look! It's the scholarship wimp!" the redheaded ringleader of a group of girls squeals. "Are you wearing that to school? Don't you have any respect for our school?"

"Do you have any self-respect? Just look at what you're wearing." I turn away and focus on my books. Saying that was a bad idea. The girl is Lilith Boucher, the 'it girl', and she's just going to get the same guys as yesterday to chase after me.

"But Kaden, she could be a great asset to our club, see?" The second twin whispers. I loosen my grip on my textbook and anxiously listen to what they're saying about me.

"I just-she doesn't seem right."

"Yeah, but look at what she just said to Lilith."

I smile as I listen to their whispers about me.

***

At lunch, I stroll over to the STEM club's room.

"Oh, hey," Baron greets me.

"Decided to join?" the raven-haired twins ask in unison.

"Not quite."

"I don't think I've introduced you to everyone yet," Baron says, "This is Sebastien," He points to a boy programming a small robot. "He represents the 'T' in our name." He takes me over to a small bridge.

14

"Normand?"

"What, Baron?" A guy with tanned skin crawls out from underneath a table and looks at me. "Is this the girl you were talking about?"

He holds his hand out, winks and smiles, "Normand Chevalier."

I shake his hand, "Rikki Dubois."

The twins spring up from whatever they were working on.

"A lovely name," one says and kisses my hand. "I'm Kaden. Kaden Mace."

"Are you designing a bridge?" I make a big deal of turning away as I face Normand again.

"Yes! I'm using basic materials to test how strong they are."

"And I'm Kai Mace." The second twin shoves Normand out of the way to shake my hand awkwardly.

Baron drags me over to a tall guy in the corner reading a book. "And last but not least, Marvielle!"

"What's up?" the boy grunts from the corner

"So, this is your club?" I ask.

"Yeah, this is about all of us."

The twins pop up in front of me smiling evilly.

"Rikki of Dubois, you are hereby invited to join our club of Science, Technology, Engineering, and Mathematics," they say in synch with each other. "Do you accept our invitation?"

"Umm, sure?"

"Wonderful." They are a bit too creepy, I think.

"Umm, what?" I ask as I slowly edge towards the door. Marvielle gets up and walks out the door. I tail him out quickly.

"They're really not that bad... they just don't have a lot of social interactions with others," Marvielle apologizes for them. He walks away, leaving me alone in the hallway.

"What?" I call after him.

***

I walk in the door out of breath.

"H-hi Marianne!"

"You're late," she grumbles.

"No, I'd be late if I ran in the door a minute later, it's only five-fifty-nine."

"Okay, okay! Your clothes are over there. Go change." She points at a bench with a blouse and black pants neatly folded on it.

"Thanks." I pick them up and change in the bathroom and adjust my tight bun. The clothes fit fine, although the blouse is a little loose. It suits me better like that anyway. I walk out.

"Rikki, you look fantastic," Nadine says.

"Thanks, Nadine, you look great too!" A lot of my coworkers start showing up. Marianne scolds all of them for being late.

She sits us all down to have a talk, "Alright, who wants to serve hors d'oeuvres?"

Nadine and I put our hands up.

"Okay, Rikki and Nadine," she says, marking her clipboard, "Anyone else?"

A few others including Pierre, the guy Nadine likes, raise their hands.

It's Pierre who drives us over to the courtyard where the ball is being held; he and Nadine sit together in the front seats.

In the courtyard, I admire the fairy lights dotting the trees and lampposts. The area is cordoned off with black rope. Benches exclusively for the rich and those working for them sit around the premises. A table full of food is set up in the middle of the garden.

I pick up a plate of mini-tarts I'm supposed to offer to people. Guests arrive so I have to lower (and in some cases, elevate) the tray to them so they can take whatever looks good.

I see Willow walk in. She's wearing a fluffy cloud-blue dress that matches her eyes and could probably pay for my rent two times over. She looks stunning and draws a bunch of the boys' stares.

"Rikki!" she squeals and hugs me.

"Be careful! If I spill this, I will lose my job."

"But then you could just work for me!"

"But then I would have to pay your rent as well, and I do not think your family likes me. Also, I like this job very much."

16

"Well, they wouldn't have to like you. You'd work for me, not them. When you work for me, you wouldn't have to pay rent!"

"That sounds amazing, but your family still hates me."

"Well, maybe my parents, but why would Andrew hate you?"

"He pushed me into a fountain and ruined all my drawings when I was fourteen."

"He did what?" Willow smashes her fist into her hand. "Oh, he is going to suffer for that." She looks very intimidating. I shrink a couple of centimeters next to her.

"It is okay, Willow. That was three years ago, he is probably different. I doubt he even remembers."

"Yeah, but now you never make art anymore,"

"Yes, because I do not have anything to work with." I roll my eyes at her.

"I'll be right back."

"What?" She strides off in her usual manner and holds up the base of her crystal ball gown.

"Willow?"

I feel a hand land on my shoulder, I look back and am about to flip the person off my shoulder before I realise who it is. I smoothly switch to French.

"Hey, Rikki!"

"Oh, hey Baron."

"What are you doing here? You didn't strike me as a rich socialite."

"I work for Le Grand Gourmet. What are you doing here?"

"I'm a rich socialite," he says, and laughs.

"Of course you are." My eyes do a barrel roll at how obvious it is.

"So, what have you got there?"

"Petites tartes. They're little pie tins filled with coloured filling. Is it really that hard?"

"Mind if I sample?"

"It's kind of my job to serve them, so no, I guess I don't mind." Nadine walks up to me, nudges me and winks. I scowl in her direction.

"Who was that?" Baron asks, clearly oblivious that Nadine thinks that we're an item.

"A co-worker," I grumble.

"She's cute. Think you can get me her number?"

"Sorry, there's already a guy she likes, and I'm the president of their Fan Club."

"Cute." He smiles and looks back down at me.

"Me?" I raise an eyebrow.

"What? It's true, we all agree."

"After knowing me for two days? You've been discussing this?" Is this what they do with their club time? Discuss how cute their peers are? This isn't a girl group. Yet.

"Even Marvielle," he nods.

"What even makes me cute? I'm a sarcastic teenager, when did that make me cute?"

"I think it's mainly your size."

"It's not my fault I'm vertically challenged!" I throw my open hand in the air, nearly whapping him on the head.

"Hmmm." He grabs a glass of champagne. He sips it loudly.

"That's champagne," I tell him. He takes a larger sip, making sure to slurp in my face.

"So, am I in the club?"

"Yes, of course you are. How could we refuse someone as cute as you?"

***

"Ooh, who was that?" Willow nudges me slyly.

"A friend!" English. Again. Because why would someone like Willow, who is completely able to learn a second language, and who lives in France which is a French speaking country learn French?

"That was a little quick."

"You are not the first one who thought we were an item," I grumble.

"Let me guess. Nadine?"

"Yes," I sigh.

"I'm telling you, that girl doesn't sit right with me. You shouldn't trust her too much, okay?"

"Keep your friends close and your enemies closer. Willow, I will be fine, I'm French."

"Just be careful. Oh, yeah! I got you this!" She holds a heavy plastic bag to my face. Inside it is a new sketchbook, pens, paints, and pencils. Expensive ones, too.

"What's this? Willow, how much was this? I need to pay you back."

"No, no, your rent paid for this!"

"What do you mean?"

"I took the pay from your rent, two-hundred euros this month."

"What? No, Willow, I will pay for these, here, just let me get my next paycheck so I can pay you back. And that is not how that works."

"No! Then I'll have to keep deducting your rent! I know how much that upsets you!"

"Willow, you are too nice! You are not going to survive in this world!"

"No, I don't think you're going to survive. Rikki, come on, you need to find someone. You know Andrew is single."

"No! I am fine, really!"

"So, you still care that he pushed you in a fountain!"

"What? No! I am over that, really!"

"So, then you'll go on a date with him?"

"What-" She puts a finger over my lips.

"It's okay, I know." She walks off without another word. What have I gotten myself into?

Andrew

I sit in the cab watching the horizon of Paris whip by. It's dark out, but everything is lit with a glow. This is the city Topaz was born in, her hometown. I smile. Even though she may not be with me now, I have a little piece of her with me.

Willow cares a lot less for me than she did when I was still in school. She would jump on my bed to wake me, and she would hug me. Now she either ignores me or yells at me, not that I'm not used to it. I yell at myself a lot.

That reminds me, I should have a little talk with that 'Corbelle'. I doubt she even knows what she's doing. She's probably just some kid, too loud and reckless. She should try being more like Topaz.

Rikki

Willow decided she would drive me home after the party. I could drive myself home, but it would technically be illegal without a driver's licence. Which is nearly impossible to get without some form of birth certificate. Which I don't have.

"Isn't Andrew coming tonight?" I ask her.

"Yeah, he has a key." She pauses. "I think."

"Oh, that is no good, is it?"

"Probably not."

We drive by the apartment. A blonde guy sitting outside the lobby. Willow flings open the door and cries out.

"Andrew!" She pulls him into a hug, he pushes her off.

"Hey, Willow." He nods at me. "Rikki?"

"Yes." I give him a little wave. I wouldn't be able to pick him out of a crowd either.

Willow grabs his ear, "So, what was this about pushing Rikki into a fountain and scaring her creativity away?"

"What?"

"Willow!" I grab her arm. "It does not matter."

"I think you at least deserve an apology."

"It is okay Willow, really." I fake a yawn. "I am really tired anyway. I am going to go to bed."

"Okay, but in the morning-"

"Willow, let it go."

"Fine, g'night."

"Bonsoir." I wave my hand in the air like I'm waving someone off or flipping them off. Both of which I'd do to Andrew Smithe.

I buzz the keypad and walk up the stairs. I open our door and go up to my room, my door locks slowly. I change into my suit. It's superhero time!

I need a better catchphrase.

***

I sit on the needle of the Eiffel Tower. I've never been able to do this in public. The view is beautiful, especially when it's dark like this; all the buildings are lit up. It's like Paris is covered with fallen stars. I sit there, enjoying the breeze for a few minutes.

I run across the rooftops near the Musée des Archives Nationales until an alarm goes off, the blaring sound echoing off the rooftops. I swoop down and land gracefully on one of the museum's many window ledges. I force the window open and jump through. The sound of the alarm bounces off the darkened walls. I follow them to a door that leads me to an empty basement. Whoever was here is long gone. They were good too, no traces or hints. There are people shouting outside. The door gets kicked open. Splinters of wood fly by my face.

"On the ground!" a woman yells in French.

"Whoa, whoa, whoa! Hold on officers. We're on the same side here. Plus, the ground is covered with rat feces," I say holding my hands in front of me. A couple of officers lift their feet to check for rodent poop on their shoes.

"On the ground!"

"Here's the thing: I can't. If I do, you'll take my mask, and you are not prepared for the stunning ugliness that will follow. Trust me, I know."

"On the ground!" About a dozen officers are shaking loaded handguns at me.

"Look, I'd give you an autograph, but I don't have a pen," I gesture behind me. "I'll go get one."

I run in that direction, but it's no use. It's a dead end.

"Listen! I recommend you all close your eyes right now and not because I'm about to show you my face!" I warn them.

A bullet hits the wall a foot away from me.

"Whoa! Trigger finger! That could have hit my face and I've only got one of these!" I point to my mask. "I need my mask for my face and I need my face for all sorts of face related stuff!" I say. "You know what, this has been fun and all, but I need to get going, I'm just your friendly neighbourhood- uh." Do I even have a name? "Never mind who I am!" I laugh awkwardly.

I make a portal out of there as fast as possible. I haven't used my power since I left the Monastery last year, it feels more exciting, brighter, and more powerful in a terrifying sense.

I gaze at my surroundings. They're my usual ones. My flat bed, desk, and shelves. I relax. I think I really am allergic to bullets.

***

Now everyone's excited about how Paris's new hero turns out to be its new supervillain. It turns out that the thief from last night stole a stone stick (dated to roughly 3000 B.C.E.) from one of the drawers in the basement. They've called me insane and dangerous, which is fair, I guess, but they've started comparing me to Tonnerre which I think is completely unfair. That guy is so stupid.

"Rikki. What are you doing here?" The twins pop out of nowhere.

"Eating my lunch. It's break-time and I don't usually go home."

"Come on, you're missing club," they growl in unison. Grabbing my arms, they drag me over to the lab.

I resist the entire time, but they eventually push me through the large oak doors. They slam behind us and Baron greets me: "Hey, Rikki," he says.

"Good afternoon," I respond begrudgingly.

"Got her," the twins say together.

I break free of their grip. I pick up my bag they dragged along with me and I take out my research files.

"Is that all of it?" the twins ask.

"Yep," I smile. "When you think of all the probabilities, it seems a lot more complicated than it really is. Though it's insanely complicated." They brush past me and grab it.

"What's this?" One of them holds the sample of my blood I used to try and find the rest of my family. (It didn't work.)

"Oh, that's not supposed to be in there. It's from a different research project I started but didn't finish."

"Could we use it?" they say.

"Uh, no." I forgot I left it in the file.

I casually grab my files from their hands and ease over to an empty table.

"Here, you'll need these." Baron hands me a box of safety glasses, a lab coat, and a box of phials, beakers, and chemicals. "You can keep them. We all have our own."

"Oh, thanks," I take the box and drop it on the table. I put on the lab coat and the safety glasses.

"Do you wear the same clothes every day?" the twins ask.

"No, of course not, I wear variations of the same clothes every day."

"You should get some more feminine clothes," they say.

"Why?" I begin to focus in on my work, placing all the phials and chemicals in certain positions on the table.

"Well, you are a girl."

"So?" I drop and pour chemicals into the phials.

Baron covers their mouths before they can respond. "They're just ignorant," he reassures me.

They break away.

"What was that for?" they whisper to Baron.

"Do you want to mess this up?"

"No, sir."

"Sir?" I start laughing at them.

They scowl at me.

"Kai, Kaden, don't you guys have a band event tonight?" Sebastien asks.

"Yeah, and don't you need someone to serve food?" Normand perks up.

"You're right." The twins stroke their chins and consider me.

It seems as though whenever I come in here I always end up slowly walking backwards out the door.

"Doesn't Rikki work for Le Grand Gourmet?" Marvielle says out of nowhere with a grin.

They all smile evilly at me.

I desperately grasp for a doorknob against the large wooden doors.

***

"Rikki! Use proper posture when serving the guests!" Marianne lectures me for the one-hundredth time. "This may be last minute, but these people are paying good money especially for you."

This was the doing of Baron and the twins, who decided it would be funny if I served food to everyone during their little band event. They invited the whole school and forced me to wear a skirt. *Not* okay! I am seriously pissed at them! I'm going to kill them!

Baron walks up to me and takes an appetiser from my tray. "You know you look really good in shapely clothing."

I grumble at him. Normand chose the uniforms: skirts and not-so-loose blouses.

He walks away as the twins step onto the circular stage at the front of the room. Kai goes for the drums and Kaden grabs the guitar in centre stage. A bunch of others I don't recognise step on as well. They start to play a cover of an old American pop song in English.

And they're not bad. Then the twins step down to mingle and mock me. Kaden walks over to me.

"Nice skirt," he laughs.

"And here I was about to congratulate you on your guitar performance," I mumble and place the plate of food on a nearby table.

"That was Kai."

"Please. I'm not as stupid as everyone else. You're Kaden, the guitar player."

"I'm Kai."

"But Kai is more reclusive. You both are, but he only speaks to you. You like to take more action which is why you play the guitar. It grabs more attention than the drums." He looks surprised.

"How did you-?"

"I have a unique way of thinking. Plus, his tie is red, not blue."

I smile at him and walk away to attend to other hungry people.

***

I walk on the empty roofs of Paris. I'm alone except for the shadow in the corner of my eye. When I see them move, I dodge the attack and latch onto my enemy's back. They desperately try to shake me off to no avail. I try to choke them but they throw me off into a wall.

"You're strong, aren't you? Wait... what the hell?" I exclaim in French. I get a look at their face and everything blurs. There's nothing except for him.

"Tonnerre?" I yell.

"What?" He asks loudly in English as he takes a step closer. It's definitely him.

"What has happened?" I ask in English. I look at his costume and I feel the colour leaving my face. I jump up and stand on my feet.

"You are Tonnerre?" I sigh and grab my forehead. "This is a terrible joke." I mumble in French.

"Who the hell are you?" He asks. I walk up to him and slap him. He grabs my hand so tightly he threatens to break it.

"A superhero," I sneer at him, "unlike you."

"Kid, you don't know what it means what to be a superhero. You should stop before it poisons you."

I slap him with my other hand. He grabs it.

"I know better than anyone. Even you." My voice hardens to ice. "Also, I am not a kid. I am sixteen."

"How so? Please enlighten me." He pretends to be interested but looks away.

"I wonder what Topaz would think?" I smirk as he throws me back into the wall, hard.

"Aie," I manage to squeeze out.

He punches his hand threateningly, "Lots more where that came from if you mention her again,"

"Who? Topaz?" He punches me in the stomach. My stomach's being squeezed out, but it's light compared to what he's capable of. I have scars to prove it.

"I'm the one asking questions. Got it?" He chokes me against the wall. I nod weakly but surprisingly quickly. Whatever will put my feet back on the ground.

"Who the hell are you?" he demands.

"I'm an... uh... s-superhero," I stutter under his grip.

"What's your name?" I pretend to faint like a little girl. He takes the bait and releases me. I kick him in the face throw myself away from him.

"Surprise!" I yell at him and take a deep breath of that sweet, sweet air.

I back away a few more steps away from him as he wipes the blood off his face. Then I charge at him. He just manages to dodges but I easily recover and get ready to block.

"You got better! It is a lot more fun, now! If only you knew how to fence." I grin at him.

It's his turn now. He comes in at full force; I dodge, jump onto his back, and flip off of him. He nearly slams into a wall, but he eludes at the last moment.

He's angry now. He grabs me and flings us into the clouds violently. I try to swallow my fear of heights, but he sees right through it.

"Is this what you're scared of?" he laughs. He laughs at *me*. He's definitely not himself. It's like he's mind-controlled again. "And what if I drop you right now?" He loosens the grip on me. Instinctively, I latch on to the arm holding me up. "Well, aren't you clingy."

"T-that's not funny!" I yell and look down at the minuscule lights of Paris.

"Now, I'm going to ask you some questions. If I don't like the answer or if I get a wrong answer, I'm going to drop you." He shakes my hood and brings me up to eye level.

I nod tensely and swallow hard. If he drops me, no more Corbelle, no more Rikki. I'll be more of a burnt pancake at the feet of the Eiffel Tower.

"Who are you?" He questions.

"I'm Corbelle." I breathe weakly. Everything is so tiny from up here. I squirm in his grasp uncomfortably.

"Who were you before that? What's your name?" He presses on.

"Topaz! I was Topaz!" It tumbles out of my mouth before I can even think.

He drops me and I feel the wind rush by me. I feel like barfing and crying. I'm paralysed. There's nothing I can do. I'm going to die, and my best friend won't do a thing about it. I hate him. I hate him, hate him, hate him.

Andrew

There's no way that girl could be Topaz. She's too reckless, too crazy, too stubborn.

I launch down to save her. Drops of water flick me in the face. Is she crying? She should not be a superhero, she's too weak.

I carefully grab her, making sure not to give her whiplash. The current takes us to the Eiffel Tower. It's completely empty so no one will bother us.

The girl takes a breathes deeply many times and collapses on the ground. I kneel to check on her.

"You really do care," she says. "You should become an actor, an actor would suit you, Tonnerre."

I slap her lightly.

"What kind of man slaps?" She smiles and gets up. She stretches like it was nothing and leans against the metal fence.

"I don't know who you are, but you need to stop," I tell her harshly as I clench my fist and stand up.

"No, I need to start, people need me. San Francisco has a bad guy, New York has a few heroes, Tokyo has superheroes, London has a hero and there's a giant hero team. It's time Paris had a hero too." She looks me in the eyes. "Remember that magic stick that got stolen yesterday? That is an ancient killing weapon. I am staying, I will find it and I will break it." She smiles at the last part.

"No, you're going to stop playing superhero. *I'll* stop the thief."

"How do you know I'm not the thief? It was all over the news that I was, and I was raised by thief."

"You're not the thief. You're not nearly stealthy enough."

She gapes at me, offended. "It is really me. I am Topaz, I am just... different. I'm not the same, I guess that's just what being stabbed in the heart does." She gives me a smile and shrugs.

"Kid, I knew the real Topaz. You're nothing like her. For starters, you're way too short and- "

She throws a ball of bright light at my head. I duck away and it disappears into a puff of yellow smoke.

"I am not short! I am vertically challenged!" she yells and stamps her foot down. "Why do people keep bringing it up?"

It's her. Her power's the same.

I hug her which completely surprises her. For a second, I think she's going to hug me back, but she pushes me away.

She looks away from me, "I should go."

"Wait!"

"What is it? Did you find something to dye your stupid hair?" She drops out of here using her bright yellow magic. I missed that colour so much.

Kaden

We all walk up to Rikki's apartment to see how she's doing and to drop off her extra work.

Sebastien presses the buzzer for apartment 37. A grainy voice answers in English:

"Hello?"

"Hello?" Baron answers, trying to imitate the strong American accent.

"Who is this?" They continue to speak English despite our obvious accents.

"What?" Baron goes back to speaking French.

"Rikki..." They say even more stuff but in English so it flies way over our heads. We all recognise Rikki's name, though.

"Hello?" Rikki's familiar voice answers in French, thankfully.

"Hey, Rikki! Are you alright? Do you need to go to the hospital?" Kai and I say in unison.

"Yeah, yeah. Guys I'm fine, I just wanted to take the day off."

"Can we come up?" Normand asks.

We glare at him. We still haven't decided on a suitable punishment for him. Everyone in the group knows she's not in school because of his stupid 'uniform' adjustment.

"What I was just asking, is there a problem with that?"

We frown and glare at him, causing him to take a few steps back.

A blonde girl practically the opposite of Rikki walks into the lobby. She opens the door and we walk through.

She's wearing a tank top with skirt and tights, makeup, short, loose hair, and she isn't lugging around a huge bag like Rikki usually does. I smile at the thought.

"Hello." Her French is pretty terrible. She holds her hand out to Baron who shakes it.

"Are you Rikki's roommate?" he asks.

"Yes." She smiles and nods.

"What's your name?" Normand asks, popping his head out so he can check out the blonde.

"Yes," she replies. She's clearly not bilingual like Rikki is.

She opens the locked door preventing us from entering the stairwell up their apartment. We walk up several flights of stairs to a hallway covered with white doors with silver locks and handles.

How can she afford this? We've all seen her clothes. You can tell every piece of them is second hand.

Kai

Willow doesn't open the door. She takes out her phone, taps it, and speaks in it: "Can you hear me now?"

"Yeah," I answer.

"Good." She looks all of us in the eyes somehow. "Rikki needs to leave your club. She doesn't know it yet, but she can't stay in your club." Her voice is harsh.

"What? Why?" Baron asks, dedicated to the members of the club he started. Marvielle seems completely unfazed as usual but everyone else is completely confused as Kaden and I are.

"She has no free time anymore. All she does is work on that stupid formula. I know that it's what will get her into a fancy university, a good job, and a family. But she's been so tired recently. I haven't seen her eat since yesterday. She's so focused on that idiotic formula. Please, take her out of your club, it's having a dangerous effect on her."

"Her 'idiotic formula' could save lives, you know that, right?" Sebastien counters, practically spitting out the words.

"But what about *her* life?" Willow says harshly. "Don't say anything about this to her, alright? If you do, you're dead. She already has enough to worry about."

She puts her phone away and opens the door.

She yells something excitedly at Rikki and spreads her arms out for a hug. This girl would be an amazing actor. She can change emotions as if they were light switches.

Aaron

Ever since I came to the Monastery, I loved the tale of the Chaos and Harmony. It's as old as the multiverse itself, and has always needed a protector or protectors since the beginning.

When the multiverse was still young, many vile things threatened its existence. It knew that it needed to protect itself, so the young multiverse took a bit of the power it still had from when it was first created, and put it in two beings.

In the same universe, two different children were born at the same time. One as pure as the light and one as immoral as darkness itself.

The light child knew she was destined for great things. At the age of seventeen, she knew she had to find her opposite and was well-aware of the evil that plagued the multiverse. She knew exactly what she needed to do to stop it.

The dark child also knew what he was destined for, but decided to do nothing about it. Though he was fair, tall, and good-looking, others found him repulsive. He wasn't surprised his mother perished in childbirth. He knew that it must have something to do with the way he was created.

Harmony, the child of light, went in search of Chaos in the opposite of places in which she was born, she searched an enormous city, completely unlike the small village she had grown to love. She searched anywhere she could, took any information she was offered, until she came to the residence she was told belonged to Chaos. It was the most rundown building she had ever seen. It looked as though it was built in the ruins of an abandoned shrine.

Chaos had not meant to save Harmony, he had not known why she was so enticing to him. Harmony was experiencing the same feeling, she noticed, as they looked into each other's eyes. And in that moment, Chaos could feel the darkness leave his body as he was cleansed from the Evil.

With a feeling of powerful energy, both were engulfed in the powers of light and darkness, they fought valiantly against the beasts, and won.

For the next million years, they defended the many universes together. And eventually died together.

The End

I'm one of the few male Harmonies, of the Prophecy. Harmony is usually female. With Chaos, I'm supposed to protect trillions of people, maybe even beyond that.

When she was Topaz, she wasn't nearly as trusting. It's not like she trusts me now, but she's more appreciative and laughs openly. Though she may be my Chaos, she doesn't want me to know her name or what her face looks like, so I've decided to keep that feeling mutual. I think she may appreciate it, but it's not like I'm not going to fall in love with her. It's too late now, Cupid struck me with that arrow hard and I know that she loves me too.

***

The story was created to explain the phenomenon of Chaos and Harmony to the children. It is not the actual legend or Prophecy, for the original has been lost through time and is probably untranslatable to any human language. The battle of Good and Evil is as old as time itself but they weren't always human. Before humans existed, a different race that lived throughout the multiverse took responsibility for the Prophecy. In fact, the only reason we, the humans, have the Prophecy is because of an ancient race of aliens that bestowed it upon us in the early years of civilization. Many great books were based off of it and even some religions.

When I turned ten, the high priest told me all about the Prophecy and how I was the Harmony and how I had Chaos. They didn't find her until we were fourteen though, and she was quiet until news reports were plastered all over the internet about a superhero in San Francisco with the exact same powers I have aside from the fact that they're yellow and bright, not black and dark. If you've ever seen a Yin Harmony, you'd know how they each have a little bit of each other, it's our powers. Everything about hers is beautiful and bright while mine are evil and terrible.

She decided to use the most explosive and obvious way to come out of the shadows. It didn't take long for us to meet after that. I thought for sure she might be some narcissistic little girl but I was completely wrong. She was like a ball of rage who couldn't trust anyone, like a caged animal.

But now it's different. She's different. That Tonnerre guy is gone. He was so annoying, thinking he had the right to her heart. He was wrong. Her heart belongs to no one, not even me. Yet.

He tried to get her to avoid the Prophecy, like it would change just for him. He took my place beside her but she still didn't accept him despite his persistence though. Perhaps he's dead. I don't care enough to find out.

I'm so happy with how she's changed. After she nearly died in San Francisco, she lost all of her memories. Something about trauma, I think. But whenever we talked about our pasts, she always described hers like patchwork. There were bits and pieces of it scattered everywhere.

I couldn't keep a secret from her. I cared for her too much. I told her to go see the Oracle, where she would find all the answers.

In the book the high priest gave me, I found that we'll live life for one million years until all evil is wiped from the multiverse. It also shows some methods to turn average spirits into demons or into angels and other skills that don't seem as important at the moment.

Rikki

All the guys in STEM club have been avoiding me all day. I haven't seen them since yesterday when they checked in on me and even then they were more than eager to leave.

I walk into what I'd hoped was an empty classroom, brushing past some jocks and cheerleaders who didn't go home for lunch. They all seem to turn away at my sight. It's not like I don't expect it, the school itself is a cliché. I find an empty table and sit. I take out my lunch of a croissant and start to eat. My hands search my messenger bag for my research.

It's gone! *All* my files are missing from my bag. I nearly choke on my lunch. As fast as possible, I head over to the lab.

I shake the handle vigorously. It's locked! I bang on the door but no one answers. Where are they?! I start slamming on the door.

Should I use the power? The hallway's empty and there aren't any security cams. I *need* that research!

My index fingers sharpen into little needles of yellow light which I shove into the lock while I watch for anyone walking through the hallways.

I've done this countless times with Tonnerre, sometimes, he would just break the door down. I would always tell him, "Where's the finesse in that?" and we would always laugh. Past tense. Idiots don't tend to laugh when they're trying to live as a tortured soul.

The lock clicks open. I throw the door open and rush over to my table. I let go of my breath again. It's here, thank god. Phew. I grab the files and inspect them. I freeze. Someone's been looking at them. The papers aren't in order. I'll scan them for fingerprints later. Cramming them into my bag, I run out of the lab.

Willow

Paris, the city of love. How can there be love without chaos? This wand, it was exactly what I was waiting for, with it I have the power to create a new Paris and a new world.

Mother promised me this kind of power. She said I could do whatever I wanted with it so long as I brought the girl to the lab and under the knife. I've got next to no idea on why we couldn't have just gotten her those two years ago but thanks to that idiot's butter fingers, we lost her. But good things always come to those who wait.

I grin and hold the stone wand between my fingers.

Rikki

The breeze is rather warm tonight up here, on a roof near the Louvre. It's so peaceful, hopefully not for long. I get up after a long enough break and race across the rooftops of Paris. It doesn't look like Tonnerre's going to show his mug tonight.

A blue blur flies past me.

"What the hell!" There it is again! "Tonnerre, I *swear* you'd better not be messing with me or I'll-" I yell in French instinctively.

"Or you'll what?" a voice behind me says in French before grabbing me. He's too French to be Tonnerre. "We got her, Velocity!"

"Who are you? Okay. You know what? Screw this." I bend down and fling them off my back in front of me. They skid on their back before coming stopping. I try to kick them in the face but my foot is slips off something hard, I take a look at the guy in front of me. He's just a guy wearing a motorcycle helmet. I drop my stance in an instant.

"Seriously? How did you even get on this roof? Who are you? Are you a bad guy or something?"

"No. Aren't you?" He rubs his head.

"Not since the last time I checked." I look at my costume and shrug.

The blur comes back and whips me in the head.

"Seriously, what the hell!?" I look in the direction it went and rub my head simultaneously.

The boy clicks his helmet and whispers something I can't hear.

The blur speeds around in a few circles before stopping beside the first guy.

"Hi!" He waves at me and sticks out his hand. "I'm Velocity," I shake his hand.

"Velocity? Is that English?"

"Yeah, do you speak it, thief?" The boy with the motorcycle mask asks me with a hint of threat in his voice.

"Yes, I'm fluent and it's Corbelle."

"That's Nuit." Velocity points to the guy in the helmet.

"Okay, you have super speed?" Tilt my head at the Velocity guy and ignore Nuit.

"Yeah, he creates shadow weirdness." Velocity points at Nuit.

Nuit shakes his head in disagreement. "No, I create... shadow clouds."

"See?" Velocity looks at me to back him up.

"Shut up," Nuit growls.

"Listen, are you sure she's good? I saw on the news last night she stole a stick from the Musée des Archives Nationales," Velocity says.

"I'm right here," I say as I try to interrupt their conversation. They ignore me.

"I don't know for sure but-" one of them stammers. I lost track of who was saying what.

I throw a small knife of light in between them. Now I have their attention.

"If I was a bad guy wouldn't I have already ran away by now or tried to kill you?" I ask them.

"Fair point," Velocity concedes and nods.

Nuit shakes his head in his hands, refusing whatever Velocity has to say to me.

"So, you make shadows," I point to Nuit, "Are you stalking me, Harmony?" I ask him. My voice is already shaking out of anger.

"Who the hell is Harmony?"

"Never mind, you're clearly not him. It was stupid anyway." I shrug. Harmony can barely speak a word of my language. Nuit stares at me confused

"So, what can you even do?" Velocity asks after what seems like an eternity.

I smile at him through my scarf and I create an explosion of light just above our heads.

"Crap!" I laugh at them as they fall backwards.

"What was that?" Velocity asks.

"That's what I do. It's like a lightshow on *very* powerful steroids." I tell them in between fits of laughter.

"Do you like, control the sun or something?"

I cringe in disgust, I've been trying to avoid the Prophecy, not be recognised by it. "No, I have the powers of the darkness. Kind of. It's hard to explain," I mumble.

"Hard to explain or you just won't?" Nuit asks harshly sensing the disgust in my voice.

"I don't want to talk about it." I match his tone and frown.

Kaden

"Is that a lighthouse?" Kai points over to central Paris.

"What, uh, what is that?" Corbelle asks.

"I'm going after it."

Corbelle grabs me by the collar and pulls me down to her height, "Uh, no, you're not. We need a plan. How new are you guys to superheroing?"

"Okay, what should we do?" Kai asks. I make a face at him, easily betrayed.

"Well, that 'stick' is actually a thirty-two-year-thousand-and-eighteen-year-old magic wand extremely capable of defying all senses of any laws of physics or order, so I would recommend keeping an eye out for it."

"Got it." I roll my eyes at Kai who's already completely trusting a stranger in a weird costume we met only three minutes ago.

"How are we even going to get over there?" I ask, annoyed.

"I have super speed," Kai says.

"I can create walls of light that I can jump through to another place," Corbelle shrugs while grinning wildly.

"What?"

"Uh, yeah, I can basically teleport." I can barely make out her smile, but I see a Cheshire grin through her scarf.

"That's cheating," I tell her with my arms crossed.

"Not if it's your power," she smirks at Kai as he smiles back.

"If that stick is really that bad, shouldn't we go and check on it?" I ask.

"Yeah, we should,"

"Plan?" she asks.

"Do you have one?"

"Uh, not yet."

"Then let's go." Velocity takes off, leaving us in the dust.

"There is no way he's beating me." In a flash of flight, Corbelle is also gone.

I need a super power with travelling capabilities.

Rikki

I drop down on to the Champs-Élysées of Paris just in time to see fifty-meter tall cyclops.

"Shoot." Velocity stops beside me in a gust of wind.

"I thought the crazies stayed in San Francisco."

"San Francisco?" he asks.

"Yeah, I used to live there."

"What do you think that *thing* is doing?" Velocity gestures up at the giant.

A black and white blur shoots into the eye of the giant.

"Shoot!" Velocity covers his head.

"Oh my god!" I yell in surprise. Really, Tonnerre? 'Oh hey, it's a giant, let's smash it's giant head open!' What is wrong with him?

The giant stumbles and falls. I struggle to create a shield that would protect the entire Champs-Élysées, Velocity, and myself before it slammed onto the street. I breathe heavily as I try to keep it up.

"What?" Velocity looks up. "Woah! Okay, those are some pretty powerful powers." He holds his hands out in front of like that'll protect him if I'd want to kill him.

I work to curve the edges of my shield to form a sphere around the giant's body and try to lower the sphere.

Velocity speeds to the other side of the sphere to look at the thing's eye.

Tonnerre floats down beside me.

"So-"

I punch him in the face as hard as I can. He stumbles backwards dumbly. Pain shoots through my hand. I cradle it in my other hand but manage to keep the giant up in the air.

"What were you thinking?! Did you forget about all of Paris?! Specifically, the fifty people you could have just crushed?!" I yell at him in English.

"But-"

"But what?! You're so possessive over San Francisco, you forget you do not even own it. You are just a a psycho's science experiment!" I hold my breath bracing myself for a blow.

He just stands there. I think he's going to hit me, but he shows no signs of anger or any other emotion.

Velocity watches us from the other side of the bubble. I hear the rev of a motorcycle engine and Nuit does a doughnut before stopping in front of me and Tonnerre.

"What the hell is that?" he asks in French as he points at the mess of wet dirt.

"A potter's sweetest dream," I say not softening my glare on Tonnerre. "I'll get rid of this. Goodbye," I hiss at them.

As I form a wall of solid light over to the Seine with the giant. I split it into five pieces and spread them along the river. I sit on the edge of the river and lie down underneath a bridge. It's so quiet and still down here at the Île aux Cygnes.

"Hey, I was looking for you." The idiot steps into the shadow of the Parisian Lady Liberty.

"Go away. You are ruining my sulking," I groan.

"Look, I'm sorry about that." He rubs the back of his neck.

"And nearly throwing me off the Eiffel Tower."

"Yeah, but I caught you."

"And choking and winding me." I add that to my list of awful things Tonnerre has done to me in the short span of a week.

"Okay, and that," he sighs.

I kick my legs. They're hung close enough to touch the Seine's watery skin.

"But I didn't mean it." He sits beside me.

"It sure feels like you did." I pat the bruises at my sides. I wince at the one on the center of my belly. "I thought you pulled your punches," I groan.

"Haven't had a lot of time to do that since I've been doing all the-"

"Terrorising of citizens?" I summon a sphere of light to illuminate the river's curves and ripples.

"Come on, I didn't-"

"Then when was the last time someone was especially happy to see you?" I spin the ball of light. "Aside from your grandmother."

"Well..." He thinks for the moment he has in his brain. "uh-" he taps his head. "There was this one-"

"Did they have any relation to you?"

"Okay, fine. No one's been especially happy about this new side of me."

"Because if you suddenly turn into a brooding idiot who breaks people's legs, who would question it? Life is supposed to be all sunshine and roses, no?" I roll my eyes at him.

"It was one time," he mumbles.

"And then there was that time you caused a fire in an animal shelter," I continue.

"That was an accident. And I saved all the animals." He buries his face in his gloves.

"Also, when you crashed into the library and injured all those old people."

"I thought it was an evil base in a warehouse," he groans.

"Should I even mention that time that you were drunk?"

"That wasn't my fault, I-"

"Who else would have gotten drunk and lit a firetruck on fire?!" I sit up and look at him and throw up my arms. This is what bad decisions personified looks like.

"To be fair, I don't actually remember doing that." He grins awkwardly, remembering something he doesn't.

"I mean, if you were to even light something on fire, why a firetruck? Do you have something against the colour red? Or did you just not like the sounds of the siren? What could you have against firetrucks? You are an American boy, is your childhood not based on cowboys and trucks?"

"I haven't been a kid for a long time, you know."

"Clearly you have the mind of one. You are like an angry toddler," I sigh. "In fact, I should not even bring toddlers into this. They have a lot more sense than you do."

46

"Ouch."

"Ouch? Is that all you have to say for yourself?" I shake my head. "Mon dieu. C'est vrai. Tu es un idiot."

"I like your new suit." He smiles like he's trying to make it up to me.

"Do not try to pepper me with compliments. I will not forget what you did." He really is an idiot. "Why are you even here? Are you going to try and kill me again? Please do not pretend like nothing has changed. We both know that everything is different." He silently nods and swallows his words.

A barge honks as it flows past the bridge. It's fairy lights glow in our eyes and fade.

"What time is it?" I ask rhetorically, pulling out my phone. The screen glows a deep blue with white digital numbers. "Oh merde, it's already three!" I yell at my phone. I open a portal as fast as I can over the water's edge and jump in.

***

You know what's just great? Waking up with only having about three hours of sleep and then missing breakfast. It's just wonderful. I haven't run this hard even as a superhero to make it to class on time. You'd think the power of teleportation would give you a little more speed, wouldn't you?

STEM club is still avoiding me. I haven't seen any of the guys during school at all since I stayed home. It's Friday today and I assume they would have a meeting but the room is still locked and empty. I prop myself against the door and sigh. I change my position so my legs rest against the wall in the air. I always think better when I'm upside down. My hands shuffle around my bag to find the book I'm reading.

Footsteps echo down the hallway. I tilt my head to face these intruders. It's the entire STEM club. They spot me and turn back quickly.

"Hey, are you guys avoiding me?" I yell down the hall but receive no answer.

I bounce up and chase after them. When I catch up to them, they've stopped beside the washrooms, taking a breather.

"P-pause," Baron says, gasping for air.

"That's not how a chase works." I throw my hands in the air. "I want answers, why have you guys been avoiding me?" I will use the spork in the bottom of my bag if they don't answer. It's probably infected with some terrible disease.

They stare at me quickly then slowly duck into the boy's washroom.

"Cheaters!" I slam against the door. "Argh!" I throw my hands in the air and walk away in defeat.

Hesitantly, I open my homemade device which is slightly illegal in at least seven countries. I've nicknamed it 'Diamond' (it fit with Topaz).

I check my messages on the device for any from Tonnerre or Tonnerre. I don't really have anything else to do since I'm being ghosted.

There's a bunch of desperate ones trying to see if I'm still alive, I smile to myself. Blackmail for later. I scroll through the messages on the way home. I blow the hair out of my face.

They were all pretty desperate. Some read 'please respond' or 'you can't be dead' the last one read 'I love you'.

I don't look at the rest. They're the exact opposite of what I thought they would be. I really must have messed him up. I'm sorry Tonnerre.

Rikki

I walk along the rooftops, slick from the rain. I love the feeling of it falling on my face. I'm near the Eiffel Tower, I stop to enjoy the view of the lights.

"Nice to see you, Corbelle."

"Bonsoir, Hurrishit." I face the idiot behind me and sigh. "I had thought for sure that you would have gone back to San Francisco after our talk. Are you trying to make Paris your own as well?"

"Only the parts worth it."

"Anything you have not touched?" I groan.

"No, everything that isn't Paris, you've already corrupted it."

"What?" Do all Americans make this little sense? "Like I corrupted your heart?"

He punches me in the mouth. I wipe blood from my mouth but smile; it hurt but it was worth it. He always resorts to violence.

He tries to punch me again but I'm too quick for him. He looks surprised, I did get faster. I throw my light triangles at him. None of them make contact but they warn him about the blast I set off in his face. He barely dodges it. I launch onto his shoulders and, as I flip off him, I kick him in the back of the head. He grabs my other leg and throws me to the ground.

"Aie," I mumble and side kick him in the stomach. Now we're both out of breath, but we keep fighting, determined not to let the other win. I land on my hands, kick his head again, and handspring behind him while dodging his attack. He side tracks me with a second surprise attack. He grabs my leg and propels me into the air with him.

We're high above Paris now, very high, too high. Too high. I make eye contact with the ground and instantly regret it. I close my eyes as tight as possible.

"Aww, little bird afraid of heights?"

"Little b-bird could kill y-you." I wearily say in English, I whisper a little prayer in French to anything, anyone. I'm not going to be picky.

"Not when she's in the air like this."

I take a deep breath and slowly open my eyes. Not enough. *Not enough.* My eyes snap shut again.

"Really, you distrust me this much? You think I'm seriously gonna drop you?"

"Y-yes."

"Open your eyes." He sighs.

"No," I mutter and push away from him forgetting that we are in the damn clouds. The clouds are rushing by. I can't even scream. Tears stream down my face.

No! *Help! Please! Someone! I'm drowning in the air!* I can't slow down, I can't call for help. I'm seriously drowning! I close my eyes. I feel sick. I'm dizzy. I'm going too fast. Arms wrap around me. I want to struggle, but I can't. If I do he won't save me again. I'll die.

Darkness surrounds me. No. Not him. Anyone but him.

Andrew

Where the hell did she go? Did she run away? I just wanted to talk to her. It was just a little test to see if she was still scared of heights. I didn't mean to drop her. But this is really unlike her, not like I'd know though, I haven't seen her for two years.

She was there a second ago, I was about to catch her but she disappeared in a black cloud. Oh god.

I slap my face and grip my forehead.

I hate that guy. I swear, I'll kill him when I find him.

Aaron

"Hey Sunshine, long time no see."

"Do not call me that," she mutters.

She's already slapped me twice. I think she's angry at me, but I can't tell through her scarf and mask.

"Oh right, that nickname's reserved for Tonnerre," I follow her closely.

"No, no one gets to call me that, not even Tonnerre," She insists.

"You're still in contact with him then?" I look at her slowly, eyeing her up and down for any lies or truths.

"He renamed himself Tonnerre." She sighs, staring straight forward down the hallway.

"What? Was that him with you?! Did he drop you?"

"No." She drops her hand into her palm and sighs. "I dropped myself."

"Was this a cry for attention? Perhaps love?" I pull her chin close to mine.

"The only attention hog is you." She pushes away from me but I continue to follow her down the hallway of the Monastery like a puppy.

"Oh, you wound me, my lady."

"I am not your lady. So, stop."

"Never."

"I already knew that, did I not?" She sighs as she shakes her head. "You are worse than Tonnerre was."

"Probably." I scowl at the mention of him. That guy's a jerk. I follow her past the wooden doors. "What is it about me that you find so repulsive?"

"There is nothing especially repulsive about you. It's just that... I do not have time for anyone," she shrugs.

"But... if you did in some completely hypothetical situation?"

"Well, then we would have to see."

She flicks my nose and smiles.

I love that girl.

"Thanks for the talk, but I need to get home. I have homework." She adds and smiles.

"Right, homework."

"Exactly." She winks at me, it feels like a stab in the heart. A yellow flash fills one of the many hallways of the Monastery.

I was never like this around her when she was Topaz. I know it's cruel to say, but I think nearly dying was the best thing that ever happened to her.

Rikki

As I jump onto my bed, my pillows spill onto the floor. I need them so I jump from my bed to pick them up and rearrange them carefully.

I tug off my costume and ease into my pyjamas. I bet Tonnerre is freaking out right now. He knows about my prophecy, and he's met Harmony. He kind of hates Harmony; at first, I thought it was because he thought Harmony was a rival for my love, but now I'm not Topaz and he's not Tonnerre, I'm not sure if he even hates Harmony anymore. But I think Harmony hates Tonnerre. This is so confusing. I hate boys!

I open my window and listen to the rain pattering on the roofs creating waterfalls down the walls of buildings. I smile. There's a thud on my roof, a big one. Willow may have heard it from her room. I climb out my window to see whatever had fallen. A boy wearing a motorcycle suit is sprawled against the hard metal roof, his helmet about a foot from his face.

Is Nuit really Kaden? Holy crap. He is.

Kaden

Where am I? It's warm. Didn't I fall off that building, onto a roof, when it was raining? Is it morning? Where's my helmet? I spring up.

Oh crap. I'm not wearing my mask. Just my face. No mask, no helmet.

Where am I? I look around the room. It's not a villain's lair, it's too light blueish. I stand up cautiously. Where am I? There's a girl sleeping on a desk. I look at her face. Wait, is that Rikki? Oh god, Rikki knows my secret identity.

Crap. I scrape my face with my hands and look at her again. I need to focus. What do I do now?

She moves in her sleep and I freeze completely. She moves her head to face me and opens her eyes.

"So... you're a superhero?" she mumbles.

"Yeah?" I stammer, a little shocked she knows what it is. Girls don't tend to be geeks or even be with geeks.

"Then where's your mask?"

"Uh-" I start, tapping my face again but feeling nothing again. I smile back in response.

"Sorry, I added some additions to it. Do you want it back? I'm pretty proud of it so don't break it." She yawns. She stands up and walks grabs the black motorcycle helmet. Her hands touch my gloves as she places it in my hands carefully.

"Did you-?"

"Of course not! Why would I unmask you? I'm not that kind of person." She waves her hands in front of her chest and shakes her head. "You were on my roof without your helmet." She points to the black sphere in my hands. I look at my blurred reflection in the black plexiglass and frown.

"Oh." It should have stayed on or, better yet, I should have stayed on the parkour course Kai and I planned out for practice.

"Are you alright? I wasn't sure if you were hurt or not."

She touches my side and I freeze. I try to ignore the bruise that she's pressing.

"N-nope, I'm fine, no hurts." I wave hands through the gap in between us.

"That's good. Are you going to be able to get home alright?"

"Yep. I should be fine." I shrug and fit the helmet over my head.

She looks me up and down like she's thinking of any other improvements to make.

"You seem to be taking this pretty calmly."

"Oh, I'm seriously freaking out inside. I have like, a thousand questions." She grins and shakes her head softly.

"Ask away." I shrug.

"Really?"

"Sure."

"Are you really sure? I mean I'm not kidding, I have a thousand questions."

"I'm pretty sure."

"Okay." She takes a breath like she's numbering them off and deciding which one she should ask first. "How did you get your powers? And how long have you had them?"

"Uh, first question. I'd rather not to tell you how I got my powers. I don't want you to copy my mistake. It was kind of painful getting powers."

"So? I'm sure it can't hurt that much. Besides, you did it."

"That doesn't mean you can just risk your life!" I grab her shoulders and shiver at the thought of the needle.

"Then, why did you?" she asks, watching my helmet carefully.

I shut my mouth faster than she can roll her eyes. I look over to her clock for a distraction. It's already three o'clock.

"I should go. It's late, and you should sleep,"

"What about you?"

"I'm a superhero. I don't need sleep."

She laughs. "So, when can I see you again, superhero?" She grins.

"Today, at school?" I kiss her hand like Kai did. She giggles and pulls her hand away.

"Alright, but you're an idiot."

"Can you not tell anyone that I'm a- you know..." I point at the block of black on my face.

"Oh, yeah, sure, of course." She smiles reassuringly.

"Okay, I should get going." I open her window covered with an old white curtain.

"Bye."

I fall out her window onto a pile of dumpster garbage and lie there. That hurt a little.

"You okay?!" She waves down at me.

Rikki

Well... Now I know Nuit's secret identity. Would that mean Velocity's Kai? Ugh! *So* stupid. Boys are stupid. But he's right, I should probably get to sleep. Tomorrow's Friday and I have a test so I should get some shut eye before failing it.

I wonder if he knows my identity... He couldn't. Not even Tonnerre knows. How did Nuit even get his powers? Is Vaccine loose? No, no I am not going back to that terrible city of San Francisco. Besides, that would be impossible. Didn't he die after he nearly killed me? And he gave Tonnerre his powers. I'm lucky he turned out good, but what if it was just temporary? What if he's only finally turning into what inevitably happened to all his victims? Is he finally turning evil? What about Kaden? Is that going to happen to him?

I rip my sketchbook off my desk and drag a pencil across the new page, creating a web. I write Tonnerre in the middle, Vaccine off to the side and link them with a line. Kaden/Nuit is also possibly linked with Vaccine. I draw him on the page, adding Velocity.

Wait, how could Vaccine die after I did? The police couldn't do anything and he had complete control over all of his guinea pigs except for Tonnerre.

I prop open my laptop and open the police files. The forensics say he was killed with a forcible trauma to the head with a blunt object like a piece of cement. Tonnerre. Tonnerre killed someone.

Andrew

Vaccine rips his sword out of her. She crumples to the ground. The yellow eyes on her costume widen. She thought she was invincible.

"No!" I fly to her side and catch her before her blood hits the concrete. "No, no, you're gonna be alright, stay with me, Topaz."

She coughs blood off her mask and rolls to the side that didn't get shot. "Ça fait mal." Her yellow gloved fingers feel the divot in her side. "Oh... je vais mourir." Her voice is faint. Her head hangs back against her neck.

"No, no, hear the sirens? They're coming and they'll save you. You're gonna be fine."

"Y-you're crying, don't cry. It's going to be alright." She sighs. It looks like she's trying to smile, like she wants her last moments to be filled with someone happy to see her go.

"No, no." I grab her hands and squeeze them.

"Please don't cr-" She doesn't finish. Her hands go limp and her voice cracks.

"Topaz?" I look at her. "Topaz? No! Please don't leave! Topaz?" I set her down, and her body turns into a bright yellow dust which dissipates in the sky.

No, no! She's not gone. She's going to meet me at patrol tomorrow at the chapel. She's going to laugh and be happy.

"She's gone you know, she's not coming back." Vaccine sneers at me.

"You did this to her!" I take a step towards him. "You're going to know what it feels like to die."

"What are you do-"

I grab a shard of metal from the rubble all around us. "You're going to know what it feels like to be stabbed in the heart." And he does die. But it doesn't make me feel better.

Rikki

It looks like the cyclops is back, and found it's friends, they're all crowded around the main street. They're all based on each other. All of them are at least ten meters tall and made of what I hope is clay. They all have gaping holes in their heads filled with a light like mine. They're mostly body; their limbs aren't very long so they don't have a very long reach.

Nuit and Velocity have already joined me.

"So, the thing's back?"

"Yep, can't you see?" I say.

"Oh my god, you did not just-"

"I did, and it was great, so don't worry, eye only have one cyclops pun." I wink and look back over to the monsters.

"I hope you die." Nuit/Kaden says.

"Don't worry, my fate's already going to be worse than that." I shrug and smile wider.

"There are at least five of them." Velocity returns from his speedy scout. "What did I miss?"

"Corbelle made the worst pun ever."

"He tells lies," I add. I step down from the vent I was standing on and walk over to them.

"Are they doing anything yet?"

"No, they're just scanning things with their... eyes."

"Which means we shouldn't interfere." I want to make sure the same thing doesn't happen.

The ground shakes as one of them releases an optic blast that the others seem to follow. We all look in their direction, startled.

"So...?" Velocity asks.

"Go time."

"Agreed." Velocity takes off and I follow via my portals.

"Oh, come on!" Nuit yells. I smirk.

"Last one there's a rotten egg!"

"You idiots!"

***

I don't even know if these are living things anymore. I honestly doubt it since every time I cut one, it regenerates with more clay.

"Uhhmm, anyone have another strategy?" Velocity yells above the clay spilling. Their blood is technically clay, right?

"What if we use water?" I ask, among the clay-shed.

"What?"

"Water versus Clay equals Water," I shrug as I cut through one's leg. The body falls back into place and turns back into an ordinary leg. "Oh, come on!" I yell at its face. It looks down at me and seems to charge its singular. "Oops." I whisper and jump away from the now-crater.

"What?"

"It's a simple equation, how dense are you guys?" I yell as I avoid more craters.

"Uh, problem with that plan... they seem to be following us."

"You don't say?" I grab Nuit's shoulder and vault over him. "I'll distract them." I add.

"Really? They're pretty big."

"I'm sure, I got this." I assure them as I leap into the air and land on a yellow platform.

I fall through a portal I strategically placed at eye to eye level with the cyclopses (cyclopi?).

"Peek-a-boo!" I laugh ta them as I try to swallow my fear of heights

I send a huge explosion into the sky. They take the bait and fire up at it. My hood ripples in the wind as I drop into one of the giant's eyes. I create a force field to shield myself, but I pop out the back of its head like nothing's happened. Eeew.

It catches me off guard. All the other golems aim their glares at me. My shield almost forms before I'm tackled to the ground.

"Merde!" I scream before Tonnerre pins me down narrowly avoiding the blast had under control.

I'm annoyed and tell him so with a few more swears.

"Well, sorry for saving you," He mutters coldly.

"Get off of me," I hiss.

"Are you sure that's what you want?" He grins and lifts his eyebrows.

I kick him where it hurts. He rolls off me in pain and breathes heavily.

"Hhh..." He stammers, grabbing his family jewels.

I blink before all the cyclops stare at us. "Oh." I grab him and we teleport over to a roof near them. "When I need you to get off, you get off." I lecture him. "Or things like this happen."

He looks shocked for a second, but grabs me and flies off the roof right before a light similar to mine floods it. My eyes widen, their blasts are zeroing in on us. They can track us. They sentient.

"We must get to the Seine!" I quickly switch to French after spotting the other guys. "Guys, mind speeding this up?!"

"Well, sorry but, we don't have water powers."

"Can't you use your clouds or whatever to soak up any water?" I ask, tapping the water.

"I don't know! It's not like I've had time to practice using my powers!"

"Fine, I'll get this." I sigh and begrudgingly, I release spores of my power. They disappear into the water silently.

"Is something wrong? You seem worried." I ask Tonnerre in English.

I look back into the river and extend my focus. Water's kind of heavy and really runs on your patience.

"Nothing. It's nothing." He shrugs and turns back to the water.

Blinding yellow bubbles filled with water ascend from the water.

"Woah." Kaden breathes out, despite Nuit's usual gruff outer appearance.

"She sure makes your power seem weak, huh?" Kai nudges his brother's side and chuckles.

"Are you alright?" Tonnerre asks me. He can see the struggle and shaking in my arms.

"Why would I not be? I did not kill anybody," I mutter coldly.

"What?" He asks, looking at my face closely.

"Nothing," I mumble. I should probably focus on the task at hand. It's already difficult to pull giant air-orbs filled with water into the air.

I lift the bubbles up higher, struggling a little. I haven't had to do this for a long time.

***

"Velocity!" I yell at his black hair and bright blue mask but keep my eyes tied to the bubbles.

"What?" His head twists to face mine in a fraction of an instant.

"Ever heard of the Archimedes screw?" I ask him. He should, he's a senior in a special smart school in Paris.

"What?" He looks at me weirdly and it clicks in his mind. "Oh! Yeah, I know it!"

"You think you're fast enough for that?" Nuit asks, turning to his brother not as quickly.

"Maybe. I haven't tested it so we might unleash a hurricane on Paris." He shrugs and speeds to the other side of me to get a closer look at the bubbles.

Tonnerre twitches. He must understand his past in any language.

"Too late, he's already here." I snicker as I pull the bubbles over Kai/Velocity's head.

"I am not a monster so stop treating me like one." Tonnerre says in English. I stare at him in pretend dumbstruck. He's right, he's not a monster, he's a murderer.

"Do monsters kill people?" I look at him, practically spitting the words.

"What?" Maybe he's monsterer. Or a murster.

"Never mind. We have to stop the golems. They're even more annoying than Tonnerre."

"Sure," Velocity says and Nuit nods. Tonnerre stays silent obviously not understanding our French.

"They're coming this way." He blurts out. He points to the skyline at a giant head of clay.

"We're going to have to hurry this up. I can handle this for a bit but I can't buy you too much time." I raise the bubbles and run towards the clay monsters.

My anger at everything, Tonnerre, the Prophecy, everything, is bubbling. My speed doubles as does my rage. I direct it all towards the giants. Light explodes around us all. Something snaps inside of me. The light seems to laugh like I've done this before.

My legs lift off the ground and into the air. I'm flying.

The bubbles break and water soaks everything. The cyclopses start to melt, their heads collapsing within themselves rendering them powerless. I don't stop. I can't.

My arms sharpen into long, glowing blades. The giants topple with my assault. Fireworks blast out of my chest and make contact with the already dead giants.

I fall to the ground and stare at the massive puddle of clay. The blades disappear, leaving my arms pinned to my sides and the sparks disappear.

"Corbelle!"

"What happened?" Kaden asks out of shock. I'm not completely sure if they saw the entire thing or just the ending.

Tonnerre says nothing and just watches me silently. He looks to the puddle and back at me.

"Are you-?"

"I'm fine," I push them away and stand, "I'll be fine."

"What. Did. You. Just. Do?" Tonnerre hisses, grabbing my shoulders. He must have seen the entire thing.

The puddle ripples from behind his head. The blades form once again. Shivers run down my spine.

"Impressionnant." A girl in a white suit and skirt complete with a top hat, bow tie and mask claps through the puddle.

"Perhaps you are worthy enough to be my enemy. You have a twist on you," She begins in French. She clicks her tongue and looks at my sword-arms (Swarms?).

64

"This was your idea, you crazy-" Nuit tries to interrogate her like the police shows he watches. I sigh and turn to the clouds. They have more sense than any of these guys.

"It's Reine Blanche." She corrects him in a sweet tone.

"White Queen?" I sigh. Why do all the villains have better names than the superheroes?

"Exactly." She coos.

***

"So, you are all the protectors of Paris?" She sneers at us. "Is she the only one with real power?" She points at me. I want to dig a hole, hide in the hole, and then bury myself in the hole. I want to be anywhere but here but I stand my ground.

"Obviously." I roll my eyes. In hindsight, probably not a good idea.

"Not." Nuit adds scowling at me underneath his stupid helmet. Black fog seeps down from his fists.

"Take this seriously!" She grips her white parasol tightly. "Or I'll make you!"

"Sure, you can." I laugh. "What are you going to do? Make it rain cats and dogs? I'd better be careful not to step in any poodles then." I'm already being told how my life is going to end starting from when I'm seventeen. I'm not giving up my choices earlier than I have to. I'm going to be whoever I want until I can't anymore.

"I warned you!" She spins her parasol in the air and points it at me. Its tip is hard to see now but I think it's shaking, then growing brighter. The tip explodes, racing towards me and only me. Tonnerre tackles me and Velocity whips around trying to grab the parasol from her. Nuit is just there. The glare increases and suddenly, she's gone.

"Get off," I hiss. I jump out of his grasp and look at the now electric mud puddle on the ground. I glare at Tonnerre. "Stop saving me."

"Didn't know the demon queen would have a preference." He nags trying to piss me off equally.

"She does, and murderers aren't any of the kinds of people she likes."

He slaps me. "I am not a murderer."

"Then what do you call Vaccine?" I blurt out the word and he steps back. "A casual assault? Yes, I found out. What made you think I would not?" I huff. I'm annoyed that he's still surprised at my intelligence. It's not like it takes any brains to search the internet.

"You died." He insists. Excuses, excuses.

"I did. It hurt." I've got admit, being shot in the stomach and then stabbed through the chest is rather painful. It's not exactly a walk through a rain drenched park.

"No. You were gone. You died in my arms. You were gone to me for two long years. You weren't alive and now I'm supposed to pretend like that didn't happen?"

"It did happen. But you were not as close as you thought you were to me. Did you think because I fought alongside you I could tell you my name?"

"So? What about me? I loved you and you died. That hurt." He crosses his arms over his chest and glares at me like I should understand. I don't.

"So does being shot." I cross my hands over my chest too.

"How long are you going to hold that over me? I'm sorry you died, I'm sorry I killed someone, I'm sorry I changed, and I'm sorry I'm not the boy you love anymore."

"I never loved you and I never will!" I throw my hands in the air. "Why is that so hard to believe?!"

He takes a step closer. "You get angry because I don't give you enough credit. Yeah, I noticed that you act differently than you did."

"It was because I died!" I throw my hands up higher into the dark sky. "My life flashed before my eyes when that sword was pulled out of my chest. I didn't like who I was, so yes, I guess I changed a little bit."

"Sword-?" Velocity asks. He understood; too bad Tonnerre doesn't.

"You wanted an excuse to get mad at me, to get out all that rage you're directing at the Prophecy. You want to get rid of it but you needed something to vent on, so you chose me."

In frustration, I slap him. His face colours, but he doesn't look angry. I slap him, using my power. I draw blood, but he doesn't look angrier he just looks thirsty for more. Or maybe that's just how he looks on a day to day basis.

"Is that it?" He looks back at me. "You're being forced to become the greatest evil in the multiverse, and all you can do is slap me!"

"You want me to hit you?" I put my hand down and let my power float away as a presence, like a ghost.

"Hit me!" He screams, nearly spitting on my mask. "Aren't you mad?"

"No, I'm not going to hit you! If you want to be punished, do it yourself." I turn away with disgust and run away. I scale a building and run across the roofs. I don't stop running. Even when it burns. I just keep pushing. He was right for once. I have a lot of rage I need to get out of my system.

***

I drop to an arched roof. From my perch, I watch Paris, still dozing except for the swarm of media crowding Velocity and Nuit at the puddle. He must have left. I close my eyes. I could die and who would care?

I feel a presence and look around. It's Tonnerre.

"What do you want?" I frown at the shadow obscuring the bright light of the half-moon.

"I want to talk."

I sit up and look at Tonnerre. "I do not want to talk," I hiss. I see a cut that's engulfed his shoulder entirely in blood. And pain. Probably pain too. "I came here to be alone, not to suffer from your idiocy," I snap. "You are bleeding a lot, is your healing factor working still?"

"Well, yeah." He shrugs but winces at the movement of the pain.

"Then why are you here?" I roll my eyes at him. "You should be healing at home. Away from me."

"I told you, I just want to talk," he insists.

"Then talk once you have gotten yourself healed." I wave my hand at him to tell him to shoo.

"Corbelle," he huffs. "I just want to talk for like, fifteen minutes, tops."

In my fanny pack I find some gauze and alcohol wipes.

"Here. Take them and leave."

I drop them on the roof and walk away. My knees bend, ready to leap off to the next roof.

"Wait! What do I do with... this?" He holds up the white gauze and dangles it in the wind like he's teasing it.

"Do you not know first aid?" I turn back to him.

I grab the collar of his costume and unzip part of it.

"What are you doing?" He blushes as I wipe the blood off the skin of his shoulder.

"I must clean the cut, it would help if you were not delirious." I tell him.

"I'm not."

"You are," I insist. I press harder on the cut to tell him to stop.

He winces but doesn't receive the message through his thick skull. "I'm not."

"I am not doing this if you're going to be like this."

"Be like what?" He smiles.

"You are delirious," I continue trying not to let him bother me. The alcohol wipe presses harder into his cut causing him to yelp.

"What are you doing?" he breathes.

"Sit down. I cannot reach your shoulder." He plops down on the metal roof obediently and I kneel.

He unzips his jacket a little more.

"Aww, is the little bird blushing?"

"No, I am not blushing over something as simple as cleaning a cut." I really hate him.

"Really," he sighs, realising I'm not here to have any fun.

68

I inspect the cut, it's not deep but it's magic. I clean his shoulder with the wipe. "Does it hurt?" I ask.

"Yeah."

"Good, it keeps you awake."

"Not a coffee person?" he chuckles, holding his chin with his good hand. He looks at me for a response but I frown and look at the cut. "Is this what it takes to get your attention? Because if it is, I'll have to get hurt more often."

"What is wrong with you?" I drop the wipe and put my hands up. I can only take so many one-liners.

"What do y- "

"When you are with everyone, you are a total *connard* to me, but now that we're alone, you're being how you used to be. Why do you keep messing with me?" I pick up the gauze and tape. "I am not a toy."

I press the gauze on and he flinches.

"I don't know why." He hangs his head.

I put my hands down on my knees and sigh. "You need help," I mumble, also hanging my head. "A lot of help."

"That's why I'm so hard on you, I need you. I need you to help me." He leans in and he almost brushes my lips but I shove him off and take a step back.

"Stop," I tell him as I put my hands in between us.

"Why?" He throws them aside and grasps my chin.

"Stop!" I push him away again and repeat step two. "I do not think we are allowed to rip off a seedy romance novel."

"That's not a reason," he insists.

"I just- I do not want this," I hiss. *I hate you.* Is what I mean to say.

"So, is this is about protecting me?"

"I want you to stop saving me." *Get out of my life.*

"Is this because I got hurt?"

"Yes and no." I lull my head around my neck slowly.

"I'll be fine, I've got super strength,"

"That is what I'm scared of, we do not know the full capacity of them. If Vaccine gave you your powers, there could be a delayed mental setback like most other victims." I change the topic quickly.

"We? So it's a 'we' thing now? And it's not like you know the full extent of your powers yet either."

"It is not that that I am worried about. Have you thought about the mental anguish all the people Vaccine experimented on? It has a mental offset that damages not only the brain but the neural link to the spine as well. Plus, there is no known cure." I look into his confused eyes. "If there is a possible link between you and him, maybe I can make a cure for you. I may also be able to find a loophole for me too."

"I know that." He rubs his forehead against mine. "But it means I'm gonna have to be a lot harder on you, and I don't want to lose you."

"You do not have a choice whether you lose me or not." I throw him away from me. "But that is not why you are here, yes?"

"No, it isn't." He scratches the back of his neck thoughtfully. "About what happened earlier tonight, what was that?"

"I... lost control over the power." I look at my hands in horror.

"I thought that wasn't possible, I mean, it hasn't happened before." He looks at my face. "Has it?" His eyes fill with shock. "When?"

"Do you remember that time you got hypnotised by Siren back in San Francisco?"

"Vaguely, it was pretty weird. Like watching your life go by from out of your body."

"So, she flooded the city with a lot of water. She was flooding it completely, even the bus stops were covered with water." I put my hands up as high as I can to show him how high the water was rising. "There was a lot of water in downtown."

"And then?"

"Then we had a, how do you say? A boss-battle. She targeted me and all the people escaped and then she almost killed me but then I released the control I had over the power." I re-enact the battle with my fists. I wave my fingers in the air to show how I lost control and sort of exploded. "Then I exploded."

"Why do you keep calling it 'the power'?"

70

"Because it is not mine. It has a mind of its own. It must listen to me but sometimes it does not. When that happens, I lose control and I everything explodes." I hold my hands up to my eyes.

"But when you turn seventeen do you think you'll get complete control over it?"

"No. I am not going to become Chaos. I cannot." I sit by the edge of the building and angle myself carefully so I don't look down. I look across the sparkling city.

"It looked like you were enjoying it."

"Hmmm?" I turn to him. My black braid catches the air and swings out of my hood. My fingers pull my scarf higher over my mouth. It's like a second skin protecting me from the cold.

"Losing control like that. You were smiling from underneath your scarf." He sits beside me and looks at his hand. His cut already looks like it's mending itself together.

"How could you tell?" I wasn't smiling. It was the power.

"I've known you long enough to know what you look like, mask or not, when you smile. It's like the entire world lights up."

I roll my eyes. "You are unbelievable," I groan.

He smiles as he looks at me. "I'm just trying to cut this tension." He says, trying to sound reassuring.

"What tension is there to cut?" I ask with a shrug. I pull my scarf down. I've got nothing to fear, Tonnerre's good people.

"Are you sure about that?"

"Paw-sitive."

"What?" He asks, shaking his head. "You're a bird, not a cat. Unless you're terrible at making costumes. Oh wait. You are." He laughs and punches my shoulder.

"Aie." I rub my shoulder, grinning. "You see what happens when I have made a pun? I am very bad at puns, no? I cannot make bird puns."

Andrew

I wish everything could be like this again. We talked for hours until the sun came up, then parted ways. But, her prophecy is about to happen, and I can't be with her for that part of her life. My nineteenth birthday is coming up and I'm expected to take over the company despite the fact I continue to tell him I have no interest in a company that sells lies and false hopes. I thought it was obvious since I keep stalling and dropping out of my university courses.

I get up and dress casually. Outside, I admire the building I bought. Willow doesn't know I have it and I plan on keeping it that way. It's late Friday morning so most people in the area have work or school so the sidewalk is empty. I wonder what it's like to work or go to a regular school. I've never had to go. I've mainly been homeschooled. The only friends I really had were my tutor, Willow, Aaron, and Topaz. I haven't seen Aaron in a few years, not since Topaz died. I think he still might be in San Francisco, but I don't know. I pushed everyone away when Topaz died.

Suddenly, someone crashes into my back with a large thud. Stunned, I turn around and find a girl on the ground.

"Are you alright?" I ask them.

"Oui, ça va bien, merci." I extend a hand to her and pull her up. "I am so sorry."

"No problem." I mumble. It is though. I'd prefer it if weird strangers I didn't know didn't crash into me every second they got.

"Oh, school! Sorry, I must go, I have a Science test! Thank you! Bye!" She sprints past me and her massive bag whips against me. She doesn't even give it notice. What a strange girl.

Rikki

I am so late. No more all-nighters ever; Coffee and alarms did not help. I should be more prepared than this. Why don't I live closer to the school? I already missed the train so I'm already guaranteed to be late. I'm going to be late for science which is my favourite subject. I need to go faster. Sprinting is clearly not enough, bikes are faster. I should've ridden my bike. The path is really uneven so I should be more careful not to trip and bump into any more people.

The doors are so heavy, my aching muscles can't *handle* them. Funny, I just made a pun! Handle! Crap. School. Late. Go! I sprint to the lab, breathless.

"Ms. Dubois, is there a reason why you're so late?" The teacher asks as she taps her clipboard impatiently.

"My bus was late?" I smile awkwardly.

A bunch of people snicker, mainly the 'popular' group. I roll my eyes directly at them and face the teacher. A few of them laugh harder at my reaction.

"Please sit down." The teacher urges me pointing to the one empty chair.

"Yes ma'am." I nod obediently as I take the empty place beside Kaden and in front of Maya.

"Bus?" He whispers, knowing I usually take the train.

"Shut up, I wasn't the one on the TV this morning." I sigh as I take out the textbook out of my backpack and flip it open to the page number on the white board.

"Saving the city is better than being late for a test." He rolls his eyes.

"I'm not late yet. I've still got three minutes." I whisper. "And shut up."

Kaden

The school is shaking all around everyone. Even my vision is blurring. My head's throbbing.

"Is this an earthquake?" someone asks. I don't know who, but I know it wasn't Rikki who looks completely unfazed, excited even.

"Students! Please remain calm. We have practiced drills in case of emergencies like this." The teacher holds onto the board at the front for balance and addresses us. It's like she's trying to reassure herself that everything's going to be okay.

"No way! This has got to be a supervillain attack like I saw last night on the news."

"Yeah, I'm getting a live news feed! Huge bear things are attacking downtown!"

"What? That's crazy!" Someone shouts in disbelief like this is the single worst April fool's joke in the history of mankind.

"I know, but it's true!" The girl with the phone says, louder than anyone else.

"This is so awesome!"

"I bet Corbelle is behind all this." The class's conspiracy theorist says quietly amongst the yelling.

"Okay students! The principal wants us all in the gym. Let's go!" The teacher stands up very slowly like she's testing for bad ground. Everyone crawls out from under the desks. Faces are relatively the same, either scared or nervous. Other than Rikki who looks wildly evil. I know she isn't Reine Blanche, but maybe... She notices my stare and corrects her expression so she looks like everyone else. We follow the teacher out the door into the courtyard, then into the gym with all the other classes. I slip out just before entering.

"Kaden where are you going?" The theorist asks.

"Uh-just need to use the bathroom really quickly." I nod and point behind me to the school. "I'll be right back."

"Hurry up! Ms. Bailly's about to check in with the teachers." She points over to our principal.

I sprint off to the bathroom.

Rikki

Tonnerre is already there by the time I drop in. He's grappling with a goblin beast thing trying to step on him. Its head is... Grey and furry topped with an oversized black nose. I don't know how to put it... it's like an adorable bear that illegally drank some Alice in Wonderland juice.

"Need a hand?" I ask him.

"That's a pun isn't it?"

"I must start somewhere." I shrug with a stupid grin on my face.

My shield separates him and the rock goblin. When he frees himself, I throw the shield in the air, flipping the bear on its back. Tonnerre flies beside my platform and stretches.

"Know where the others are?" He asks about Kai and Kaden.

"No, how would I?" We go to the same school and the majority of my classes are with them.

"You guys seem like the same age." We are. Sort of.

"So?" I ask like it doesn't mean anything.

"So, wouldn't you guys use phones or something to contact each other?" He takes out his own phone and points to it in case I didn't know the English word.

"No, we met two days ago." I shrug.

"Do they already know about the Prophecy?" He grits his teeth together. He thinks it's just something only he should know, like a secret between the two of us but it isn't. Everyone at the Monastery knows about it so how is it a selective secret? Why does it matter if I tell anyone?

"No, and I will keep it that way."

The bear manages to flip itself back onto its legs and screams, it's horrible and high pitched. I can't hear anything else. I try covering my ears but it's no use. Wind rushes by me. Am I falling? It's getting louder. I fall to my knees and squeeze my eyes shut. Tonnerre can tell I'm in pain and so is he. He says something I don't hear as he also tries

76

to block out the noise. I can't hear anything over the scream. I watch him launch off the street through the slits in my eyelids.

The noise stops abruptly. I look up to see Tonnerre wrestling with banshee-bear. He's struggling to hold its mouth shut.

"Move!" I yell at him.

He punches the bear down and flies beside me. The bear makes an effort to scream again but it's muffled by my force field. My skin prickles at the echo of its scream.

"Koala bears are vicious, aren't they?" He says. His fists are still ready to punch something.

"What is a koala bear?"

Reinforcements bound towards the bear. Their screams hit Tonnerre's ears before mine. The force of the pavement hits me full force. I touch my ears tenderly and my fingers are covered in blood. The world starts spinning and turns black.

Andrew

"Topaz!" I focus on the oncoming koalas. "I could use some backup!"

I look towards her, lying motionless against the pavement. She's taking in painful breathes, so I know she's alive. My main goal right now is to make sure she doesn't die.

One of her friends whips past me, does a U-turn and stops abruptly beside me and asks me something in French.

"What?" I don't understand what he said.

He gestures over to Corbelle and speaks slowly. "G-good?" He asks hesitantly.

"I think so, but we need to make sure she stays alive." I nod to him.

"Plan?" He tilts his head to his right shoulder and cracks his knuckles.

"Punch things."

He looks behind me and sighs. He jumps up and takes a leap forwards.

"What-?" He rushes away in a gust of wind.

All the bear things watch me. They don't seem to be provoked. Were they just waiting for Corbelle?

One steps towards her. I punch it in the face which seems to provoke the rest. Again, they release a high-pitched scream, the same one that messed with Corbelle. It's painful, but thanks to my healing factor, it hurts her more than it hurts me.

Velocity races behind me. The rev of a motorcycle follows him.

"We good?" I ask him. I put a thumbs up in the air to try and tell him what I mean. He nods but his friend on the motorcycle only points to Corbelle.

A rock thing crashes into the wall beside us. I grab Corbelle and fly out of their reach. Velocity and Nuit speed down the street.

I set her gently down on a roof. I leave her there and return to beating down the rock creatures just won't stay down. Velocity is using his speed to gain as much advantage as possible. It's mostly working. Nuit's releasing a cover of thick black clouds. Our siege is works only to push them back.

Corbelle struggles to stand up.

"What are you doing?!" I hiss at her trying to push her back down to the ground.

"What are you doing? Having all the fun without me?" She sounds distant and hesitant. She shakes her head like she's getting the water out of her eyes but drips of blood fall out.

"You need to go home! You're not in any shape to be fighting. You need to lie down and rest!" I push her down again but she sits back up again.

"Do not worry, I got thi-" The monsters realise she's awake and let out their shattering scream again. She screams in agony and crumples to the ground. Her ears are dripping with deep scarlet liquid.

Rikki

Stupid banshee-rock-bears. Stupid ears.

Every time I get up they let out their screech but when I'm done they stop. They can't keep screaming forever but if I get up they'll scream and I can't last that long, let alone out last them. I could use a shield and I could protect myself but they don't work astoundingly well against noise. Plus, there's five of them. Another drawback to shielding myself is that it would limit my power to the inside of the bubble. Maybe if I surge the power... no, that would hit anyone on the ground.

Use your brain Rikki! Think! Think!

What if I make a run for it? If I keep playing dead, will they notice? I need to get out of here now.

The light floods my eyes even though they're closed. The breeze stops and I'm in my empty classroom again.

I open my eyes and stand up. I tenderly feel my ears. They're not bleeding too much, but it's really noticeable. None of my blood is on the floor which is good news.

They must be hitting the bears really hard. I can hear their explosions from here. The shaking hasn't stopped either. I didn't notice it when I was unconscious. What can I do?

I'm not any help over here and I wasn't any help over there, I can't think! Not with that stupid... rumbling...

I look out the window. The things are closer, they're practically on school grounds but they're not screaming yet.

What do I do, what do I do, what do I do! I'm racking my brain for an idea, anything, I need an idea. But what if I... Wait, that'll work.

***

I rip my locker open and grab my purple scarf and dark blue sweater. I really hope no one remembers my ugly clothing choices. I wrap the soft woolen purple scarf around my head like a hijab and slip the sweater over my head and costume. This should work. They won't recognise some weird multi-coloured superhero.

The schoolyard is engulfed in chaos. Tonnerre is single-handedly taking down three rock-banshees leaving Velocity and Nuit with one each.

"Wow." I mumble from atop the school's roof.

I leap off the roof and flip down to land. "Nailed it." I yell in French. I join Tonnerre and fight one of his three bears.

"You're wearing that?" He points to my sweater.

"Yes, they won't recognise me in this." I shrug and vault over the jaws of a 'koala bear'.

"Nice plan." He smiles and throws another on its side. The concrete crunches underneath its weight. What do these things eat? Themselves?

"Thank you, I am genius." I nod cheerily and sit on the koala's belly.

"Really?" He asks, still grinning as he takes down another. I reach to scratch my furry bench underneath the chin. It seems to enjoy it and tilts its head back further. I stand up and rub it behind the ears.

"Hey, I think it likes me!" I laugh.

I shield a bite from a jealous koala bear and create a bubble in its mouth.

"Corbelle!" Tonnerre yells at me trying to run at me.

"Wha-" A bear bites me from behind and holds me tightly in its jaws. This is gross. Superheroing is really hard.

Kaden

Tonnerre goes really to town with these guys, which is helpful for once, unlike that girl that just got bit by a grey bear. I think he's protecting her. What a sweet couple. I should tell him that after all this.

"Does anyone have a plan?!" I yell in French above all the punching and bear slobber.

"No, we're just going to wing this!" Kai smirks. He loves this.

There's not a lot I can do. Making clouds isn't that useful for short range combat. I'm blocking the things' sight and Kai is using his speed to hit them extra hard.

"Is she doing anything helpful?!" I yell at Tonnerre pointing at the girl being flailed around by a bear.

"I...am the... most powerful... person in the universe, so, uh, yes." She yells as she's being thrown around the yard. "Also help, please."

"What!?"

"I'll explain later." She sighs as she gets thrown to the ground by a bear.

"What talk?" Tonnerre asks from underneath a bear.

"What?!" I hate it when these stupid Americans butcher my language.

"Uh-"

"Whooo!" And the girl is conscious after being bit by a two-ton furry monster and swung around like a rag doll. I'm way out of my league.

"Cor?" Tonnerre asks seeing whether she's alright or not. I think if she can survive being maimed by a giant bear she should be fine by now.

"Yeahm, whas the problem?" 'Cor' rubs her head and looks around at the bears.

"Giant monsters are attacking a school." I tell her as I release more fog from my fists.

She looks around. "Oh. But I think they're bears. Tonnerre called them 'koala bears.'" She springs up and launches onto the back of an attacking rock thing. Woah.

"These things are uncomfortable." She groans, the regret placed all over face.

"That's what she said." Velocity chimes in with a grin.

"Not to you!" She adds with an even bigger grin. She decided, since sitting wasn't comfortable enough, just to stand on the back of a giant, furry bear.

"Hah!"

"Focus!" Tonnerre yells in French at all of us. He punches a bear straight in the jaw and knock one of its teeth out. Corbelle winces but turns back to her faithful steed.

"I'm just waiting for you guys to finally chip in." Corbelle chirps happily as she scratches the koala's head while standing.

"Are you being serious right now?!" I ask. How can she say that? She pretty much just joined the fight and she's not even wearing her regular costume.

"I'm delirious." She responds, rolling her tongue and laying down on her bear. Kai snickers.

"Velocity, are you being serious right now?"

Kai punches the face of a bear thing at the speed of sound. It slams into the ground loudly. "One down!" He yells. "You guys had better catch up!"

"I got this one." Corbelle shields a bite from atop another. She ducks under its head to kick it in the neck. She slides off her bear and drops underneath the attacking koala bear and vaults onto its back. "Ok, that didn't work. Probably because I don't have super speed." She holds onto it tightly as it violently tries to shake her off. "Anyone mind if I just wreck this whole thing?"

"No-?" Tonnerre stammers as she looks at him expectantly.

"No." Me and Kai respond quickly. When she wrecks things, it can be rather entertaining.

"Good," I can sense a smile in her voice as light completely floods the area.

Rikki

Light floods the area. Not my light. It's blue, much prettier than mine. It surrounds me for a moment and it circles just me but repulses as quickly as it became captivated.

"You're not a hero..." A girl whispers in French from the middle of the hazy blue smoke.

"Who are you to say?" I ask while I lean into my bear's thick fur.

"I'm Sage and I'm Paris's greatest hope for protection, not some thief." she leers at me.

"Why does everyone bring that up? It's not like I've tried to steal the Mona Lisa recently!" I say, plugging my bear's ears. He doesn't need to hear some jerk insult his momma.

"Face me thief!" She screams. She lunges at me but I dodge gracefully by jumping off the bear into the air and above her. A banshee-bear lurches at me. I lose my footing and fall but Tonnerre catches me.

"Aww, my prince charming." I laugh in English and stand up. I wipe the grey fur of my once pretty blue sweater.

Sage charges at me again. Tonnerre lifts off the ground with me in his arms.

"Nope, nooope, put me down! Now! Please!" I struggle in his grasp. he lets go and I drop.

I'm kind of starting to enjoy the feeling of the air. It makes me feel like hurling but it's better than me being in water. I'm like an actual bird in some ways. Wait, no. Ducks like water. I'm like a cat... water and air don't suit me but I need them to live, but if I have any more exposure, I would drown in either substance.

Ovals of my power circle around my head and I expand them, making them go faster, and faster, and faster. They don't slow my fall, at all. Of course. Of course they won't protect me from dying. Of course.

I force the presence of the power way down underneath my short little legs. I give it a face, not a literal one but I make it visible. I've never done it before since I've always been scared too to. I was the only one who had to deal with its burden, the only one who could see it and feel it. It's like a cloud; it feels like one too. I'm about five metres from the ground. I close my eyes and brace for impact.

My butt bounces off of something soft-ish for once. I hope that was the cloud. I look around. Everyone seems to mirror my surprise. Even the three bears have stopped.

Tonnerre takes the ground and smashes another bear's head into the ground. Only stunning it. Two bears left now.

"What was that?" 'Pure' girl asks pointing to where the cloud of power used to be.

"Uhhh-magic?" I shrug to add emphasis as I wipe off any lasting smidges of power off my hazy blue sweater.

"Anyway, you're coming with me, thief." She grabs me by the collar and lifts me off the tiled concrete.

"No, I'm not." I grab her wrists and twist. Pain stings through her arm and she lets go instinctively. "I would know." She holds her arm and looks at me with a new rage.

"You're coming with me." She grabs my arm tightly and the bears snap back into action. One head butts her. She goes flying over the school's fence and into the bushes in a park somewhere.

"I did not know the 'Protector of Paris' could fly! Maybe I should step down, what do you think Tonnerre?" I laugh in English. He just grunts at me. Maybe he's just not in a talking mood after all this bear fighting. "Wow, wonderful insight. Although that is what I would have expected from you."

The remaining bear opens its mouth. I flinch and prepare for a piercing scream. Tonnerre notices and steps between me and the bear. I love the gesture, but I'm not sure it'll help.

No scream follows. There's nothing; it's quieter even. Hesitantly, I open my eyes slowly to see giant bubbles everywhere.

Did the bears dissolve into bubbles? What is going on? Why are there suddenly bubbles?

I reach out to the one closest to me, I tap it and it ripples, it makes me laugh. A new feeling surrounds me as the bubble swallows me.

"Uuuh, help?" I wave my hands to balance myself. I thought it was just hugging me but that's never the case. I punch the wall of the bubble to try to pop it but I have no such luck. I sigh. This is probably the worst prison I've ever been in.

"Cor!" Tonnerre tries to pull me out but gets stuck in as well, we both fall in and land with a thump.

Andrew

I can't believe I'm falling for her. I didn't notice it at first, but I do now. It's like when she smiles it makes me happy. It's like it's only us. I try to react when it is only us around but I can't. That would put the plan in jeopardy.

***

We're pretty high up in the air, I think Cor's having a panic attack, she's breathing heavily and has braced herself against the side of the bubble. Every few seconds, she looks behind herself and jumps to another side of the bubble.

"Think you can pop the bubble?" I ask her.

"Noooooooon." Her eyes are squeezed as tightly shut as possible. She lets out another breath and whispers something in French. Something about 'dieu'.

"Don't worry, I'll catch you." I reassure, holding out my arms.

"Noooooooon." She whispers clenching her fists together and releasing them slowly.

"I won't let you fall. I promise." I touch her shoulder, she slowly opens her eyes and gives me a panicked smile and barfs all over the bottom of the bubble.

"Ooooh no." She quivers.

"Ok, clearly you weren't meant for air travel." I lift in the air to evade her past lunch, breakfast, and dinner.

"No kidding, Sherlock." Her voice may be weak but she won't stop making quips. She takes a deep breath and stands tall or at least she tries to.

"Stand back." She takes her arms from her sides and throws them up for balance like she's trying to be an airplane.

I do as she says. I watch her arms sharpen and change into bright yellow knives. I see the discomfort beneath her mask and scarf. I've never seen her do this before.

She starts stabbing the bubble, slowly but building up her speed. It doesn't work, the bubble's too stubborn.

"This is not working." She sighs, looking at her hands. He blades disappear back into fists and drop to her side.

"Why don't you just teleport?" I offer trying to reassure her with a prize-winning smile.

"That will not put an end to this. I will just keep getting stuck if I run. It will show her I can't fight, that I'm scared of her. Why should I be scared of her? She's just an insane lady with a magic wand. Nothing scary there, yes?"

I know why. But I can't tell her.

"Sooo, can you blow this bubble?" I ask, looking around the bubble and how high we are. Whatever can distract her from barfing all over the enclosed place will work.

"Not without killing you." She sighs, stroking her chin. She's definitely thinking of a better way already.

I pretend to sound like I'm thinking.

"I have nothing, are you thinking of something?" She asks. She shrugs and sighs.

"Trying to."

"What if I- uh, no, that wouldn't work." She mumbles quickly. "Oooooh, we're getting pretty high." She mumbles as she pins herself up against the bubble again.

"It looks like we're almost to the top of the Eiffel Tower." I look down on the giant triangular tower.

"Shut up, shut up, shut up!" She yells at me and covers her ears. She looks up above, into the sky and breathes heavily. "Je n'aime pas."

"Heh." I smile at her drastic measures.

She shakes her head and tries to focus. "What if I do open a portal though..." She still presses her yellow eyes closed. When I first met her, I thought she was some weird freak with yellow pupils and a French accent but she's a lot more than that.

"But you said-"

"Yes, but this is our only chance of getting out." She sighs with her eyes closed.

"Okay, do you know where we're gonna end up?" I ask, grabbing her shoulder tightly. The last time we teleported didn't really work out so well.

"No." She says quickly in a whisper like she's hoping I won't hear.

"No? That's not very reassuring."

"When have I ever been reassuring?" She smiles weakly and exhales.

"Touché." I grin back.

She grabs me and takes a deep breath. I know what happens next, I close my eyes and brace for the light. A breeze blows through my hair and I know it's over.

"Uuuh." She keels over onto the grey stone. I hold back her braid and she barfs again. It's surprising that that much food can fit into such a small person.

"You know where we are?" I ask her, looking around at the buildings. I sort of remember them and then I look at the massive bronze statue.

"No, you?"

I look around, we're not in Paris anymore, but at the park in San Francisco. My teeth girt together. I don't have a lot of happy memories from here.

"Yeah, I think we're in San Francisco." I sigh but try to keep my optimistic tone just for her.

"What?! Oh no..." She groans and stands up only to fall on her knees again. I let go of her braid.

"They made a statue of us." I look up at it as she continues to groan.

"They made a statue of us?" She looks at it disapprovingly and strokes her braid like she's checking for any leftover pieces of discarded food.

"Yeah, that's what I just said."

"Noooooooooooo." She whines and leans her back onto the two-year-old grey concrete, away from the barf.

"I think they did a pretty good job." I look at my bronze eyes in the statue. There's no way I'm goign to look at hers but in way, my prayer to her was answered. After all, the real her is just groaning on the ground behind me.

"I look so stupid, the artistry is soooo bad." She yells and pulls on her face with her yellow gloves.

It's almost daylight and some people are staring at the weird costumed freaks in the middle of the park. I remember that, before she died, if people saw us in the park they'd sometimes buy us coffees and thank us. They thought it was a token of appreciation to their heroes.

"Cor? I think we should probably go." I kick her boot.

"Yes," She notices the stares as well. "But at least we are in the same universe." She mumbles as she stands up. That's happened before too. The one time I've passed through an 'alternate reality' as she put it.

"Oh yeah, thank god for that." I roll my eyes. At least we're still in one piece.

"Can you say anything without... how do you say... sarcasm?" She groans and rolls her eyes at me.

"No."

"How shocking." She sighs. She stands up and stretches her arms.

"Oh my god," I groan as I smack her lightly on the back of her head.

"Ow, what was that for?" She rubs her head and glares at me. I'm pretty sure she also mutters something in French but I've got no idea.

"Bad puns about my name."

"Aw, but you used worse ones on me and you were two years older than me." She shrugs. "And that was an accident."

"I still am two years older."

"Whatever." She frowns and scans my face like she's making checking if it's an English swear word. "Je te hais tellement."

Rikki

"Where should we go now?" Tonnerre asks like I should know all the answers.

"I do not know! I thought this was your city." At least that's what he tells me all the time.

"So, you admit it." He smiles and leans closer.

"Why are guys so possessive?" I sigh and throw my arms in the air. They're all idiots. I walk away from the park and stick my tongue out at the idiotic statue. Why did they make a statue of me? They could have at least hired a better artist. They practically butchered my figure, I mean really? I single handedly saved the city at least seven times.

"Where are you going?" He peers over my shoulder, looking in all directions.

"I want to check out all my old places. Alone. By myself. I'll meet you at the old chapel at seven o'clock."

"Aren't you scared about missing your school?" He's offering me more bait. He obviously wants me to spend more time with him.

"Eeeh, I can make a lie in time." I shrug. "Besides, I think the other guys can handle it, yes? I don't need any more press time." I spy a building ledge overlooking the park. It's a good place to open a portal to. "Adieu." I mutter before I disappear.

I open on the ledge and look around. This will also give me time to put some pieces together about the links between Tonnerre and Vaccine. If he hasn't suffered any side effects or setbacks yet, then it means Vaccine had a reason to care about him. What's the relation?

I can't find anything. Where's my old apartment? I'm pretty sure I still own it. Probably.

There are no recognisable roofs in this neighbourhood. I'll have to keep looking over everything until I find my house or something recognisable. The old chapel is nearby. It's only one in the morning in Paris, so I have a while still. I wonder where Tonnerre went. All the buildings have either been replaced or renovated. There's a familiar roof on the corner of the horizon. I vault over to it, quickly changing my path. I kind of feel like I'm fourteen again.

It's the only building that's remained untouched aside from its new windows. My roof hatch is still here. I thrust it open and jump in. It's exactly how I remember it. I smile at my terrible apartment. Everything's the same as I left it. The floor is still held together with the deteriorating carpet. Everything is coated in dust. I trace my finger along the edge of the old table I had to balance with books. I stay away from the fridge. I don't know what's inside of that box of malicious intent and I don't want to know.

From my bureau, I pick out a short skirt and sweater to replace my costume and blue sweater. A final touch to my outfit are some aviators. I slip them on and grab my old backpack. I stuff my costume in it along with any bills I can find. There's nothing I really need here. All the stuff worth anything to me is in my new apartment.

I strut out the building's and in to the streets. I cross the footbridge and look down. I had to hide there once, it was wet and I panicked. I thought for sure she would find me but I was smart. She never taught me how to swim so she never checked. I keep walking towards downtown, passing by my old school. It still looks like the prison I thought it was.

I hear voices behind the school's steel bars.

"I think I recognize her." Someone one points and whispers at me in English from the shady schoolyard.

"What, her? Oh yeah, she seems familiar." Another shrugs quietly.

Someone grabs the bars of the fence separating the school from the world. "Do I know you?" They ask me. I'm pretty sure they're a dude.

"Uh, I used to go to school here?" I ask more than say. I mean, I haven't been here in two years. How would they still remember me? I don't remember any of them and why should I?

Their hands try to grab my sunglasses from behind the fencing but I take a step back and avoid them.

"Rikki?"

I remember that voice.

"Hey, Taj." I smile awkwardly and lopsidedly while I push the glasses farther up the bridge of my nose.

"What are you- where were you- how-" He sputters, spitting in nearly every direction.

"Um, I need to go." I start walking away from the school. I am not going to care. He betrayed me. He laughed at me. I grind my teeth together like Tonnerre does when he's especially angry. I need a drink.

"Rikki, wait!" He yells behind me.

Nope. I am not waiting for that asshole. I get bullied and he doesn't stand by me, he helps the bully. The stupidest idiot. I walk past the schoolyard without a second glance. How dare he talk to me.

I stroll over to the Capricorn Cafe, I spent so much time working here. As soon as I open the door and step in, the fragrance of java and espresso hit my nose. It's sooo enticing. I order the darkest roast, and drop a five on the counter.

"Rikki?" It comes from behind and I recognize that voice. Shivers run down my spine as I freeze up. I should've brought a hat too.

***

Again, the voice calls my name. He's probably wondering if I still speak English.

I still don't turn around. "Sorry, I think you are mistaken." I say quietly. Another shiver drops down my back and connects to my neck.

"Rikki?" He says like a parrot. It's like he can only say my name. Not, 'Hey, are you Rikki?' Or 'Excuse me, but do you know a Rikki Dubois?' No, instead he just repeatedly calls my name.

He grabs my shoulder and I try to shy away. I'm legitimately tempted to open a portal away from here. He drags me shoulder around so he can get a look at my face. He peers into my face long enough for him to know it's me.

"Hi, Aaron." I mumble quietly with a frown-ish smile.

"Wow, it's really you." He's a lot taller than before and his hair isn't as stupid. It actually looks pretty good. Actually, it even looks a little like Harmony's.

94

"Yeah, yay..." My voice is really weak right now. I wave my finger up in a little celebration. But I don't mean it. I just came here for a coffee.

My coffee is ready, and my tongue is tied. I can't speak around him. I didn't really leave on very good terms unless you count blowing away to a secret castle in the mountains.

At the side counter and grab my drink. I get a meter away from the door before Aaron stops me. I take a deep breath and sigh. "Have I given back your jacket from when I borrowed it all those years ago?" I ask, a little irritated.

"Yeah, but what does that have to do with anything?"

"Then why do you keep bothering me?" I brush past him and walk through the door onto the sidewalk. It's cold, really cold.

"God dammit." I hear him mumble before he runs off. I take a long sip of my coffee.

Some guy in a cape is jumping over roofs while another is just in the sky imitating me when I was Topaz. It's getting colder. Does he have ice powers? I think I'm going to watch since I probably won't have to step in.

I find a bench outside of a boutique and sit down ready to admire this battle between superheroes. I look at my breath appearing from my mouth.

"Blizzard, your tyrannical terror of ice will stop with me!" The guy in the cape yells at the other.

I can't hold my laughter inside of myself. I let it all out at once and they totally notice.

"Rikki?" They say simultaneously. How many people know me here? I wonder if I can brainwipe the entire city and make them forget.

"Uh- bird!" I point behind them and run away. I make it to an alleyway before the guy with the ice powers tracks me down.

"You're really here. It's really you" He breathes.

"Yes?" I look up at him. He's created a bridge of ice to mend the gap in between the buildings. He stands on it and looks down at me.

"But-you've been gone for years! Why now?" He grabs his blue mask and yells in frustration.

"Uhhh... world travel?" I stammer. "It takes a lot of time, you know. Those large oceans. So wide and blue." I spread my hands out in front of me like I'm measuring a great expanse.

"That doesn't explain why you left so abruptly." He looks like he's frowning but I can't tell.

"Why do you care so much? It is not like you know me." I shrug. "Mon Dieu, you totally know me, do you not?" I sigh and hang my head. I mumble a few French swears and watch the guy in the cape tackle 'The Blizzard'. Well, all's well that ends well. I walk out of the alley and just keep walking until I get to my apartment.

***

I drop by the chapel an hour early with another coffee and donuts in my hands.

"Hey." I look behind me, it's Tonnerre. It always seems to be him. Just for once, why can't it be a handsome prince charming? Not some moody bottle blonde.

"How did you know I would be early?" I ask as I take a bite of a donut hole.

"There's been some serious changes in San Francisco." He mutters and sits beside me.

"Yes, you are not the only superhero. That is new." I chew the bite of chocolate dough thoughtfully. "What was his name, again?"

"It's Supreme. And I'm not exactly a superhero here." He grits his teeth together and scratches the back of his neck.

"Right, breaking that guy's legs, getting drunk and setting a firetruck on fire, and killing Vaccine *are* the makings of a supervillain."

"How did you find out I killed him?" He turns to me with a serious look on his face. I can barely keep my act together and keep my laughter in.

"You seem surprised." I shrug. "Besides, I have my ways. So does any other woman."

"I guess I shouldn't be, you are pretty smart." He drops something on the ground and grabs a donut hole.

"And illegal." False birth certificates and fake ID is getting harder to make these days.

"Speaking of illegal." He hands me a glass bottle out of a six-pack of them. "Want one?"

"Soda?" I tilt my head and read the label. It's difficult to make out due to the mashed-up font.

"Something like that." He smiles.

I pop the lid open and I take a sip and just as quickly, spit it out. "This is disgusting! You know I hate alcohol."

"I just wanted to mess with you." He grins wider and rubs my head. Great. Now my hair's scuffed up again. Does he know how hard it is to stuff my crazy locks into a measly braid? I frown and grab a hole of a donut. I stuff it into my mouth to get rid of the terrible taste of alcohol.

He opens his own and takes a swig of it.

"If you keep at that, you may try to set another firetruck on fire." I grin meanly before turning to a more serious topic. "Can you think of any link you have with Vaccine?" I add quickly. Probably not wise to bring this up now.

He spits out a little of his beer. "Where did this come from?"

"I was thinking about it today. Do you not think it is more than coincidence that you haven't had any mental or physical anguish from your powers?"

He pauses for a second, "Yeah, but do you really think I have a possible link with Vaccine?" He asks and looks right at me.

"You were the first... it might have been faulty or a prototype." But I know it wasn't.

"Hmm... could be." He breathes into his beer and looks away. What could he be hiding?

We sit there in silence for a few minutes until he takes a drink of his beer and asks if I'm really European.

"Yes, I am. I am perfect." I click my tongue and nod.

"Aside from the Prophecy?" He clicks his tongue too.

"Aside from that." I shrug and stuff two donut holes in my mouth at a time.

"So, what about your secret identity?" He asks, trying to sound casual but obviously failing.

"What about it?" I ask, spitting donut dough everywhere on the roof.

"Why the secret?"

"I want to have my own life until I can't. If that means a mask, then so be it, I will wear one. I will wear it until I cannot." I stuff another donut in my maw. I never have these in France. "What about you?"

"Well..." He sighs, "...Secrets need to be kept secret." He mutters and focuses on the horizon again. I tilt my head and look out on it too. There can't be anything especially interesting there, can there?

"Is someone after you? Your family?"

"Kind of..." He takes a quick sip. I can tell he doesn't want to talk about this since his eyes are avoiding mine. He's still hiding something.

"Do you need help? I have friends in high and low places. If you need help, I would be more than happy to aid you."

"No, no. It's fine," He mutters quietly. "I don't really want to talk about it."

"But you must need to, I mean, are they in danger? There must be something I can help you with- "

"Just shut up already!" He yells at me. "I don't need your pity or your help, alright? I already told you to stop talking about it!" He drinks the rest of his beer and throws the empty bottle onto the roof. It shatters into a hundred jagged pieces that spray everywhere.

I get up quickly and walk away from him. I smooth my hair down and swear under my breath. I can't be around him when he's like this.

"Sorry to interrupt-" The guy in the cape from earlier says. "-but I am in dire need of brew." He flies onto the roof and walks over to Tonnerre.

"How did it go with Blizzard?" I ask him with a devilish grin. Tonnerre's words quickly fade.

"He got away thanks to you." He turns to Tonnerre and ignores me much to my dismay.

"You still fighting that guy?" Tonnerre responds.

98

"He is so annoying!" He grunts and picks up his own brown bottle. "What's with your girlfriend?"

"She's not my girlfriend. Just a friend," Tonnerre mutters coldly.

"I didn't know you made friends with villains now." He looks at me and frowns. "You're keeping really weird company, aren't you?" He turns back to Tonnerre and washes down some putrid liquid.

"You don't know where it begins." Tonnerre sighs.

"I am right here," I mutter quietly. They're clearly enveloped in their own conversation. I check my watch. It's not even seven yet which means we're not leaving soon.

"Isn't The Blizzard Taj Rishi?" Tonnerre asks.

"Yeah, Taj Rishi. He was a student at San Francisco Highschool." That makes my ears burn. Not only did Taj turn evil, but they're talking about my old high school like that's what they would have expected. Sure, it's a lot like a prison but it was my school and it couldn't be that bad.

I bound off the chapel to a lower roof. I need to find Taj.

***

Why is it so easy to find idiots in this town? I mean, Taj chose a warehouse by the river. Cape Man is an idiot for not finding him. I hate this place.

My knocks echo throughout the warehouse. I've already changed into my civilian clothes.

"Go away!" Taj yells at me. "This is private property! I'm gonna call the cops on you!"

"What are you going to do? Freeze me?" I sigh and lean against some rotten panels by the door.

He swings the door open. "What are you doing here?" He's still wearing his stupid blue costume except for the mask.

"Wow, you really are a supervillain." My tone is unmistakably sarcastic.

"Rikki, is it really you?" He takes a step closer into the flickering light outside the door.

"Yes, is everyone an idiot in this town?"

"I thought you were dead." He moves his hand close to my face and I swipe it away with the back of my hand.

I tell him I went back to Paris.

"Paris?" His confusion gives me a small amount of satisfaction.

"Yes, did you never listen to a word I said? Or were you too busy making fun of me behind my back?"

"Rikki, it's not like that I..." But I cut him off and play my favourite song.

"Who cares about a hater," rings out my phone. *"I don't give a damn about a traitor!"*

"Sorry, that's my boyfriend calling. I think I should probably pick it up." I say it as harshly as possible and click the pause button.

"Ok, that is just- that is just- I don't even know." He shakes his head.

"Bye," I start sauntering away. I want him to know how well I'm doing without him. I don't need him. I never did. I don't need anyone. I'm a superhero.

"Rikki wait!"

"No! Stop being a supervillain. Use your powers for good. Help people who really need it." I don't even look at him."...then we may talk." I walk away. He knows me well enough to know not to follow. I wish Tonnerre knew that.

Andrew

"You're late." I tell her. Miles left half an hour ago and before that, in between the both of us, we drank the last of the beer and ate the last of her donut holes.

Corbelle lands on the roof. "Shut up." She mutters. She's tenser than ever.

"Where were you?" I ask. She doesn't just up and leave without telling anyone first.

"I was seeing an old friend, why does it matter?" She grunts and kicks a rock off the roof.

"Didn't go well?"

"I do not have many friends." She picks up another rock and throws it into the distance. It doesn't make it very far. It skids off the ledge of the roof and drops into the alley.

"I can tell." I hear it drop and echo off the dumpster at the bottom of the alley. "You don't seem very popular."

"Like I am the one that drives everyone away." She throws a rock above my head. She picks up another and aims a little lower.

"I get it. I snapped. I-a lot of things are going on right now and-" I catch it before it hits my face and throw it back at her. She curves out of its way, creating a yellow wall to stop it. It cracks in half and falls to the ground.

"You needed to yell at something."

"Right. You of all people would know," I mutter and scratch the back of my neck.

"Would you like to go back or are you staying in this horrible town?" she asks quickly to change the topic. She picks up half of the rock and throws it at me.

"C'mon! It's not that shitty."

"It's sooo bad! I have never seen so many tattoo places in one block!" She yells and throws her arms up to the heavens.

I laugh. "Okay, it's made a few changes to accommodate the incoming hipsters but that's just business."

"I am not kidding. What happened to this city?!" She sighs and throws her half rock at my head.

"You died." I miss the catch and it hits me in the eye. "Damn!" I yell and try to drown out her laughs.

"Not untrue." She shrugs with a smile.

"Are you kidding me! Of course, it's not untrue! You died over there!" I point towards downtown. It's still not the same since that battle. It's just different, darker.

"I know." She mutters and hangs her head for a moment. "But I am ready to go back to Paris and stay in my bed forever. Are you coming or staying, Windy?"

"I'm coming, Sunshine, give me a minute." I finish the last of my beer and slowly get up. She comes over and offers her arm as support. "I didn't drink that much," I tell her, though I did.

"It does not matter, going through portals is very... barf inducing. Especially when it goes through time zones." She nods from under my arm and pulls me forward.

"I've never barfed all the times you've teleported me," I mutter and lift my arm away from her.

"It is not entirely the act of walking through the portal or 'teleporting' as you say. It is mainly the change in atmosphere." She grabs me by the collar and pulls me away from the edge of the roof.

"I'll be fine." I assure her.

"Your funeral." She shrugs. Her platforms close underneath and over us, and we're back in Paris. She lets out a sigh of relief.

A bubble moves up my throat and she seems to sense it. "Are you well?" She asks and dives under my arm to hold me up.

I bend down and barf all over a Parisian roof. After a second of pure agony, I stop. She steps away and looks at the pile of barf like she's judging it. "It's not that bad." She shrugs. "But I think my roommate is freaking out since I have not shown up yet after an emergency at my school. I need to go. Do you know your way around Paris?" she asks and tilts her head to meet my eyes. Her raven braid tumbles out of her hood.

"Yeah, I'll be fine." I slowly sit, swallowing the bile in my throat.

"Are you sure?" She checks me over.

"Yeah." I nod my head.

"Adieu." And she's gone. She didn't teleport. She didn't have to. She just ran away. Like everyone does.

Rikki

Willow is going to be *so* pissed. Or maybe she'll be understanding and be all 'Oh, it's okay, Rikki! I know you're secretly a superhero so you can do what you need to never mind what I feel about you disappearing when an average person would die.'

My window squeaks little louder than usual when I push it up. My footsteps seem a little heavier. God, I feel like a kid sneaking in late at night, but that's exactly what I'm doing.

I shake my boots off and slip off my mask and scarf at once. I dive straight into my bed and lie there for an eternity.

My bed is so comfortable. I just want to just stay here forever. Screw the Prophecy. I can just stay here forever. Harmony will understand.

"Rikki? Is that you?" Willow mumbles as my door creaks open slowly but not slow enough.

"Uh-yes!" Quickly, I cover myself with blankets and desperately try to drag my costume off, "Do not..." she opens the door. "...come in!" But she's in.

She looks around. "What are you doing?"

"Science?" I say as more of a question. I mean, what else would a lonely kid do in the middle of night, alone in their room?

"That doesn't look like Science. What are you doing?" She pretends to rub her eyes. She's not really tired. She's been up this entire time.

"Sleeping?" I throw my head back into my pillow.

"You know what? I am too tired to deal with this." She picks up my mask, turns it over and asks what's this?

***

"Uh," I think quickly... "That is what I am planning for Halloween." I laugh inside my head. French people don't celebrate Halloween. It's an American holiday.

104

"Oooh, really?" She coos as she completely believes my lie. Crisis averted.

"Yes. Let me sleep, please. I am very tired." I sigh and pretend to close my eyes.

"Okay, but I want to talk about this in the morning." She moans and walks up to my door.

"Yes, Willow, just let me sleep," I moan louder.

She turns to leave but then asks, "You're single, right?"

I should just answer if it will get her out of here faster. "Yes, Willow. Just let me sleep." I roll my eyes at her, this is only the third time we've had this conversation this week.

"Hmmm, I should set you up with Andrew." She smiles through the dark.

"Willow nooo. I'm too tired for this and it is too dark in here to hear you," I groan.

"Fine, but you owe me girl talk, and the girls and I are having a sleepover here on Sunday."

"What?" I roll over just as she leaves. The door closes.

Ugh! Willow why!? I don't want anyone! I just want to stay single! Tiredly, I change into my baggy pajamas and drift off.

***

Longest night ever. My bags have bags.

My phone is buzzing non-stop, which does not add to this glorious day. I pick it up and drag my finger against the screen. As I do, Willow walks in through the open door.

"Morning Rikki... You realise that's a banana, right?"

"What?" I look at my yellow and irregularly curvy phone. "Oh. So, it is." I put it down and rub my eyes. Yep, it's definitely a banana. She places a more rectangular shaped object in my hands.

"Here's your phone."

"Oh, thank you." I smile up at her from my mattress. "Bonjour?" I mumble.

"Is this Rikki?" Someone asks in French.

"No... this is... I'm tired." I rub the back of my head and look at the banana. Why is there even a banana in my room?

"Is this a bad time?" They ask from wherever in France they are.

"Kind of, but it's alright. Who is this?" I mumble.

"Uh, Kaden." He pauses and argues with someone on his side of the line.

"How are you?" I ask and look at my clock. It's about ten in the morning.

"Uhh- no I'm not going to just say that! Hey stop, give me the phone!" I blink as I listen to them bickering.

"Rikki, this is Kai! Kaden has a huge crush on you and wants to go out with you on Sunday."

"Kai nooo!" I hear Kaden yelling. Their poor parents.

"You were going to have to tell her sometime." Kai yells back. It sounds like he still has possession over the phone.

"So, Sunday?" Willow grabs my phone and shouts in English amidst my wild grabs.

"Oui?" He mutters, obviously puzzled. "Dimanche, six heures?" He asks in French.

"Okay bye." She hangs up and squeals.

"Willow, quell le enfer?!" I yell at her. "Why?" I grab my phone from her hands and cradle it in my arms.

"You have a date!" She screams as she dances around my room happily. I really hope she never does again.

"It is not that big of a deal." I try to reassure her so she stops.

"Yes, it is!" She screams and grabs my shoulder with a massive smile all over her face.

"No, Willow." I groan. "It is just a casual meet up in which I will meet up with a casual acquaintance and have dinner with him. That is the definition of a rendez-vous."

"When was the last time you went on a date?"

"I do not know. Maybe two years ago?" I thought my first date (which was with Taj so I hope you understand) would also be my last.

"What?! Yes, it's a big deal! It needs to be perfect! I need to dress you up!"

"Willow nooo," I groan uselessly. I hate getting dressed up. She always goes overboard on everything. She uses makeup that'd cost my rent and tries to fix my ugly. Then, she stuffs me in a tight dress that costs ten times my rent and to top it all off, she puts *something* in my hair that takes about a week of constant showers to get out.

"The girls will help," She says with a reassuring smile.

"That doesn't make it better!" I yell. Why was this date planned on Sunday?! My brain is suffering major whiplash. "Willow," I mumble finally.

"Yeah?"

"Get out of my room!" I throw a pillow at her but it misses her. She gets the idea anyway.

***

I get dressed and walk along the street. I don't have a shift today, and I don't think I'll go out as Corbelle until dark. It seems like all the superheroes except me are either bent on TV' time or 'accidentally' stay long enough to be cornered in by reporters and camera crews. I think it's so stupid. Why would you want yourself on TV? You'll be more popular with people and supervillains. It would just draw more attention to yourself and it would attract an unnecessary spotlight from governments. Though sometimes it's nice to get your name out there.

I have my new sketchbook and pens with me. Some distractions from being a superhero, an occult in the making, and a teenage chemist would be nice. My music is extra loud. I like it like this since it reminds people that I don't want any interaction. I just want to be me. No mask, no prophecy.

I slide between two buildings and drop down a narrow flight of stairs. I use this way all the time. It's mainly secluded, and is filled with greenery, the perfect spot to draw. When I don't come here, I sit on the rooftops of Paris and draw the view.

The rock I'm sitting on reminds me of riding one of those bears.

My pencil hits the paper, but it doesn't describe anything around here. Instead, it does a light sketch of San Francisco. Of course, no drawing of San Francisco would be complete without its famed superheroes.

"Looks good," a guy says in English from behind me.

I snap my book shut and look behind me. Someone else is here. They shouldn't be here. No one ever comes here. I mean, it's practically impossible to access without knowing the secret pathway. Of course, there's the possibility of flying in but only Tonnerre can do that. And Sage, I guess.

I recognise him from Friday, I knocked into him.

"Oh, uh, thanks," I mutter in French.

"Are you a professional artist?" he asks in English, another tourist. He must have gotten lost.

"Me? No," I laugh nervously, "well, I don't know, I don't exactly have a future planned out for myself."

"I know how that feels." He shrugs with a smile. It doesn't look like he and the smile are very acquainted. It looks misplaced on him.

"Yeah?" I ask, not really interested. From my experience with Americans is that as soon as you get them talking, they don't stop. Hopefully, he gets so distracted with his own voice that he won't notice when I escape from the way I came.

"I'm eighteen and have no idea what to do with my life."

"That's pretty bad," I mumble as I open my book and dully print the tips of the trees. San Francisco has a lot of trees. I've been thrown into many of them.

"Really?"

"Oh, well, I guess at least you do not have to look forwards to an empty future since yours is going to be filled with adventure and surprise!" I say in a sunshiny voice while I outline some of the churches and the singular skyscraper/watchtower.

"Aren't you a little beam of light."

"I know! For fun, I do community service and I help the poor and I recycle all my recyclables. I am a very good girl." I sarcastically bat my eyelashes.

He laughs and then gestures to the sketchbook, "So, how well do you know that 'Tonnerre'?" He points to my page and presses on where Huricane's head is.

Andrew

"Uuh-" She stutters uncomfortably, "I heard about Tonnerre in San Francisco and then he came to Paris so I decided to draw him," She stutters.

"Why?"

"His powers seem interesting, yes? I've been having a little bit of a hard time lately so why not focus on someone who doesn't have regular problems, right?" He shrugs like she's scrambling for an answer. I bet she's got a crush on me when I'm in the mask.

"Didn't he break that guy's legs?"

"It was completely uncalled for to break his legs for just robbing a crappy coffee joint."

"But why him? What about Corbelle?"

"Who wants to draw a thief? Besides, she is kind of boring, don't you think?" Corbelle is the opposite of boring. She is unpredictable and amazing.

"I guess..." I stammer. I wouldn't call her that after knowing her for these few years.

She takes in my blonde hair and piercing blue eyes.

"So, do you have any other problems or will you leave me be?" She huffs and stares back at her drawing.

"For starters, there's this girl-" I sigh.

"Ooooh," She says without any emotion and sighs. I glare at the girl on the rock.

"I've known her for years and loved her for just as many but-"
She gags.

"I like her, but I can't tell her, I can't tell if she loves me or if she doesn't."

"Just tell her then. See what her reaction is." She says simply and returns to her fanart.

"It's not that simple," I say annoyed.

"It is not? But I guess I do not really have anyone to love so, I wouldn't know." She shrugs, sighs, and picks up her book. I could take a hint that she wants me to leave but I'd rather not at this point.

"Lonely?"

"No, I like being alone, I can think." She glares at me and gestures to the ferns by the rock stairs.

"Yeah?" I edge her on.

"There is this guy who likes me, but I can't tell him I don't like him." She sighs and sticks her tongue out in defeat.

"Then just tell him."

"I cannot, he is one of my friends, I do not want to ruin our friendship." She sighs. "I'm really starting to sound like some whiny teenager."

"I wouldn't have noticed," I tell her.

"That is because you are some guy who I just met." She rolls her eyes and sighs.

"Love at first sight?"

"What happened to that girl you were just talking about?" She lazily looks at me again.

"She's questionable."

"How so?" She doesn't sound like she really cares but I continue.

"It's hard to put into words, well, there's another guy, he's her... fiancé." Well, Corbelle has Harmony but she doesn't really like him.

"You like a girl who's about to be married?!" She shouts starting to actually look interested.

"No, it's not like that, it's, argh!-"

"Argh?" She asks and realises she's not really interested so she turns back to her paper and pencil.

"She's amazing, she understands me better than anyone, she a genius, and I think she's pretty,"

"Think?"

"And she's just... incredible."

"Wow. This is exactly why I don't love anyone. All the boys I know are either completely lovesick for someone else or are too lovesick to be healthy."

"I'm not."

"You are." She sighs with a frown.

Rikki

The guy leaves after a little while, thankfully. I can't put a name on him, but I think I remember him from somewhere.

My sketch is slowly evolving, I added some colour to give it life and to pretty boy's request, I provide a night city background to it. Maybe I should actually show it to Tonnerre. Maybe not.

A droplet of water smears the edge of my book, I stare at the intense clouds in the sky. Thunder. I've never been scared of thunder, but I've never been completely comfortable with it. I mean, it's Tonnerre's name.

I sigh. The one day I didn't pack my obscenely tiny umbrella. I close my book and search for a covered area. There's none over here but I should be able to find a cheap cafe off the Champs-Élysées.

The streets are crowded with tourists and locals alike. Pickpockets and grifters often lay siege to this area. I've been grifted before, or at least they tried to. I gave them a good mouthing off in French afterwards. They looked so shocked. I had to laugh at them.

I step into an old cafe, it reminds me of Capricorn and San Francisco. In the window, I spot a Help Wanted sign. I walk in and apply on the spot.

***

Well, I've got a new job now. Rikki for the win.

I quickly broke the news to Marianne via text messaging. She took it way too well, I was almost offended. The shifts here anyway, no late nights spent working rather than jumping across roofs catching magic animals and monsters. What a great time to be alive.

I sigh and lean against the counter. The bell on the door rings. A customer.

"What would you like?" I mutter.

"I'd like a frappuccino, please, if you're not too busy being the nerd you are." Maya Lesage. What a beam of sunshine.

I rattle off a few of the additions... whipped cream, cocao, milk, vanilla, and soya.

"No, I'm on a no-soy diet," She mumbles as she scrolls through her phone.

"What kind of diet is that? Isn't the point of a diet to be soy-friendly?" I ask her critically.

"Is it really your job to question your customers? What happened to 'the customer is always right'?"

"Fine, fine. That totals to five euros," I grumble, wishing I hadn't asked. She taps an over glorified card on the scanner. I roll my eyes at her.

"Excuse me?!" She noticed. "I am your customer! You must treat me with respect!" Her sass is even greater than mine, it's startling.

"Yeah, sorry. I was just thinking of a funny joke a friend of mine told me a while ago." I roll my eyes again, just a little more stealthily.

"Well?" She gestures at me.

"What?" I ask. "Did you come to your senses and want soy after all?"

"Let's hear it." She flicks her giant cat-eye sunglasses off her nose and lays them on the counter along with her five-euro bill.

"Why didn't the skeleton compete in the talent show?" I ask her.
"What-?"

"Because it didn't have the guts!" I start laughing at my own joke, she stares at me dumbly and then it hits her. She lets out a little snicker while my laughter fills the shop.

She leans in from the other side of the counter. "You know, with all your science stuff, do you make any chemical combustions?" Maya whispers to me.

"You mean explosions?" I whisper back.

"Yeah, you think I can buy some?"

"You want to buy explosions?" I look her over carefully. She's wearing a pink suit and matching skirt.

"No, I want to buy bombs."

"From me." I point to myself. "You want to buy bombs, *not* explosions, from me."

"Yeah," Maya nods and looks around the shop for any prying eyes or ears.

"I can't believe I thought you were a priss," I mumble to myself. "What do you need them for?"

"I can't say right now; can I meet you after your shift?" She looks around suspiciously.

"Uh-sure?"

She walks out and flicks her sunglasses onto her head, frappuccino in hand. The girl who just asked me for a bomb. I watch her walk down the street. My school life just took a dark turn.

The bell hanging from the door frame rings again and Kai walks in.

"Hey," I mumble as I lean carefully against the corner. Is he going to ask me for explosions, too?

"Oh, hey Rikki, I didn't know you worked here," He looks at me. "Are you alright?"

"Yeah, fine. Also, to answer your first question, I do as of today." I shrug mildly.

"Did you quit catering?"

"I don't like skirts," I glare at him and scratch the counter violently with my finger.

"What about dresses?" He asks with a sickening smile.

"You want something or are you just annoying me?" I glare at him and tap the cash register impatiently.

"A little bit of both." He shrugs. "How much would it cost to get you to wear a dress to school?"

"What do you want?" I sigh and lean on my arm.

"A London Fog, please." He smiles politely for once and drops a handful of change on the counter. I curse at him as I count it.

"You're a euro short," I mutter at him angrily. Today's a Saturday, not a Mathday. Mathday's aren't even a real thing. I just made them up and they already suck.

"Here." He takes out a bill that would've paid for the whole thing in the first place, and puts it on the counter. I throw my arms up in defeat and glare at him. I turn away and grab the other side of the counter.

"You know, you're not the best barista," He says as he peers over my shoulder.

"Really? Well, you know, you're not the best customer."

"You should lose the sarcasm and scowl. Then you'll be almost human." He shrugs at me.

"Where'd all these jokes come from? Last week you were the quietest person I knew." I raise an eyebrow at him as I mix his tea with whipped cream and vanilla.

"A lot can happen in a week," He mutters and looks around the solidary and silent shop.

"Yeah, I know the feeling." I nod at him and let the tea sit.

"Oh, yeah that reminds me, you want to come to our next performance?"

"Sure, depends on the hours though," I mumble as I turn back to the tea. I glance at the printed recipes hanging above the mini-fridge.

"What are yours?"

"Four to seven on weekdays," I mutter as I stir the tea once again.

"How much are you getting paid?"

"Millions of dollars, I won't even need another job." I shrug as I pass him his hot tea.

"It's so hard to get a simple answer out of you." He rolls his eyes at me. "You're as bad as... Corbelle," he mumbles, I hear most of it.

I tap the cash register and retrieve his change from its dark chasm of coins and cold, hard cash.

He takes a sip of his tea. "Are you excited for your date with Kaden?" He asks, changing the subject.

"Why have I been forced into this?!" I yell at him and dig my nails into the wooden counter.

"So, you don't want to go on a date with Kaden?"

"Well, you see- " I laugh awkwardly. "It's not that I don't want to go on a date with him, it's just that- "

116

"Friendship troubles?"

"Yeah, well, I like Kaden, but we're friends, right? And only friends." I make an X with my arms to emphasize the point. "A relationship is the farthest thing from what I want, right now. Please don't tell him I said that, by the way."

"I'm his twin. It's like you're asking Santa not to give out presents."

"Santa isn't even real." I mumble under my breath. "Please? I haven't even told Willow."

"So, what's so wrong with him?" He asks and takes another sip of his drink. "Are you into girls?"

"What? No! I just don't want a relationship. How hard is it to understand? I *don't* want to be with someone. I don't want to be with anyone."

"Whatever you say."

"This isn't the dark ages! I don't have to have a guy!" I yell at him and the entire world.

"But what about the guy's feelings?"

"I just don't know." I shrug.

"Okay, I won't tell Kaden, but you should tell him before he gets any more false hopes." He walks out leaving me to mull in the silence and solidarity of the shop. I need more friends.

Maya

The cafe door swings closed and Rikki turns the sign to 'closed', obviously not seeing me walk up to the door and bang on it. She turns with a start and unlocks the door. "Thanks," I tell her as I walk in to the quaint little shop.

"So, you want bombs?" She looks me over as we stand just inside.

"For a friend," I insist. "Also, you missed a spot." I point to a dirty table she hasn't wiped down.

"A friend?" She asks and looks me over again.

"Well... a boyfriend." I nod.

"Your boyfriend needs a bomb?" She looks at me sceptically and sighs. She leans against the table I was pointing to and produces a cloth. She wipes it quickly and efficiently.

"Not a big one, a smoke bomb." I roll my eyes at her.

"What could he possibly need a smoke bomb for?" She yells and throws her arms up, spraying dirty water everywhere.

"Look, can I just buy one?" I don't want to explain anymore to someone like Rikki. She wouldn't understand.

"One? You *always* buy more than one." She grins evilly and tucks the cloth back into her apron.

"I'm impatient, alright? Can I just buy some smoke bombs already?" I yell at her.

"Hey, hey, calm down! Do you want the whole city to know?" She walks behind the glass case containing greasy, old muffins and scones. She grabs notepad and a pen from behind the counter. "How many?"

"Fifty?" I ask. I'm not sure if that'll be enough but I hope it lasts me long enough to lay off the drugs.

"Sounds fun," She grins at me as she leans against the counter.

"How much?" I dig out my wallet.

"Nah, I don't want money. But you do owe me a favour, got it?" She points a finger gun at me and shows me the gap between her teeth with a grin. If she took out her bun, she'd look a little like Corbelle.

"Okay," I say and tucking my matching wallet back into my fancy bag she couldn't afford in a thousand years. What does she mean, a favour?

She starts wiping some more of the tables. It doesn't look she cares about my livelihood or making the bombs.

"When can I have them?" I ask her, annoyed.

"When I make them," She mumbles. "Probably Monday." She shrugs. "It could change."

"Alright, I'll wait till then," I mutter. Maybe I can wait that long but... I can't stand the pill.

When I get home, I swallow the little blue capsule with my eyes squeezed shut. The brief feeling of sickness passes and I'm no longer Maya Lesage, I'm Sage. I don't even know my powers. My source is completely anonymous. All they do drop off my monthly dosage in a package overlooked by my parents. All I know is that they chose me for a reason. They chose me to protect Paris. Not some weird emo freak.

The thing about taking the pellets is that they also affect how I act until they wear off. They usually make me more focused and agile but they make my balance wobbly so now I have a tendency to fall down. I'm not even going to mention all the times I've had to been wheeled to the school nurse for fainting in the middle of Math.

Rikki

Is it just me, or is there a lot of cats around? I've tripped on at least three, one landed on me, and four are following me.

They're just cats and yet they're *everywhere*. I look around, there's no one. I duck down a narrow alley. The cats follow. My feet leave the ground and I cling to a cold metal fire escape painted dark blue. The cats make efforts to follow but fall off the ladder. I snicker at them. I never liked cats.

All the windows on this side are obscured by curtains so it's safe to teleport. All the shadows disappear beneath my light. The breeze is gone, replaced by my mellow walls. I drop to my desk and flip open my computer. Its lights hum and drowsily go on as I tap open the browser.

A newsflash hits me over the head. My hand falls from my chin which slams down against my desk. I sit up, rub my sore chin, and look at the live footage.

"Tout l'hommes sont chats!" A woman yells onscreen. That explains all the cats. All men are cats.

I ignore my headache and slip into my costume. What is wrong with this city? It's almost as bad as San Francisco. But... it's actually kind of fun.

***

So! Paris is being overrun with cats. All the guys in Paris have been turned into cats. Is Reine Blanche behind it? That's who I think is the main suspect.

There are damn cats everywhere. Tonnerre is a cat. Nuit is a cat. Velocity is a cat. I am *not* a cat. Why am I the only female superhero in Paris?

In the distance, there's screaming, nearby cats join in, and then more. A chorus of screaming cats is rising above Paris. It's hitting my eardrums with force. It's nothing compared to the bears' screams but it's not silence.

Bubbles are flying up in different places all around Paris. None of them around me thankfully, but they're close. They're beautiful in a dangerous way and I kind of want to touch one again. I reach out tentatively. Abruptly, Reine Blanche's face appears on the bubbles right before I touch the nearest one. I lean back and scowl at her face. I don't know if she can see me or not.

"Protector of Paris! I have a challenge for you!" She grins evilly as a projected image. "I have turned all your partners, not to mention all the men in Paris, into Felis Catus, otherwise known as the common cat. I challenge you to protect all cats and remaining people from any further threats. If you survive tonight you can continue to the next test. Bonne chance." All the bubbles and her face explode in a giant pop that pierces my eardrums and echoes across the rooftops. Big problems.

Someone screams near the Eiffel Tower. Bigger problems.

Maya

I stepped on a wet roof! That was almost as stupid as Kaden Mace. I'm Paris's superhero. I should be better than this. Better than Corbelle.

Light suddenly covers the roofs closest to me. Is that the sun rising? In the middle of the night?

"Are you all right?!" Corbelle falls out of whatever light show just happened on the corner of the horizon. She's clearly flustered.

"Corbelle." Not, Corbelle. She's so annoying with her yellow power and terrible quips. What's she doing here? Reine Blanche obviously meant me when she addressed the protector of Paris.

She looks exasperated. "Why don't you pitch in for once? I've been saving various cats and random women from completely random stuff, and you're just standing here. Does. Not. Help." She bends down and breathes heavily. I have never seen her this serious.

"Alright, what do I do?" I ask her, taking whatever suggestions she may have so long as they're sort-of sane.

"Don't let anything die!" she yells before falling backwards off the roof.

"What?" I yell back and lean over the edge. She's gone. What the hell is wrong with this girl?

Rikki

This city has problems. Its problems have problems. Its problems have problem's problems. I just saved seven cats from one car and one lady from seven cats. Why is this so hard?

Bears are randomly stalking the streets. *Why is this happening.* I'm trying to avoid all animals other than cats and women.

The streets are dryer now. I've got a better grip and a faster pace. I slide down the corner of a street. *Bear!* I scream in my mind. A bear is holding some cats hostage. I'm not going to stop, that would give away my advantage of speed.

I slide to the ground and extend my legs in front of me. I drift under the bear and grab the cats. I whip my legs around so I'm standing and start running away from the bear.

"Mon Dieu! Mon Dieu! Mon Dieu!" I yell as I race away from the brown monster. I don't bother looking behind me since the cats' screams give it away. The bear is following me.

I can't vault off or onto anything. The pile of hissing furballs twist in my arms. I hate cats.

Can bears climb? I've seen videos, but they can't climb buildings can they? Running isn't going to be quick enough. The bear swiftly gains significant ground over my short legs. I can almost smell it. I can't *bear* it.

Time to go old-school. I form a wall of light in front of us, the cats start struggling in my grip.

"Stop squirming!" I yell at them as I jump through the portal onto a roof. I didn't plan this out, I need to steady my thoughts. This is getting dangerous. Something's wrong with me. I need to focus. My headache's only getting worse.

Aaron

I knew something was wrong. I warned her. But did she listen? No. She acts all flirty and friendly, but she hates me. I can tell. If she really cared what I thought, she would have been more careful.

I scoop her up in my arms and take her back to the Monastery. She's out cold. She's so quiet. She's at peace for once.

I don't trust Tonnerre. I feel like he's playing her, using her. I don't know if I should tell her or not. If I do, she might shrug it off and she'll tell him and he'll advance his plans or something. I don't know what his plans are, but I've sent some priests to watch him.

She mumbles some French in her sleep. I pull us through the distance between the Monastery and Paris. I step down the stairwell in the Monastery to the Oracle's room and knock on her door.

"Harmony, to what do I owe the pleasure?" She groans at me and ignores the girl in my arms.

"Chaos collapsed on a roof," I seethe at her. I place her down gingerly in front of the Oracle on a padded mat.

"Young love," she sneers at me and puts down her magic spell book in one of the many piles in her room.

"Just do whatever magic you do- if you're not a phony." The Oracle and I always shared a hate for each other, Chaos's always been close with her despite it though.

She places a hand on Chaos's forehead and glares back at me. "It's called exhaustion, idiot. She hasn't been drinking or eating enough." The Oracle pats her head again. "And she has a fever."

"How was I supposed to know that?" I ask her and kick a pile of cloth. My foot hits something hard and I double back in pain.

"You're the one stalking her."

"Hey! I was just in Paris and I decided to check on her."

"She's as old as you and more mature than you. She doesn't need to checked on, but you on the other hand," she mutters.

"She's my Chaos, I think I have some rights to visiting her."

"Je peux t'entendre..." Chaos mumbles quietly and twists in the Oracle's arms.

"Shhhh, honey, you're alright, just sleep," The Oracle flattens an orb of magic over her forehead and she falls back onto the Oracle's lap.

"Jealous?" She asks; she knows me too well. I may hate her but she's always been the creepy old lady in the basement.

"No." I hiss, trying to conceal the obvious truth.

"You can go, I've got her now, she's in good hands."

"You think she wasn't before?"

"I know she wasn't before. Now, go. Before I make you." I turn to the door. She's made me leave before and it was not pretty.

"One last thing, did you peek under her mask?" She asks me, making me freeze in my footsteps.

Rikki

"Where am I?" I ask in French and sit up. Do I have a fever? I think I'm burning up. It feels like my head and body's on fire. Where am I? Seriously, where am I? I... Paris. Crap. Paris may as well be in flames right now.

Mask. Am I wearing my mask? I scratch at my face. It's there.

"Hello Carmen, feeling better?" The Oracle asks in French. She seems to know every language I guess that's one of the many perks of magic because, you know, *magic*.

My neck turns around so quickly it cracks, "Ow," I grumble and massage it carefully.

"Don't worry. It's just me. How are the cold packs working?" She walks in and takes a sip of her tea. She looks down at me and takes another sip of her tea. She goes through tea like I go through coffee; at an alarming rate.

She removes the packs wrapped around my forehead and squeezes them. "They've melted! How are you feeling honey?" She looks down at me with worry.

"A little dizzy and very hot. Where am I?" I wipe my bleary eyes and swipe off my mask. She already knows my face and my name because, you know, *magic*.

"You're in the Monastery." She takes another sip of her hot drink. It smells like cinnamon.

"How did I get here?" I ask her and rub my eyes. My internal clock in screaming wake up but my eyes say no.

"Harmony found you." She takes a long sip.

"What! How did he know I was in Paris? How did he know where I was?" I throw one of my legs down on the makeshift bedding.

"Calm down. He just wanted to check up on you."

"Check up on me? I don't to be checked on!" I yell at her, throwing my hands at the shallow ceiling.

"That's what I told him."

126

"If anyone needs to be checked on, it's him! I mean seriously! Who lets some teenager go out alone, at night to see some girl? What kind of system are you running here?"

"If he didn't, you'd still be on that roof with a fever and not enough food."

"I've been eating," I insist defensively and sit up. "I eat a burger like, once a week. I eat lots!"

"Not nearly enough." She pokes my stomach. "Too skinny." She pokes the air out of my stomach and I burp.

"Well, I'm fine." I say and slowly stand up, but a wave of dizziness and nausea hits me and I fall back.

"This is why he checks on you, even though he knows you hate him. He knows he needs to check on you since you don't check yourself." Oracle always knows what's going on. You can't hide anything from her. She's always right because, you know, *magic*.

I barf all over her dark blue (now a little green) carpet and bend over. She holds my hair out of the mess.

"You don't take care of yourself. Don't you have a roommate? Hasn't she noticed your daring endeavours?" She asks me.

"No-" This morning's breakfast lands on my makeshift bed. "Thankfully not. Willow would completely freak out."

"What about that male mistress of yours?"

"He's not like that!" I yell. "Why do I have to date someone! He is *just* a friend. There's nothing between us."

"That was a little defensive."

"No, it wasn't," I insist and bring my hands up to my chest angrily. "It was truthful."

"You like someone." Like I said, she knows everything because, you know, *magic*. "I can see the blush on your face, you may as well admit it to any unwanted ears listening."

I hug my pillow tightly.

"You haven't told him?" She asks me.

I hide my pink face in its fluffy surface. If I hide my face maybe she'll forget me.

"You should. You love him don't you?"

"But what if he doesn't love me?" I mumble. "And it's not like I've seen him recently, it's been two years." I add. I think of his red hair and blush some more.

"You haven't loved anyone before, have you?"

I shake my head without even thinking. I look away.

"There's no shame in admitting it. I haven't ever loved anyone, I think it's better like that." She looks to the ceiling with a cloudy look in her eyes. Or maybe that's just how her eyes really look. I don't really pay attention.

***

The Oracle left me to sleep but I'm not going to sleep. I just want to go home. She used her magic to stop me from teleporting or portaling away. I'm under curfew. I hate this.

What's happening in Paris right now? Is Sage handling it? Is everyone dying? What's even happening?

My fever is just as bad. I made her give me human medicine, I don't want to be healed with magic. I'd like to stay on the side of science for as long as possible. Too bad fever medicine sucks. I feel exhausted and I want food. But how did I get sick? I'm outside all the time! My body is used to this. I didn't eat anything weird and I haven't been exposed to any weird bacteria. But she is right, I didn't eat much. God! I feel like a toddler, I'm acting like one too. If she gives me magic then I'll be better. No, that's the medicine talking. Stay strong, Carmen. I can't stay strong when I'm like this. I don't even feel warm. I just feel cold. I just want to go home. I don't want to be here. I don't want this prophecy. I don't want these feelings. I hate my life.

Andrew

A cat. I was a god damn cat. What the hell. I hate this place so much.

Where's Corbelle? She's always here first. She'd be fighting these things first.

Nuit says something in French and the other one agrees.

The girl says something about being a hero or saviour, I don't know. I should have paid more attention during French twelve.

"Funny, it was Corbelle wasn't it?" I ask, responding in English to whatever she said.

"What?" She asks in English. "No." She says and shakes her head.

"Where?" I ask, making to say it slow and easy to hear.

She says something quickly then continues with something along the lines of: "...Arc de Triomphe."

I jump off the roof, "Go home." Where's the Arc de Triomphe? What is it even? Paris is so weird. I wish she'd just come back to San Francisco.

Would she just disappear? She's sixteen so she'd probably want to ditch everyone. Oh god, does she think of me as a father figure? Or an older brother? She'd want to ditch me then.

Where is she? Even when we were in San Francisco, she would always tell me or leave a note when she couldn't make it but she is a teenager, she doesn't need to tell me when she needs to go or when she can't make it. She's not some kid.

"Corbelle!"

I don't even hear the echo. This is completely unlike her, but do I even know the real her? I don't even know her name. She's an amazing actor and she's smart. She could be anything, anyone. The girl I know might not even be real.

Rikki

I smell like barf. I hate this. So much. I'm not supposed to get sick.

"I want to go home!" I kick my sheets and roll around in the new bed of pillows.

"Not until you're better," The Oracle insists.

"Why not? My roommate will take care of me!" I shout, throwing stuff everywhere.

"You're staying here."

"Please?"

"No."

"I need to go, please!" I'm begging now, "I command you to let me leave." I don't like forcing her to do what I say, but thanks to an older magic, she has to do whatever Chaos or Harmony says.

"Hrmmm. You can use your power just fine, I never put any protection up." She begrudgingly mumbles. "But if you leave before you're better, I will send Harmony to see you occasionally."

"I'm going," I tell her, trying to officially end the conversation.

"You really love that red-headed boy, don't you? I can tell." She's trying to add to our later conversation. Why does every girl I know wants to talk to me about boys?

"I'm going." I don't want to talk about this. Ever. In a million years. And then some.

I use the power to open a wall of light. I know it shouldn't make me smile but... I can't help it.

Paris is not being overrun with bears or cats. It's actually quiet. Is everything normal? I feel better but not a hundred percent. I still feel dizzy, so parkour won't be a very smart thing to do. Oh well.

I vault to the roof parallel to me. My landing is not perfect. I could do better, I've done better before. Where am I even going? I know I'm not going home. That seems to be the only thing on my mind.

Why can't I think straight? It's not because of my fever, or is it? I have no idea.

"Tonnerre!" Why would I even try that? Paris is filled with people in sound absorbing buildings, of course, he's not going to hear me. Why did I even bother?

"Hey," Tonnerre calls back in English. I throw a triangle at him. He swerves just in time.

"Sorry, instinct," I relax my arm and shake my wrist out. It's still ready to throw more at him.

"Your instinct is to try to kill anyone who scares you?"

"Anyone who surprises me and it was a shot to your shoulder."

"Wow, what Parisian optimism."

"What American naivety," I correct him, bringing up my chin as an act to try to be a snob.

"I don't know how to respond to that," He laughs.

"Maybe it's your American stupidity," I correct myself and stare at my gloved nails. The leather is starting to peel.

"Spoken like a foreigner."

"You're the foreigner, bald eagles and whatever." I say and spread my arms around, gesturing to all of France. "This is not America."

"Maybe," I pretend to think about it though I do really hate both nicknames. Of course, I can deal with something friendly and personal like sunshine. After all, it's just a friend thing, right?

"Are you alright? You look like you're burning up. Your face is all flushed." He puts a hand on my forehead. "Wow, your head's freezing. How do you feel?"

"Stupid prophecy," I groan and wave his hand away. "It is probably just a small sickness or something."

"I'm not sure you'd want to have an actual fever though. They really, really suck. You get to stay home from school which in nice, though."

"How do you get over one? Just in the case that I get one."

"My mom used to give me home-made chicken noodle soup. It would always make me feel better." His gaze drifts away from mine. He must have some happy memories of his parents. He's lucky. I think about my mother and look away.

His blue eyes focus back onto mine again, "Is there someone to take care of you?"

I cough out of surprise. There isn't anyone, really. There's Willow, but she has her own problems, she doesn't have time to worry about mine. I can barely handle my own troubles.

"Not even that Harmony guy?" he asks with a hint of worry on his masked, movie-star face.

"No, no. I can take care of myself." I wave my hand. "But how did you become not a cat?" I want to change this subject as quickly as possible. I don't need him in my business.

"There weren't any actual threats. They were all illusions; Sage axed them all and when she did, I think we all turned back into humans. At least that's what I think she said."

"Good. Also, I am not going to be able to patrol tomorrow." I add and sigh.

"What? Why not?"

"Well, I have a date but-" I sigh as I try to explain like I did with Kai.

"You know what? There's something I need to do, right now."

"Tonnerre, wait." He takes off, doesn't even stutter, he's just gone. "Oh, come on," I groan. His wind hits me just like he would. Why is this so difficult?

What day is it? It's Sunday, right? Yeah, I think it is, Willow's going to be freaking out. Who wouldn't be after their roommate disappears twice in the same week? Not Willow. She's going to be on full freak-out mode.

I shove aside the curtains across the entry to my room. Everything in my room is colder.

"Rikki?" Willow asks as she walks in my creaky door. I need to put a lock on it but that wouldn't do anything to stop her from coming in.

"Willow. I was just going to go to sleep," I laugh awkwardly as I kick my mask underneath my desk.

"Don't scare me like that! Where were you?" She grabs my shoulders briskly.

"I was at a friend's house." I point behind me at the window and make the shape of a house with my hands.

"Really?" She nudges me in the stomach with her sharp elbow and winks.

"It was not like that!" I yell at her and sigh. I drop on my bed and spread myself around on the blue sheets.

"Are you ready for your date tonight?"

"Date? Oh, yes. I will be fine," I grumble and lazily look at my closet. I'll have to wear my dress.

"Well..." Willow looks at my closet too and scratches the back of her head.

"Well, what?"

"You're not the most graceful person... I think we'll give you a hand with getting ready."

"Just let me sleep," I groan. I haven't had enough coffee to be considered awake.

"You hear that girls?" I hear her whisper-shout to the living room. I forgot about the sleepover.

***

"Willow I don't think lipstick is supposed to work like this," I tell Willow and her little party of daddy's girls.

"Relax Rikki, I know what I'm doing." She continues to drag a stick of cherry coloured compound across my face. Another girl brushes the other parts of my face with a soft brush. My hair is being tugged by another girl while another searches online for a new dress. I never bother to learn their names; they're always different whenever there's a sleepover. From what I hear, Willow hangs out with all the investors' kids from her dad's company. Every time she does it, she gains extra shares.

"Willow I cannot afford this," I beg. I'd rather be in the fiery pits of hell than here.

"No, we've got this. We're rich."

I sigh. Whenever my timing is bad enough to be caught in the middle of 'makeovers', someone always yells 'Nerd Makeover!' and they do my hair and makeup and put me in a dress.

"So, who's this guy?" one girl asks Willow as she crunches on some designer potato chips.

"He's a member of Rikki's science club."

"Oooh, scandalous." She grins and focuses back on buying an over-priced piece of fabric that's probably too small.

"It is not like that!" I yell and throw my arms up from the chair. The girl doing my makeup scolds me and pulls my hair like I'm a little doll for her to play with.

"You think he would like black?" The girl on the computer asks.

"No! Do not choose anything black, please!" I beg. "Anything but black, please!" I insist.

"He loves black, right?"

"Knowing Rikki, I'm sure he does." Willow smirks and looks through her makeup bag. I don't want Kaden getting the wrong idea. If I wore a black dress like his costume, he would be the kind of person to take it the wrong way.

The girl taps the computer. "Done." She smiles.

"Wonderful." Willow coos as she tries to take my hair away from the other girl.

"I asked you not to!" I yell at them all.

"Too late hon." They always call me that, 'hon'. They want to put me in a dress, do my hair and makeup, but they don't care about me, the person underneath that façade. I hate that Willow's family forces her to hang out with these people. They're intolerable. They're the true definition of snobbery. They always complain about everything no matter what. "This is *so* small!" Or "This drink isn't sweet enough!" But my favorite is probably: "These clothes aren't expensive enough!".

The doorbell echoes through the living room as the dress is dropped off.

"This dress was based on that new superhero, Nuit." The girl on the computer says blatantly as she continues to tap on it.

"Really?"

"Yeah, one of a kind."

That's even worse. "No!" I yell and groan. "There's no way I'm wearing it!"

"Here, hon, try it on!"

They push me into my room and force me into the dress. "This does not fit!" My arms pin down to my sides in frustration.

"It fits fine Rikki! You look great! Look in the mirror," Willow encourages me.

I spin around in the mirror. It looks how it feels. Very tight.

"Try on the jacket and hairpiece that came with the dress!"

They pat a black bow into my hair and Willow stuffs my arms into a leather crop jacket. I've seen this dress at least a hundred times in New Navy. Either this is a fancy rip-off or New Navy ripped off the designer. I can't wear this.

"Oh! Oh! He's here!" Willow looks out our window onto the street.

"Quel?!" She drags me out of my room, out of the apartment, down the four flights of stairs, out of the lobby and into the street. She pushes me out and slams the door behind me.

Kaden stands before me in a suit, looking like he'd been through a similar ordeal.

"Hi," he mutters.

Kaden

We sit at the restaurant in silence. Baron and Kai told me to come here, they said it would be perfect for any girl. Unlike her usual self, Rikki looks uncomfortable and hesitant.

"I like your dress," I try to start some kind of conversation with her.

"Yeah, Willow chose it," She mutters and looks around at the red, velvet drapes and the running waiters. She takes off her jacket and it hits me: the outfit was based on me.

"I love it."

Her cheeks turn rose as I grin at her.

"Is that bow part of it too?" I ask and look at the top of her head.

"Y-yeah."

"Is that a little mask on it?"

"I think so..." She stammers and bends her head down so I can get a better look. The bow's been elaborately braided into her hair on the top of her head.

The waitress comes over and straitens her white apron. "What would you two like to order?" She asks sweetly.

"I'd like a steak with rose lemonade." I tell her and fold up my menu. I place it on the white table cloth and she picks it up.

"I'll have salad and a water, please?"

"Rikki, you don't have to choose the cheapest thing on the menu, I got this, you don't have to pay for it," I try to smile at her.

"Okay, uh, can I also have a rose lemonade then?" She laughs and hands the waitress the menu.

"Sure!" The waitress's excitement is almost as annoying as Corbelle's. Maybe she's Corbelle. Of course, she's not as short as she is so she probably isn't.

"Thanks..." Rikki gazes at her hands and fiddles aimlessly.

"So, I can guess I'm your favourite superhero?" I ask her with a wide grin.

"I-I'm sorry Kaden," Rikki stammers and hangs her head low.

"What are you talking about?" I laugh a little nervously. What is she talking about? She avoids my eyes. "What is going on?"

She still won't meet my eyes. Now I'm really curios. "It's just- I'm not ready for a relationship yet. I've got a lot on my plate right now and I have bigger fish to fry instead of doing things like *this*."

"What- Rikki?"

"I'm sorry." She gets up and quickly walks away.

"Rikki?" I get up and run after her. But I shouldn't. She doesn't want me. She wants someone else. I shouldn't go after her, that's not my job. She left her jacket and it's raining outside. I hope it starts to really pour.

Rikki

I wore flats tonight because I thought I was going to wait until the end of the date, after dancing, to tell Kaden how I felt. But I didn't, I couldn't. I didn't think I'd need my black flats because I was going to run as fast as possible away from a boy who was going to buy me dinner, in the rain. How did I forget my jacket? I knew it was raining, I knew I would have needed it.

My back droops against another solid wet brick wall, I take a deep breath but I can't hide a sigh. I smooth my soaking hair out of my face.

"Hard night?" A certain blonde asks me in English from up in the sky, about a meter above me.

"Yeah... I told a guy who asked me on a date that I didn't love him," I groan and suddenly stop. I probably shouldn't be talking to him without wearing a mask. There are only so many short, Mexican-French girls who know both French and English.

"Wait. Do I know you?" He asks and floats down closer to the wet sidewalk.

"I hope so, I have only spent two years of my life fighting with you," I mumble and instantly regret my words. "I mean- "

"Wait, Corbelle?" He floats and smashes into the sidewalk and steps up to me.

"Stop! I am not wearing my mask!" I tell him as I cover my face with my arms and walk a few meters away. His footsteps stop where he is.

"Oh... Sorry. I just got a little excited."

"Well, I do live here, in France along with thousands of other people who could also have superpowers so it cannot be that surprising to find me, no?"

"I thought you were on a date tonight. Did you get stood up or something?" He asks.

"No, I just left," I say simply and sharply. I just don't want to talk about all this drama and romance.

"What do you mean?"

"I cannot handle all of this! Everyone expects me to balance the world in my arms but I cannot!" I yell and look at my hands and turn to him. "I can only take so much before I snap!"

"You're always putting things before yourself, saving the day, but here you are, getting down about some drama. Corbelle, it's okay. You don't have to take in all of this at once."

"... You're right," I sigh.

"I get that a lot." He smiles and nods.

"I am afraid not very often from me, though." I hide my eyes with my loose hair, grin back and nod.

We sit there in silence aside from the splattering of the rain. It pours and pours, it cries and cries. It teases the sun and brings out the light in everyone. It seems as though I'm the only one who notices. Everyone tries to block it out, with umbrellas and staying indoors. Neither of which work. I learned to embrace the rain and to relish in it. I just can't right now. I'm too cold and wet to do so.

"You're cold aren't you?" He says finally, breaking the rain's pleas and whines.

"A little..." I look up at the rain and smile as it hits my eyes.

He pulls out a yellow compact umbrella and drops it into my hand. "Here."

"Thanks." I open it and swing it over my shoulder and walk silently to my apartment.

Kaden

People have been whispering about Rikki and me all day. I thought if I booked us at a restaurant owned by Maya Lesage, the school would have been whispering about how cute a couple we were, but no. She chose to break up with me on our first date so that's what the school is whispering about.

"Hey! You left without me today!" Kai sprints to catch up with me.

"You should have woken up earlier."

"What's up? Is this about Rikki?"

"I didn't tell you about that!"

"I talked to Rikki before your date-"

"I'll see you later."

I walk past him, making a point to be rude. Not okay. My twin was talking to my girl behind my back right before we had a date.

I just want to get this over with.

My eyes stick to the ground. If only I could just use my powers... I could hide everything, my shame, my disappointment, and my anger. If only I could just keep my eyes on the ground. The school is quieter today. Now they have something to feed on. They're like parasites, living on the discontentment of others.

The classroom door screech open. Everyone looks in my direction except Rikki. This is a new Rikki, one I've never seen like this. She's not wearing her usual baggy clothes and sneakers, but a black sundress and a yellow cardigan. With the sneakers. Her hair is more elaborate too, and she has with a matching yellow hairband in a braid.

I ignore her and she returns the favour, looking at her book and jotting down notes. She doesn't seem to care that she dumped me and that the school is whispering about us.

Rikki

Make no mistake, the school is talking about Kaden. Not about me, just about how they're sorry for him and things like that. Instead of whispering and gossiping about me, they're avoiding me in the halls.

Everywhere I walk, crowds of people split apart to evade me. I'm on my way to the lab to set up the first phase of plant testing. I already know how it's going to go, getting to the lab I mean.

I walk in and STEM doesn't even bother giving me a glance. My sneakers slap the floor on my way to my station.

I open my lab box and choose the small phial containing my recipe. Slowly, I pour a drop mixed with half a cup of water into one of the two marigold plants I brought this morning. I water the other one with regular water and none of the mixture. I let my breath out and relax. I didn't spill any.

"Hey, Kaden! Can you hand me the cutters?" I may as well groom and water some of the other plants since I'm done with my work.

He doesn't respond, just shrugs me off.

"You too? Jeez!" I walk over and grab the cutters harshly, "I thought you of all people would be smart enough to break a cliché." I keep pruning and watering. No one pays any attention to me even by the time club was over.

Outside, thunder cracks through the pelting rain. Great.

The rain grabs at my face as I pedal home on my bike. The chain freezes and my bike tips.

"Dammit," I hiss as I pick myself back up. I swear and kick it. I try to push it forwards. Nope. It doesn't work. I stare at its fading and peeling purple paint pleadingly. "C'mon, please, just this once," I whisper to it. "I promise I'll take to the shop as soon as it's sunny again." I give it another thrust but it doesn't budge. "Ugh!" I throw it into a puddle and sit on a rock underneath a strong pine needle tree. The puddle reflects my hazy frown. I shove my soggy hair out of my face and make an effort to smile, but that's not me in the reflection. That's a girl with a normal life, a girl who has normal friends and normal interests. She's just the girl I want to be.

***

"Ooh, Rikki that wasn't good for your fever," Willow coos as she takes her hand off my forehead.

"R-really?" I'd missed all of school today because of a little cold. "Willow, I cannot move," I groan from underneath an enormous pile of blankets.

"Yeah, that's the point, Rikki, if you take off the blankets you're gonna disappear again and your fever is going to get even worse."

"Fine," I groan and sigh. "May I go to my room?" I ask her carefully.

I trudge up the stairs nearly tripping over the four layers of blankets Willow has bundled me in. My door opens slowly as I body check it open. I fall to the floor in my room in a pile of pillows and sneezes while the dust settles.

"Careful!" Willow yells at me from the bottom of the wooden stairs.

"Yes..." I sneeze. So stupid. How could I have gotten sick? I drag the pillows and blankets not already piled on my being onto the floor. I drag myself onto them and relax for the first time in a few weeks.

Shoot! My plants! They didn't get watered. And homework! I can't sleep yet.

My eyes are closing. What's wrong with me? Even on my worst nights, I'm twice as awake than I am now. I'll just take a small nap.

***

Where am I?

The wind whirls my dress about my legs. Butterflies fly where the wind once was. This can't be real life. There's a two-nicorn at least twenty meters away from me.

143

"Where are you?" Tonnerre asks faintly.

"What-" I turn to face her. Not her. Anyone but her. I hate her.

I take a step towards her and punch her in the face. She dodges then trips me. I fall to the ground heavily.

"You always were slow, Carmen." She steps on my back making it crack.

"Mmmrm!" I can't speak.

She kicks my face, breaking my nose. I scream louder than I ever have.

"You always were weak, Carmen." She kicks me over with her foot and uses her heel to crack my ribs.

I can't even hear myself cry. The pain is rippling through my body, branching out to every finger, every tooth, every toe.

"You know, Carmen, I never saw any skill in you. You're lucky I saw your powers."

That hurts, more than the nose. I hated her and she took me away from our family but she was the one who cared for me, the one who made me feel better. She was my only real family.

"I always hated you."

As I stare at her through teary eyes, her face changes shape and instead of her freckled, a young tanned and masked one stares at me coldly.

"You were always useless," Tonnerre gripes. His blonde hair reflects a red glare in the air, one that I caused.

He steps on my windpipe and crushes it. With my last breath, I scream, I cry, I do whatever I can.

My illusion breaks and I'm back in my tiny room. My eyes are wet and swollen.

Everything is cold again which means I'm probably back to normal. I take a deep breath and wipe away my tears. I shouldn't be crying over a stupid dream.

Kaden

No. I am not going to do it. I cannot do it. Don't do it. Don't you dare touch that window. You can do it, Kaden, just walk away. Just walk away.

My hand taps on the glass of Rikki's window.

She looks over at me and walks up. Her window doesn't open very easily, and screeches in my ears. I instinctively cover them.

"Hey..." I start.

"Hi."

"What do you want?"

"What? You're the one who knocked on my window," She tells me with a tired grin.

"You opened the window."

"Because you knocked on it, idiot!" I don't say anything as she glares at me suspiciously.

"Are you sick?" I try to rub her forehead, but she swats me away.

"I'm fine," She insists and turns away.

"No, you aren't! You're burning up!" I grab her shoulder and turn her back so she's facing me again.

"I. Am. Fine," She hisses at me with a hard frown and eyes like daggers that bite at me like bears.

"No. You. Are. Not," I try to match her tone and face but I can't measure up to her moodiness.

"Yes, I am."

"No, you aren't! You can't keep treating yourself like this! I don't know why you do this to yourself, but you need to stop! Or I'll make you!"

"I don't need your help."

"Rikki!" I shout at her as loud as I can and she shuts up immediately. "You are not fine, you're sick and have a fever. If you come to school tomorrow, I will do everything in my power to make you go back home and embarrass you."

"Kaden-"

"No. I'm not finished. You're going to listen to me and you'll agree or I'll show up to school with 'Rikki' written all over my clothes. I will."

She glares at me.

"I'm not kidding Rikki, I have sharpies on my desk."

She sighs and stops arguing.

"Good. Eat some chicken noodle soup and some medicine and you'll feel better."

I jump off the ledge onto her roof. I've had some practice doing this when she was out.

"Get better!" I yell at her.

Rikki

I'm at school again, Kaden hasn't shown up and our first periods aren't together so he won't know that I'm at school before lunch and by then I'm sure I can make a plan to avoid him.

I run in the hallways and ignore all the chatter as I head to my first art class. I haven't had art yet.

I walk down the hallways watching the growing morning shadows dancing on the lockers.

"Rikki? I thought I told you to stay home today," Kaden stops right in front of me, nearly causing me to knock into him. With all my planning, I didn't even avoid him.

"No, a superhero came to my room last night and told me not to go to school." I sigh.

"Well, I'm sure you agreed with him knowing that someone who saves the city would probably know how to protect its citizens."

"I'm sure a naive spineless little girl would do that exact thing, wouldn't she? Because, of course, why wouldn't she just accept orders from a strange dude who just broke into her house?"

"A smart girl-"

"Woman," I correct him.

"A smart *woman* certainly would."

"Too bad that smart woman is stubborn too as well." I shrug and pull my messenger bag closer to my hip.

"No kidding- " The loud shrill of the school bell echoes across the lockers and walls and interrupts him. "Crap! I've got Math! I gotta go!" He rushes past me."

Oracle

This has been bothering me: *Fate. Hate. Destruction. Revenge. Joy.*

Over and over. I try to look into Chaos's past and this is what the Fates give me. Nothing but this. Over and over. On repeat, on repeat. Nothing but that. I looked into Chaos's future: *Fate. Hate. Destruction. Revenge. Joy*

Again, and again and again. Nothing but that.

Fate: When she completely becomes Yin. Hate: She hates her fate? But there's revenge. So, a person. Destruction: This is the grimmest, whatever she shall destroy, it is clearly going to be something significant. Revenge: She'll get revenge on whoever she hates for whatever reasons. Joy: Her revenge will give her some ill-begotten contentment.

This is all very alarming. I can't tell Harmony about this and there's nothing I can do about it aside from watch. Hopefully, she doesn't change too much.

Rikki

Math. Math. Mathity math. Why are you so difficult? I've been looking at this paper too long. I know what all the little signs mean, but they only look like little blobs right now. Same with my English homework. An essay about something I'm passionate about. Being a superhero? No, that's probably not the best idea, I mean, what if the teacher knows I'm lying about how it feels to fly through the air? Chemistry is the only plausible thing that pops into my head.

Maybe a change of scenery will do me some good. My window opens with its usual squeak. I really need to get some oil for it. The last thing I need is for Willow to catch me sneaking in from patrol.

I shove my papers and work messily onto the flat roof before clambering up myself. It's still tonight. Not even a breeze to chill me. It's not even that cold, in fact, it's kind of warm.

My ribs shift slightly on top of the hard roof. I should've taken out a few pillows to cushion my stomach.

I chew the back of the pencil. *Chemistry*. What's so good about chemistry? Why should people care about chemistry? Wait, no... What if I did Paris? Or Paris and chemistry?

"Hey," Kaden mumbles as he sits down beside me and looks ta my paper and pencil.

"Busy," I tell him and focus back on the blank piece of paper.

"You're eating a pencil. Didn't know you considered that as busy" Kaden tells me and grabs the paper out of my hand.

"Homework. You should be doing yours too."

"I know. I did it."

"You cheated, didn't you?"

"It wasn't copyrighted," He shrugs beneath his black helmet and black leather jacket.

"Some superhero you are. I can hear the headlines already: 'Famous superhero Nuit accused of plagiarism!'" I wave my hands in the air at the non-existent but future newspaper.

"How much have you done on your essay?"

"Lots." I grab my piece of paper from his gloved hand, nod and pretend to work.

"That's it, isn't it?" He points to my blank piece of paper.

"No. Those are your grades," I sigh and tap my pencil against the roof.

"Wow. Walked straight into that one, didn't I?"

"That, you did."

"So, what's your topic?"

"Paris. Or Chemistry." I try to throw the loose hairs that fell from my bun away from my face but they fall right back down. I sigh.

"Do you want some help?"

"Oh my god, yes."

"So, this is your first year at the school right?"

"Yeah," I sigh.

"So, last year, our English teacher was amazing. She taught us all about influential writing and stuff like that. She had a special recipe for the perfect essay: Who cares? Why care? What if no one cared? No one could ever get lower than an eighty-six in her class, she was just that good a teacher."

"Wow."

"Yeah, can you base your essay off of that?"

"Let me just write it down."

I scribble the teacher's recipe on the paper and link all of it to chemistry.

"Remember, opening paragraph, CD, CM, CM, repeat, repeat, repeat, closing paragraph." He reminds me.

Facts about chemistry, my thoughts about chemistry. Chemistry, chemistry, and more chemistry. I'm almost sick of it.

"How does this look?" I ask him after completing about three pages of single-spaced, painstakingly written chemistry trivia.

"It's not bad actually."

"Thanks." My hand's throbbing just like it did when I hit Tonnerre. I shake it wildly through the air like it's got a mind of its own.

"What time is it?"

"I don't know... twelve o'clock?" I shrug. It's not a big deal, I usually stay out until three or four.

"And you're sick. I forgot about that."

"Oops," I shrug with a stupid smile.

"I'm wearing the 'Rikki' shirt tomorrow," He mutters with a serious look on his face.

"What? You already made it?"

"Yeah, I had art today last period," He grins.

"Fine. But I want that soup you promised me," I sigh and drop down onto my windowsill.

"Okay, okay. I'll get you soup."

***

Okay. Time to jump out a window.

Everything is still... so still. Nothing has changed. I've been reading headlines of a fire around here somewhere. I can hear the sirens. Oh. There goes a firetruck. Its blue lights bounce and reflect off windows and curved roofs. My legs leave the ground before I ask them to. The moment of weightlessness. I always love this moment, a split second of worry-free movement between hell and heaven. I land on my feet, the pain of hitting the ground spreading through my legs. I curse myself. I should've rolled, but that would've ended with me as a pancake on the road. I spring into the road just quickly enough to latch onto the back of the next truck. I climb up the doors to the roof and stand up tall.

The firetruck takes a sharp turn around the corner. My feet skid across the sleek red metal and trip against a metal ladder. My back leans over the edge. In a moment of slow motion, my hand reaches for the same ladder I slipped on. My hand grabs it and holds on to it with every ounce of my strength. I should be more focused than this. Even with this sickness, I should be more watchful. Crouching on the firetruck's roof, I let out my breath and breathe in again. Something lands on my tongue. Something hot.

Embers waft and dance through the sky. The sky's on fire. My eyes widen. How could this happen?

Andrew

Where is she? She's always first to a scene. Something's been going on with her.

Looks like another firetruck is coming. I can see its glaring blue lights through the clouds, and I cringe at its siren. There's something different though, a lower scream, not even that much of a scream, more of a *"Whooooooo!"* Oh. I see. She's riding the firetruck.

I glide down to meet her. She's going to want to hear about the fire. The truck screeches to a stop and she gracefully flips off. She always does things like that as though she's dancing, her movements are always graceful and beautiful no matter what she's doing. It fits her perfectly. She practically dances through life.

"What happened?" A look of horror is frozen on her face.

"A fire broke out a few minutes ago," I answer her, "do you have a plan?"

"Save everyone inside." She sprints into the building. The entrance is fully enveloped in flames, it looks like the entrance to hell. Yellow and orange tongues of flame lick the building leaving permanent black shadows staining the walls. Ash floats through the air.

"Wait!"

"What?" She slows to a stop, and looks back.

"It's dangerous."

"So, is being a superhero," She rolls her eyes at me, "we are used to this, no?" She throws her arms up.

"Okay, but... just wait for me."

"You better hurry-" She starts as I fly in front of her, brushing past her. "-up."

We charge forwards. The building's frame creaks with every step, it even seems to sway. I walk closer to Corbelle. If she falls through I'll have to catch her.

"Watch out!" Corbelle yells at me and throw me out of the way.

I look up as a piece of a large wooden pillar, covered in dust and fire, comes crashing down. Corbelle ducks to my left and, before I can react, grabs the pillar before it hits me. Her black hair whips against the pillar.

I hit the column from her arms and throw it back into the surrounding fire. She lets out a relieved breath.

"Are you alright?" I ask her as she keels over and catches her breath slowly.

"I'm fine. I used the power."

"Uh, your hair's on fire."

"What?! Put it out! Put it out!" She throws her arms up and wildly tries to swat away the flames quickly eating up her black braid.

"Stay still," I try to tell her as I grab the braid.

"My hair is on *fire* and you tell me to 'stay still'?"

My gloves rub against it quickly but it doesn't work. I grab the top of her hair, the part closest to the neck, and wave it furiously in the air.

"Is it working?" She asks shakily.

"Almost extinguished." The last little bits of embers have almost left her hair and I brush them away. "There," I say and drop her air. It's a lot shorter than it was a few minutes ago.

She pulls her hood back up, "Is there anyone in here?!" She shouts up to the ceiling and upper floors.

"You should use French, we're in Paris."

"Yes, but this is a lab. There are scientists from all over the world working here."

"You're right." When is she not? She always does her research, almost always knows what's going on. Almost.

Rikki

"Can you fly me up to the next floor of this building?" I ask Tonnerre in English and stare up at the flaming ceiling and falling wood.

"Sure, I think I'll have to brace the structure, so you'll be on your own afterwards."

"That is good. Thank you." I nod as I fit my scarf over my face as an attempt to protect myself from carbon monoxide poisoning.

"No problem." He grabs me by the waist and drags me upwards. I wonder if he has the same feeling of weightlessness when he flies or is it like an anchor, like a building pressure he releases when he flies or is it the other way around?

He punches through the flaming ceiling and lets go of me with one arm. "Are you going to be alright?"

"Me? I will be fine. Did we not extinguish a fire when we first met?" I shrug with a careful grin.

"This is a chemical fire, a lab fire. We don't even know if anyone is still in here."

"You're so cute when you're worried about my safety." I squish his serious face, "Parisians eat pain for breakfast. I'll be fine." I jump away from him and onto the wreck of the second floor as he flies back to the first one.

"Is anyone up here?" I shout around in French, "Anyone?"

"Up here!" A woman yells down in English between hoarse coughs.

"Which floor?" I yell up in English quickly. She doesn't sound like she's got much time left.

"I'm on the third floor! Please hurry! He's stopped breathing!"

My fingers sharpen into needles without even thinking. The presence. It's like the past Chaos is trapped in it. I take a running start and crash onto the flaming wall.

I scale up it carefully. I need to choose the pieces of wall that aren't in danger of collapsing on top of me. I'd prefer not to die today.

My claws sink into a wooden panel. I pull myself up. Over and over and over until I reach the third floor.

"Where are you?" No answer. Not a good sign. "Hello!"

My eyes search the room. A woman in a lab coat lies slumped over a man in a corner.

"Non, non, non, non, non," I gasp as I run over to them and listen to the woman's breathing. Her raspy breath is faint compared to the crackles of the fire all around us. The man is not breathing! My hands push against his chest quickly.

"Un...Deux...Trois..."

Another flaming piece of wood crashes down and makes the building shake. "We need to go now! Snap out of it! If you keep trying this, you're going to kill yourself and that other woman!" I tell myself in French.

I grab the woman's limp body by the armpits, and check her shallow breathing. I jump out a broken window.

"Dépanner! S'il vous plaît, cette femme a besoin d'aide!" Some first responders sprint to my side with a stretcher, I lay her down gingerly.

"Was there anyone else inside?" Someone asks in French.

"Y-yeah... there was a man... Oh no." I open a wall of light back into the flaming remains of the lab and look for the man. There's no sign of him. Just a pile of flames. I'm too late. I just let a man die.

I sit down. How could I let that happen? I'm a failure. I'm exactly how she said I was.

But I need to keep going. I can't give up.

I jump out the window. The wind's back. It feels amazing, it whips at my hair and adds to the weightless feelings but it doesn't shake the empty feeling.

"There... there wasn't even a body left."

"You can't save everyone." The nurse tries to give me a reassuring smile, but I shake it off. I shouldn't have let that man die. It was my fault.

156

I look around, three ambulances wait at the corner as well as two police cars, and four firetrucks. A policeman gives them a signal to start spraying and they convulse as a powerful whip of water hits the flaming mess. Security and press cameras follow my every move intensely. I still flinch whenever I see those flashing lights.

A detective taps me on the shoulder. "I appreciate what you did in there. If you hadn't gotten to that woman when you did, she would've died," she says.

"But the man..."

"What man? On the lab records, only one person was working here tonight, no visits, no nothing."

"But..."

"Kid, you seem pretty young and it looks like you took in a lot of smoke. You got there where the firemen and women couldn't. Paris thanks you for that, but you're young, you need to be lucky every time to live, but disaster only needs to be lucky enough to find you once."

I swallow everything, "Thank you officer, but I'll be alright, I've got a partner to help me out."

"Good, I don't know where I'd be without mine. Mace!"

"Yes, ma'am!" A raven haired man runs up to us,

"Soares Mace meet..." Kaden's and Kai's brother?

"Corbelle." I shake his partner's hand, the man who shot at me in the museum.

"Soares here will be your go-to whenever you need police help. I am confident you'll make the right choices and save Paris when you need to."

"Yes, detective... sorry, I don't believe I ever learned your name."

"Chief Corre."

"Yes, ma'am!" I mock a little salute to her. She scowls at me and walks away to speak to the other officers.

"So, you're the one who shot at me?" I smile slyly at her, he doesn't that older than me.

"Please don't have me fired," he pleads.

"Too soon." I say, faking a smile.

Andrew

"Tonnerre?" Corbelle calls over to me.

"Topaz?"

"I am over here! You can let go of the building."

"Coming!" I carefully let go of the piece of drywall. I walk over to her. She avoids my eyes. I ask her, "What's wrong?"

"I let a man die." She looks downhearted, so sad.

"...It wasn't your fault." Gently, I put my hand on her shoulder.

"No, you were not there... if I had been faster I could have saved him. If I had wasted any more time that woman would have died." She brushes my hand off and takes a step back. She looks like she's about to cry. "It is my fault."

"It's okay."

"No, it is not. That man had... comment dites-vous... a family, he had someone he loved and now he is gone forever."

"No, you tried your best, remember what you said? If you had been slower the other person would have died."

"But only one person was supposed to be here this night."

"What? A ghost?"

"No. Something illegal. I will look into it." She turns away, she looks like she's about to jump off a ledge.

"It wasn't your fault you know. It's the opposite. Imagine if you weren't there at all, more than one person could have died. Firemen could have been trapped trying to save the person."

Her silence affirms iwhat I've said. She knows that I'm right.

Rikki

I run away from him and make it to the top of a few roofs. I should be home already. It's late even by my standards. I need to do some research on the lab, only one person was supposedly working but two died. Is it a riddle?

My wrist cracks softly as I pull up my window. It's quiet for once, good thing I oiled it. In my washroom I take off my mask. My eyes are red and swollen from the smoke and my throat burns. I really am going to have to stay home tomorrow. I'll get Kaden to bring me some notes, he owes me.

The smoke bombs! Crap! I forgot to make the smoke bombs! Why am I like this? I don't even have any liquid nitrogen for them. I can't make them tonight I already have too much to do. I'll have to do it tomorrow... it already is 'tomorrow'. I'll go get them. My mask slips on and my window slams against the wood as I jump out. There's always at least one hardware store open this early in the morning. I follow the glaring orange lights to the House Depot closest to my house. I release my platforms and drop to the street. I walk in and hiss at the painfully bright lights.

I walk over to a red headed guy not much older than me reading a magazine at the cashier.

"You sell liquid nitrogen here right?"

He stares at me. Suddenly, his chair collapses, with a crash knocking over a chocolate display.

"You okay?"

"Y-you're a superhero!" he stutters, dumb-founded.

"Last time I checked."

"How about that liquid nitrogen? I'm only in a huge rush."

"You need it to save the world, right?"

"Kind of?" I give him a shrug, emphasising my case.

"Yes! Coming right up!" He trips over the chocolate.

He grabs his phone out of his pocket and clumsily taps it quickly. What is he-

"Jim! There's a superhero at my store! I'm helping to save the world! Call me back, bye!" At least, that's what I think he said, he's talking at about a hundred words a second.

He slams a massive silver and white metal vessel on the counter, his hands shaking as fast as his speech.

"I only need two-hundred milligrams."

"Take it all!"

I tap the nozzle on its smooth curved lid, now covered in dents from excited bumps. "Okay. Pass me that *Fine* water bottle? It's a limited-edition solid copper ones right?" I hate their water bottles, they're off balance and useless. They'd make better baseball bats than water bottles.

He nods vigorously and swipes it from the counter but hits it off. Before it crashes into the ground, I catch it without a sweat. I twist open the lid and carefully slide it under the nozzle and press it. Fog sweeps around us from the sudden change of atmosphere. Good, it's fresh.

"Shoot, I didn't bring enough money... only twenty euros," I mutter.

"You can pay with a selfie with me!"

***

The swelling in my eyes has nearly completely died down, but my throat is still a little chaffed. I'll need some cough medicine at some point.

I walk up the concrete steps that seem to reach for my feet. My eyes squint from the ever-present sunshine, it's so annoying and bright. If it was night already, I could chat with Tonnerre about the new things I found out about the Smithe Industries and the lab from last night.

Back at school, everyone's in class already.

Science. Yes. Love that chemistry.

I walk into the crowded classroom, I already missed advisory, but I'm on time for Science, trying to remain invisible. I take my place beside Kaden, my shoes squeak against the floor as I slide into my chair.

"Hey." He gives me a lazy wave.

"Hi. Not wearing the shirt today?"

"Feeling better?" He ignores the question.

"No, I've been diagnosed with Ebola."

"Good to hear. By the way, I handed in your essay. The teacher was very pleased with it."

"You did what!" I whisper-shout at him, "What the hell!"

"But it was really good."

"That doesn't mean you get to hand it in for me." I hiss at him.

"Mr. Victoire really liked it... I think he wants you to enter in a city-wide competition."

"You know I would never do that. Why didn't you tell him that?"

"I didn't want to crush his dreams so early on."

"He's an adult!"

Maya interrupts our bickering by tapping my shoulder. "Rikki, can I talk to you after class?" Maya asks me with a hint of nervousness in her voice.

"Sure. I have them ready. Come by my house later." I wave her off and scratch at the desk.

"What was that about?" Kaden asks.

"Nothing. Clothes. You wouldn't understand."

"You never talk about clothes, believe me, it shows."

"It doesn't matter."

"Yes, it does."

"I believe it's called 'none of your business' Kaden, also known as manners. Maybe you should buy some, you certainly have the cash."

"Buuuuuuuuurn!" Maya whispers at us and I high-five her awaiting hand. I wink at him with a smile of victory. He looks really annoyed. I'm showing a little too much Corbelle. I glue my eyes back to the counter until the teacher walks in.

"Good morning class, today we're going to work on a project involving the periodic table."

My muscles respond to the words 'periodic table' before I can stop them. I burst out of my chair, sending it smashing into the ground.

Kaden

"Rikki, you okay?" I ask her.

"Help. Me."

"Just sit down slowly. Maybe, no one noticed."

"Oh, sure, no one noticed me jumping three feet out of my chair. Of course, why would anyone notice?" She says sarcastically. I pull her back down.

"There. Just try to calm down."

"Yeah, thanks for that expert advice."

She burrows her face in her arms.

"Hard night?"

"You have no idea."

"My fault?"

"Partially."

"Well, want me to make it up to you?"

The teacher has noticed our conversation. "Ms. Dubois, Mr. Mace, would you like to include us in your conversation?"

"No ma'am."

"No Ms. Boulay." Rikki always knows their names.

"Well, pay attention!" Ms. Boulay frowns. "Our project isn't entirely based on the periodic table." Rikki rests her head on the table, "We're going to work on the science fair; other students from all over France will be competing. It's up to you to represent our school. You may choose your own partners and your own topic. You have this class to sort that out. You may go."

Before I can say anything, Maya grabs Rikki's shoulder "Rikki, can you be my partner?"

"Sure," Rikki says absent-mindedly as she carves her nails into the bench.

I glare into Maya's my smirking brown eyes.

"Hey, Rikki, wanna go for lunch with me?" She asks, further trying to piss me the hell off. "My treat."

"We can have a picnic by the Seine just underneath the Pont de Bir-Hakeim."

"Great idea."

"I just have to stop by my place to pick up some things."

I can't believe this. She's planning my ideal date with the ideal girl I would ask out and Rikki agreed! What does Maya have against me?

Maya

"Have you ever wanted to jump into the river?" I ask Rikki. "It's very refreshing."

"Was there a reason you went into it aside from it being wonderfully refreshing?" Rikki sighs.

"A dare."

"Are you kidding? I can't tell if you're being serious or not."

"Why would I be kidding?"

"It's almost if you're every stereotype of a popular white girl brought to life."

"Yeah, right," I sneer. "Can I have my smoke bombs since you're so bad at small talk."

She rustles something out of her black messenger's bag. "Here." Her hands shove a paper bag almost filled with little pellets. "Be careful, as soon as they come into contact with oxygen, you won't be able to see, so make a plan before firing one of those suckers." Her hands distract me. They're covered in scars and cuts.

"What happened to your hands?"

She examines them for a moment and pulls them back. "Nothing. Just some housework."

"Oh," I mutter.

She takes a long slurp of her grape soda. She's the only person I know who can actually drink that stuff. "So, your boyfriend," she starts.

"What about him?" A barge floats past the bridge we lean against, the sound of the water calms me.

"Well, he uses smoke bombs! Why do you hang around someone like that?"

"He's the only person who cares. He's the only person I've really held feelings for a long time." My eyes drift away to the still river underneath the bridge.

"It's okay. I know how that feels. Really." She grabs my hand and squeezes it.

"What's it to you?"

It's her turn to look into the river now. "I've had a really... difficult childhood. I was raised by my mom. I did love her, but I just wanted to impress her so, so badly. But I never could. But now, my best friend, this guy, I kind of hate him, but he has feelings for me."

"That's pretty good."

"Really?" Her sarcastic tone is back, I didn't miss it all that much.

"You'd be surprised how often it happens. Just wait, in a few months, you'll be in love with him too."

"In anime," she mumbles.

"In real life. And anime."

"You don't say."

Rikki

I need to find Tonnerre. I found out so much about the Smithe foundation and the lab. I have been waiting all day to find him.

My feet leave the ground for a moment while my power and I pass over an empty alley.

"Tonnerre! Where are you, you pain!" I groan as I stop at our usual hangout.

"You called, Sunshine?" He says in English. Behind me.

"Yes! There you are. I have much to explain."

"How much sleep did you get last night?"

"I had a lot of coffee. Now allow me to explain." I spread out my hands and create a three level cylinder with four tiny spheres inside using my power. "This is the lab with the people. There is you, me, Dr. Rosewell, and the man. I tried to get a DNA sample of his remains but too many police. Only one person was supposed to be in the building last night."

"What if the man was visiting?"

"No visits. Their work was too confidential. And the lab was bought out by the Smithe Industries last month."

"What? That's got to be a..."

"They were engineering and testing samples of Achelium, a key ingredient to Vaccine's serum. That is suspicious, no?"

"What? No. Maybe they were just-"

"The police findings of the blaze were inconclusive. They were not working with flammable substances. Everything was working. But the sprinkler system did not turn on. Is that not strange?"

"Corbelle, calm down, I'm sure this is just some misunderstanding. maybe you're going through some things and..."

I slap him as hard as I can. I guess this is why Maya asked about my hands, they're covered in cuts from hitting and grappling onto things so much. I even leave a tiny mark on his face this time. I feel a little proud.

"I am perfectly fine! How dare you say that! Every time I start to think you are finally becoming a good person, you ruin it! Honte à toi! J'espère que tu vas en enfer!"

"Corbelle-"

"Leave me alone!" Paris leaves my eyes for an instant as I teleport over to the Pont de Bir-Hakeim where Maya and I ate lunch at. I hope I blinded him! "That *connard*!" I can't believe he said that to me! He is such a jerk!

***

I need to hit something. Now. He is such a jerk. I can't believe him. Every time I think he's finally a good person, someone I could finally be with, he completely ruins it.

My research needs furthered exploration, anyway. I need to expose more links between the Smithe's and Vaccine. Chief Corre said I could come over to the station whenever I needed to. Or I could train. There're no boats around at this time of night. But I want to actually fight something. I'll have to look around for some muggers or robbers to beat up.

My boots grip against the roof's metal exterior. All I want to hear is the crash of broken glass. I look down to the street, happy couples walk on the near empty, dimly lit sidewalks. C'mon mugger, show your face. I just want one little hit.

Gunfire echoes in the streets. Pigeons steal my air. A toothy smile grows beneath my scarf. I follow the noise to another alley.

"You hear me! I'll fire again if you don't hand it over!" A young woman stands over another shaking a gun in the other's face.

"Hey, is that you, Jahylmei?" I ask her in French.

"Jail-me?"

"Okay, sure thing, whatever you say, evildoer." I flip off of the roof. The wind rushing through my scarf and hood.

"Step away and no one gets hurt!" She waves a gun in my face. The other woman makes a break for it.

"Run!" I yell at her.

The woman with the gun grabs the other by the neck, gets her in a chokehold, pointing the gun at her head. "Take another step and her brains are on the wall!" She shouts.

"Woah. Calm down. You do not want to do this. Believe me, this is a bad idea."

"Stay where you are!" The woman being choked starts sobbing, huge wet tears, Niagra Falls. "Shut up!"

"I'm not going anywhere. I'm not moving, see? You can let her go, okay?" I try to calm her down. "It's alright. You can let her go."

"No! All I wanted was-" Tonnerre smashes her on the back of the head with a bottle and silences her.

"What are you doing!" I yell at him in French. "I was handling that!" He stands there dumbly, not understanding a word I said. I rub my head and look at the victim, bits of glass dot her ruffled, bleached hair. "Are you alright?"

Tears circle and confuse her eyes. "I-is she dead?"

"No." Tonnerre says.

I walk over to her still body and press my fingers into her neck for a heartbeat. A soft ripple hits my fingers. "No, she's going to be alright. Do you have a phone?"

She takes a deep breath, "Yes."

"Can you call the police and tell them what happened? Tell them Corbelle was here."

"Okay." She's still crying.

"Do you want a photo?" I offer her a smile and she nods with a weak smile.

Andrew

She poses for the picture with the young woman. She's always so quick to change her emotions. Her face can go from completely pissed at me to happy and optimistic for a photo. She's unbelievable.

I watch her wave the girl away.

"Why did you do that? I am not a child. I can take care of things."

"Some great handling you did back there."

"I am not stupid! Why do you never give me enough credit? You always treat me as though I am a child even though you act like an angry four-year-old."

"I take things seriously. You act so naively at least half the time. You're never serious, but as soon as I step in, you freak out like I'm the bad guy."

"Maybe you are. I have not killed anyone lately."

"Wow. Seriously? You want to go there? Fine. At least I never stole from people."

She looks up at me with pure anger all over her face right before she punches me square in the jaw. "You do not know what it is like on the streets! I had to do whatever necessary to survive, so yes, I did steal, but from people who had so much money! You have never had to steal, did you?"

I don't respond.

"I asked you a question!" She hisses at me.

"No. I never had to steal."

"That is what I thought. Stop following me joli garçon." She storms off, up the side of the building. She certainly has had a lot of practice doing it.

I need to find her. I launch into the air, but she's already gone. Damn, she's quick.

170

Rikki

At least I got to punch something. Idiot.

How could he possibly have been involved with Smithe industries? Is he their lap dog? I need to check the San Francisco police records again.

At home, Willow should be asleep by now but I get out of my costume anyway.

The computer hums as it's lights switch on. I need to go through all the police files involving Vaccine's death all over again.

I click on my downloaded copies of the files. There's are so many errors and holes in the information. I didn't notice them before. I'll have to check the online copies.

"INFORMATION BLOCKED BY SMITHE INDUSTRIES."

I don't care. I need to look at that evidence. My fingers make their way through the firewall.

"ERROR 404, PAGE NOT FOUND." How is that possible? Did Smithe buy out the police? San Francisco really is corrupt.

I flip open my sketchbook and look at the webs. They've already almost filled the page. I've linked Tonnerre to Smithe Industries, Smithe Industries to Vaccine, Vaccine to Kai, Kaden, and Tonnerre. It makes so much sense but it also doesn't. How did Kai and Kaden even get possession of the serum without going insane? What could Smithe have over Tonnerre? Money? A job? His family? What is his deal?

I spin in my chair trying to make sense of it all until all the colours blur into one smudged monotone. I wish I had a punching bag.

Andrew

"How much does she know?" I yell at myself for the tenth time. Does this mean she could find out my real name? She linked the lab to Smithe. And she found out the lab was testing Achelium. Does she know my secret identity? What if she hates me? Maybe I should just tell her... but that could potentially mess up the plan.

Rikki

Today is a special day. For Americans. Hallowe'en anywhere in South, West, North, or East America, October thirty-first in France. I had to break the news to Willow this morning that she couldn't force me into a matching unicorn onesie. What. A. Shame. I couldn't convince her to change out of hers though. She told me I owe her a favour for tonight. I swear if it's a date I'm going to murder her. No more dates.

I'm late for school again! My attendance is going straight to hell with no possible hope of resurrection. I keep missing due dates for assignments and missing entire classes without any excuses aside from 'my train was late'. With any luck, I'll graduate with a B average. I'm so screwed. If I have any chance of finding a loophole in the Prophecy and somehow create a normal life for myself, I'll need a proper education.

I wheeze into advisory five minutes late. The earliest I've been all week. I need a better alarm system.

"Hey, there hot stuff. Try to contain your excitement because I'm going to need your help on a superhero case."

"Really, Kai?" I laugh before covering my mouth. "Oops."

He looks really nervous now that his col guy persona is gone. "What?" He looks around the school, but it's just us. I always do a subconscious check. "What are you talking about?" His mouth quivers as small drops of sweat fall to the floor between us.

"Oh. Did Kaden not tell you? Oh, crap." I say and hit my head, completely regretting my words.

A smug look flashes over his face for a moment before hardening. He's probably congratulating himself at not being the first twin to drop the secret.

"What did he tell you? You know what? This is a bad place to talk. C'mon." He grabs me by the waist, throws me over his shoulder and runs off me at high speed. Everything blurs into a solid white wall. I know it's moving but it also isn't. It moves with us. And then it's over. Like a life. It's there, then it's not. Bam. Gone.

The light wall fades around us and he drops me.

" -what." Kaden sits on a bed eating something out of a bright pink plastic container. "Kai?!" He bounces off and chases him into another room.

"Um." All I wanted was to go to school today. That's all I wanted.

Kai

What did Kaden do? Oh my god. He told Rikki his secret identity right out of the gate! How is he my brother? If it were anyone else, not Rikki, we would be in so much danger. He is such an idiot!

"Kai!" Kaden yells at me as he follows me into my room.

"Go away! I'm changing!"

"You brought my ex into my room. What if I was doing something else? What the hell are you doing with her?!"

"You know what?" I turn on him. I have every right to be as angry as he is, "You revealed my secret identity to some random girl you met that same week! What the hell are you even doing with her?"

"Stop acting like I meant to put you in danger intentionally! It was an accident! But there's no one else I'd rather know. She's been completely trustworthy so far. She even upgraded my helmet!"

"But what happens when she gets the right incentive? She's not rich! She goes to our school on a scholarship!"

"Why does that matter? She's smart! She could give them fake names!"

"But why should she give fake names when she can get more money for real ones?"

Like a ghost, she stands just in-between where we thought she was and where we are. The door hangs slightly ajar. "Listen, I'm just going to go then." She sweeps her loose hair out of her eyes and strides out.

"Rikki, wait." Kaden goes after her. Of course, he would.

"Would you just let her go? She doesn't want to be here. She just wants a normal life and that doesn't include us."

"I can't be bribed you know," she yells back. "I'm not that weak. But I thought you were a superhero. Sorry for thinking too much of you." She's really leaving.

"Rikki! Wait up!" Kaden chases her but turns back immediately. "Where did she go?"

"How should I know? You're the one who went to follow her!" I yell at him.

"But she's gone."

"What do you mean she's gone? No one can just disappear like that! How could she have done that?"

"Because of you!" Kaden yells at me points his finger right at my nose. "It's always your fault!"

"How is this my fault all of a sudden? You said she'd give a fake name! In that 'hypothetical' situation, would she have accepted the bribe?"

He shuts up immediately. He never thinks about what he says as long as he wins an argument.

"Ever think that she might not take the bribe?" I shove him out the doorway and slam the door in his face. He didn't win this time.

Rikki

Why did I jump out the window? Why didn't I just use the door? That was so stupid. What if they saw me? How am I going to explain that? *'Oh, yeah, don't worry, I've been jumping out of windows higher than that since I was ten.'* No. That would be terrible. But why would they say those things about me? I thought Kai and I were solid. And there wasn't even school today! Why am I so disorganised? I need to google it, I really need to.

Well, I have nothing better to do. It's barely dark outside and it's too early to start eating.

A sigh escapes from my lips as I open my laptop. I've only had it for seven years. *"How to be organised"*, c'mon search engine, what'cha got for me? Oh man, I just love articles written by people who tend to have no idea about the subject. I just love them.

I've read at least seven articles, all of them essentially saying to get a good night's sleep, relieve stress, and plan things out ahead of time. You know, the usual. The exact things I don't do.

There's a slight ringing from my clock, the only proof that I have any degree of organisation. It's blue light illuminates Sage's figure flying by my window. What's going on?

I'm changed and outside within three minutes. Practice, lots of practice.

My feet hit the metal roofs as I follow her 'pure' trail. For a good twelve minutes, I blindly trail a luminescent blue-ish fog. How often does this happen? I'll have to ask her about her powers.

I end up at the Eiffel Tower. I drop from my golden circles onto the closest roof. What's happening? There are lights *everywhere*. They're multicoloured. They flash. Like fireworks but they're all coming from an ominous square set-up in the middle of the tower's base.

What's going on? I summon my circular platforms again, vault onto the nearest one and run to the others. A guitar riff hits the air. My rubber skids across my magic. It's a concert. I'm overreacting about nothing, it's just in my head. The music's pretty good though, I love the beat.

I swing myself onto the top of the set-up stage made of black metal pipe. It's not half bad, but the stereos could be stronger. I watch a female singer on center stage. The crowd goes wild.

I've never been to something like this. My whole body wants to move to the electronic strike and the shrill of the guitar.

"Come here often?" Sage sits beside me.

"Nope, this is my first."

"What? You've never been to a live concert?"

"Nope, this is new to me."

"Then how did you know about the concert?"

"I saw you through my window, thinking there was a monster or something, I followed you."

"What do you mean your window? Like, your civilian window?"

"Uh, yeah, what other window is there?"

"Wow. I just never knew you had a secret identity."

"Why'd you think that?" I smile at her. Of course, I would have a secret identity.

"I've never seen you without your mask, I mean, you've never talked about your secret identity."

"Because it's a secret." I look at her sceptically.

"Well, duh," She rolls her eyes behind the fog obscuring her facial features, "But even Tonnerre has told us at least one thing about himself."

"Really? Huh." I shrug while she looks me over with a wide grin on her face. "What?"

"You have a crush on him," she cackles.

"What? No, I don't!" I screech at her, "I just never took him for the talking type, that's all!"

"You totally do! Omg! I need to tell the guys!"

"What? No! That's not necessary!"

She holds a rose gold rectangle tightly I desperately try to grab it from her hands.

"No!" I yell, almost grasping its case.

"Calm down, Corbelle!"

Maya

I wish I felt this happy regularly. Everyone is practically brimming with happiness, even Tonnerre, despite his silver scowl.

I guess this is another part of my powers? I'm an empath?

Tonnerre brought a box of baked goods, probably to make up with Corbelle, I think they had a fight, but she's still holding a grudge against him. Damn she's stubborn.

"So then, she planned my perfect date with the girl I have a crush on," Nuit says, reaching for a bun.

"How are you going to eat with your helmet on?" Corbelle asks, her mouth full.

" ...shit."

Velocity laughs, more of the sound that comes out of a sick horse actually. I think he knows Nuit better than the rest of us, maybe even his real name.

"It's a shame they kicked us off the stage," I complain.

"To be fair, we were causing a huge disturbance." Corbelle laughs.

"Yeah, but we're the ones that save the city," Nuit argues.

"I'm not trying to butt in, but we should play truth or dare," I suggest, sipping my coffee.

Tonnerre says something in English that none of us understand.

"I guess I'm translator?" Cor sighs.

"That's right!" I laugh at her.

"I hate you guys," she hisses.

"Well, not Tonnerre."

"You're right. I hate him significantly more. Don't tell him I said that. I'd prefer not to have my brains smashed against the sidewalk."

"Relax, he barely understands any French. But you still have to translate."

She rolls her yellow eyes, the ones that match her power, I think I'll ask her about that if she picks truth.

She mutters some English and he nods I know about as much about English as Tonnerre knows about French.

"Okay, Corbelle, you first. Truth or dare?" I ask her,

"Umm... dare?"

"You should- "

"Take off your mask!" Velocity yells,

"What the hell, dude." Nuit punches him in the arm.

"I was just kidding!"

I roll my eyes with such gusto, they almost pop out of my head.

"Anyway, Corbelle, you should photobomb that couple down there." A happy couple poses for a selfie underneath the roof we've set up camp on.

"Gladly." She smiles evilly as she kicks a handstand off the roof and silently flips behind them into an alley silently and unnoticed. We all lean in far over the edge. She evades being seen from all angles in the shadows, except for those eyes of hers, which glow like jewels in the darkness. As does her toothy grin.

Her eyes sneak out and, smoother than silk. They slip behind the couple. She's under the shelter of a nearby dumpster. Her smile disappears behind the scarf she pulls over it. She's going in for the kill. But the corners of her grin grow as her fingers launch into 'bunny ears' in the background of the photo. In a flash, the phone clicks and Corbelle's gone in the same flash of light. We lean farther over the edge. Where is she?

"Mission accomplished," she laughs from behind us with a big grin, almost throwing me off the edge.

"Damn!" Nuit exclaims.

She struts over to the box of baked goods, plops down and stuffs a macaroon in her face. "Nuit's turn."

Kaden

"Aren't we supposed to spin a pencil or something?" I ask them.

"Come on! It's not like we did that when I went, it's your turn Nuit."

Corbelle jeers, exactly what I would expect from her right now, exactly what I would expect from Kai right now. What's his deal? I thought I really knew him but he just keeps proving me wrong. He watches me glare at him and returns the favour.

"Okay, can we not kill each other tonight, please?" Corbelle stands in between us; sometimes it's like she's the one with super-speed.

"Who wants to call it?"

"I'll call it." Kai grins at me.

"I still have to choose truth or dare," I huff and stall for time.

"Then choose... if you dare."

"I'll take truth," I mumble. Sage snores, her back hunched around the chimney. "But it appears our host is currently unconscious." I gesture at Sage.

"It's okay, I got this." Corbelle walks over to her. Her eyes close as her fingers sharpen, curving around an invisible tennis ball which explodes with a pop in her hands.

"What? Oh my god!" Sage's surprised face is priceless, "Oh. Did I fall asleep?"

"Yeah. Awake now?" Corbelle can barely stop laughing.

"How do you even do that?" Kai asks her.

"What do you mean?"

"Your powers... how do you even use them?"

"Um-"

Rikki

"Well, there's this one thing I kind of have been meaning to tell you guys, uh, it's just that it's... really hard to explain," I stutter.

"What are you telling them?" Tonnerre asks in English. He's pretty much just been watching us this whole time.

"I am telling them about the Prophecy, there are some things about it that I haven't told you about."

"You shouldn't."

"Why?" I glare at him. He's been eating my ear off about what I 'shouldn't be doing'.

"What'll happen when they realise they've got a celestial being on their team? It could spread information to some unwanted sources."

"I've got to tell them sometime, not everyone is like you."

"You don't even know their names, their real names."

"It's not like I know yours."

"But we've known each other since San Francisco."

"So? That does not mean we tell each other everything, no?" I throw myself against the metal chimney beside Sage.

"Uh, what are you guy talking about?" Sage asks as I switch back to French.

"Nothing. Anyway, my power comes from an ancient mystical prophecy. Pretty much when I turn seventeen, I die," I mumble.

"You die?"

"You're not seventeen?"

"I'm sixteen years old." My teeth rip off another part of the croissant.

"Do your parents know about this?"

"No. Well, just my mom but she doesn't really care. She's gone anyway. My family doesn't really matter when it comes to my power."

"How can you say that so nonchalantly!" Sage nearly screams at me.

"Because I've accepted it. I never knew them and I never will." I sigh and lean against my knee.

"But, but!"

"Says the girl who freaks out over one little death."

"Oh, I'm sorry, I thought you were a superhero, Velocity."

"That wasn't me." He points to his brother.

"'One little life' matters you idiot. I'm not upset over my parents because I got over it. I almost died. I got rid of all my sadness and anger at everything. I changed."

"You almost... died?"

"Yeah, but... this isn't where I wanted this conversation to go. It seems like whenever I put on a costume, it's like I never left San Francisco." My timer beeps in my fanny pack. "Oh, I need to go. See you guys later."

I jump off the building, feet first.

Bad idea. Bad idea! Regret! I start screaming as a black hole opens from underneath my feet.

***

"Can you not?" I ask him, tired of going through this same charade every time.

"Would you stop putting yourself in such dangerous situations?"

"I have not been having a good night, so I would suggest taking a step back Harmony." I look into the black pits of his eyes. I've never seen his mouth, only his eyes and his red hair.

His hand grips around my arm. "But I don't think you understand, this is dangerous."

"I've already had this talk. Please do not force me to listen to it again."

"But maybe you need to hear it again. The last time I saw you, you collapsed on a roof because of a fever. You almost fell to your death."

"Would you stop? I get it, I am risking my life. I made that choice. You made the choice to be a coward and I made the choice to help people." I cover my mouth. That came out wrong. "I know that I am putting my life at risk." I try to ease the sharp daggers in my voice. "I knew that two years ago and if you weren't there to... heal me, I would have died. But this is my choice. Not yours."

"I don't care."

"Yes, you do not. The only reason you care about me is because of the Prophecy. If anyone else was Chaos, you would whine about their safety, not mine."

"Chaos, I--"

"I am sorry. That was uncalled for. I have had a rough night and would just like to go home. Please excuse me."

"Chaos, would you just listen to me?"

No. I don't want to listen to you. That's the point.

My arm convulses as I pull out a wall of light from the presence.

Aaron

To heal her. Because that's all I did. She was the one in San Francisco, defending it against bad guys. She was the one who got stabbed and shot, the one who was seconds away from dying. If she hadn't come here in her last moments. I'm glad she made the right choice though, to get over here. We were able to save her, even train her, but without her memory it was like a piece of her was missing. I couldn't stand it. I told her to see the Oracle, but she wasn't the same. She came out a better person. She laughed almost all the time and told jokes the times she wasn't. But now she's in Paris, her supposed hometown. With Tonnerre. I don't want her to die, not by the hands of a Smithe anyway, especially not *Andrew Smithe*.

Topaz

Feliz día de los Muertos, everyone! That's the only Spanish phrase I remember from the good old days way back when I had a happy family. On that note, why was I born here, in Paris, the city of love? The thing I suck most at? I hate romance. If it was a person, I would probably kill them.

But what am I even waiting for? I'm not leaving, it's like I'm on pause. Am I waiting for the Prophecy? Am I waiting for morning?

Why don't I jump from here? Why don't I jump from the top of the Eiffel Tower? Why don't I? My knees jitter as I stand on the tall pole that towers over my bright city. Just a jump. That's all it would take for your fear and yourself to take flight. It's kind of funny actually. My knees kind of jingle as I slowly extend my legs, careful.

"Hey, it's actually not that high up." The breeze is- The breeze carries my scream. The breeze is strong. Very, very strong. Strong enough to throw a person off of the top of the Eiffel Tower. Don't ask me how I know that.

The power explodes around me as I forget to hold onto it tightly. It slips away from my grasp and swirls around me.

Andrew

Where did she go? Even she can't disappear mid-fall but that was only the last time I checked. I've at least cruised atop a third of Paris, I still need to veer around the Eiffel tower and outer Paris. I'm almost there though and I've stopped two robberies on the way. And still no sign of Corbelle. What is up with her? She's been so different since she died.

And here we are, at The Eiffel Tower. Only supposed to stand for twenty years but lasted for more than another hundred and stands tall in the present day. She always sulks out here. Now I just need to look for a teenager cursed with magic, hiding in the shadows. The Eiffel Tower closes at midnight, she'd be there. She's always there. Alone.

Something's off. The lights are... different? Brighter?

Lightning rips at the bleak, paper gray sky and thunder rolls through my ears. The wind picks up vigorously. This is really strange.

Unearthly groans and hisses are starting to pour out of the shadows, the kind that tears at your mind, that breaks your sanity apart.

All the wind is doing is roaring it past my ears and carrying it to the base of the tower. Dried leaves caught in the wind are being twisted into a whirlwind beneath the tower.

This definitely isn't normal. Even the hisses seem to agree, they've gotten louder and they're also circling the base of the tower. What kind of supervillain uses the very calls of hell and wind as a weapon?

What is... that?

***

What the-?! Where did everything go?! What's going on?!

"Aw, man." I peel off my mask and rub my eyes. There's nothing in them but they sting like I've been watching something a little too closely or like I've been staring straight at the sun. The heat of sun is left on their lids, a glare that hurts. But it's not my eye lids. Looking at everything is hurting and making my eyes bug. Only one person can leave that damage.

187

"Corbelle!" My raspy voice doesn't even stand a chance against all the shrieks and hissing.

The glare starts to slowly fade, as do the screams. I squint at the tower's silhouette is hazy and barely recognizable but it's the tower's.

My eyes squeeze shut as I try to un-addle them. The second time works better than the first. Corbelle's frame stares at her hands with such horror like she just killed someone.

"Qu'est-ce que j'ai fait?"

"Corbelle!"

"Tonnerre?" Her figure tries to see over the line of roofs. "Que s'est-il passé?"

"Um, sorry? I don't speak French! What are you saying?!" I still can't see her face but she can see mine. My mask covers my face as the first drops of water land on the streets of Paris. It's poetic in a way.

"Euuh, tout ce que je me souviens..." Sunlight burns my eyes for the second time tonight as waves of her power disappear into the rain. "Qui je plaisante? C'était génial! J'ai eu le contrôle!" Her sulky mood wavers as she throws her arms up into the rain with laughter. What did she do?

"What are you saying?" I grab her shoulders and stare into her eyes. They're a brighter yellow.

"Uhh, nothing! It doesn't matter!" Her fingers pry mine off her shoulders before she takes a step back, still smiling.

"I think it does."

"You're in a mood, aren't you?" She sighs and looks at me like I'm the person she finds more disagreeable than anyone. "I hate it when you're in a mood."

"Did you just use an abbreviation?"

"You mean like, you're or don't?"

"Yeah, you never use those."

"Why can't I?"

"Because- " Why can't she? "Because it's not you!"

"Because it's not me? I don't want to fight right now, Tonnerre. I can see you want to be left alone so I'll just go. if you want to talk like a normal person to a certain degree, you seem to know where to find me." Her sunlight floods my vision again and she disappears into the shadows.

A mood? I'm not in a *mood*. If anyone was in a mood it would be her.

Rikki

"Rikki! Wait up!" Kaden's running behind me. He's probably under the impression that I'm wearing my hood up because I'm listening to music. If there was a way I could knock out that idiot without getting expelled I would have done it twice by now. I hate them both. 'She could take a bribe' when have I ever done that? Sure, I did that once. I was a snitch once. I'm sorry I ratted on the woman who took me away from my happy family.

"Rikki!" He grabs onto the sleeve of my yellow rain jacket. It's cloudy today and I'm not taking any chances. Even my jeans are supposedly water proof.

"What did you do to your hair?" He looks at me in horror as I glare at him as to snarl 'Look at me again and I'll peel out your insides as you watch in horror'. But he's right, I did do... something to my hair. I cut it (myself, I'm pretty proud). I looked at some pictures online before so it didn't turn out too terrible. The main thing I was worried about was Willow's reaction which came this morning. It was not pretty. It's not my fault I accidentally used a hipster's selfie as my inspiration. I shaved it at the back and cut it to half-length at the front. And I gotta say, I look pretty badass. Too bad I have to wear an itchy wig plus my regular mask to patrol now.

It's feeling pretty good to catch all these stares.

"Rikki Dubois?"

"Present!" The teacher looks at me like I'm growing a tree on my face, mainly because this has been the first time I've been on time since the second week of school. Not because of my hair or anything.

"Alright class, you may head to Science. Rikki, I'd like to see you right now please." I look around for support but everyone has already left. Even the air in the room is stale.

"Yes, ma'am?" I walk up to her desk slowly.

"This is the first time you've made it to homeroom on time in over a month."

"Yes ma'am."

"Can you tell me what's going on?"

"Well," I can't tell her about any of the stuff that makes me late like the monsters, villains, muggers, or massive koalas (yeah, those things are back). "uh, you see, uh- "

"I understand, you must be missing your parents, correct?"

"What?" How does she-

"I looked at your files and I see that you're living in a condominium with a roommate. Do your parents live in another part of France?"

"Wha- Oh, uh, yeah, they live in Bordeaux!" I lie, staring straight into her eyes.

"Really?"

"Yes." Please believe me. Please believe me. Please believe me. Please bel-

"My parents also live there," she informs me.

"Oh. Cool." Yes! Yesyesyesyes!

"Well, I won't hold you back any longer, you may go to Science."

"Thanks, Mrs. Humbert!"

"Oh, and Rikki?"

"Yes?" I stop in the door frame.

"I like your hair."

"Thank you!"

Maya

Rikki walks in slowly then ducks behind some desks avoiding our teacher.

"Ms. Dubois, I can see you. Please don't cower in my class." Almost everyone around me laughs at her. The 'it' group. I hate them.

"Sorry, Ms. Boulay."

"I understand Mrs. Humbert has spoken to you about your current situation and its difficulties, but I would appreciate it if you were not to make a show of yourself."

"Yes, ma'am." She hurries to take her seat in front of me amidst the laughs. I don't understand how she can just ignore how nearly everyone behind her is making fun of her and laughing at her. Even Kaden is trying to ignore them.

Zoé nudges my side. "Isn't this funny?"

"No." I respond. She snorts like a pig and nudges me again. I never asked for these looks, red hair, blue eyes, skinny, tall. Every single girl in this group is just a variation of hair and eye color.

" ...so, then she- "

"Quiet in the back please! I'm trying to teach!" They lower their voices to mumbles and look away from the front of the room.

"Hey, Rikki." I lean over the edge and whisper into her ear.

"Ms. Lesage!"

"Sorry, ma'am."

"Anyway, if you'll allow me to continue- "

"Of course, ma'am."

"Thank you, Ms. Lesage. Everyone, you may group with your partners and discuss the science fair."

"Hey, Rikki." She turns and faces me and I get full blast her new haircut.

"Oh my god."

"I know," She shrugs, "my hair. Yeah, I accidentally- "

"It's trendy."

"I know- Wait, what?" She gives me the 'eyebrow' look.

"It suits you. You look nice."

"Was that sarcasm?"

"Rikki, no."

"But- "

"Let's focus on the science project, okay?"

"Yeah, let's do that."

"So, accelerated growth."

"Yeah," She pulls out a stack of files so comically huge, I could make a very rude joke about them but the teacher is listening. "I've managed to make some progress on the acceleration front, but I want to get results in a matter of minutes rather than hours. Because at this rate, my marigolds, doused with the formula, grow at a faster rate but only by a few hours. It's impressive but not enough." I love how she never tries to dumb anything down like everyone else does for me. It's like she really knows me.

"To win."

"Right."

"Can I look at these?"

"Sure." She passes them over and I paw through them.

"You're wasting a lot of the procedure on making sure that they're equal."

"It's a very important part of the process- "

"If you, hmmmm. What if you focused on what the plants want, like sunlight. I know it sounds stupid, but maybe?"

"You know what that's actually- I need to write this down! I've got an idea!"

"And you need to announce it?" Her finger pushes against my lips.

"Shhhh. I'm thinking." Rikki scribbles down some unintelligible lettering and numbers. "We're going to need some calcium extract, beans (lots), sticks, and pots. If I add it to our current mixture, we'll win easily."

Rikki

"Sir, calm down, what's going on?" Ms. Boulay has been shouting into her phone for at least half the class. It's distracting us from doing anything. Most of the class has been loudly making jokes or laughing at me. It's almost as annoying as Kaden. Ms. Boulay's face keeps changing from bothered to shocked to fearful. Did someone die? Her fingers shake as they tap her phone's screen. "C-class, there seems to be an unfortunate disruption downtown and I've been instructed to send everyone home immediately. Stay away from the main roads."

"Ms. Boulay, what's going on?" A boy sheepishly asks from the front.

"There's a monster. A very large monster. Now go home now! Everyone! Out! Out!"

I barely have time to grab my bag before being shoved out of the dimly lit classroom into a dimly lit school hallway. A monster. A very large monster.

***

The horror frozen on everyone's face is all the same. From the window, we can all clearly see the silhouette of something straight out of a nightmare destroying buildings all over downtown. This is bad. This is worse than San Francisco. Way worse. No one notices the waves of golden light and my disappearance. I hope.

Stress is coursing through my body. It's been a while since I've felt this kind of challenge like. Actually, the first time I've faced a challenge like this.

The yellow wormhole opens on top of the beast. I stick the landing and grab onto one of the thousands of spikes on its back. It's like a dragon from a fairy tale except for some frightening appendages such as the thorns covering its back, legs, and head. Its scales shift violently underneath me. It already knows I'm here.

Blue and white streak through the sky.

"Tonnerre! Catch!" He barely has time to look at me before I briefly balance on one of the rough spikes and then launch as high as I can off the monster and into the smoky air. The monster really has noticed me. It's at least half the size of the Eiffel Tower. Its scales part and reveal yellow teeth with small spots of red blood. They pull into a grin as it watches my current situation: falling straight into its waiting jaws.

"Tonnerre!" His eyes meet mine for a moment... and instant before the monster's jaws snap, meters away from my feet. Air rushes through my wig. I don't have enough focus to teleport and Tonnerre's still too far away to save me even though he's already at full speed. He just doesn't know it yet.

I'm not going to die. I'm not going to die. I'm not going to die by being eaten by a nightmare dragon.

Wait! What did I do last time I fell?

Andrew

"Corbelle!" Agh! Where is she? This is happening again! "Corbelle! Where are you?!" I can't see anything, again because of her. "Corbelle?" Everything is yellow. "Shit!" I rub my eyes. It worked last time. This is not good. Where did she go? Why isn't she responding? "Corbelle, listen to the sound of my voice! Where are you?"

The hisses and groans aren't as loud as they were last time which is nice but not by much.

Colour is starting to return to my vision and silhouettes somewhat.

Did she get eaten? "Corbelle!" She got eaten! No! This can't happen again! I can't lose her again! Not again! I don't want to be alone!

Please no... I don't want to be alone...

Kaden

Crap. This monster is bigger than it looked at school. It's bigger than the school by so many meters. How am I even gonna be able to help with this? I create clouds, not knives. This is more of everyone else's problem instead of mine. When Kai asked me if I wanted to be a superhero I said yes because I thought it would be easy. This... this is what death means. I'm going to die. It's just been slightly delayed by- is that Corbelle? Is Corbelle a god? She's literally lit up like the sun, literal waves of light are swirling around her and she's flying right above the monster's jaws. Everything else is bland and in shadow compared her. Everything about her is glowing and floating as though she's a deity. The monster looks as transfixed as I am.

"Nuit!!" Kai yells out my name, "what are you doing?! You scared the hell out of me!"

"Yeah, Nuit, what are you doing? It's bad enough having Corbelle acting like this, but you too?"

"Uh, yeah, I just- "

"You guys know who they are?" Sage points up to the cloudless sky where a steel vehicle with two solid red W painted against its side floats. Three people fly beside it. It's the Warriors of the World!

Maya

"The warriors of the world." Nuit breathes. They look down at us like the gods they are. They say something in English I don't understand.

"What are they saying?"

"I don't know! Corbelle's the one who translates, not me!" Nuit yells.

"Then where's Corbelle!" Velocity yells at him. His anger is rising as high as Nuit's. It's almost overwhelming how similar their traits and personalities are. It's like they're related.

"She's busy!!"

"And how would you know?!"

"Alright, shut up! Can you guys stop arguing for a minute? I think I can patch my way through to the Warriors of the World!" I scream that at them. God, they're intolerable. They're like parents.

"What?"

"Wait, you can do that?"

"Yeah, I-I think I have a degree of telepathy. It's not much but they've got an actual telepath on their team, right? So, she'll be able to hear and he'll patch me through to them."

"You can read our thoughts?"

"No! Are you even listening to what I'm saying?" I yell at them.

"What am I thinking?" Velocity smiles.

"Oh my god. I am surrounded by idiots."

Hello, hello? Can anyone hear me?

"Is it working?" Velocity asks.

"Shut up!" I yell at him.

Hello? Is anyone there?

"It's a bust. It's not working." I sigh.

"What do you mean it's not working?"

"I can't do it. We need Corbelle."

"That's not an option," Nuit mutters.

"What are you talking about? Of course, it's an option! Where the hell is she?" Velocity yells at him like he's a dog.

"Well, she's busy!"

"Doing what exactly?" Their emotions are in danger of melting down. Corbelle was right, they really are grown up toddlers.

Nuit doesn't even say a word despite his anger, he just points up at the sun. "Why do you think the monster hasn't noticed us or the Warriors yet?" At a closer glance, the sun has a disturbingly familiar human body in it. Cleary unfeminine and stubby. It must be Corbelle.

Rikki

"Children, you have done well. Stand down and let us professionals take the lead." One woman beside the aircraft yells at me, keeping her distance. Why? Does my breath smell?

"Quickly! I can't keep it distracted for much longer!" Gravity is starting to seep into my legs and the light seething through me is fading too. I can feel myself slowly sinking towards the monster's waiting jaws.

"Venus, Luna, Mercury, you're on crowd control! Everyone else, you're with me! That includes you wolf cubs!" Wolf cubs?

Everyone on the ground is mesmerised by the arrival of a real superhero team. The Warriors of the World, I think. I've heard tons about them, I was particularly obsessed while I still lived in San Francisco. I wanted to be one of their members. Their success rate is one hundred percent! It's still impressive!

Crap. Distractions are not helping. The distance between me and the monster's snapping jaws is rapidly decreasing.

"Uh, I have a problem! I can't hold this any longer!"

"That's all right, girl. You did the best you could!" Girl? They're acting like this is what they would have expected from me! I'm going to show them what I can really do.

"Everyone close your eyes!" I shout at them.

"What?"

"Just do what she says!" Tonnerre yells from above, "She knows what she's doing!"

"Trois..." I whisper to myself, this is going to take a lot of my power. "Deux... Un!" All the light inside of me swells and explodes out of me. I can imagine that it's very bright. If I could see. My eyes have been consumed by the light.

And then it ends. All my power, for the time being, has been spent blinding a giant monster.

"Whoo... Tonnerre, catch." I can barely force those words out of my mouth before I start to fall towards a blinded monster shaking off what look like tiny ants. The buildings look so distant from up here.

Where is Tonnerre? Isn't he going to catch me? That idiot always catches me.

-

"Corbelle, hold on! I'll get you to a hospital." Something hazy blue and yellow shouts.

"Hospital? But I'm in the middle of the air! There's no hospital." I giggle. Hosptial. It's so silly.

"You stretched yourself too far."

"It's okay Mr. Cloud, I'm going to be okay. I have super powers! I'm floating above the clouds like the magical being I am." I touch Mr. Cloud's face. It's so squishy.

"Corbelle, you're delirious."

"No, I'm not. This is the most real I've felt in foreveeeer."

"Where do you keep your energy shots again?"

"You don't need an energy shot! You're a cloud! Hah ha! A cloud!"

"Here they are." I hear a clicky-click and an ouchie in my shoulder.

"Oww! Why'd you do that... Mr... Cloud."

***

What happened? Ugh. I feel like throwing up. I'm so dizzy.

"Tonnerre?" I look at him, expecting an explanation.

"Oh, thank god. I could not take another minute of that." He mumbles but maintains a scowl.

"Why did you prick me? I had the weirdest nightmare and- " I look up at the monster and the other super heroes in the midst of defeating it with brute strength. "-it's not a dream. What happened?"

"Well, you went full power and wore yourself out."

"I remember that. What else happened?"

"You went all delirious and I had to give you one of your energy shots from your bag and- "

"Wait, where are we?"

"I don't know, on a building in downtown?"

"Oh man, we're pretty high up, you know."

"Cor, calm down, it's okay. I'm right here."

I take a deep breath. "You're right, you're right. We should go help them."

"That's not what I meant. You're in no condition to-"

"That's stupid. You know me well enough to know that I'm going over there right now to help."

"There is no use arguing with you. Ever." The edges of a smile on his lips disappear as quickly as they appeared.

"Okay then." I respond slowly shuffling to the edge of the building's flat gravel roof. He grabs me like I'm his bride. "What are you doing?" I hiss.

"You're in no position to be using your powers right now."

I kick my way out of his grip. "I don't have time for this." Waves of my light surround me and carry me to the monster. "Mon dieu!" Pain shoots through my whole body like it's being torn apart from the inside. Tonnerre was right. I inhale sharply and collapse on the smooth concrete. "Aie."

"You okay?" Sage asks in French as she gives me a hand.

"Just peachy." She hoists me up easily from the concrete.

We stand about seventy meters away from the monster. We really are ants compared to it.

"You ready?" She asks, watching my glazed over eyes.

"Yeah, let's go." My legs launch into a full-on sprint towards the rock-dragon-monster. Swords replace my arms. My leg slips forwards as I slide underneath the dragon-beast's humongous foot. It's bigger than a mini-van but my power, from my experience, can cut through anything. Including giant-monster-stone-dragon-beast feet. I don't intend to completely cripple its leg but I don't want it to be completely able to move and squish me.

Maya

Corbelle is probably the stupidest of us all. She's cutting at the monsters leg with her powers. I mean, who does that? It's a monster!

"You coming or not?" She asks, already running towards me before the monster screams in pain, sending a rumble across Paris. "Scratch that! Run!" She grabs my arm and pulls me up a series of platforms she created out of her power. It's causing her a lot of suffering and she's still doing it. She's crazy.

"What are you doing!" I screech at the idiot who's going to have me killed.

"We're creating a distraction." The monster is still eyeing us, it's glaring at us. It knows we're the ones that hurt it.

"Crap!" The ground rumbles beneath us as the monster limps its way towards us. "You really are insane!"

"Oh, relax. It's not like I'm going to kill you."

"Oh yeah, and a giant monster running towards us is the least of our problems."

"Least of mine."

I look at her. "What kind of problems do you have!" I yell at her.

"Ones that involve a lot of big and bad." She takes a deep breath and releases yellow sparks out of her hand.

"Like 'giant monster destroying Paris and about to eat us' or 'I'm going to die' problem?"

"Oh, I don't know, it's hard to explain but it looks like we've got some time so we could-"

"It's coming!!" I shake her shoulders violently. She needs to do something! What am I going to do? Fly at it?

"Rude."

"Rude! I'm being rude?"

"Shhh, child. Let the grownups do their work."

"I'm older than you!"

"C'mon the monster's almost here. Let's rock and roll!"

"You did not just- " the world around me disappears in a puff of yellow. "Hey!" The yellow holding me up disappears, leaving me to fall to my untimely death. "Hey!"

Rikki

Sage should be fine. I made sure that Nuit was underneath her before I let her fall. I hope he caught her, but there's no time to worry about that. I need to help stop a monster.

"I'm going to jump on its head! Does anyone have a problem with that?!" I yell in English. I don't wait for anyone to agree before I vault into the air. Since I blinded it, it won't be able to immediately eat me. I think it's mainly using its smell as its sense of direction and because I was down by its foot, I don't think it got a whiff of me. Probably.

"Oof." My stomach automatically deflates as I land on the massive spikes at its nose. I pull myself up on top of its head.

"Tonnerre! Get that girl off the monster! She's in the way!" One of the Warriors of the World yells.

"Got it." He mumbles, ascending from the monsters head to reach me.

"Aw, come on Tonnerre, and after all I did to help?" I yell at him.

"You're not being particularly helpful right now, you know."

"I'm plenty helpfu-" My feet shift precariously on top of the monster's violent shaking of its head. "Zut." Is the one word I'm able to make out before falling off of the rock dragon and back into the open air.

***

My stomach is tied in a knot. Then another knot. By the time the third knot, also known as barf, breaches my throat Tonnerre's caught me.

"Oh thank god." I breathe.

"It's funny, you know? A super hero afraid of heights." He grins, carrying me by the arms like a wet cat.

"Remind me to kill you later," I groan and cover my eyes.

"Oh, come on, I'm not that bad."

"You know what they told me?"

"That Tonnerre was a total jerk?"

"They told me that falling rocks but I've been trying it lately and it actually sucks, but that's also true."

"Hah. Funny."

"It sounds like you didn't find it all that funny."

"Oh yeah?"

"Tonnerre! Put your girlfriend down and give us a hand!" A lady lasering the dragon with her eyes yells at us.

"Uh- "

"Did she call me your girlfriend? Aww."

"Well- "

"Go! She's waiting for you! I'll torture you later."

"Bye- "

"Go!" I duck behind him and push him over towards the battle. I can't help that much anymore. I just really need a nap. For days. I need a long nap.

Andrew

Maverick doesn't even need to say 'torpedo' in her usual Texan accent. I already know what to do. She gives me the nod as soon as I fly up to their- our hovercraft. I've done it before, it was my job almost whenever we've faced an omega level threat: smash through its skull.

This one's made of pure rock judging by what I've seen from all the cuts we've been giving it. I'm going to have to take a 'running' start.

I fly around the monster's head a few times before lifting above the clouds. I take a breath and reverse directions. Every week I practice this with the Warriors. I think they were impressed by my show after Topaz died. They told me she was holding me back. Until today, I haven't seen them since. The clouds part with my oncoming force. Sometimes when I go this fast, I pretend like nothing changed, like I've just gotten my powers in San Francisco, like the girl of my dreams is just waiting for me below. But no such luck.

The monster leers at a bright light, luring it farther and farther away from my targeted area. Corbelle. Not the person I had in mind but she was, once upon a time. Never mind her though. She may be the center of my thoughts but she won't distract me from my mission. I curve towards the monster's head again.

The smash or crunch is usually the same. A solid sound as I break into its skull and into its brain. Sort of like a bullet. That would have been a better name than Tonnerre. I've been covered in monster brains after but they're either easily washable or my healing factor takes care of it. The goo is always gross though. This one is no different.

It's actually warm for a moment as I enter its head but then I'm outside and it's cold again despite being covered in its brains.

I look for the bright light again but in her usual fashion, she's teleported away before I can even talk to her. I'll have to check the Eiffel Tower tonight. Until then I'll hang around with the Warriors of the World like I used to.

Rikki

I can't believe he did that. After everything. He knows how I feel about killing and he still killed it. Some things never change.

I teleport into my room. This is always a risky strategy because (one) it gives off a lot of light and (two) I have no idea if anyone could be in my room. So, if Tonnerre or someone else was cruising through my neighborhood and saw a bright yellow light coming from someone's window, of course, they would come and investigate. Then they'd see me, still halfway in my costume, eating rice crackers. And if one of them, especially Tonnerre saw, I wouldn't be able to hide my secret identity from them. And who knows what Tonnerre will do once he knows my name is Rikki Dubois. But it's not like I don't wonder what his name is. He's tall, blonde, and his eyes are blue. There're tons of people I know who match that. I've sort of filtered it down to anyone eighteen years old and ones that used to live in San Francisco. It really hasn't helped a lot. San Francisco was filled with blonde, blue eyed people. It was really annoying because a lot of them were total jerks. And I went to school with a lot of them.

I duck underneath my blankets and change into my baggiest pajamas. I snap open my computer and plop down before my half empty box of dried mochi. What I'm planning is pretty big. And very illegal.

Andrew

Where is she? She's always here this late. At least I haven't been blinded yet. I've checked every inch of the tower and nothing. She's not here. But she's always here. And when she isn't, she's not very hard to find.

I wish I still had her contact in my phone. Why did I delete it in the first place?

Because I sent all those depressing messages... that she has probably seen by now. Crap.

Smooth move, Smithe.

But, really where is she? She always meets me. Is this because I killed that thing? She always gets pissed at me because I killed that 'one thing' and then she makes a big speech about "we're heroes, we don't kill those we want to save." But I'm not a hero. I haven't been since she died.

Kaden

She's been avoiding me non-stop. Even when I tap on her window she shuts her curtains. I know it's because I said those things but she doesn't need to take them that seriously. I mean, why should she? They're just words, not sticks or stones.

"Rikki!" I run into her.

"What the hell, dude!" A girl who is clearly not Rikki yells to me.

"Oh, sorry, I thought you were someone else." Rikki doesn't have nose piercings.

"You mean that new girl, right? She's in the cafeteria right now." She takes her phone out as her pink-haired friend glares at me. I knocked into her as well. The girl continues. "She challenged Lilith in front of everyone. They're going to have a massive fight at the end of the day." She shows me some live pictures of a dwarf facing off against a giant.

I shove them out of the way and sprint into the building. Lilith always fights dirty. In fact, she's never fought at all. She always gets her cronies to face off anyone she wants.

This isn't the first time she was challenged. Last time that happened, the challenger ended up in the hospital with a concussion and a week suspension. Lilith's family also has a degree of control over the administration of this school thanks to their blue blood. She's easily a triple threat: Popularity, Money, and Corruption. Rikki doesn't stand a chance.

I throw everyone to the side. They've all circled Rikki and Lilith. They give way as I push through until I can smell Lilith's million-dollar breath.

"Rikki!"

"Aww, mommy's come to save her baby. Isn't that sweet?" I feel all color rush to my ears. They're burning red against her flaring eyes. Rikki's been doing some good work against her.

"Oh, do you mean the principal? 'Cause she's coming straight for you. Lie-lith" Nearly everyone laughs at her. "Speaking of saving bacon..." Rikki slithers out of the circle and disappears from view.

She knows how to make a good getaway like Lilith knows how to whip up some fake tears.

"Lilith? Are you alright?"

"It-" she sniffles, "it was horrible!" She leans against the principal's chest and cries into her suit.

"Okay, everyone get to class!" Everyone scatters away like rats when they're discovered.

If anyone was Reine Blanche, it would be Lilith.

Rikki

Lilith? Please. She's a twig. She may tower over me, but she's not exactly a super hero with super strength (not that it would make any difference). I don't usually go around starting fights, but when I do... It's not like I originally started the fight. She's the one who tripped that freshman and had her henchmen stuff him in a locker. She's a real piece of work, a beautiful and popular girl turns out to be a total jerk and bullies everyone around her. Willow watches about a hundred different variations of that plot on TV.

During the fight, I'll have to pull some punches. I already know I'm fighting her henchman from the constant flow of gossip so I won't have to pull many... just enough to make me look like something other than a weirdo with powers.

The clock is ticking as I try to think. It's almost three thirty and I don't have a solid plan to beat her. But I could call in some favors from a certain client.

***

I didn't get to talk to Maya face to face but I sent her a text which, knowing her, she's probably looked at in the middle of a class. I hope she doesn't have detention right now. She's a crucial part of my plan.

"Hey, Rikki!" Another senior high fives me, "Thanks for standing up to her. I'll send you flowers while you're in the hospital."

"Thanks." Hospital? There's no way I'm going to a hospital.

I turn away and walk to the parking lot.

The window doesn't distort any of the people surrounding it. Out of the crowd, I spy Lilith standing on a lawn chair. She's wearing designer sunglasses and sipping on a large coffee. She gives me a smug wave from her throne.

I charge down the stairs two-at-a-time. The doors open before me as a chorus of recording iPhones follow my every move. People who don't even go to the school clear a path for me. Maya gives me a nod. I nod back, a grin growing on my face. Everything's going according to plan.

212

The parking lot is empty of cars, it's inaccessible by cars so it's an ideal place for a fight.

As I walk through the crowd to the centre, I hear various whispers:

"Are you sure that's her?"

"She's tiny."

"I feel so bad for her."

"She's going to get destroyed."

"Why would she ever challenge her?"

I roll my eyes at them. I'm small, but I pack a punch. A punch that can knock out Tonnerre if necessary. Sometimes.

"Nice sunglasses," I smirk at Lilith.

"Of course, they're Marcel Celeste. Nothing you could ever afford, scholarship wimp- Oh, you were being sarcastic."

"So, we going to get this show on the road? I've got places to be and world problems to solve." I crack my knuckles. Not so good for my knuckles but it's intimidating. I know that from experience.

"Pierre! Michelle! Get your butts out here." Two guys even taller than her head towards us, cracking their knuckles. One's ginger and tall, the other's brunette and even taller.

Like real henchmen.

***

The taller one lunges at me. Smoke erupts from where he thought I was. About time, Maya. I jump over his head, lean onto his back, and bounce at the other one. His face hits the ground. How does dirt taste, foul villain? I elbow thing number two in the stomach. Wind hits my face and carries them both away from my punches. I manage to mouth a solid 'What are you doing?' to Kai before he disappears into the crowd in an instant. What a bag of wind.

"Pierre? Michelle? You big idiots! Say something!" Lilith cries out.

The smoke makes me cough. It stinks of the Mace brothers. This isn't the smoke I designed.

Kai runs a lap around the parking lot, sending the smoke and Lilith's idiotic sunglasses into the air.

"Rikki!" Lilith screeches and looks down at me.

"What?"

"How did you- no one's ever- I mean-"

"I gotta go, early shift." I grab my messenger bag out of the dust and step over the unconscious bodies of the lackeys making sure to kick dirt in the air. As I walk off, I hear the astonished whispers of the crowd: "Did you see that?"

"I bet my lunch money on Lilith!" Someone from my class whines.

"Shut up!" Lilith cries out over everyone's murmurs. "I want a rematch!" She points at me from her throne.

"No thank you!" I laugh at her as I turn, drawing up more dirt into the air. I look like a dancer.

People from both sides back away and clear me a path.

"Y-you, coward!" she screams again.

"But I fought. All you did was bat your eyelashes from your lawn chair." I give her a little wave and a ta-ta before walking through the crowd and onto the bike route.

The fight drew a lot of attention, but it was a really crappy idea.

I guess I'll hear tomorrow whether I'm expelled or not.

***

This isn't the first time I've broken into a skyscraper. It's not the first time I've avoided the cameras in the shadows and not the first time I've been stuck in a ceiling, clipping wires. It's not like I would *regularly* do this for fun or even regularly do this, but I need to know if Tonnerre really is the Smithe's lapdog. The security around here is tight but this is central Paris. I've almost been discovered twice but it wasn't too hard to get to the basement of the French headquarters of Smithe Industries.

I always liked hanging upside down. Usually, it's because I have to. My current plan is to snip some wires cutting the lights to the building so I can place my 'Diamond' device on one of their servers to suck up all their data on me, Tonnerre, Vaccine, and anything involving Achelium. Of course, the lights'll hopefully work as a distraction for most of the security guards but I can deal with the rest without Tonn-

"They were right. All the pretty girls really do illegal things," he says from below me. There he is on the concrete floor inside one of the most brightly lit and famed buildings in Paris.

"Are you here to stop me?" I pop my head from out of the hole in the paneling in the ceiling.

"Depends, what are you doing here, Corbelle?"

"I'm trying to- " I grunt, pretending to untangle some cords and wires. What do I tell him? He'll be *really* angry it if he knows I'm investigating him. "I'm trying to find links between Vaccine and Smithe."

"I already told you, Smithe Industries has nothing to do with Vaccine." I can hear the disapproval in his voice along with a tinge of guilt.

"Oh? And how do you know?" I glare at him, upside down.

"Well... what proof do you have that they're connected?"

"Seriously, you don't think it's suspicious that an unregistered man was inside a Smithe lab dealing with a highly volatile and dangerous substance?"

"I'm sure they've got an explanation."

"Yeah, right!" I snicker, "like I'm just going to walk up to Markus Smithe and demand an explanation about his possible links to Vaccine." I smile at the thought of punching that guy in the face "Heh." I turn back to my work.

"So, what is it that you're specifically doing in the basement?"

"Cutting the lights."

"So, you can do what?"

"Shut up, I've... almost... got... it." I nearly touch the purple wire. My fingers lengthen and snip it along with a red wire behind it. "Crap." The lights flatline after flickering for about a minute.

"What did you do?"

I flip out of the ceiling, grab his hand, and run towards the stairs.

"Hopefully nothing, but we better not hang around to find out." A siren blares through the fire door separating us from the rest of the building. "Double crap!" I drop his hand and burst through into a deeper darkness.

"You set off an intruder alarm. Wait, your eyes- "

"Glowing, I know. It's been happening for a while." I sigh at him, it's been obvious for even longer. I pull my scarf over my face to distort the glow. If only I could do that over the whole power... it could be a way to prevent my curse from taking over.

***

To a certain degree, I'm invisible right now so I've got better chances of sticking to a wall and chasing my own way to the hard drives which should be on this floor. Tonnerre's just going to be an obstacle. I prefer to do these kinds of missions alone. But he wouldn't understand.

"Corbelle?" He whispers.

I silently glide across the floor towards what should be a heavily locked room filled with beeping and flashing lights. White lab coats sprint past me in the utter backness. They're oblivious to my being there.

"All according to plan," I grin to myself. My body hits the end of the hallway, my stomach taking the blow of the doorknob. "Aie," I whisper.

My fingers lengthen, with finesse and focus. The alarm is sounding because of my carelessness. One of the locks clicks open. Now for the other two. A fingerprint scanner. That's cool.

I scramble for the Diamond in my fanny pack and press it against the scanner. I love algorithms, there's just this magic of them especially when you get one for say, a lock, just right and it goes all according to plan. Because that makes me a wizard.

The last lock, a code. I rip the keys off and cut to the circuit board. If I move some of the wires around just right... Presto! Magic!

The door buzzes, absent to the other chorus of buzzes throughout the complex.

"Oh,"

That's a lot of computer drives. And this is only one floor. This is the main dock, but not the only hub for the Smithe computer servers. Shoot. This is going to take a while.

216

Andrew

The lights are flickering back on.

Was this also part of her plan? To ditch me in the dark and let me be arrested by my own family? She doesn't know my name though. And it's not like I'm going to tell her anytime soon. She talks about my father like he's the grime she scraped off her boot. But back to her 'master' plans. They rarely ever go to plan. When she was Topaz her plans were *perfect*. Simple and eloquent. She always ensured they would work. But as Corbelle, her plans aren't well-thought-out or even well planned. There's always an element of improv in them, and she doesn't always execute them properly. Did she even look at the floor plans of the building? Or know about the different alarms? Because she set off the trespasser-alarm. She's such an airhead. How can I care about her? But I do. It's just how things work.

I know those weight and mechanised stomps. Security is coming heavily armed for us, or me. Thanks to the current advances in technology and thanks to some of our- Smithe Industries' investors, the Powers Group, we now have Mechanised Intelligent Compact Bots. Or otherwise known as M.I.C.E. which are giant robot dogs. They practically make the building shake, figuratively and literally. And thanks to my influence on the CEO of the Powers Group's son, they now make little squeaks along with an unintelligible "Intruder, stand down." Which is exactly what I'm hearing as three turn the corner of the white, plant infested hallway.

" -Intruder, stand down."

"Override code eighteen-AS-slash-T."

All three answer correctly with my name. Their front legs bend with a creak as though they're doing the downward dog. A bow. That's what my dad told me they'd do. It's what my mom said they'd do if they heard my override code. They would bow to their superiors, like they should. As they did. Just like they both said.

They trample past me towards the server room, just a few doors down. Where Corbelle is right now if things aren't going according to her plan. Damn that airhead!

I fly over their metallic toothed jaws towards the room of hard drives. She left the door wide open. Idiot.

"What are you doing? The M.I.C.E. are coming!" I warn her, slamming the door shut. If I use my override code again, it's going to cause an error with the million-dollar bots. "Aren't you done by now?"

"No! This takes time! Which I did not have enough of!"

"You had ten minutes!" The M.I.C.E are initiating their 'tank' mode, pretty soon they're going to bust through.

"Have you noticed how many hard drives are in here or the encryption software?" She pauses to look at a screen. "Because this is going to take me a few more minutes! I need much more time!"

"How much? I can't hold these things off much longer!"

"Uh, give me three minutes! Then I'll take us out of here!"

"Not sure we have that long! Can you do your thing?"

"My thing? No! I don't have nearly enough focus to do that!"

The M.I.C.E. take their ram formation. One in the back, two at the sides. "I can only going hold this door closed for another minute!"

"Almost done! Only a few more seconds!" She says hurriedly.

"How many?" I yell and grip the doorframe and door together.

"Dix... neuf..."

"Just hurry up! They're about to bust in!"

"Intruder, stand down," All three command.

"They're here!"

"I still need a few more seconds!"

The first M.I.C.E. smashes through the door and pins me down, spraying the door's concrete everywhere. "Corbelle!" I yell at her.

"Distract it!" She tells me and waves her hand.

"It's a tank! I'm not just going to distract it!"

"Turn it on its back! Stall them three more seconds, yes? Un... Deux... Trois... Done!"

"A little problem here- " The other two burst in destroying what was left of the door. " -now we're screwed."

"Maudit!" She drops her thing into her bag and lunges at the M.I.C.E. on top of me. Her power smashes its head, but only leaves a dent. They all look at her. "Maudit." The one on top of me scrambles against my chest to chase Corbelle. She barely jumps over its beating jaw and crumpled head. She almost slips off of its back before landing beside me silently.

"Quickly!" She yells at me, grabbing my arm and dragging up.

"Mother- " Pieces of yellow surround us as she sticks her tongue out at the M.I.C.E.

The view changes from the room of hard drives to the miniature streets of Paris. I caress her hand but she pulls away quickly. "What are you doing."

Now's a good time as ever. "Corbelle," I look her in the eyes, "There's something I need to tell you."

Rikki

"It can wait." I tell him, looking away. I pull out my Diamond and check the info. All of it's downloaded. I'll have to scan through it at home. "I need to get home as soon as possible."

"No, it can't." He takes a deep breath and looks at me. "What I want to say, Corbelle, is that I love you."

"Aw, thanks Tonnerre. I love me too," I grin absentmindedly and keep scrolling through the files. I burst into laughter but still look at him in the eyes. "Theat's a joke, right?" My stomach is even starting to hurt.

"Uh, no." He looks at me like I just punched a kitten.

"Wait, you're serious?" I stop laughing in an instant and my silence nearly kills the stars in the sky. "So, all this stuff about making a point of being a total jerk to me, was...?"

"Well, yeah." He's going to say it again. "I love you." No. "Don't you love me?" Nonono. How can he say that to me?

"Ew," I say under my breath so he doesn't hear. "I don't know what to say," I say, a little louder so he can hear. Why is this even happening?

"What?"

I sigh. "You're unbelievable. I can't even- I mean, after everything, after how well you know me. You did not listen to a word I said? You know that I do not like to kill and yet that's what you do. You know that I don't feel," I wince, "*that* way for anyone. We are heroes, not murderers." I say quietly, looking away from him and his stupid blinding blonde hair. My eyes melt into the Eiffel Towers metal. Why did I bring him here? To my special place?

"Why are you like this, Corbelle? They killed you! And you don't want justice?" He argues back.

"There is a difference between justice and vengeance!" I yell and clench my fists tightly.

"Why are you this complicated? Why can't things go back to normal?"

I glare at him, he glares down at me. He only likes who I was. Not who I am. I cross my arms. "This is my normal." I'm not going to give him the satisfaction of hitting him. "If you want *your* normal back, then just go back to San Francisco. It is not like anyone will miss you." I stand my ground and stare daggers at him.

"Topaz will miss me."

"Too bad she's me." I grin at him as I jump over his oncoming fist. "Le sort est-il brisé?" He hits me again and again but misses each time. "You almost hit me." I land on his face with both my feet. "Almost."

He grabs me by the hood and throws me off the side of the tower. My stomach lurches towards the ground.

Just like I've practiced, I open a portal back up the side of the tower and salute him. "Ooooh, c'est dommage."

Andrew

"We hate each other and also not hate each other. It's very confusing." She jumps away from my punch and latches onto a stretch of metal. She sits on a circle of her power above me and sighs at me like I'm the insane girl who dresses up like a living shadow.

She can't believe me? I can't believe her. She's right, she's crazy, she goes from being a great person to a down right psychopath in seconds.

"You're right, we do hate each other."

"Exactly."

"But then why do we always wait for each other? I know you wait for me too." I ask her, pointing at her.

"I do not." She rolls her eyes. "It's not waiting for you as much as waiting for a faithful dog or cat." This is what I'm reduced to by her. A cat.

"Then why do you wait for me if I'm just a cat? Is it because you're lonely?"

She looks at me in disgust and rolls her eyes again. "I am not lonely, I have many friends." She scoffs.

"Then why are you always out here and not with them?"

"Why are we talking about this? We were just at each other's throats," She groans. "Can we go back to attacking each other?"

"Why are you changing the subject?"

"Why do we even talk to each other?"

"What were you really doing in the Smithe building?"

"What were you doing in the Smithe building?" She turns my own question against me. I'm about to ask her again but I'll choose something she'll respond to.

"You first."

"No."

"Why not?"

"Because."

"What has gotten into you?"

"I just want to know what you were doing in a random Parisian skyscraper. I have my reasons but why were you there? Are you connected to the Smithes?"

"What? Of course not! I heard something suspicious and I thought I'd check it out. That's all." I scratch the back of my neck as she eyes me carefully.

"You're hiding something. It's plain to see. If you tell me what it is, perhaps I can help," She says slowly and carefully like she's waiting for my reaction.

"Why do you always think that? Why can't you trust me?"

She walks around me on her bright yellow platforms. "Well, trust is a very special thing. You can give it to everyone you meet but once someone breaks it, it's very hard put it back together again. I am not going to let my trust be broken again."

"I would never do that." I lean into her, trying to mend the gap but she evades to my left and slaps my cheek.

"Don't." A black braid shimmers underneath her hood. It reflects her beautiful and imperfect smile. The braid of raven hair, the color of the starry sky, drops at my head. "Stupid wig," She mutters under her breath. She's somehow managed to shimmy herself up the slanted rusted metal of what she and the French people call a national monument. Her moony glowing eyes stare down at me from above they're full of grace and not just because of her power.

"So I was wondering," I start. I've asked this question before but that was two years ago and we were both different people. "Why do you wear your mask?"

"You're asking this again?" she sighs.

"You remember?"

"I told you it was because... I..." she scrunches her nose and taps her forehead. "I completely forget."

"So, can you tell me your name finally?" I smirk tilting my head as I lean closer to her lips.

"I don't think so." She interjects by pressing her gloved hand over my mouth and throwing my chin into the air. "I don't feel very kissable today."

"So, another day?"

"How about never?"

"So, is that your answer to the mask thing?"

"No."

"Then what is it?"

"That's it, no. I'm not going to tell you." She shrugs like it's not the big deal it is to me.

"Is it because you don't trust me? Because, Corbelle, I've known you for three years."

"No, I trust you." Her arms move around in a circle. "I can trust you with my life."

I scratch my neck with a twinge of guilt. "But not enough to tell me your name?"

"It is a stupid name, it's not like it really matters." She shrugs but her arms tense up. I can almost see the power tether itself to her.

"Then why don't you tell me what it is?"

"Why don't you tell me yours? You seem very anxious to know mine." She looks like she's about to bite me. Her teeth grind like they always do when she's had enough of me.

"Fine!" I reach for my mask but drop my hand weakly. My fists grip together in defeat. If I tell her mine, she'll tell me hers. My fingers reach up again but drop once again.

"What?" She asks, annoyed.

"I can't do it."

She rolls her eyes at me and swings behind the slated pillar to another part of the tower. It's like it's made of old rejected and over-sized triangle Rubik's cubes.

"Ugh, come on Corbelle, it's not that bad." I fly over to the next rusted triangle but she's gone. "Corbelle?"

"I didn't fall." She says, annoyed that I'd even imply.

"No, I didn't mean it like that-"

"Then what did you mean?" The gravel in her voice has lifted but her glare remains. Her legs drop from the bottom corner of the triangle above me.

"I just- "

"You? You what?" She asks, obviously not wanting me to respond.

"Can you not?"

"Can I not what? Interrupt you?"

"Sure," I mutter.

"Knock knock," she grins at me with a fat cat smile.

"Who's there?"

"Interrupting cow."

I roll my eyes at her, of course, she makes a knock-knock joke in the middle of a conversation. "Interrupting cow wh- "

"Moo!" she shouts. "What did you expect?" At least that's what I thought she said, her voice drifted off in the middle of her sentence.

"Corbelle?"

"Wrong answer." She yells from above.

"Where are you?" The air pushes me upwards to where she should be. My instincts pull my eyes down to the ground and the air below me. The trees look like green dots amongst all the cement. There aren't any black spots on the ground so I can trust she hasn't fallen yet.

A rock bounces off my head.

I watch her from below as she scales another step of the tower's many triangles without breaking a sweat. I'm pushed higher, I stop so I'm hovering beside her next triangle.

"Cheater," she sneers as she struggles to mount the base of this triangle. She climbed through the inside of the pillars. I lend her a hand but she slaps it away.

"I don't need your help."

"And you never did," I sigh, annoyed at her continuous stubbornness.

Rikki

He looks at me differently, like this is the first time he's ever seen me. A twinkle in his eyes explodes.

"Um, are you okay, Tonnerre?" I take a step back. The power surges into my arm and turns it into a small mallet. It shakes until I tell it to stop. Why would it even choose a mallet? Everyone knows axes are so much better.

I've seen this look before. It's happened in San Francisco, he got mind controlled by a girl who could control water. It went downhill from there and I ended up with a scar shaped like an x and a fresh tetanus shot. Because getting your shoulder sliced open by your best friend is fun. So much fun that I felt like barfing up clowns. Wait no, I mean-

"I think I should probably head home, you know, I'm a teenager and I have school still and yes." My boots edge closer to the open air.

"Oh. Uh, sorry, was that getting a little weird?"

"No, no, it's fine. My timer's about to beep anyway." I paste a fake smile on my face with ultra-strength crazy glue. I can only pray it holds. Plus my eyes are moments away self-destructing on themselves.

My legs liquefy in the sea of air and the pull of gravity. I am never going to get used to this. Falling equals very scary. Very scary equals yellow stain on the costume. Yellow stain on the costume adds to my big heaping heap of problems that I keep shoving more heaps onto. So, it's a triple heap, maybe?

Tonnerre's stare burns the back of my head. He's ready to rescue me in a moment's notice. Should I feel safe? 'Cause that is not what I'm feeling.

All feeling dissolves from my body as I teleport into my room and take off my mask. I wonder how the other superheroes get their masks to stick on their faces, glue? I've heard of kids doing it. It's not like anyone hasn't at least tried on some variation of a costume. I have. That's also why I no longer use glue. Of any kind.

***

The moon rises over the city through my window. Why? Why is life so complicated? Why can't it be like a math equation? At least that way you'll know what the result will be. I take off my wig and scratch my head. It feels a lot cooler.

The clatter of my window shatters my mood (it wasn't me, actually). I throw my white blankets over my head and launch up the ladder to my bed. My pillows fly everywhere. You're asleep. Don't move. Or is that for dead people? That's for dead people. What do people do when they sleep?

"Rikki?"

Don't move. Stay still.

"I know you're awake. I just saw a light in your room."

Yet another reason of why I am never teleporting to my room again.

"No one's here." I muffle from under a comically large pile of blankets. Probably the only thing I've faced tonight that won't kill me.

"Rikki," He sighs, "would you just talk to me?"

I roll in the blankets so that I'm facing away from him.

"Rikki! Stop acting like some spoiled princess and talk to me!"

The blankets pull me over to him long enough for me to give him a glare and offer a rude motion with my hand. "I learned that in America," I mumble, not sure whether he heard it or not. I roll back and wait for him to leave.

"Rikki- "

"Stop that. Can't you tell I don't want to talk to you? I hate you." Even I wince at my words. I didn't mean that but it's too late. He's already struggled through my window. Crap. This was not in the answer or equation.

Kaden

Everyone has been whispering about Rikki this morning and my ears are burning. 'I hate you' has been ringing in my ears since last night. It's not just that she said it that pisses me off it's the tone she used. Like she's been thinking about it for a while. But what I've finally realised, is that I hate her too. I can't stand her. She acts like everything isn't a big deal and she acts like she could carry the weight of the world.

"Kaden! Kaden, you've been avoiding me for- " Rikki chases after me down the street.

"Stop. I don't want to hear it." I hiss at her. Now it's my turn to ignore her.

Her shoes stop behind me. She's just going to stand there and wait for me to turn around.

"I'm sorry! Okay, I get it. I'm a headstrong dummy with issues. I'm sorry. I'm so, so sorry. Please don't leave."

"I told you, you idiot, that I did not want to hear it. Leave me alone, bitch."

A gasp drops out of her mouth but then she replaces it with her signature 'I don't care' face. Her hand quivers and pulls into a fist but she pockets it quickly. Her free hand reaches for her hair as she brushes past me but fails. I think what surprised me the most was her lack of remorse like this is what she was expecting me to say. It makes me feel used, after all Kai and I did to help her she doesn't even cry that we're no longer going to care about her. We were just her pawns.

Her hands move to pull up the straps on her worn-out backpack, second hand I bet. My designer runners move to step on her faded sneakers caked with layers of dirt. She trips and falls into a dirty brown puddle. I'm not the only one to laugh at her attempt to climb back on to her stubby little legs, the whole schoolyard seemed to chuckle as a collective. Salty tears still don't drip down her cheeks she just shrugs it off and walks away into the darkened school building. I can't let her do it again. I can't let her go to *my* school. Filthy bugs like her should be kept out.

Rikki

Okay, crappy start to the day. Probably the crappiest. Ever.

I blow the mud off my nose. I guess it didn't get to him that I didn't mean it. Too bad.

My loose jeans stride into our advisory classroom.

"Aah, Rikki Dubois." Lilith sighs, lounging all over the teacher's desk as all my classmates except for Kai and Maya hurl slurs at me. Some of them racial, some of them sexist, and some of them just against me.

I throw my bag down onto my desk and scratch my head, not violently, more of like I was silently planning how to blow up the classroom.

"Hey, everyone look! The bug has lice!" Kaden walks into the classroom after me and points at my head-scratching. I've only had lice once, it was not very fun or pleasant.

"Are you sure she isn't one?" Lilith chimes in with her stupid horse laugh.

"Guess it takes one to know one." I ask her while I count the cars out the window.

Lilith growls at me. I'm not kidding she actually made the *grrrrrrrr* sound.

"Lilith, what are you doing in my classroom?" Mrs. Humbert walks in with her attendance in her hands. The class goes silent like someone waved a magic wand over them telling them to shut up.

"Yeah, she's black like a beetle!" Kaden chimes in. Too bad it took him that long to think of a comeback, he should really stick to science.

"Mr. Mace! What was that?" She looks at him, her jaw lower than humanly possible. "Who was the directed at?" She snaps. It's kind of obvious it was me, I'm pretty sure she knows it too. But I'm not going to say anything to help him.

"Uh, no one." He shrinks into his seat, the weakest smile on his face. No one has had that effect on him before (from what I know).

"Who!" She snaps yet again, sending everyone to shrink into their seats.

"He said it to Rikki!" Cedric squeaks.

"Thank you, Cedric," she says kindly but switches to her true dark side as she turns back to the jerk hiding behind his bag. "Kai, you may go to the principal's office and be sure to take your brother with you." Of course, they're twins. Because Kaden is Kai and Kai is Kaden today. I thought today couldn't get any more confusing.

"What did I do?" Kai asks and looks around the room.

"Kaden, if your brother had something to do with this, I'm sure you did too."

"He didn't do anything!" I yell at the teacher and stand up, sending my chair flying backwards into the wall.

"Ms. Dubois- "

"He didn't," I insist and nod. "It wasn't him. It was all Kaden."

"Did he do anything?" She takes a breath and looks at me. Her fingers nimbly push her glasses up the bridge of her nose.

"No," I mutter and look down.

"Exactly."

"What?" She's sending him to either detention for a month or a suspension because he didn't want to bite the dragon/ his twin brother/ Lilith kiss-up.

"Ms. Dubois, please, don't make me send you with them." I snap shut. I can't get a suspension, that'll mean bye-bye school for a scholarship student.

They stand up slowly and walk out of the classroom with the teacher shooing them out.

"Anyway class, we're ready to announce the prizes to the Science fair! To first place, an eight-thousand-euro scholarship! And to second place, one week of studying abroad in New York, America!"

The class lets out a collective groan.

Kai

My brother is an idiot. *An idiot!*

So, he figures since we're twins that I'd jump off any ship just for him. That I would abandon Rikki because of something she said to *you*. Not me. She didn't tell me 'I hate you'. She told you she hated you while you were in her bedroom in the middle of the night. It's like we share a brain and I'm the only one who uses it. I mean, the middle of the night? In her bedroom? And this isn't the first time? Of course, she hates you, you idiot! And because of you, we're stuck in detention for the next month!

That's exactly what I would say to Kaden if we were speaking at the moment. I gave him a pretty similar mouthing off as soon as we left the solitary classroom.

"What were you thinking?" I yell at him, "You can't just yell racist slurs in front of a teacher! And about a classmate, a friend!"

"It wasn't that racist." He mumbles.

"That's beside the point!"

"Then what is the point, Kai?"

"How could you say that about Rikki?!" I scream at him.

"Wow, look how defensive you've become over her. She's as old as us, she can take down someone twice her size, and she's a genius. She doesn't need our help. She hates us."

"No." I stop on the orange and yellow stained sidewalk. "She hates you. Not me." I pause for a second and soak up the annoying dramatics I know him for. "-And I'm done being your twin. You can't make both our decisions. You can't just hate our best friend because she told *you* she hates you. Leave me alone." I mutter.

"I thought I was your best friend," he says. What a drama queen.

"No. You're not even my brother anymore." I cross the silent road of our high-class community to the other side of the street with the golden lampposts and villas.

Rikki

"Hey guys," I drop down to our usual concrete roof plaza. "Am I late?"

"You always are." Kaden/Nuit grumbles at my general direction and continues to look dramatically into the horizon. He reminds me of the Great Gatsby.

"How far did someone shove a stick into your butt?" I ask with a smile.

"Shut up," he mumbles.

"Wow, that far? That's pretty crazy. Seems painful, too." I shrug.

"Did anyone ever tell you how annoying you are?"

I tap my fingers slowly. I'm pretty sure he rolled his eyes under his giant black helmet.

"What are you doing?" He asks with a sigh.

"Counting," I smile.

"Oh my god," he says, except with less pauses and more annoyance in his voice. He tries to grab his throbbing forehead but forgets about the massive black block on his head. "Can someone please take her away from me. Sage? Tonnerre?" He asks and looks around the plaza.

The mop of blonde looks in my direction, not with a frown or a scowl but with the faintest of smiles. "Hey, what's up?"

"The sky." I point up to the dark and ominous looking clouds.

"Did you know you're a terrible person?" He says with a wide smile, but I can see the pain behind it. He didn't forget about last night, but he wants me to play along and pretend to. Last night was clearly a mistake.

"Are you alright?"

"Why do you keep asking me that?"

"It's okay if you aren't," I mutter and look at my feet. Sometimes I'd like it someone asked me that once in a little while.

"I'm fine."

"Okay, okay," I mumble and sit down with him.

"Okay?" He lifts a golden eyebrow at me, "What did you do?"

234

"I didn't do anything!"

"Then what's wrong?" He sighs at me.

"Nothing. Why would anything be wrong? I'm a superhero." How could he understand?

"Whenever you start a sentence with 'okay' something is always wrong."

"*Nothing* is wrong." I match his colorless sigh.

"Just spit it out, Corbelle. This isn't about your name again, is it?"

"No, 'Crow' isn't as stupid as Tonnerre."

"Hey!"

"What's going on?" Sage whispers French into my ear.

"Oh, nothing. It's fine we're just debating."

"Then I'll just leave you lovebirds."

"We're not- " She smiles and turns away. "Really?"

"What'd she say?" He asks in English.

"Nothing!" I groan. "Mon Dieu!"

"Anyway, what I was *trying* to say was the Warriors of the World are looking for new members. You're the only Parisian superhero they haven't recruited. Plus, they have a special interest in you."

"Because I am black? I have heard the incidents but I am not in the mood to joke, Tonnerre."

"I'm not joking."

"Oh." Have you ever felt the world crash around you? Like a bone-and-soul crushing feeling that won't let you escape. Like your final death trap. The three times it's happened to it's been worse each scenario:

1) When I found out the woman who raised me took me away from the rest of my family and raised me to be her own little thief.

2) When the Oracle gave me back *all* my memories.

3) Now.

I smile like this isn't a big deal and it's just a big joke on me.

Andrew

"Non. Je ne peux pas.."

"What do you mean?" I ask her.

"Exactly what I said. I can't. I am not a murderer and I never will be."

"Corbelle, we're not murderers."

"Four hundred and eighty-six people. That is how many are missing because of your little club. Would you like to know how many are confirmed dead?"

"We save the world."

"No, you kill!"

"Then what are you doing to save the world? All you do is watch Paris!"

"At least I do not kill!"

"You will! You're Chaos! You're a ticking time bomb! A time bomb that could- *will* kill millions!"

She draws in a gasp and winds her hand back. Her light covers it and turns it into a small hammer. "How can you say that?" She breathes. "You say it like you're so sure it will happen but I am in control!"

"Then what about those energy bursts?" I scream, "What about what you're doing to your hand? Is that you too?"

Shame covers her face as she hides her hand in her bag. "What. Is. Wrong with you?" She says slowly and quietly like everything I do makes her mad.

"What's wrong with you, crazy?" I glare down at her. Why can't she see the point of joining the Warriors? We've saved the world countless times, travel the world, and get paid well doing it.

"Maybe you should look in a mirror," she seethes from underneath her scarf.

Rikki

All I could do was watch him slap my face from out of my body. He was too fast to stop and even if I did block him, his arm would break from the impact of it hitting the shield.

"What kind of man slaps?" I say in French, carefully nursing my bruised face. He didn't hit me too hard so he's got to have some sense.

His chest heaves. He's not done throwing me around like a ragdoll. It's like I'm still seven.

"Calm down," I breathe, "It is okay."

"No, it isn't! You can't just stay in this bubble you've made! You're not immune, you're not safe from anything! People die! And what have you even done to stop yourself from becoming Chaos?" He screams at my mask.

"I've done so much- "

"But have you really?"

"Stop! This is not your problem, it's mine. So, stop acting like you're in control!" I yell at him.

"You're right. If you don't want to accept help when it's offered, you don't have to listen to me, you don't have to listen to the Warriors of the World, you don't have to listen to the only people who care about you." He grabs my shoulders.

"Everyone has joined?" I wipe his giant hands off.

"Except for you."

"Fine." I shrug.

"You're abandoning everything."

"No, I'm not. I came here for a fresh start which you ruined."

"So, is this it? This is your choice?"

"Did you not hear me?"

He grunts but not really. It was more of a sad sigh he tried to disguise as a grunt. The building shakes as he launches off into the dark gray cotton balls. My eyes follow him until he hides from them.

"Guys," I look at the others, starting in French, "did you join the Warriors of the World?" My spine tingles as I say the club's name.

"I did," Sage says slowly, waiting for my approval and the others'.

"Same here." Velocity says, nodding at her.

"Yeah, we all joined. Isn't that what Tonnerre was talking to you about? Trying to get you to join?"

"Uh, yes, he was but- "

"Guys, she's not joining." Dammit, Kaden.

"What?" They both screech at different pitches, Kai, surprisingly at the higher one.

"I just don't agree with- "

"Killing?"

"Yeah," I whisper, twisting my hands together and untwining them in the same motion.

"So, you're not going to help? You're going to stand by and watch people suffer?"

"What?" I stare at Sage and wave my hands and shake my head. "No! Of course not."

"Then what are you going to do?" Kaden sighs.

"I'm going to stop them the friendly way."

"You sound like a ten-year-old." Kai rolls his eyes.

"I meant friendly to the civilians, do you have any idea how many people are missing because of your new little club? Plus, jail time is a punishment that will ruin your life, trust me."

"Why? Is that where you've been for the past two years?" Kai asks.

"What are you talking about?" I ask him.

"I can understand some of your English, you know. I know you've been gone for two years and something about a sword."

"I was legally dead for three whole minutes because that sword was stabbed in my chest. Tonnerre saw everything, that's why he's like this. That first year I was missing was spent in a coma, the second in a state of amnesia and rehabilitation. I've never been in jail but if you want to know that little story I have about it... I just want to warn you that it's a little dark."

The twins look at each other and nod.

"I want to know," Sage whispers to me as I sit on a sloped piece of the wall protecting us against the wind.

"As you guys know, my parents are dead and I wasn't exactly adopted." They all look like they're on the edges of their seats, listening to my tragic back story. I haven't even told Tonnerre the full story about it so don't expect me to tell them everything. "Now that I think about it, I was technically kidnapped in that hospital. The woman who stole me raised me as her little thief. She taught me the basics of gymnastics, defense, offense, and pickpocketing by the time I was half my size. Next thing I knew, I went on 'missions' with her, breaking into mansions, banks, and museums all over the world. Anytime she made a fraction of a mistake, she'd take it out on me. I still have some of the scars. It wasn't until I was thirteen I found out she wasn't my mom, I had enough stashed away to find my own permanent residence and put her in one. For all I know, she's dead, stuck behind bars." Of course, this isn't what it really is but why would I tell them the truth? I barely know them.

"Oh," Sage murmurs.

"Uh- "

"Ugh, sorry, I should have told you guys the shorter version. I am such a drama queen." I sigh at myself, trying to ignore the two visible sets of bug eyes.

"You don't want to kill her?" The boy in black asks.

"Of course, I do. But it's better for her to rot there."

"For her to suffer?"

"I prefer to put it as 'reflect on her actions for a very long time'."

***

Here's the truth: My mom was an international thief starting at the ripe age of sixteen. She learned her skills thanks to years of gymnastics and practice. Whatever she stole, she'd only keep part of it. She gave the rest to people who really needed it like homeless people or orphans.

She was always good at picking good targets to steal from until of course, she met my father. She's pretty great at faking emotions like her excellent daughter. Happiness, sadness, surprise, love. All of them were easy for her to manipulate and fake until she met dad. They met at a fancy party mom had planned to pick out some stuffed wallets at. He walked up to her in her dark blue dress and said 'I wouldn't expect to see someone like you at one of these things. You're too real.'

About eleven months later, they had a baby. Carmen Rikki Dubois. My full name. Mom had decided to submit to a normal life with my dad and finally settle down rather than run around in the middle of the night breaking into people's houses. Mom and I even moved to Mexico with him. We lived like that happily for a few years. They were perfect together. I thought they were really in love but like mom and the universe constantly remind me, true love doesn't exist. They had a massive fight when dad found out about mom's past. Afterwards, mom ran away with me in her arms and came back to my birthplace, Paris (some parents call it a divorce). While I was going through puberty, we found out I had very explosive powers so that was another thing. Skip through a few years of her training me in gymnastics and fencing, and I'm nearly grown up.

We travelled all the way to San Francisco in America to grab a few bucks from Smithe family who are comfortably sitting there, unwatched. Mom goes in to grab it while I hide. I decided that it was finally time for me to 'spread my wings' so I hid under a bridge. That's basically my life story. Of course, there are still the things that actually happened in San Francisco but they're not really that important. I was a really dumb hero then I got really hurt and practically died and then I got better then, finally, I end up here, in Paris.

I told them a different but equally dramatic story and yet they still ditched me. At least I'll have a lot of time to think by myself. What. Fun.

"J'ai l'ennui!" I whine in French making a point to drag the I on much longer than necessary.

I'm so bored that I've started re-organizing my room since I've got nothing to do thanks to the other nine-thousand superheroes. I've started with the seemingly endless piles of random papers. Late night Rikki tends to skimp out on her duty to caffeinate herself so things can get pretty messy if she's not careful. My desk was probably the worst hit by her messing spree but I know I/she didn't make some of these messes. Someone has been through my room and was looking through my papers for something. At least I'm not going to be bored?

"Willow?" I yell down the stairs a little desperately.

"What's up Rikki?" She bursts through my door making it slam against my wall, "What's wrong?"

"What's behind your back?"

"Oh, I was doing some cleaning and- "

"You don't clean though."

"Well, why did you call me?" she snaps. "Sorry." She reacts, choking on her own words. She covers her mouth and gives me an apologetic look.

I wave it away absent mindedly. "Someone has been going through my papers, specifically my school work involving the growth serum."

"What? And you think that was me?!" There's barely a hint of guilt on her face before she wipes away watching my suspicion. "Rikki, I would *never* do that. It has to be one of your friends."

"I will- "

"I'll."

"I'll-" I roll the 'L's a little bit, "-ask them."

She walks out the door, turning on her heel and hiding whatever she was 'cleaning' with against her stomach. She's a culprit.

My hands shovel through pounds of paper trying to find some of the missing ones which turn out to be my sketchbook, a rough recipe of the serum, and the sample of my blood. All of which *can't* go missing. They just can't.

***

Suspects on who stole a sample of my blood which if you filter and activate it properly, you could channel it into raw energy, aka, the power. But this isn't the only thing I'm worried about, my sketchbook and a recipe of my growth serum are also missing.

Willow is probably the biggest suspect. She knows my day schedule like the back of her hand, and she's got access to my room whenever she comes to our apartment. But I don't know what her motive would be.

Kaden's next. He's got motive, he quit the Science fair with Kai and partnered with Lilith who also hates me. They'd love me to mess up and fall flat on my face, literally and figuratively. He's probably stolen the recipe and other missing items trying to replicate my serum and to make it better as their application for the fair. They don't even need to replicate it though, Lilith is richer than rich. She has more yachts than the United States has guns. No judge has a will stronger than an easy five million. Plus, Kaden has the ability to break in through my lockless window apparently. I should put a book between it and the frame to keep it closed.

Lilith's third but her motives tie in with Kaden's.

There could be Tonnerre somewhere in this too but he doesn't know who I am or that I'm Corbelle. If he did, he would probably completely destroy the apartment.

"Hey, Rikki." I snap to attention, "You okay? You look a little dazed." Maya asks, running over to my side.

"Oh, yeah, I'm fine. It's all good." I respond, she's got no motive or access so it can't be her.

"You really need a break, what're your grades again? A pluses?"

"In Science," I mumble.

"In all the Science related subjects and English. We all know how the teachers praise you."

"No, they don't."

"We should go shopping! You obviously need some new attire!"

"No-"

"Hey! You know what?"

"What is a word that is commonly used at the beginning of a question," I grumble.

"Oh, please. Spare me your scientific words." She does the finger quotations thing with an accent as she says scientific.

A giggle escapes my sour face before I snap it shut like a feeding grizzly bear waiting for a salmon. I want fish for lunch.

"There you are. You should stop being such a sour puss, your face will stick like that, you know."

I bear a grin that shows all my teeth at her like those weird toddlers.

"You don't want your face to stick like that either." She squishes my cheeks together, giving me fish lips, "You've got such a pretty face when you smile. Usually." Her finger tugs at the corner of my lips.

"Want to know where I got these scars?" I whisper to myself.

"Nope still ugly." Her warm fingers drop me and she walks away.

"Hey! At least I look ten times better than Lie-lith."

"Try a hundred times."

"Aww, that's sweet of you."

"You're supposed to tell me how pretty I am now."

"I'm sure Kai will tell you." I wave him over.

"Please, I'm saving myself for someone better than Kai."

"Ouch," I say as he walks up to us underneath the brown, yellow, and red leaf salad above our heads.

Maya

Something's off about Rikki. I don't need to be Sage to decipher that. All through science she was focused on Lilith and Kaden, who are apparently an item now.

"So, are you nervous for Thursday?" I ask her.

"No, why?" She mumbles as her blood-shot eyes quickly look away from the sickening couple.

"Did you forget?"

"No, I'm the ultimate genius I never forget anything I'm an elephant times ten," She rolls her eyes and sighs. "What's on Thursday?"

"The Science fair entries are due on Thursday."

"That's not a funny joke. Wait. That's not a joke, is it?" It takes her a second to process. Her fingers grab my shoulders at a startlingly strong grip and shake me. "I need to come to your house and we need to work on our progect."

"Take a deep breath and calm down, Rikki. And take it easy on the hair, not all of us cut it impulsively."

"Sorry but this is really important," she mutters and stuffs her hands in her greasy black hair.

"You want to go to New York, right?"

"Yes," she hums as she lies her head on the table. "I really want to go."

"I could tell. You can't pay for it by yourself, can you?"

Her eyes pop at my knowledge. "How did you know?" She hisses at me quietly.

"For starters, you're a scholarship student, I've seen in you in all the second-hand stores near the rented condos, and you rarely eat out. It's pretty obvious. Don't your parents ever send you cash or anything?"

"No," she groans and digs her head into her ancient laptop and lazily types the keyboard.

"So, that's what the job is for?"

"Job?" she stutters as she tilts her head and looks deep into my eyes. "What job?"

244

"Yeah, your barista gig." I roll my eyes at her. "You didn't forget, did you?"

Her eyes grow to the size of golf balls, her blurry brown eyes growing even more bloodshot.

"Did you?" It's my turn to grab her shoulders and shake her. "Did you?"

"Sort of? Mostly?"

I sigh, "I can lend you some money, I just got a really well-paying job."

"I don't need your money or your charity, Maya. I could just get a new job even if I did."

"You can't survive without money."

"Two words. Instant. Ramen."

I sigh at her. How does a person like this even exist?

Rikki

It took us five minutes to sprint from school to Maya's mansion, it's probably one of the biggest houses I've ever seen. She lives in a castle.

"C'mon, Rikki." She drags me by the arm and presses the keypad to the solid black gate surrounding Castle Lesage. The two halves slowly edge open violently. By the time it opens enough for us to squeeze through, she just stands there. I make a move to walk through the gate, but she holds me still.

"We're supposed to wait for the gate to entirely open," she states, completely monotone.

I groan and wait the extra ten minutes we could have used for our project. "Crap," I whisper.

"What?" She turns to me.

"I forgot the plants. I'll get them. You just wait here." I drop my bag by her feet and sprint down the empty sidewalk. It takes me a minute to reach it once I make to the top of a roof and run all the way to the school.

One of the school's back doors squeak open as I push through it and run to the STEM room. They all stare at the alien intruder known as me. Knowing Kaden, he's spread the word to them to hate me. Everyone glares at me as I strut over to my plants. At a closer glance, all they are is brown stems.

"No! Did you guys forget to water them?" I ask around, looking at each of them. They all bury their heads into their work, pretending like I'm not there and like they didn't just murder a pair of defenseless marigolds.

I pick them up, sigh, and leave. I slam the door behind me.

***

"Got them," I say, breathless.

"Good," she mutters as she pulls me through the open gate and then into the castle.

"And *who* are you?" A tanned, bald man with a stylish mustache sits up from a desk in the all marble interior. Everything is shiny and organized and perfect. I look around. Her parents are billionaires. Trillionaires. They own a mansion in Paris made of Marble with a secretary. And probably a butler.

"I'm a friend of Maya's," I offer as I moon at every lavish corner of the place. A cold black-steel railed marble-footed staircase sits in the middle of the house. I can't help but stare at it.

"Maya doesn't have any friends," he scoffs at Maya. Her face matches the color of her hair. "You're just some street rat looking for food, right?"

"Is that because I'm black?" I break the spell and snap out my phone, pressing record.

"What are you talking about I- "

"You called me a street rat. I have it on video. Give us free passage and I won't upload it. If you're lucky."

He drops into his seat and shuffles some papers into illegal disarray.

"Which way to your room?" I ask, looking around in ecstasy.

"This way." She pulls me up through the middle of the grand staircase.

If I thought the first floor was fancy, the second is (insert synonym for fancy here). It's practically a castle, where's the moat and drawbridge?

She drags me to the third white door on the right and throws it open carefully.

"In." She shoves me through and closes the door silently behind us. I land on her massive bed. It's at least half the size of my room and blanketed with everything I would ever need to survive minus food and water. I kick off my sneakers and roll around in its fluff.

"Wow," she pops.

"I want your house," I groan, muffled by blankets, stuffed animals, and pillows.

"Too bad you can't afford it." She picks up a purple and yellow tiger.

"Correction, I want your bed." I grab the tiger from her hands and hide it in the many layers of cushion. It's my hostage. "I am the holy burrito. I am all knowing." I roll on to her back and squish her.

She laughs and picks up the box of plants. Her frown worsens. "What happened to them?"

"STEM club killed them," I mumble.

"Ugh, that idiot. What a jerk. To think I used to have a crush on him. Hmm. How much progress have you made?"

"Well, I turned it from theoretical into the seeds you see before you." I produce the super seeds from my the file after much difficulty wrestling out of the layers of blankets and pillow things. "With the improvements I've made, they should grow within the span of a few hours."

Maya

"All we need to do now is to write it up," Rikki says and sits up. "That's my job, right?"

"You're the one with top marks in English so, yeah, I guess that's your job. Woah. *That's* your computer? It's a Mac!" she moons as I walk over to my desk.

"Yeah, so?"

"This would have made everything go so much quicker! Why didn't you tell me?" She jumps off the bed and lands beside me silently. *Silently*.

"I didn't think it was important, don't you have a computer?"

"One that's incompatible with nearly all the programs we needed to use for the fair!"

"Well, sorry."

"It's not your fault, you didn't know." She sighs at me.

"But I could've!" She can't act like I'm stupid just because of my hair color and social standing.

"I didn't think it was important." She takes a step back.

"You didn't think it was important to tell your partner about your crap computer that can't even help us with what computers are supposed to help us with?"

"It's all I can afford." She calms down taking a deep breath, but I'm not ready.

"And who's fault is that?"

She bites her lips together, grabs her bag, files, and plants. She slams the door as she leaves out my door.

"Don't let the door hit you on the way out!" I call back.

Rikki

Great going Rikki, you lost yet another friend. What's wrong with you? I hop down the stairs towards Mr. Moustache.

"What'd she do? Throw you out?" He says as he shuffles some papers. Why does he even need papers? He works at a door.

"I left," I tell him.

He chuckles, "Sure you did."

Today has been a massive test of patience. This week has. At the beginning, all my super friends left for some murder club. Then one of those same friends turned against me and started bullying me. My club killed my science project and now I'm down another friend. This's what I blame for what I do next.

My fist smashed against the white desk. If it was any thinner I would have broken it.

"I. Left," I hiss and turn to slam the doors shut behind me. I'm not waiting for that damn fence to open again. My muscles grip the brick surrounding the mansion and launch myself upwards to freedom. I hate this stupid life. Tonnerre's right, I haven't made any progress for my cure. I'll have to look through that book again.

Little drops of dark gray land on the sidewalk around me. It can't rain now. Even if I run I'm a good ten minutes away from the apartment. At least now the plants will get watered.

***

By the time I'm finally at the apartment, I'm soaked to the bone. Willow frets over me for as long as she can before I wave her off and go upstairs.

"You're going to get sick, Rikki!"

"I don't really care anymore!"

My door closes quietly. I sigh, no superheroing tonight. With the Warriors of the World still in Paris, it's a major target on my back. But this means I get to finish the science project. *Yay.*

Rain patters on my roof and around my window.

I drop my bag and change into some dry clothes. I've got a lot of research to type out. My computer flips open as a take out a bag of chips. I grab the files from my (thank god) water proof backpack and drop them on my desk.

I groan. I don't like writing.

It takes me two hours to type in the half of it before someone knocks at my window. The light blue curtains part to make room for Kai to open the window. He grunts as he steps through wearing a soaked white V neck, black backpack, and jeans. He's carrying a white plastic bag.

"What. Are. You. Doing," I hiss and try to shove him out.

"Hey, hey! Don't throw me out! I'll fall to my death!"

"What a shame that would be."

"I've got croissants if you let me in!"

"How dare you tempt me." I can smell them from here. They smell like heaven.

"And you can have them right after you say sorry."

"How did you even know I love those."

"I see you eating them every day at club and everywhere, really."

"Fine. Sorry for being mean." I reach for the bag but he lifts it way above my head. I extend my arms as far as possible while he laughs. I jump up and grab them from his hand. I open the bag and take out the white styro-foam box filled with deliciousness.

"Didn't you bring any plates? Or napkins?"

"Didn't think we'd need them."

"We? Don't tell me this is a date," I groan.

"No, even if you were wearing proper attire this still wouldn't be a date." He gestures to my old shirt splattered with 'San Francisco's Heroes' and faded fluffy pants.

"I'm going to get some plates." I open the door slightly and step through. The coast is clear, Willow isn't anywhere. The drawer opens quickly and not so quietly. I take out two silver forks and carry them upstairs.

Kai looks out the window.

"What's up?" I ask him and look out as well.

"Reine Blanche."

"Oh no. I'll just have to eat these croissants all by myself. What. A. Shame."

He doesn't laugh.

Kai

I use the teleportation device the WotW gave me to get to their floating base. It's crazy, I've never been in something so big! The blue lights shine over the clouds like spotlights! We're celebrities. Some of the big American newspapers have already published stories about the new recruits for the Warrior of the World! Their telepath has even fixed the language gap we have! I can't believe Corbelle would ever miss this but she's weird that way.

Thousands of doves fly below the glass window on the floor of the briefing room. Reine Blanche leaving her signature behind.

"Maverick, the girl I was telling you about is causing trouble again," I speak to the leader. The telepath stands beside her silently, wearing her usual green attire.

"Who, White Queen?"

"Yes," Tonnerre walks in slowly. I haven't seen much of him. He only really hung out with us when Corbelle was there. "she's causing havoc with birds. She's got something planned."

"Great, and I thought tonight would be quiet. Emerald Thought, please call our teammates to our aid," she says with a grin, gesturing to the woman at her side.

"Of course," she mutters softly.

"Oh, and we have a little initiation you and your friends still need to go through."

"Initiation? I thought we had already joined."

"We just need to know we can trust you." Several more costumed heroes walk in. I could name them all and their super powers. I've been obsessed with them since I was five.

"This is the new kid?" Arctic asks. She's got ice powers.

"One of them," Heat Wave mumbles. Fire's his game.

"How many are there?" Toucan asks. He's the one with plant powers.

"There's four, I think. Excluding Tonnerre, of course," Goliath, the size-changer says, ruffling Tonnerre's hair.

"There's three," Tonnerre responds, his voice full of hate.

"Oh, yeah your stupid little girlfriend didn't want to join." Goliath laughs at Tonnerre's scowl.

"She's not my girlfriend." Tonnerre punches him in the gut. Goliath falls to the floor in a heap and just lies there for a moment before growing to three times Tonnerre's size.

"You think you can beat me?" He yells in a low baritone that matches his height. His size has an effect on his voice. "Think again, idiot!" He lifts his giant fist over Tonnerre's head. His power slows him down too.

Tonnerre easily stops his fist and brings Goliath to the ground again.

"Stop!" Maverick screams. Everyone freezes. It's not her power but she's good at it. "We have a mission and if we act like this all the time, we're no better than that Corbelle bitch." Tonnerre flinches but doesn't say a word. She glares soundlessly at him.

Kaden and Sage walk in at the best time possible.

Andrew

"Wonderful," Maverick stares at them, snapping the scowl off her face. "The other recruits are here."

"Uh, hi," Sage mumbles, sensing the mood in the room.

"Hey, we just wanted to let you know about- "

"It's okay, Velocity already briefed us," she interrupts, "But we were hoping you'd join us tonight," she cooes falsely.

"Really?" Nuit asks.

"Of course," she responds. She's got to be talking about the 'initiation'. "We have to make sure you're made of the stuff we want for our team."

"Do you want us to use our powers?"

"No, we want you to take off your masks, tell us your names. We need to know we can trust you with our secrets."

"Sure." Velocity peels his mask off. "My name is Kai Senet Mace. Is that good enough?" The girl wearing blue looks at him in shock so does the other one. A few of the warriors look surprised but not as shocked as they are. I guessed they would do it, but I don't know about the girl.

"Kai!"

"Wait, if you're Kai, does that mean- ?"

Nuit sighs and pulls off his black motorcycle helmet. "Yes. My name is Kaden Searle Mace."

"What?" What's her name? Sage screeches.

"Why, do you know us?" One of them asks.

"Sage. It's now or never." Maverick glares.

"You're right, you're right." She waves away the smoke obscuring her face. "Maya Lesage. It's a stupid pun."

Nuit looks at her and she looks back as bug eyed as possible. Velocity looks at Maverick, ready for whatever she throws at him.

"Wonderful." She claps her hands. "Everyone made it! You're now official members of the Warriors of the World. I, Candace Gunter, welcome you with open arms." She grins her terrible grin. She's the worst person I know. And not because of her body count.

Rikki

I promised myself I wouldn't put on a costume of any kind but it's getting pretty weird out here. White Rabbits have been flooding the streets for hours. I threw bread crumbs at them earlier form the roof. That also attracted some of the hundreds of albino pigeons circling Paris. From my constant news reports, the Warriors haven't done anything despite them being in Paris. But neither has Reine Blanche. Why'd she even call herself 'Reine Blanche' if all she does is do magic tricks? Why didn't she choose to be 'The Magician' or 'Le Magicien'? She's like Tonnerre. 'Thunder' in French, but is he French? No. He's an American idiot, like the other Warriors of the World.

The rabbits are doing something new. They just stopped running (hopping?) through the streets. The wave of white just paused. What are they doing now? Climbing on top of each other? Are they creating a beak? A mouth? If Reine Blanche wanted to send a message, she shouldn't have chosen something like rabbits. I mean, who chooses rabbits for anything? It's just stupid.

A third layer of rabbits pile on as lopsided lips for the mouth-beak. This is too weird.

"So, you think you can hide heroes?" The mouth thing lets out a screechy, evil laugh. A screevil laugh. Why is it even in this neighborhood? My computer beeps an update. 'Giant Rabbit Mouth Seen All Over Paris!' Okay, that explains it. "You think you can stop what I have planned?"

I was never good at keeping promises.

***

I land on the one piece of sidewalk not taken over by furry white rodents filled with carrots and poop. The rabbits scurry away from my feet.

"Aw, c'mon guys. I gave you bread crumbs, I thought we were cool!" They don't respond they just scurry down the street. "West?" I tilt my head.

Okay, this is different.

I chase after them. Hopefully, they're leading me to her.

Three human bodies land in front of me. The asphalt cracks like glass under their feet. Looks like the Warriors of the World sent their flyers against me.

"Corb- "

"Corbelle, you are to stand down and surrender- " One in a red costume says in American English.

"Hey! I thought I was going to say that!" Tonnerre's not part of the group. Neither is that leader-lady, Maverick.

"Well, you should have been faster!"

"I'll show you fast!"

"Will you now?"

"Idiots, shut up! You let her get away!" I think that's what the last one said, while they were bickering, I climbed up onto a fire escape. They're probably the most helpful thing made of metal ever made.

The three Warriors lift into the air again leaving nothing but the wind and blurs. They're going to search for any black spots on the roofs of Paris. Otherwise known as me. Yay but not so yay.

Three dots linger in the sky as I slink down and edge against a building, following the rabbits. I swear if they lead me down a manhole, I'm going to punch every one of them. My name's Rikki, not Alice.

***

I didn't even know Paris had abandoned warehouses. But they apparently do because that's the only place villains do their villainy these days. Is it sad to say I miss mobsters?

The ancient, and I mean ancient (Probably as old as Tonnerre), wood crumbles beneath of me. My nails dig into the wood as I climb higher. I'm almost at the windows at the top of the building.

They're too dusty to see anything except for the sea of white rabbits piling in. I creak one open and step through. There's an entire loft I can stand on. It's like a barn. Except with more villainy than animals. Or more animals than villainy. Do evil rabbits count as villains or animals?

Either an earthquake or a sudden tremor knocks me onto my feet. I fall onto the wood.

"Aie." I need to add more padding to my butt.

Did it stop? I peer out the windows way above the giant barn doors. The Warriors of the World. The rabbits echo my mood. I'm pretty sure that ninety-five percent of them just bared their teeth at the doors. Do rabbits have a good sense of smell? Maybe that's why so many are left to make more little bunny rabbits.

The lead lady, the one with the accent and laser eyes, strides up to the doors, her club following her. They assemble a V in front of the giant wooden doors. I spot Nuit, Velocity, and Sage in the back. It's too late to hold my scowl back now.

Purple bursts through the doors and they step through in slow-motion.

"Reine Blanche, your tyranny over Paris is over, I- we- "

"Uh, Maverick? She's not here." Someone in red beside her pokes her shoulder.

"Tch." I sneer. Do all superheroes go into deep monologues after making some bizarre entrance? I stand up and lean against a heavy wooden pillar connecting the loft to the roof and the roof to the floor. If crap goes down, I'll have to break it down.

A blonde in the darkest blue costume stares up at me. He doesn't scowl. He just stands there like he's trying to speak to me with his eyes. *'Why?'* He asks.

I pull down my scarf and frown at him. I can tell it eats at him. He turns away to watch Maverick bicker with the super-murderers behind her. He's in the third row. Not her right or left-hand people but not in the back either.

A shrill laughter breaks through the shouts, bickers, and eye contact. She *is* here. A bunch of rabbits climb on each other to create a pedestal of rabbits. A flash of dark red flashes and suddenly, she's here.

"Really? You brought *them* here?" She grimaces, speaking in English and pointing at the Warriors. It's unclear who she's really talking to.

She looks into my eyes, straight at me, like she can see the real me. I shiver. I hate it.

"Oooh, and it looks like we've got a straggler." She smiles at me, flicking her wand. The wood beneath me breaks. I fall through and land on a cushion of rabbits.

I hate these things.

Andrew

Corbelle tries to stand up but rabbits grab her wrists. She throws them off and aims one at White Queen.

"I think we may have gotten off on the wrong foot. I'm White Queen, a pleasure to make your acquaintance." She smiles at Corbelle's scowl. "It's incredible to be in the presence of someone with such immense power, may I call you Chaos?"

"No," Corbelle replies, full of ice.

"Then whatever should I call you?" She bats her eyelashes beneath her white mask and skirt.

"Your end." Maverick hisses, trying to draw her attention over to us like we're the real threat. But deep down, we all know Corbelle is.

"Oh. The big bad Warriors of the World." She turns to us and raises her wand. God, I swear if she turns me into a cat again, she's not going to hear the end of it.

A rabbit hits White Queen on the cheek. Ash sprays the back of my head. Only a blackened hole remains from the doors behind us. Corbelle pats the rabbit in her hand and grins wildly at White Queen.

"Want another?" She grins wildly, "I'd make a rabbit joke no one would carrot all."

"So, not-so-Chaos maybe we got off on the right foot after all." She lifts her wand again.

"Maybe." Cor throws the rabbit at the wand, "Or maybunny not." A few people groan behind me. I'm pretty sure all of them are from France.

Maverick breaks formation and lunges for the wand amongst the rabbits. They clear a path before she lands. I don't watch her fall, all I hear is a thud before Corbelle tackles White Queen.

"Warriors! Grab that bunny!" Maverick screams, pointing at a rabbit with a stick in its mouth. "And grab Corbelle and White Queen!"

Everyone launches into action. Goliath grows to the size of the roof. He's not fat, he's more skinny and lanky than anything which makes him easy to knock-out. His red glove reaches for Corbelle who's managed to twist White Queen's arms behind her. He grabs her by the back of her costume and brings her to his face.

"Hey!" she shouts. "Put me down!"

"You're this 'celestial being'? You're tiny!" He pokes her in the stomach. She spits in his visor, brings her legs up, and kicks herself out of his grasp. She lands amongst the rabbits and glares at me.

"Tonnerre! What. Are. You. Doing." Maverick hisses, a piece of rabbit shit hanging from her chin.

I know it's too late to stop White Queen by the time she reached her wand. I watched her grab it from behind Maverick's pissed off head.

"Shit," I whisper.

"What. Is. It?" she seethes, her eyes flaring with rage.

I rocket through the roof, barely missing White Queen's red blast I can't say Maverick's as lucky.

Rikki

Their leader poofs into a snake. A green little garden snake, harmless among the harmless. Tonnerre hasn't done anything useful this entire time aside from open a stylish skylight through the roof. As for the rest of the Warriors of the World, they're scrambling. They don't even know their fearless leader's been reduced to a small heap of hisses and yet they're falling apart.

Reine Blanche got her wand back despite my attempts to stop her (I can still taste the rabbit hair). I've got no idea where she could be, her costume is completely white and so is the majority of the warehouse.

A giant red and black fist closes around my body in a single, quick motion. Crappity crap.

"So, you thought you could escape from me?" He lets out a low laugh. It shakes the building and the little rabbits just long enough for me to catch a glimpse of blonde.

"Let me go! There's an actual villain that should be stopped!" I whap him with my one arm that's free.

"You think you can just charm me with that little French accent, but I'm not Tonnerre," he chuckles. "They've got their mission, I've got mine."

He takes a step towards the wall. This must be how that girl felt in King Kong. He crashes through the wall like it's cardboard. Rabbits and superheroes alike spill out into the crisp fall afternoon.

He presses the side of his goggles, "Maverick, I've got her." He rumbles.

"Chaos!" A blonde shouts from the ground. "A gift from me to you!" She waves her wand around and fires it at me. I close my eyes and brace for the blast.

My wrist feels cold like someone just put it through ice water. My eyes flip open one after the other. I stare at it. A silver bracelet covers half of my arm, a little piece of topaz sits in the center of it. Okay, then.

It shakes my arm and moves to my hand. The silver lengthens into a giant épée with a topaz tipped handle. Okay, then.

I swing the épée at the giant red and black hand. It hits home and stabs him between one of his knuckles.

He screams in pain and drops me. The magic sword turns back into a bracelet as I plummet towards the ground. I land with a little less grace than I should have and roll onto my back.

"Pain..." I groan in my native language. A rabbit hops on my chest. "Well, aren't you hoppy?" I ask it, unsuccessfully trying to sit up.

The giant guy's back to a normal size and the rest of the Warriors are still fighting rabbits.

I stand up and survey for Reine Blanche but no luck. She's gone. But she gave me a silver bracelet which I've got no idea on how to pry off. Maybe I can sell it with my arm still attached.

My arms lock behind me in a moment. Whatever invisibility and I had with the Warriors is gone. I wildly try to step on the feet of my captor but every time I land, it's got no effect. All my thoughts feed my bracelet. I need the épée, not a bracelet but I haven't been feeling a lot of luck recently.

"We've got you now," he tells me.

"This is what you really are, isn't it? This's where you've felt the most at home?" I ask him.

"They've accepted me where *others* won't."

"I just don't accept that this is you, that this is who you want to be."

"It isn't. But he died when you did."

"Am I the only one who still believes in the Bejeweled Storm?" That's what he called our old team-up. Topaz and Tonnerre. He gave me top billing.

" ...You've got two seconds to teleport." He whispers.

"Wait!" I whisper-shout. but it's too late. He pretends that I over power him and he falls backward.

"Quickly! She's getting away!" he yells at the other Warriors.

"Uh-" Rich green surrounds my every move. There's nothing I can do about it. It tightens around my waist and arms like a snake.

"I've got her," a woman wearing all white and green remarks.

I struggle, trying to kick my way out, trying to squirm my way out, trying anything to get my way out, but the chains won't budge.

"It's useless to even try," she doesn't even have any emotion in her voice. I use her droning dialogue to check out the Warriors. There's the growing guy who grabbed me, the green lady (I'm calling her the Vermillion Vixen), a bunch of randomly dressed people, Nuit/Kaden, Velocity/Kai, Sage, and Tonnerre. I especially eye the last four. Nuit's unreadable for obvious reasons, Kai just stares back, Sage doesn't even look at me, she looks to the cement. Tonnerre isn't even there. I watch his eyes, he's somewhere else. I swing my arms but it doesn't do a thing. It's useless, they're taking me.

"Let's see who this little girl really is." The Maverick lady says freshly turned back into a human. Her voice is filled with disgusting anticipation. She's preying off my fear, off my discomfort. Her finger taps my face and the other sits me down on the flat concrete. "It's a shame we couldn't recruit you for the team. We're just going to have to use our other measures." Her fingers walk up to my mask.

"I'm going to warn you once," I mumble.

"Oh?"

"Let me go and I won't explode your little club. Don't believe me? Reine Blanche was impressed by my power. You called me a celestial being. Do you want to make me angry?"

Maverick grunts and whispers to her left-hand person.

"No," she responds after a short eternity. "But we're not done." She snaps her fingers. "I haven't seen your powers once today, how can I be sure you still have them?" She grins.

"How can you be sure I *don't*?" I say, matching her twisted grin. The Vermillion Vixen tightens the green chains on my arms. They feel like they're about to pop off.

"I'm not. But I'm sure you'd prioritize Paris's lives before your own."

"What?"

"You have a choice, you can come with us, no fighting, no resistance, and our hovercraft won't blow your city to little bits." Her bottom teeth crook on each other as she smiles.

"What?" Sage screeches, stepping up towards Maverick.

"Ms. Lesage, is there a problem?" Her words chill down my spine.

"Maya? I thought you of all people would be a super*hero*."

She squints at me for a moment like she's remembering something then shock washes over her face. She knows it's me.

I purse my lips and shake my head slowly at her. But she nods barely in response.

"So," Maverick snaps, "what's your choice? Kill millions, or sacrifice yourself?"

I stand up slowly in response.

"Excellent," She coos, pushing me towards a red spaceship.

"You've got a piece of rabbit crap in between your teeth," I respond, taking another step forwards.

Maverick doesn't say a word, she just falls behind us. Tonnerre takes up leading me to the ship while she digs at her teeth.

266

Maya

Rikki Dubois is Corbelle. I should have seen it sooner, they're practically identical in looks. They're both small, dark skinned, and have a slight gap between their two front teeth.

Corbelle, or Rikki, sits in the back of the ship, right beside the giant door we use to exit for battle. Maverick deemed the rest of the ship too confidential for Rikki's eyes. I'm the only one who knows that Corbelle is Rikki and vice versa. I plan on keeping it that way. It's unbelievable though. Someone as insane as Corbelle fits inside a plain girl like Rikki.

"So," she starts. Her arms are tied with green magic and tied to the solid metal wall. She can't get out. She can't find a way to knock me out. She sighs. "How much do you know?"

"Your name."

"Is that it?"

"Everything you've told me. In both of your... *yous*. That's another thing you're going to have to explain to me, who *are* you?" I ask. They may look alike. But they're not the same.

"It's simple, I'm who you know." She tries to shrug but it ends up looking like more of a head bop.

"Yes, but who? There are two different people I know. One's hard working, sarcastic, and adorable. The other's, well, she's insane."

"They're both me. Who are you? Maya Lesage or Sage?"

"I'm Maya."

"Then what's with the costume, Maya? Is this a new fad or something? Did I not get the memo, *again*?" She smiles like an idiot, the gap in her teeth as showy as ever. I know she wants me to smile with her but I just can't. I frown at her instead. "This doesn't look good on you Maya. When you're in this team, you're a murderer. It's what they do with all the bad guys they meet. What do you think they're going to do to me? They're going to try to find where my power comes from. They're going to take me apart piece by piece if they have to. They'll dissect me like a frog. It's what they do. Where do you think that monster is?"

"Please, you're just dramatizing things. Tonnerre said you would, it's your thing."

"Of course that's what he said." She mumbles. She jiggles her arms and sits on her wrists and her green chains.

"What's up with you two?"

"Why don't you ask him?" She sneers. Her arms move again like she's stretching them, she brings the just behind her knees so she's leaning into them.

"You're just like him, you know that, right?"

She grunts as I look away from her. I can't stand her. Her face, her attitude, her goddamn teeth. She's terrible. Does she even count as a human being?

"Hey, Maya."

"What?" I snap.

"Sorry."

"For what?" I turn around to meet a kick in the face. Warm thick blood rushes down my mouth. Her green chains tie around my throat and pull me up to stand.

Rikki

Desperate times call for desperate measures. Desperate times also are known as being locked in a murder gang's broom closet with another murderer. I call desperate measures choking that same murderer and dragging her around the ship until they let me out. Would I prefer this situation? Maybe. Why am I stuck in this situation? Because I couldn't pick a side. And then I did and it's totally the right side. I'm the good guy despite what they'll tell you.

"Sorry about this but I need to get out. Claustrophobia and all that." I try drag her down a hallway but she's taller than me so she's been bending down under the chain. "Now, which way?"

She grunts and points straight down the hallway to a large glowing light and chatter. "If this isn't a coffee shop, I'm punching you in the gut," I tell her in French, dragging her onwards to a hopeful coffee shop.

The quick chatter clears to either whispers or silence. "She should be here." Maverick whispers as I walk into the not-a-coffee-shop-at-all.

"This isn't a coffee shop, it's not even a Starbucks!" I exclaim.

Anyone on the Warriors of the World with any power aims their guns, hands, eyes, or whatever it is they use to kill, at me.

"Maverick!" One of the flying girls exclaims. "She's got a hostage, one of our own!" Maya seems to relax knowing they won't shoot one of their own.

"Sage, don't worry, we won't shoot you in the head," Maverick says, charging up her purple eyes.

"W-what?" she cries, standing up, and knocking the chain off her neck.

"Okay, screw this," I say in French as I roll to the other space of the red metallic wall, where they can't reach me.

I grab the closest person with a gun and pull them to the ground, stealing their firearm.

"Thanks." I pull the top part closer to me to load it. It glows a bright orange out of its black shape. It's like one of those guns from laser tag.

"-uh, Maverick? What do we do? She's got a gun."

"Shoot and ask questions later." She fires her purple at my feet.

I leap and drop the gun. My legs flip over me and I land further away from them.

"Nuit." She mumbles through a thick fog seeping from the room. I run farther away. Lasers light up the walls beside me. I run faster.

"Ooh, this looks important." I skid to a stop and run into the only room not in a fog. It looks like the engine room.

Kaden

Maya grabbed Corbelle's gun and sprinted down the hallway before any of us. It's personal for her. I guess it would be for me too if she was just choking me too. No one thought Corbelle would be smart enough to find our engine room and hold it hostage though.

"Stand down or I crash this ship," she says as we walk in the door not even glancing in our general area. She points over to the churning, glowing, spheres from the control panel. Maya lies on the floor beside her, not moving aside from her slow breaths.

"You wouldn't," Maverick sneers at her, not even noticing what she just did to Maya.

"Why not?" Corbelle smiles evilly and taps the gun's handle.

"Fire!" Emerald Thought screams at us. Everyone, whatever firepower they have, fires in Corbelle's direction. None of us even aim. That's why a stray laser hit the engine and broke it. The whole ship seemed to lurch in a single motion of sickness.

"No! You idiots!" Maverick screeches at us. "You see what you've done? We're all going to die!" She shakes Emerald Thought like it's her fault.

"Where's the control room?" Corbelle asks, she looks shaken but she's not in full panic mode yet.

"I can show you," Kai responds.

"Good," She responds, following him out, "Kaden, you come too."

What? How does she even know my name? Did Kai tell her? How could he?

"Kaden!" Kai yells from the hallway, waiting for me amongst the team's wails and cries.

I chase after them to the control room.

Corbelle's already pulled apart some of the panels checking for wires. "Found it!" she yells at Kai.

"Good." He digs around in the opposite corner of the cramped office with the solitary steering wheel and chair. "I've almost got mine."

"Need a hand?"

"No, I've got it." We're free to use French since the translator is on the other side of the ship.

"Okay, I'm starting to cut mine, though."

"Got it."

"Kaden, can you check where we are?"

"How do you even know my name?"

"There are more important matters to focus on, Kaden," my brother insists.

"Fine," I grumble as I step over my brother's legs to the board with the fancy GPS. "We're still right over Paris."

"Crap."

"Why?" I ask her.

"We're going to crash into Paris." She responds, "I cut mine, you did yours?"

"What are you guys even doing?" I ask them.

"We're trying to connect the power from the lights to the engine," Corbelle mutters.

"Maybe we can restart it since the engine controls the steering and our moving capability but not the lights."

"You guys have the stupidest system. I mean, really? You need a whole new generator for your lights? That's pretty stupid."

"Says the girl who made us do this in the first place."

"I'm sorry, I just don't like being held in a broom closet with my hands tied with magic chains."

"I thought you'd appreciate our plight for assistance."

"I didn't think you'd go as far as kidnapping people for your club."

"It's not a club," I mumble.

"Whatever," she responds. "But why keep the generators in two different rooms?"

"I didn't design the ship. But I don't see why we can't just use your powers," I tell her, kicking her legs.

"Remember how I told you about that occult prophecy about me?"

"Yeah."

"Well, I found a loophole. If I don't use my powers at all even after I turn seventeen, I may not be recognised as the 'great destroyer' and someone else will get my role."

"And that's why? But how can you be sure that that will work?" Kai asks.

"I'm not."

Silence seeps into the room like my fog. It takes over.

They each stand up and connect their wires. A flash of light travels to either end of the wires.

"Ow!"

"Damn!"

They react to the shock by holding their fingers and staring at each other for that 'okay' as the lights flicker out.

"Did it work?" I groan.

"Check the GPS, idiot," my brother responds.

I roll my eyes and glance at the monitor. "We're not losing any more altitude, we're hovering."

"Aw, yes!" Corbelle shoots her hand up for a high-five. "No? Okay, fine." She drops her hand.

"You've got ten seconds to get off our ship or we'll be persecuting you with any means necessary," I tell her. Kai stands beside me. Something we agree on.

"Fine." She throws her hands in the air and walks out. "But where's an exit I can jump from?"

Andrew

I didn't expect to see her so soon tonight. I didn't really expect to see Corbelle at all. I usually only see her once a night if I'm lucky.

I fly down to meet her at the top of the rusted Eiffel Tower.

"What's up?"

"What's up?" She looks at me angrily. "How can you be this casual? You tried to kill me today. Don't act as though I didn't see you hidden in your little club, aiming a weapon at me."

I land on the same slab of metal as her. "I had to do what I had to do, Corbelle, you of all people should understand that."

"And why is that?"

"Well, uh-" The last time I brought up her past, she slapped me.

She looks so angry at me like she could tear my head clean off. "Ugh. This doesn't suit me." She wipes away all her anger and replaces it with the emotion I know best. Disappointment.

She takes a deep breath and continues, "I'm done, okay?" She doesn't even look at me. "I thought that I could manage this. I thought I could stop you from becoming this, but I didn't think *this* would happen."

"This?"

"Everything. The killing, the Warriors, everything." She gestures all around us in a single, sad motion. "But if you want to kill people, become the very thing we try to stop. I'm done stopping you. I am finished."

"What do you mean?"

"I just need a little break, a hiatus like you say." It takes me a second to figure out what she said beneath her thick accent. "I might even quit."

"Your school? Are you going to be Corbelle full time?"

"No, are you not listening? I am not Corbelle, my name is- my name doesn't matter. What I need you to know is, that you need to leave. Murderers aren't welcome in Paris."

"But who's going to protect Paris after you've gone on... hiatus?"

"Paris won't need protection once all you crazy people leave. So, go. Tell your club." She turns away and takes a step towards the edge.

"Corbelle, wait."

"No." She jumps off and disappears into the black of the city.

"Dammit." I trail off.

Rikki

Okay, first day without wearing my costume. It feels kind of good. You'd think that I'd miss it but I don't. I don't have any new bruises or cuts for once.

I stride in through the doors with soaring confidence but every glare I get makes me shrink a bit. Maya grabs me by the shoulder, digging her nails into my skin.

"Hey!" I yell at her. She drags me away from my classroom and into a washroom. She checks underneath the stalls before releasing her grip.

"Show me." She hisses.

"What? No! Someone could walk in and- " She walks over to the tall door and jams her foot in front of it.

"There. Now, show me."

I sigh and dig the eye lenses out of my eyes. They pop out quickly. My bright yellow eyes, the only part of my power I can really control, blink back at me from the mirror. "There. Happy?"

She walks away from the door and grabs my chin. "They really are yellow."

"Well, yeah."

"How long?"

"Since I was born. I think."

"So, all that about your mom- "

"*That's* true. My earliest memory is of scaling a building or something."

"You were really raised by a thief?"

"Yeah. Born and raised."

"And you've always had that power?"

"Since I was born," I repeat with a sigh.

"How? I mean, you've tricked so many people for so long, am I the first?"

"To find out? Yeah. Probably."

"Wow. That's just- wow."

"Did you already tell your club? Should I move to Antarctica? Or will that not be far enough?"

"What? No! Of course not! Rikki, this is a big deal. You're a big deal! Chaos? That's huge!"

"I never told you about the Chaos part- "

"Tonnerre told everyone."

"Of course he did."

"Oh yeah, speaking of the warriors of the world... we're leaving tomorrow."

"Really?"

"Yeah, Kai, Kaden- " Her eyes explode, "I mean Velocity and Nuit, uh- "

"I already know. You're the only one who surprised me. Yeah." I breathe. "This has been a lot to process. For both of us, I guess."

"Well, at least you're going to win the science fair."

"Uh, no I'm not."

"Are you kidding? Growth acceleration! You could solve world hunger!"

"Lilith," I hiss.

"So? She won't buy second place. Just think about it." She grabs my shoulder and wipes reality away with her arm. "New York for two weeks!"

"We don't even know the results yet," I trail off.

"Hey, what happened to your face?" She grabs it and squishes my face by the cheeks. "You're not even wearing makeup! Could you at least try a little harder to look good? I know this is your secret identity but still. Do you even put any effort in your outfits?"

"Not really. Isn't enough that I'm wearing clothes?"

She digs her hand into her purse and brushes something all over my cheeks. "Hold still."

"What are you doing? Stop!" I pull away.

"Come on, Rikki. Did you even try to hide that cut?"

"What are you talking about? I don't have a-" I wince as she presses on it. "Fine, so maybe some glass cut my cheek, so what?"

"Ugh." She wipes some more stuff on my cheek. "There. No one will be able to tell the difference." She finishes by adding some black stuff to my eyes and lips. I finish by wiping it off once she leaves. I pop my contacts back in and walk out of the bathroom.

Maya

"First place goes to Lilith!" Ms. Boulay yells echoing the everyone's joy. This is the first time she's ever actually made anyone in the class happy aside from Rikki. "No surprise there." She mumbles quietly, hoping no one would hear. "And second place goes to Rikki and her growth acceleration formula!" Her smile is probably the one part of her that isn't completely repulsive.

Rikki's non-Corbelle smile is something out of a fairy tale. It's wide toothed genuine, not smug and hidden. She laughs and walks up to the teacher. She shakes her hand and Ms. Boulay whispers something in Rikki's ear before handing her a white envelope.

She walks back with a stride and slaps my outstretched hand and sits back down, a massive smile splayed across her stupid face.

"Congratulations to you both." The teacher says genuinely. "Now let's turn to our actual curriculum, please. Achelium. Does anyone here know that word?"

Rikki's smile disappears and dips into a frown.

"Anyone?" She looks around the room for any faces or open hands, "No one? At all?"

Rikki sighs.

"Fine. Achelium is a volatile substance that is often researched. I'm sure you've all heard of San Francisco?" The whole class nods but Rikki looks away.

"Those superheroes, right?" Christen asks. "Citrine and Tonnerre?"

"*Topaz* and Tonnerre," I correct him, still staring at Rikki.

"Tch. Whatever." He rolls his eyes.

"No, actually I meant the villains they faced. Does anyone recall them?" Ms. Boulay looks around the room again but no one raises their hands. She sighs and continues. "To gain their powers, some of them used Achelium. But now, many of them are suffering from disabilities because of the drug."

"What does this have to do with our curriculum?" Rikki raises her hand finally.

"Well, I may have been stretching the truth a little bit on saying this was part of the curriculum. Since we finished the science fair so quickly, we have a few extra weeks to work on an extra project."

"Can't we just play some games or stuff instead?" Zoé chimes.

"No. We're going to discuss the drawbacks of using drugs like Achelium."

Willow

"She quit." My brother hangs his head.

"What? And you let her? But what about the plan?" I yell at him.

"I don't know!"

"Can't you keep her here?"

"What? No!" He looks at me like I'm the weird one. "I don't even know her name or anything!"

I groan and slap my head softly. "Are you with us or *her*?"

"You," he mumbles.

"Good." Vaccine says as she steps out of the shadows. "Very good."

Kai

She walks in hesitantly, watching if we're mad at her or not.

"Uh, guys?" Kaden turned the lights off. All for the dramatics. I lean deeper onto my dark bench by the window. "Hello?" She snaps the lights on and looks right at me and smiles. "Okay, I know you guys hate me and everything, but guess what! I won the science fair!"

"Shut up," Kaden hisses from behind her.

"What?" She sighs. "What is it *this* time?" I can barely control my snicker and then he glares at me. My laughs echo across the room.

"Kai," he tells me to shut up, his voice full of warning and ice. I snap my mouth shut and grin with Rikki. "Corbeau." He starts scanning her expression.

"Wait- I can explain." Her grin turns to fear.

"No, we don't want to hear it."

"I want to," I seethe, taking a step towards her. My steps shake the benches and beakers on them.

"Guys, I-"

"What did you tell her?" We both hiss.

"What?" She raises her eyebrow and laughs. "You think-" She looks at us and laughs some more like we're the biggest joke of the year.

"So? Did you?"

"No! Of course not, your secret's safe with me." She zips her mouth.

"Then how does she know?" I take a step closer.

"I don't know." She shrugs and walks out, but stops. "But that reminds me! I'm missing part of my growth formula. An early version. Have you seen it?"

Rikki

Their faces don't change. I click my tongue and slowly outline everything. "Have you been having a salt craving recently?" I point to the sea salt chips in Kai's hand.

"Yeah, so what?"

"How long? For a few months?"

"What's your point?"

"You stole it. Didn't you?" I tilt my head at them and frown. "My formula."

"No!" Kaden exclaims, grabbing the bag out of Kai's hand and crushing it.

"Yep. That was us." Kai says, taking it back.

"That's the 'secret process' you guys used, isn't it?" Kai nods and slowly east some more of his chips. "So, you used the growth formula to-?" I trail off.

"We were aware of the side-effects of the drug, so we pretty much made the better parts bigger."

"You altered my formula?" I yell at them. "You can't just do that!"

"Only a little bit. It's so we could use it at a microscopic level."

"What?"

"Okay, so we changed it a *lot*."

"And you went into my room and stole it?"

"Kaden did." He points to his twin.

"Before you had the superpowers, you broke into my room? In the middle of the night? Why would you ever do that? How did I not hear you?"

"You know what's really strange about that though?" Kaden looks at me like he's a tortured soul.

"That you broke into a teenager's room in the middle of the night?"

"You weren't there."

"So?"

Kaden looks to Kai. "Why wouldn't you be there? In your room?"

"Yeah, that's a little strange, Rikki." Kai nods.

"I was having some trouble sleeping so I went out for some fresh air, what's wrong with that?" They look me over for any hint of lies but shrug. I'm too good a liar. "Where did you even get the stuff?" I sigh.

"The darknet."

"Do you even know how dangerous that is?"

"It worked, didn't it?"

"And yet you decided to join the Warriors of the World." Oops. Probably shouldn't have said that.

"How'd you hear about that?"

"It's all over their site, 'Parisian heroes'."

"No, it isn't." He grabs his phone and shoves the non-existent site in my face.

"Maya told me," I blurt out.

***

This week really flew by. Kaden, Lilith, and their cronies are still after me but they're not that hard to avoid if you know how to scale walls. But I honestly gave up caring because of New York, duh. I am so excited. I've never even teleported to New York and even if I did, it wouldn't really count.

Of course, the universe hates it when I get too happy so picture day didn't go as well as I wanted it to. For starters, Willow forced me to wear makeup and do my hair. Before school, I washed it all out in one of the washroom's sinks but Maya just had to walk in right then to force new makeup and hairspray on me. Then the special black dress things we had to wear were too big for me so it dragged behind me and Lilith used it as an excuse to trip me (like she needed one). Then Kaden did the exact same thing about fifteen minutes later (like he needed an excuse to). I'm still pissed at him and his brother for looking at something on the darknet and responding like, 'Hey, it's a mysterious and untested chemical. Let's jam it in our bodies for superpowers.' *Idiots.* Everyone I know is an idiot. But the real kicker about last week was that I know some of the people going to the science internship in New York. Which isn't a good thing if you were wondering.

"You're coming to my house after school." Maya sits beside me on the bench. The clouds parted so the park outside our school seemed like a good place to eat lunch alone. My flimsy sweater barely protects me from the cold winds though.

"And why is that?" I take a bite of my chocolate croissant covered with almonds. Just the way I like it.

"I need to look through what you've packed. You've never packed before, have you?"

"I'm fine. I don't need a mom." I tear off another piece, spraying a piece of almond on Maya's white blouse and black scarf.

"Did you pack a dress or something?"

"I don't need a dress."

"Isn't there like a presentation dinner thing at the end of it?"

"Well, yeah, but I'm not wearing a dress."

"Speaking of dresses, there's a masquerade in a few weeks for the heroes of Paris."

"I know." I bite a little more chocolate off.

"Then you're going?"

"No. The last thing I need right now is more publicity. Your club's after me and if they know about it, so do certain governments just itching to get their hands on a source of unlimited power."

"You could at least go for one dance."

I shove the last bit of croissant in my mouth and stand up.

"I've got coffee if you stay." She pats the steaming portable cup that came out of nowhere.

I grunt and sit my butt down. I reach for the coffee and take a long sip. It's bitter and tasteless. Just the way I like it.

"There's no way I'm dancing." I look at the little kids weaving their way around the barren trees. It's practically winter already. I'm getting closer to my birthday. I stare at my hand. I don't feel the power as much as I used to but it's there. Like a ghost. My eyes still glare yellow in the mirror so that might not change.

"Is it because you don't know how? Because I could teach you."

286

"I'm not dancing." I hiss, taking more sips of my hot, delicious coffee.

"Fine. But you're wearing a dress to that dinner." Maya adjusts her legs and crosses them. She looks so grown up in her leggings and matching outfit while I've got the looks of a fourteen-year-old.

"I don't want to," I groan, finishing it with a sharp aftertaste of coffee.

"I'll take that as a 'Yes, mother, I'll wear whatever dress you give me since you'll pay for a year's worth of my coffee.'"

"You're evil!" I hiss as I take a slurp. She gets up and walks away. "And you called yourself 'mother'!" I shout at her.

***

The ring echoes down the walls of her mansion.

"Hurry up, I'm cold," I whisper to no one, failing to fold my arms together. The black door opens after a second too long.

"Rikki, what are you doing? Get in here!" Maya stands in front of me wearing a pink party dress covered with ruffles. She drags me in and rips my heavy duty coat off.

"I am *not* wearing one of those." I point at her and spin to maintain balance.

"For someone who climbs buildings, you don't have much grace." She pokes my shoulder and looks me over.

"Oh well, I'll have to work with it."

"Really?"

"Come on." She grips the sleeve of my sweater and proceeds to drag me up the grand staircase. We stay as far away from the man at the desk and the desk as possible.

"I just need something ordinary, Maya. Nothing fancy."

"But that takes out all the fun. I bet you'd even wear a suit if you could."

"Actually." I stroke my chin.

"No. Dress."

My feet grip the flat floor and I stand up. I hate being this short. She swings her white door open and pushes me through. It slams shut like a gate. Her room is even bigger than I remember like it grows when no one's looking.

She dives into one of two doors in her room and disappears.

"Maya?"

"What?" She pops out holding a matching pink dress.

"*Hell* no."

"Fine." She hangs her head hops back into her massive closet. It's twice the size of my room. My butt drops into her deep bed. I surround my cold body for a second of pure joy and warmth then Maya walks out holding another dress. "Here, this one's a few sizes too small for me so it must fit you." She throws a miniature bathing suit at me.

"It's a bikini."

"It's the newest style, I've got one too. I just accidentally ordered the wrong size."

"*Accidentally.*" I throw the swimsuit back at her.

She trudges back into the closet and reappears with two new dresses. "These seem more your style, goth girl."

"Hey, I'm not goth! I just like darker colours."

I grab the longer one out of her hand and pull it on. I fiddle with my hair and look in the mirror.

"Not bad." I spin around with lots of grace.

"Ugh, no. Take it off."

"What? Why?" I flip the long sleeves and low cut neck, the long bottom falls below my knees.

"You look like a vampire."

"But I like it."

"No. Try on the other one." She shoves a smaller black cloth at my chest.

"Fine." I huff as I manage to drag it on. "How's it look?" I ask her.

Maya

"It's not terrible but it's a little long." The black dress doesn't outline her flatness as much as the other one did but it doesn't really show off her curves as well as it did. It's tighter at the chest and from there it cascades down to just above her knees.

"Long? It's tiny! And it's strapless!" She slips out of it and dumps it on the floor.

"I'm going to make it a little shorter, okay?" I pick it up and bring it my sanctuary.

"How many dresses do you even have in that closet?"

"I don't know." I walk up to my sewing machine and click in some black thread. I pat the dress down flat as I cut off the hem. The machine flicks on and chews the new hem closed. "Finished!"

"Wonderful." She mumbles from the light doorway.

"Try it on."

She mumbles something about jerks and tugs it over herself.

"It's perfect," I moon. "You can have it, it's too small for me anyway."

"Wow. Thank you *so* much." She takes it off and drops it with her ugly scarf.

"Okay, come on, you're not wearing *that*, are you?" I point at her crappily knitted what-used-to-be-white sweater and leggings.

"Why not?"

"Did Willow help you pack?"

"Uh, no but I left my suitcase at home alone with her which in hindsight, was probably a crappy idea." She sighs and drops on my bed.

"No, it was an excellent idea. Okay, time to go." I fluff my designer dress and grab her by the arm.

"Where are we going?"

"Outside."

"I don't want to go outside." She groans as I pull her down the stairs towards the back exit. "It's cold and- " I pull the door open begrudgingly and shove her out first. "-your neighbors are playing terrible music." She opens her eyes and looks at me then looks back out at the 'Farewell, Rikki!' banner then back at me.

Rikki

This is not an ideal situation. I'm at a party. Everyone in grade twelve is comfortably fitted in between Maya's spacious ivory fence and bushes. Heaters dot the yard (It's more like a meadow) like old-fashioned lampposts. Tables of food cover one side while a few piñatas hang from trees.

"*Maya,*" I want to say. Or punch. I want to punch her. But there are too many people here and I'm not sure whether she'll attack me back.

"Go on Rikki, go make some friends, finally." She shoves me off the patio into a group of prettier girls.

"Uh, hi."

"What are *you* doing here?" A blonde one spits at me, her red lipstick frowning. Should I know her?

"Oh, you know, it's just *my* party." I roll my eyes and pull out of their little circle.

Someone shoves my shoulder and disappears before I catch them.

I don't even know any of these people. What was Maya thinking? My stomach strides up to the dessert table. A few guys laugh as they pour themselves drinks. They all wear blue bomber jackets with our schools' logo on the back and front. One knocks into me, splashing something on my old sweater.

"Hey! Watch it!"

"Oh." He hiccups, I can smell the beer on his breath and my sweater. "I'm sorry."

So, there's alcohol at this party. That's how Maya must have gotten all these people to come. I hate parties.

I grab a plate full of cake and walk over to a secluded spot underneath another barren tree. I shove as much as I can in my mouth before Kai spots me and walks over with a red cup.

"You too?" I point to it with my plastic fork.

"Rikki, relax, it's just a little beer."

"That kind of stuff kills your brain cells, maybe it's why you've been using the darknet so much."

"Come on Rikki, be cool. It calms me down, it'll help you too." He pushes the plastic cup in my face.

"No." I throw his hand away and glare at him.

"You're so- "

"I know." I sigh, grab his cup and take the smallest sip. "Aw, that's terrible! Gross!" It's like if water could go bad.

"Yeah, you're not the kind of person who's really into all this 'party' stuff, are you?"

"I like books, not boys."

"I'm sure you do."

"Can I be honest with you?"

"Sure." He takes a sip of his putrid liquid.

"I hate this!" I look all around and throw my arms up. "I don't know anyone. Practically everyone hates me. What am I doing *here*? I could be doing anything else! I could be saving the world!"

"Calm down, Rikki, it's okay. Everyone has these moments. How do you think I feel when I'm around all those heroes? I'm not one of them. I'm a kid with a suit and science. What can I do?"

"Anything! You could stop them from killing, you could help people, you could do literally anything!"

"Then why don't you?" He takes another sip out of his red cup.

"...You're not really helping."

"Rikki, Rikki, Rikki." He sighs and grabs his temple. "You are incredibly stubborn and an idiot. It's amazing you and Kaden didn't get together."

"It's not like it's my fault."

He looks at me.

"Okay, it is but he's such a jerk about everything. I'm actually kind of glad we didn't get together. No offense."

"None was taken. I'm his brother, not him."

"Hello?" Maya's voice takes over the DJ's music. "Hi, I'd like to announce something, please." If there was a sound of drunkenness, this is what it would sound like.

Kai

"Is she-?" I look over to Rikki but she's gone. "Dammit."

She's already made her way to the table Maya's standing on. "Maya, you need to get down right now." She grabs Maya's arm and tugs it.

"But Rikki, look, the party's just starting!" She spins around and nearly conks Rikki on the head with the microphone.

"Yeah, Bitchy Dubois, let her do whatever she wants! You can't control her life!" Lilith shouts.

"Who even wanted you here, beetle?" Kaden shouts.

She looks around at the oncoming crowd and sighs. "Fine. You idiots don't want me here so I'll just go. No need for any more drama," she grumbles and pushes through.

"Young lady!" a shrill voice cuts through the crowd. "What are you doing?" it screams. The crowd parts for a young woman and older guy to come through to Maya's table.

"Hi, mom and dad!" Maya giggles.

"Maya!" The woman gasps.

"Get down here now!" The man yells at her, pointing to the ground. He's wearing a dark blue suit that matches his wife's dress. His salt and pepper hair is getting greyer every second.

"You know what your guys' problem is?" Maya hiccups. "You've all got sticks up your- up your- wait, what was I talking about?"

"Something about sticks!" Someone shouts from the outside of the mob.

"That's right!" Her words slur as she points to the guy. "You've all got sticks up your asses! Not letting anyone have any fun, it's sick!"

"Maya, please!" Her mom starts to cry. She's got to be an actress or something.

"This is my party! You don't even care where I am or what I do half the time! Just go inside, it's not like you really care!"

"Maya. Come inside *now*." Her dad grabs her arm and pulls it violently.

"No!" she screams and throws her beer cup at him. It splashes all over his suit and the crowd goes silent. You can almost see the smoke flaring out of his ears.

"That's it! Young lady, you have embarrassed me and your mother for the last time!" He wipes the alcohol off his face with a handkerchief and drags her off the table.

"Let go!" she screams and shouts at him, wildly throwing herself around like a child.

"Hey! Stop!" Rikki slides in front of them. "This is my fault, I made her throw the party, it's not Maya's fault!" The man simply grabs Rikki's head and pushes to the side as he walks past her.

Part of the mansion, a corner of the top left piece of it, topples over three people.

"My house!" The man screams.

"Alright! This is a stick-up! Every one of yous gots cash an' I know it!" A guy with a ski mask hovers over the pile of debris.

Rikki

I look behind me at Maya's dad then at the thief if you could even call him that. He's clearly incompetent. I mean, what kind of burglar yells 'I'm robbing you!' It's just unprofessional.

I can barely stifle the power before Kai creates a whirlwind around the robber. "Everyone get down!" he yells. Everyone without powers immediately ducks or sprints underneath a table.

"What are you doing?" Kaden grabs me and pulls my legs out from under me.

"Aie." I still need to add more padding to my butt.

"Stay down." He points at me and charges at the villain.

I spring up on my wrists and run at the dude.

"Rikki!" Kaden shouts at me and startles Kai who stops running in an instant.

"Whas' that?" The guy in the air rips off his ski-mask and grins at me. His oily brown dreadlocks fly in every direction. They match his stupid and sweaty white skin.

"I will kick you in the face!" I yell back. My feet grab a running start before vaulting off Kaden's shoulder with my hands. I soar through the air towards the guy and get ready to karate kick him in the mouth knocking some more of his rotten teeth out of his stupid cracked lips.

Wind flies through my hair. "What are you doing?" Kai hisses as he drops me on the ground beside some of our grademates. He zips back to the fight and brings back Maya's dad. "If you want to be a hero then get these people to safety, stop acting like an idiot."

I sigh in a heap then right myself before these strangers. "Is everyone all right?" I grumble. None of them respond, they only look at the 'superheroes' fighting the bad guy. I'm pretty sure Maya just joined the battle, I can hear more crashes from the rubble of the house and the squeals from her dad.

"W-what are we going to do!" A girl with a ginger bob bawls at me.

"I don't know!" I tell them, throwing my hands in the air.

"What do you mean you don't know? You should be trying to save us!" Maya's dad yells at me, just itching for an excuse to yell at a teenager.

I sigh. This isn't how I wanted to spend my last week in Paris.

A piece of black ivory fence appears out from the ground in front of me in a fraction of a moment. It's jagged edges reflect everyone's faces. "Okay. We're in danger." I spout quietly as I carefully trace the sharp edges with my eyes.

***

"What do we do? What do we do? What do we do?" A guy I recognise from the jocks table screams as he rocks back and forth.

"Do you have a back exit?" I ask Maya's dad.

"My house!" he cries staring at the pile of rubble. "My house!" He doesn't even care his daughter's risking her life to save his and others'.

I slap him on his right cheek. "Do you have a back exit?"

He nods and points to the bushes behind the table we're hiding under. I grab the table's legs and turn it on its side to give us a wooden shield. Too bad it means I must sacrifice all the tasty cake and dessert but if I could, I would trade places with it if it meant I didn't have to deal with Maya's dad.

"Okay, everyone, follow me. Probably." I say, looking at everyone. There aren't a lot of people left I'm pretty sure they either ran away in a panic or in a panic, ran away.

I sort of crawl towards the bushes where a couple is intimately making out. Barf.

"Uh, did you notice the giant super-battle or no?" I ask them, pointing behind me.

They don't even wince at my words.

"Okay then," I whisper and crawl past them. The back gate matches the familiar theme of the house, ivory. I jostle the silver handle but it doesn't budge. "Why won't it work?" I ask the infamous father of Maya.

"Young man, it works." He seems offended that I'd imply he'd ever owned something that didn't work. "It just needs a key."

"Oh, really." I roll my eyes. "Then where is this key? Also, I'm a girl."

"It's exactly where it should be, on our kitchen table." I could practically strangle this guy by this point.

"Then why did you bring us here?" I hiss, practically choking the light out of today.

"You- you said- "

"I don't even care." I wave my hand away. My fingers dig through the tall green bushes.

"What are you doing?" Someone I've seen around the halls asks.

"Looking for a rock." I comb through the dead and fallen bristles for at least a medium-sized stone.

"Going somewhere, pretty?" Someone says.

"Found it!" I yell at them. I look at them with it in my hands. "Oh. It's you." I hurl it at the mugger's head. "She shoots!" I yell in French, pumping my arms through the air. "She scores!" The rock hits him flatly on the side of the head and bounces off.

"Honey, all that did was piss me off," he mumbles as he grabs my arm and takes me into the air. "I'm invincible," he laughs, spitting his terrible breath everywhere.

"No." I pull my legs up between us. "Grabbing!" I yell at him, kicking myself away. "Maya?" I waiver. She better catch me.

"Gotcha." She hiccups, apparently not letting me turn into a pancake.

"Thank you," I tell her as she sets me down by the gate just in time to see the guy knocked out by Kai. He punches the robber at super speed until he topples to the ground. I kick him with my foot. "And stay down." I point at him. Kaden and Kai look at me the way they look at me like they're trying to decipher me. Maya's pink party dress now looks more of a brown with fewer ruffles and more rips.

I grab another rock and smash the handle of the gate.

"Have a good night everyone."

***

My last day in Paris has been filled with rain. It's practically drowning the city and me with it. My plane got delayed by an hour so

I'm pretty much stuck at this lousy airport for a while. Going through security, I kind of set off an alarm. I blame the power for that. It didn't take them long to realise it was just a fluke and I'm really not that dangerous. That's what they think at least.

"Here's a coffee." Maya nudges me.

"How'd you get through security? This is for people who board the plane, not annoying drunks like you." I'm still haunted by last week. Apparently, the robber got high on Maya's supply of power pills which are chock-full of Achelium. I would have stolen them if there were any of them left. The robber chugged them all before crashing out of her bedroom wall for even more cash. It's not uncommon for robbers to target that area, it's pretty rich and Maya's family aren't the only billionaires that live on Wagram avenue.

"It wasn't hard. I just had to show them my Warriors membership."

"Of course." I take a sip of the coffee. It's the best coffee I've ever had. So good. It's dark and rich. Is that cinnamon? I love cinnamon.

"It's good, yes?" She eyes my mouth, still attached to the plastic lid.

"It's not terrible." I shrug as I wipe the dribble off my chin.

"I figured. You've got a terrible taste in fashion and food." I shrug again and take another sip without a word. I don't have to, it doesn't matter what I say since she'll just keep droning on and on without me. "Wait." She inhales. "Did you pack heels?" She grabs my shoulders and detaches the coffee from my lips. I blink at her blankly. "You didn't."

"Nope."

"Wait here, I'm sure we've got some time to-"

"Now boarding!" A computer screen yells at us.

"To-"

"Welp, I gotta go. See you in a few weeks." I take a step to the glass boarding gate.

"Rikki!"

"What?" I turn back to her on my heel, nearly spilling my coffee everywhere.

"Thanks for saving my family and everything."

"It's nothing." I turn back to the gate more slowly. "Just try not to get so drunk next time."

***

Planes are now on my dislike list, along with clichés, frappes, and octopi. I thought it would be fun to go on an eight-hour plane ride filled with crying babies and stale pretzels. At least I still have my terrible judgment as always.

The JFK Airport is like someone having the terrible idea of 'Hey, what if a stadium lobby was an airport?' Of course, this is pretty much how all airports are planned out. I stare at the giant American flag and almost forget my airsickness. Almost. I spent a few minutes by a trash can before a chauffeur tapped my shoulder.

"Dubois, Rikki?" She's got a distinctive American accent. Maybe from Florida? Is that in America? I honestly have no idea.

"Uh, yes." I smile at her, wiping any leftover stuffs off my face.

She smiles back. "Alright, please follow me." We pass underneath a massive metal sculpture that doesn't quite fit the building's style.

"Are all the buildings like this?" I ask her, looking around like the tourist I am.

"No, not many." She says, grabbing my duffel bag and suitcase.

"Oh, I can take that!" I take my duffel bag from her hands and swing it against my shoulder.

"Are you sure?"

"Yes, no problems here." I smile at her. She looks a little surprised I know this much English. After all, Americans don't really bother to learn any French aside from 'bonjour' so why should it go the other way around?

She silently opens a black door for me.

"Uh, is this a-" What's that word? The long black car? For the president of this country? "-limousine?"

"Yes, the Smithe Industries ordered one especially for you two."

"Two?"

"Oh, two in English means for there to be more than one I think it's, uh, Deux? In French?" She mispronounces it in the middle and trips over the x at the end of the number. If she can't say it right, she shouldn't say it at all. A French person could mistake whatever she said for whatever so, there's next to no point in even saying it.

"I know what two means, I was just wondering who else was coming in the car."

She shifts her weight between her feet uncomfortably while holding the door open for me.

"Thanks." I smile as I duck my head under and slip in.

The back of the seat pops a bit she opens the trunk and stuffs my bags in.

"Uh, hi." I wave to the boy in the corner but he ignores me. There are too many moody boys in my life right now. "So, you're going to the internship as well?"

He grunts in my general direction.

"*Zut*, I'm just trying to make some conversation." I roll my eyes at him and lean into the leather seats. I nearly overlook the treasure trove of soda cans and salted chips. "I've heard of these." I pick up a brand. "Mr. Vickies?" I lift an eyebrow. I saw these in San Francisco but I never tried them.

"Can you pass me a bag?" The boy smiles, throwing up his hands.

I nod and toss him a bag of 'Sea Salt and Vinegar'.

"Nice throw," he breathes. "I love these." I can tell from his size. He looks a little... cheeseburger appreciative. He tears the little bag open and reaches to the bottom of the pack. His hand piles a few in his mouth as I grab my own bag. "What's your name?" He asks as I dip one on my tongue. They're really salty and kind of sour but in a good way.

"Rikki," I mumble, spilling more food remnants on my face.

"Is that a French name?" He asks out of interest.

I nod a little bit. It's not really but it sort of is. "What's yours?" he clearly wants me to ask him.

"William Copperlan the first." He holds his head up high. "It's British."

"Oh. That's why you had that funny American accent." I point to him.

"What? American accent?" he exclaims, offended. "That's like calling your accent- stupid!"

"I'm sorry. I didn't know." I offer with a smile.

"Inexcusable!"

***

He continued to snub me for a while until I asked some about England and Britain. His funny monotone slaved into a long lecture about his 'beautiful country' and his 'Buckingham Palace' then, he went on to explain all the benefits of a monarchy. And by all of them, I mean he explained every single one to me. It's harder to understand his English through his accent and by this point, I was way too tired to even listen to his strange words.

"Plus, your country, France, also had a monarchy-"

I clicked open my phone and turned my messages back on. My phone buzzed to alert me of the three hundred and seventy-four messages from Maya and Willow. I sigh and press the power button. There is no way I'm going through those now.

"-and then there's Big Ben, our superhero-"

"Superhero?" I ask, finally finding something interesting. Travel has never really been my thing aside from the occasional yearn to go either New York or Paris or the country. It's not like it's anything special. Everyone wants to go somewhere.

"Yeah, didn't you hear me? Big Ben, our superhero."

"He is a 'good guy', yes?"

"Obviously, not like those blokes you've got in Paris."

"Blokes? I do not know that word, what does it mean?"

He laughs. "It means, like, a person," he chuckles some more.

"The heroes in Paris aren't terrible, it's that club that some of them joined."

"The Warriors of the World?"

"Murderers of the World," I correct them.

"I agree." He nods, all signs of his laughter gone. "It's terrible what they do, especially when they do whatever the highest bidder asks." He bends down and looks in my eyes from the other side of the limo's seating. "Wait, you said only some of them joined, who didn't?"

"Corbelle."

"Isn't she the one with the yellow powers?"

"Uh, yes." 'Yellow powers'. That's what I'm reduced to.

"What does 'Corbelle' translate to?"

"Well, it loosely translates into Crow. But she didn't want that name, it's actually a kind of funny story, the guy who first spotted decided on her name and it just kind of stuck but- "

"Why does she wear all black?"

"Becau- I don't know." I shrug. I probably shouldn't tell him exactly how much I know about myself.

"It's pretty cool," he chirps excitedly. "I've seen some videos of superheroes around the world but she's the coolest, and not just because she's the most powerful! She can practically disappear into shadows!" Is this what a 'fanboy' is?

"She's really the most powerful?" I probably shouldn't be asking this. It's just going to go straight to my head.

"Well, yeah! She's got an unlimited source of energy, doesn't she?"

"I don't know..." Yes, I do. I'm actually not sure how but I believe it's got everything to do with my curse. And also because it's magic so I'm not allowed to question it.

"She's insane! When she does the thing- you know, the thing?" He points at me like I should know everything about Corbelle (Which I do).

I would totally show him the thing except I totally can't so I just stare back like my usual, idiotic self.

"Where she like-" He tries to imitate the sound of an explosion but ends up spraying half the limo with spit. His hands curl up and jump apart in a single motion. "-and then everyone's like, 'Oh nooooo! I'm blinded!'" He cowers in the corner of his seat and squeals ridiculously.

I giggle a little bit.

"You totally know, don't you?"

"When she and the others saved Paris from that giant monster is still quite famous all over France." They're still applying repairs to downtown Paris. Thankfully, the Eiffel Tower didn't sustain any serious damage. But the monster did. I don't actually know what happened to it but if the Warriors were involved it's probably dead. But that brings up the question of what they did with the body. What would someone do with a giant spiky-stone-dragon corpse?

***

The car stops, abruptly sending me off my seat. My arm snaps over the door handle and grabs it to cushion my fall. My fingers loosen and slip off the railing. I land face first into the seating beside William. It muffles a few of my swear words.

"You kids okay?" The driver lady opens the door and lets rays of sunlight in.

"I'm quite fine, thank you," William responds cheerily.

"...No," I mutter from inside of the cushion.

"Come on, let's go Rikki," he groans as he starts to tug on my free arm.

"Ow! Ow! That is worse!" I scream. Sadly, he doesn't hear me my muffled shouts of pain.

He pulls harder and dislodges my head out of the seat. "There you go," he breathes, shoveling his jagged hair back into place.

"Merci," I seethe as I nurse my shoulder.

"No problem." He steps out of the limo into the sunshine. It stings my eyes. I wipe the tears out of my eyes and blink until the glare leaves.

"What's this?" I ask the driver, pointing at the lavish building.

"It's a hotel," she responds with a smile like she understands my language gap.

Wow, thanks, lady. Like I can't read the words on the side of the building. Speaking of the building, this isn't what I would have expected from an American hotel. I thought they were all seedy and gross. But this one is insane! It's taller than tall. It's like a vertical ocean. All the glass on the front of the building is wavy and different shades of blue.

303

On the lobby doors, the glass curves outwards towards the street like they're opening a sea to welcome us.

"*This* is the hotel?" William asks, echoing my confusion. "It's a skyscraper!"

***

This is like a mansion plus-plus. Everyone's so nice and welcoming and every room is dressed perfectly. They're not tacky but not too full of themselves. It's a perfect balance of hotel and mansion.

My door clicks open quickly but opens a lot slower.

"Uh, hello?" I'm supposed to have a roommate, she should be in here. "Anyone?" I drag my duffel bag through the door hole.

"What are you doing? Close the damn door!" someone screams.

"Désole!" I slam the door shut and lean against it.

"Do you have any idea how cold it is in the hallways?" A girl wearing towels and holding crutches walks out of what I hope is the bathroom.

"Cold?" I offer hesitantly.

"Ice cold! I just got out of the shower!" she shouts.

"Sorry I just- " I stammer.

"Wait, you're the little French girl, right?" she asks, pointing to my chest and balancing. She's using the wall to hold herself up as she lets go of a crutch.

"Uh, yes." I notice the loud music coming from the farthest of the two set beds. I'm pretty sure I heard something like it San Francisco and probably coming from tourists in Paris.

"You're shorter than I imagined." She strokes her chin and looks me over.

"I get that a lot." I sigh.

"Hah! So, she's got a sense of humor!" She smiles. "Aaron won't stop talking about you."

I knew Aaron would be coming. There should be some other characters from San Francisco coming as well.

"Penny."

"Yeah, that's my name." She grins, pulling the towel on her head tighter. "What's yours? Sorry, I didn't check your name, only your nationality."

"It's Rikki." I give her my hand for a handshake. I hope she remembers me.

"Rikki?" Her eyes practically pop out of their sockets. She hits my hand away and jumps onto me. "I missed you so much!" she screams, holding me tight. My spine cracks a little.

"Careful, Penny, I don't have superpowers."

"You're right." She laughs and attempts to sit up. "Where did you go?" She asks, talking seriously. After all, I have been missing for two years and I spent one of them in a coma at a completely off-the-maps-secret-will-never-be-found building with my sort-of-fiancé. Then, I spent the second one without any idea of who I was and also kind of fighting things twenty-four-seven. So, why don't I just start with that?

"Oh, you know, around," I laugh and scratch the back of my neck. She had better believe me. I'm way too exhausted to falsify any more truths and continue to get away with it.

"Okay." She shrugs.

"How've your water powers been going?" I ask, spinning my finger around.

"They're going great, I've practically perfected mind-control!"

"Oh, that's... perfect!" I laugh.

"Are there other people from San Francisco here?" I ask, I already know there are. I just want to change the subject to something less I-am-going-to-self-destruct-and-you'll-know-I'm-a-superhero. I guess I'm more of an ex-hero now though.

"Yep." She nods her head. "Aaron *definitely* is. He won't stop talking about you. That guy is crushing on you, *hard*." She looks at me in the eyes. "And you're crushing on him too, aren't you?"

"Euuh, maybe?" I shrug and smile. I've got no idea.

Like clockwork, someone knocks on the door. Penny reaches for her crutches and makes her way over to the door.

"Rikki? You might want to answer this door."

"You should put some clothes on," I tell her as I reach for the door and pull it open.

"Oh. Hi... Rikki."

"Aaron..." I smile lopsidedly. I am way too tired for this-

Maya

What is wrong with that girl? She hasn't been responding to any of my calls or messages!

I angrily tap my phone and send her another.

"Sage!" Maverick screams at me. "Are you present in our conversation?" She seethes. She's been a lot more mean and ugly since Rikki beat her ass.

"Yes!" I yell back at her.

She glares at me but turns back to the giant screen in the middle of the table.

Someone nudges me in back.

"Hey!" I hiss quietly managing not to grab the attention of the bitch.

"Is that her number?" Tonnerre asks in his gruff tone pointing at the phone in my hand but not looking at me.

"Depends. Why do you want it?" I ask, not daring to look at his blonde greasy hair and crystal blue eyes.

"We have some issues I'd like to sort out," he whispers, crossing his arms over his chest.

"Do you now?" I grin. "I'm sure she'd love to hear about them."

"She would."

"And how well do you know her? Her name? Age? Where she is right now?" I egg him on. I've seen her do it all the time, it's practically her favorite activity.

"She's sixteen," he jeers at me. His fists are already shaking.

"Is that all you know about her?"

"She was born in Paris, raised by an abusive mother. She lived in San Francisco for a few months and was in a coma for a year. She's been stabbed through the heart and shot through the stomach. Her power's result from an ancient prophecy that gives her an unlimited source of power from the time she turns seventeen. After that, she'll live for one million years cutting down anyone in her way. Then she'll die and that's it." He frowns at my shocked face and continues. "She's a master at anything she tries. Fencing, gymnastics, parkour, thieving, and English just to name a few."

"Is that all you know?" I challenge him.

"I respect the secrets she wants to keep," he spits.

"Is that why you want her number?"

"It's none of your business."

"Actually, I'm the gracious and beautiful girl blessing you with the number of your little crush. Who's real name I happen to know. So, if you want to have contact with her, you'd better tell me whatever you've got planned for her because I'm her best friend. If you want to talk to her, you talk to me. You want to date her? You date me too. This is a package deal, jackass." I press my finger in his face.

"Fine," he grunts. Watching my look. "But you need to pass on a message for me."

"I love you?" I roll my eyes. All boys are the same.

"No, I already told her that. Tell her I'm sorry."

I roll my eyes again and type in the message and send it to Rikki. They're all the same.

Rikki

"So..." He scratches the back of his neck awkwardly and laughs.

"Uhm. Hi?" I laugh back, closing my eyes.

"How have you been?"

"I've been-" Hunted by a group of crazy murderers who want my blood so they can turn it into pure energy and use it for evil purposes. "-fine. How have you been?"

"You know, good. Nothing really big's happened recently." Must be nice.

"That is good."

"Yeah, good."

"Oh my god, just kiss already!" Penny yells from the open doorway. "It's painful watching you two!"

I sigh. There are giant butterflies with wings like razors in my stomach making everything I do awkward. I breathe out. "Sorry. Things have been going lightning fast right now and- " My phone buzzes in my pocket like a butterfly trying to escape from my side. It's going to infect everyone with my severe awkwardness.

"Do you want to take that?" he asks. His face matches his hair.

"Sure." I smile and press the messages button. Two-hundred and eighteen unread messages. Why do Maya and Willow do this to me? I click on the most recent one from Maya. This had better be good.

'Tonnerre wants to say sorry.'

'Koala bears have taken over Paris, again!'

Okay then. Those are two very different messages. Is she playing a game? Am I supposed to guess which one is bunk? I type my response: *'Do you need some help?'* I type in response to her French messages.

The infamous grey dots appear as she types from the other side of the world. *'No. I just thought you'd like to see what you're missing.'*

I roll my eyes at her. *'I am quite fine, thank you.'* I want her to feel the wet burn of my sarcasm. *'And koalas aren't bears.'* I sigh and send the message.

"Sorry about that. My friends are idiots." I smile.

"Trust me, I know how that feels."

"So, how have things been in San Fransisco? Any more super battles?"

"Definitely not as many as Paris."

"True, Paris is practically overfilling with idiots with superpowers," I yawn and remember them all. It's so weird I can remember them all and not my email password.

"The Warriors of the World? Ugh, those guys suck. They act like they own the world. They were in San Francisco a few months ago."

"Oh no! Did you manage to get the stench of cheap perfume out?"

"Thankfully, but just barely," he laughs.

"Yes, but they've been there so long it feels like they're really trying to mess up our *sentses* of good and evil." I smile as I make the pun.

He laughs again and notices the bags underneath my eyes. "Hey, how long was your plane ride?"

"About eight hours but I'm fine." I wave my hand away and smile.

"Okay, you've got to get some shut-eye before the opening ceremony." He grabs my shoulders and turns me towards my open door. He pushes me in and closes the door. "See you tomorrow, Rikki."

"Like I said before, you two are painful." Penny sits on her bed watching me still.

"Did you watch the entire thing?" I ask her, still leaning against the back of the door.

"Yes. The entire time I just wanted to scream. It's so painful watching you two talk to each other. You're like characters in a romance novel and it shows." She takes a deep breath and leans forward, her black hair spilling off her shoulder. "It actually hurt me which is not an easy thing to do now, I'll tell you that. You two should get married soon."

"What? Penny, I'm sixteen. In my country, you cannot marry until you are thirty-six."

"Really?"

"No, that's just the age I'm going to get married at," I groan and jump into my bed. "I'm going to be lonely forever," I mumble, already falling asleep fast.

***

I hate jet lag. I'm up six hours earlier than I need to be and I think it's killing me. In New York, it's three AM in the morning. Everything is pitch black and I'm way too scared to move. If I move, I could wake up Penny and I'm not prepared to suffer the wrath of Penny in the early hours of the morning.

I know how to move silently while walking on gravel, snow, and basically, anything that makes a sound. That did nothing to protect me from wearing a rain jacket while going to bed. No matter how I slowly I move the jacket crinkles and makes a sound like it's softly raining except not really. Of course, this wouldn't be the problem if Penny twitched every time I moved the jacket. This is like being glued to the floor all over again (long story).

If I had the power to shapeshift, this would be a hell of a lot easier. I could just change into a snake and slither out silently. It would also mean I could finally swim without drowning too. Drowning isn't very fun. I've done it enough to know I hate it.

I twitch under the jacket and Penny turns in her sleep.

This is not an ideal situation but I've been in worse. A lot worse. Like being locked in cages of angered parakeets (no, really). Those birds are bloodthirsty. Or that time I got stuck in Tonnerre's head (no, really, that happened).

My eyes hurt. I probably should have taken out my contacts before going to bed. I force my eyelids open and shut for a few moments until they get used to the pain and the darkness. I shift my head to the bedside clock. The jacket moves and so does Penny.

How has it only been three minutes? It's still three in the morning! This is an eternal hell!

***

Penny yawns and sits up after an eternity. I managed to fall back asleep after another half hour but my senses are still completely disoriented.

"Quand est-ce?" I mumble drearily.

"What are you saying?" She asks as she turns to my bed.

"Sorry," I groan. My English isn't completely functioning yet. "I asked what time it was."

"I don't know. You've got a clock right beside your head."

"I do?" I turn my head to face the small black digital clock on the wooden nightstand. "Oh yeah, I do. I forgot about that." It's nine thirty-three in the morning. "When do we need to be there?"

"At about ten thirty," She groans and grabs her wheelchair.

"Good, we've got an hour." I shed my first yellow skin of rain jacket and take a step towards the bathroom. I smell distinctively of air travel. "I need a shower." And a coffee. A coffee would be pretty good.

Penny manages to wheel herself quickly ahead of me and locks the bathroom door. "You snooze, you lose!" She yells from behind the door.

I mumble some French swears under my breath and unzip my duffel bag. I feel around for a suitable outfit for my taste. My hand touches some wool and pulls out a light pink cardigan. Willow.

There's gotta be something other than dresses and skirts in here. I've checked both my bags and so far Willow hijacked my bag and packed: a dark blue dress (aside from the one Maya made me pack), two white button-up shirts, black ankle pants, a rainbow of pastel coloured sweaters, a few tank tops, black tights, a skirt, and boot wedges. What she left in my bags that I packed was one pair of jeans, and a printed Eiffel Tower shirt. She wouldn't even let me leave with a pair of sweatpants. I can't believe her.

I grab my phone and send Willow a very angry message. I send it and throw my phone on my bed. I cannot believe her. My face collides with my pillows as I land on my temporary bed.

'You're a girl, own it!!!!!!!!' She adds a few sickly smiley emojis.

I frown at her message and pick out the ankle pants, white shirt, and a cardigan. I frown even more at the small heels as I choose them as well. "Stupid Willow," I mumble in French.

After I shower and change, I grab the room key and explore the hotel. It stretches into the sky for an eternity. Each door has its own

312

metal address in brail as well as numbers. It's a lot more luxurious than I could ever afford.

At nine forty-nine, I get lost and ask a cleaner for directions to the Terrace Boardroom. He shows me to the floor and points to the door. Thanks to my terrible sense of direction, I've been wandering this floor for about five minutes. I don't have Penny's number so I'm kind of screwed. I sigh and walk past another giant wooden door.

The metal elevator creaks open and a couple looking about my age step out.

"Hi, my name is Rikki Dubois, do you know where the Terrace Board Room is?" I walk up to them and stick out my hand with a smile.

"Ooh, look Daisy! It's a small French person!" the boy says, poking my cheeks.

"Uh, do you know where the- "

"Look, Daisy, look! Listen to her cute little accent." He squishes my left cheek with two of his fingers. This is why I hate Americans. "I thought most of them were white, though."

"Excuse me?" I laugh as I brush his fingers off. "Did you think all Europeans were white?" I shake my head while still laughing. It's hilarious idiots like this still exist.

Daisy tries to pull her boyfriend away while giving me the 'I'm-really-sorry' look and then the 'He's-not-usually-racist' look.

"Because I thought not all Americans were idiots but I guess we were both wrong," I laugh out loud as I follow another stream of people coming from one of the three elevators.

***

The room has about twenty-four places fitted with twenty-four seats. Each seat's got a name tag, water bottle, and a notebook.

I touch one and get my hand whapped away.

"What are you doing?" A guy screeches. "Can't you read? Is that your name on the piece of paper?" He screams down at me.

"Yes," I tell him while I pull my wrist of his massive hand. "It says, Penny Liu. She is a friend of mine. She'll be here in a minute." I glare and pat my seat, the one beside hers.

"Fine," he jeers and walks to his on the other side of the room.

My seat and Penny's both face the giant window behind where Colleen Smithe will sit. She's the head coordinator so she'll be welcoming us and giving us all a snapshot of what we'll be doing under her care. My chair's exactly across from hers which is a little frightening since I'm pretty much here to see what exactly she's got to do with Vaccine and Tonnerre. Also, Willow warned me about her mother so there's also that. *"Don't let her intimidate her because she'll try."* Wonderful advice Willow, thank you for that because that'll help me so much when I'm sitting right across from her in a two-hour meeting.

So, Penny's sitting beside me and so is that William kid from yesterday.

The last group of kids walks in at the same time with Mrs. Smithe herding them in. I make sure not to make awkward eye contact as she walks in. This is the first time I've gone undercover so I've got to be careful for once.

"Good morning, students," Smithe says as she sits down. Her eyes fall right on mine and smile. "I'd like to welcome you all to the first Smithe Internship. Hundreds of students have submitted fantastic science projects and engineering feats but you are the best of the best. Of the most incredible was a growth acceleration formula that could save thousands of lives." Her eyes fall into mine deeply.

I smile back at her stiffly feeling like the definition of awkwardness.

"So, I am inexplicably proud to welcome you all to this space. I hope we can all create some miracles together." She stands up and smiles at everyone. "We have an assigned curriculum for those who have yet to graduate and we have a very special lab for all of you to use. Thank you very much for joining Smithe Industries for the next two weeks." She walks out and Aaron takes her place.

"Hello, my name is Aaron Powers. Some of you may know me as a friend but here I'm going to your supervisor. This means I'm going to be your go-to guy if you've got anything on your mind but if you do anything I don't like, I'm sending you right back to whatever city you came from. Got it?"

Everyone in the room nods quickly and quietly. This is a different message than the one Smithe was just talking about.

"With that being said, here are some of the rules." Aaron takes out a clipboard and reads it aloud. "One, curfew's at ten thirty sharp. Two, no alcohol. Most of you guys are under eighteen so that means nothing illegal here. Three, I'm not going to allow any fights. If you've got something against each other, get over it. We're here to work together, not to get at each other's throats. Four, each of you have an assigned schedule. You follow that schedule. Don't and I'm sending you back home. Five, you follow the rules. Don't and I'm sending you back home." He looks around the room at everyone looking for just one person who questions his rules. "Everyone understand?"

The entire room nods carefully not to offend the all-powerful supervisor.

***

Okay, so I've gotten past all my regular school activities. They put me in a special class for special French children because I'm extra special. I'm the only one in my class. Also, the teacher barely knows any French.

"Euh... English... my name is... Cambell," he stutters hesitantly while looking at me for approval.

"I can speak English," I tell him. "You don't need to speak French so long as you speak your language slowly."

He nods and wipes his forehead with a relieved smile. He wipes his hand on his beige pants and flicks open a whiteboard pen. "So, I'm going to be your teacher for all your subjects aside from Science and PE?"

"Is that a question for me?" I point to myself. "Uh, I am not sure. On my schedule, it says that my courses are to be taught by Damian Cambell and that every second week we meet in this classroom."

"Yes, that's me, but the only subject I really know is Math so how do you suppose I teach English, History, and French? Well, I guess you don't really need to be taught French and..." he starts to drone and I start to lose my focus. My short attention span (unless related to Science) draws my focus out the lighted window of the bricked school to the gym. You can't see a lot of New York from the school but I could see all of it from my hotel room.

So, this is an American city. Well, New York at least. It's beautiful in a strange sense. It's almost as if you put Paris and San Francisco in a blender, took out the rivers and replaced the Eiffel Tower with 'The Empire State Building'. It's a concrete jungle. Everything either glitters or absorbs shine. Or it's extremely ugly. There's grime and dirt everywhere and everything is rock and metal. It's all about perspective.

I tilt my head against the window. The last of the leaves here are finally blowing away. They're rather stubborn, I find. It's like they think this year will be different from any other year like somehow they won't get blown away by the gusts of winter. They're suckers to think that their fate will be different from their ancestors.

Penny

A lone girl walks along the hallways of the white school halls. Her black bob bounces up and down with each of her steps. Her tanned fingers trace across the grey metal lockers.

"Penny, what are you doing?" she asks, her high pitched voice piercing the suffocating silence of the hallway.

"Rikki, just stand there. I'm just trying to capture your essence in a chapter of my book." The lead of my pencil smears the otherwise white-lined paper of my black leather bound book.

"Are you still working on that book? What has it been, two years?" She sighs as she walks up to my pale, wheelchair-bound legs.

"Actually I started a new one. This one depicts the nature of your sudden disappearance. I'm just finishing it now." I push my glasses further up the bridge of my nose and continue penning my paper.

"Has that not already been solved? I'm here. I'm alive. There is nothing left to solve." She shrugs easily and smiles like she practiced in her mirror at home. "It was just some travel."

"Then why didn't you tell anyone?" I put down my pencil as I press further.

"It is my life so why should they care?" Her left-hand twitches softly. I stare at it and smile. Now I'm getting somewhere.

"I mean, I was really worried, you know and so were a bunch of other people."

"I never asked you to be worried about my safety. I'm sixteen years old. I don't need people looking after me."

"But it still doesn't explain that without even living in San Francisco for ten months, you just flat out disappear."

"My parents needed me to come back to... Bordeaux for Parisian schooling. They didn't approve of my American schooling."

"And yet, here you are." I take out my phone and press the red record button. I'll have to capture this on record for any later use.

"It took a lot of begging for my parents to allow me to come here." She scratches the back of her neck.

"But, back in San Francisco, you disappeared in an instant. Taj said you were with him one minute and the next you were gone. This was at approximately the same time all hell started to break loose in downtown. Everyone thought you were dead." I breathe. These are not easy memories to navigate. "We held vigils for you. we tried to contact anyone who knew you, your parents, your siblings, but we couldn't find anything." I can feel the thick, warm water washing down my cheeks. I looked everywhere for Rikki and the fact that she's right here right now is impossible. "It was like she never existed."

"She?" The girl walks up to my wheelchair and looks in my eyes. "What are you talking about?" She smiles.

"You know exactly what I'm talking about!" I scream at her face. She staggers back with a perplexed look on her face.

"Penny-" she tries.

"No! I don't know who or even what you are but stop pretending to be *her*!" I cry. I thought I could handle it. I mean, it was like she really was Rikki. Her clothes were spot on, her voice was on the dot, her looks, hell, even her accent was identical to Rikki's but that's not her. I can tell by the way she stands like she wants me to tell her she's Rikki like she's not some foreign weirdo. I thought if I played along, she'd take a hint and we'd both pretend that she really was Rikki but I can't and she isn't. "You're not her, alright! Rikki Dubois was my best friend and she died! Alright? You can't just take a dead girl's name! It's not right!"

318

Rikki

So, my ex-best friend thinks I'm not really me and that I'm just some weirdo who stole my own identity and that I'm actually dead. Isn't this fun?

"Penny, you've got to believe me. It *is* me." I point to my chest. "Rikki Dubois, 'that weird girl who likes books more than people', remember?" I try to smile but I can't. The jetlag is really catching up with me. "It's really me, who else could I be? I mean, I know all about your water powers and your water magic, right? Why do you not just hypnotize me and make me tell the truth?"

"Why don't I?" she leers. This was obviously a bad idea.

She smashes her hands together and pulls them apart like she's stretching taffy. Water flows to her wheelchair from every direction.

"You know, that was more of a... rhetorical question." The lid of my water bottle pops open and the contents move quickly to the gathering orb in her hands. It spins and spins and ripples.

"How old are you?" she asks. Ripples shake the base of my throat and push my answer through. Sixty percent of the human body is made of water so she's pretty powerful when she wants to be.

"J'ai seize ans-"

"In English!" She barks.

"I am sixteen years old." Something gulps. It could have been my voice. I think I'm having one of those out of body experiences. Actually, I imagined myself to be a little taller than this. I should start wearing wedges more often. Those increase height, right?

"Who are you?" Her orb sharpens into a spike with her anger. She still can't tell whether it's me or not me (I think it's answer number two, personally). It reminds me of the power welled up inside of me.

"You know me as Rikki Dubois."

"What do you mean? What's you real name?" Her spike dulls and turns into more of a slope shape with her curiosity.

"It's Carmen-" I use everything I have to cough out some water to regain some control over myself. Water falls out my mouth like a mini waterfall. "-Rikki Dubois. My middle name is Carmen." I cough out, still trying to wildly spit out the rest of the water. It only adds the puddle surrounding my heels. Is it weird to say that I'm actually kind of thirsty, now?

She frowns from her chair. "What were you going to say?" Her circle of water starts to spin again.

"Nothing." I gargle as I look away. I put a hand in between me and the girl in the wheelchair. I pick up my bag and look back. "Do you still think I am not myself?" I sigh. I'd hate if I just got this wet for nothing. I'm pretty much soaked to the bone like a soggy bowl of cereal.

She makes the sound she made when she thought or like when she contemplated something. "A little bit but you haven't completely proved yourself yet so don't think I won't be keeping a look out on you." She wheels away from me, leaving me hunched over and soaking in a wet hallway.

"What?"

***

Second day of the 'Smithe Science Internship'. Progress on finding links between Vaccine and Smithe: Zero. Progress on making Penny believe it's really me: Zero. Progress in finding a decent coffee shop: Zero. I have decided I don't like American cities. I really, really want to go back home but I can't without talking to Aaron first and then I'd have to face Mrs. Smithe head on and there is no way I'm prepared to face that dragon.

I scroll through my hundreds of messages and take a sip of my terrible coffee. My head's just started to adjust to the time here. Today's supposed to be our introduction to the lab. Guess what we're using! It starts with an 'A' and ends with a 'chelium'. No, guesses? No one? Are you sure?

Willow's currently panicking about the sudden increase in koalas all over the city and whether it's okay to wear faux koala fur outdoors. I take another sip and nearly spit it out. This coffee is really terrible. It doesn't help that Tonnerre keeps sending me messages through Maya.

'I miss you' and 'Where are you?' But I think my favorite was 'Can I have your number?' It's so cute that he thinks he can just pick me up in an instant. I sigh and drop my phone. It's already December first. Where did the time go? I pick my phone back up and text Maya.

'Tell Tonnerre that his bleached hair should stay out of my business.'

She sends me a 'happy face' emoji in response. My phone springs out of my hand and buzzes about on my nightstand. The caller ID says 'Judgy Fashion Lady' which means Maya's calling me. I press the green button and pick the phone up.

"Hello? Maya?" I say in my regular French.

"Corbelle?" A blatant American voice asks in clear English. Why is Tonnerre calling me?

"Mon Dieu," I mumble and sigh. "What do you want, Tonnerre? I am busy." I look out the window. For all I know, he could be out there right now.

"Are you sick or something? Your sounds all squeaky and high-pitched."

"This is how I normally I sound. I'm not wearing the voice changer." I feel my neck just to make sure.

"Oh." This would be the moment he would scratch the back of his neck. "How are you?"

"I am fine. How are you, aside from irritating?" I sigh.

"I'm good, good."

"So, what was the point of calling me?" I ask and look out the window. White powder has started flying down from the sky. "It's snowing," I breathe and press my face against the window.

"Corbelle?" he asks. "Is it snowing there too? Sage says you aren't in Paris anymore. We're in New York. Where are you?" I nearly drop my phone. How much did Maya tell him? Are they here because of me? Why didn't Maya tell me?

"Give me back my phone!" Maya screams from the background. "Give it!" she yells. That explains how he got to call me. He must have grabbed it from her and flew up into the sky.

"So, you guys are in New York? That's interesting, but no, I'm still in France." Play it cool like ice. "Just *chilling* in France." I ruffle my short hair with my hand. It's grown a lot since I last cut it. I think I'll have to snip off the ends since they're starting to curl up.

Something that sounds like a punch rings through the background noise. "Were those some puns?" He asks.

"Of course not, I mean, It's snowing here so why would I make a pun? That's just *cold*," I mumble. I look up at the sky in case Tonnerre's just there, hovering.

He laughs and continues. "So, we're only staying in New York for a few more days. Maverick just wanted a chance to brief our... director on the situation. After that, we're going back to France to hunt you down."

I didn't really want to be back on speaking terms with Tonnerre but it's not like I've got a choice. "Tonnerre," I start. "Do you remember our last conversation?"

Andrew

"Well, yeah. What was it a week ago?" I ask. I remember exactly. I just don't want to. She called me a murderer. There was so much disgust in her voice as she said it too. I scratch the back of my neck carefully.

"Try two," she sighs. "I thought you'd have understood it by now."

"Understand what? All you said was that you'd be taking a break for a while." Sage glares at me and then at her phone. She pulls herself out of the clouds and races right at me. I dodge carelessly to the air above her.

"Or that I'd just quit altogether," she swallows the rest of her words. I look down at the clouds. She might be down there somewhere. "Guess which one I'm considering."

"Cor, you can't quit! You're the best out of all of us!" Sage listens to my words and stops charging at me. "You're the hero the world needs."

"Did I ever tell you about why I started being a hero?"

"Why?" I ask. She didn't though it's not like I asked or cared.

"In San Fransisco, on the first week you appeared, I saw you. You were racing away to fight a bad guy and I was loading a dishwasher. Our eyes met and I knew I couldn't just stand by any longer. That was the first night I decided to be Topaz. I wanted to be someone good, like you. But now you're not the best role-model," she sighs quietly. She doesn't want to offend me.

"Well, that's true." I scratch the back of my neck again. "Can I at least know your name? We've known each other for two years; don't you trust me?" It seems like every time we talk I bring this up. And she knows too.

"My name doesn't matter but trust me, it is a pretty stupid name anyway. I mean, what kind of name is- Rik- uh, I mean-"

"Your name is Rick?" She's right 'Rick' is kind of a stupid name.

"Yes? What's yours?"

"It's uh- Andrew. My name is Andrew."

Rikki

"Andrew?" That's a pretty stupid name. "As in Andrew Smithe?" An even stupider name but less stupid than Rikki Dubois.

"Uhm..." He pauses for a second. "Yes..."

"So, your name is Andrew Smithe, as in son of Coleen Smithe?"

"Yeah, that's me," he breathes. This would also be another point in which he would scratch the back of his neck.

"Well, this is awkward." That's why he had ties to Smithe! He's their son! "Wait, so have you been a secret agent working for Smithe?"

"What?" his voice quivers. It was meant as more of a rhetorical question but his reaction is not exactly what I would call 'not suspicious'. "What would give you that idea?"

"Nothing really." I lean against the glass window pane. It's freezing so it cools off my back. I take a sip of my crappy coffee. Maybe its terrible taste will wash away this conversation from my memory. "So, Andrew Smithe, where in New York are you?"

"I'm not exactly in New York at the moment, more like above it. Why?"

"Can I meet you somewhere?" I need to smooth out all this new information. "In masks," I add. I'd prefer not to show him what I really look like yet especially because of his suspicious answer.

"Uh, sure. Where do you want to meet?"

"Is there a decent coffee shop somewhere in New York? All the places I've tried are terrible." I stare at my caffeinated drink with a frown. Then I take another sip of it. "I miss Paris."

"So, you're in New York?" he asks. He probably knows about his mom's internship and that there are only a few names with 'Rik' in them. Then he'd figure out my full name then he might tell his parents then he'd be disappointed by my stupidness and then everything would just go to hell.

"Well, I'm in-" What are the places in Manhattan? "-New Jersey." What were the others? Brooklyn, Queens, what else?

"Oh, cool. Do you want to meet near the Hudson River Park? It's pretty close to Jersey. Or there's also the High Line. It's a little farther

325

away but It's really nice." I flip open my computer and check which one's closest to me.

"The High Line sounds good to me. What is it, a garden?" I ask. It looks like a garden road but also a walking path.

"Yeah, it's a park. We can meet there and then grab some food if you want." My stomach rumbles despite my best interest.

"Food sounds pretty good. What time do you want to meet? I'm kind of busy with a... job so maybe sometime around twelve?" Due to my schedule's insufficient planning, I've got a three and a half hour break right after eleven AM.

"Sure, sure. That's good with me. How will I know where to find you?"

"I'll wear a hat." I look at my suitcase and rummage through it. "It's more of a toque, really."

"Cor, it's Winter. Everyone's going to be wearing a toque."

"But how many will be wearing a stylish mask too?"

***

The High Rise: pretty much an old, dirty railway turned beautiful garden covered with snow. It's like going it's through puberty. There's next to no one here and it's started snowing again. I sigh into the clouds. I'm not even wearing a proper mask. I stole some black face paint and smeared it over my eyes and cheeks. I took out my contacts to make it easier for him to recognize me. I look pretty stupid. I even checked.

I sit down on what is either a snow-covered planter or a bench. It's hard to tell what is what in a white wonderland.

A man dressed in a fancy dark blue sweater walks up to me. His blonde hair is only slightly bothered by the heavy hat weighing it down. He looks me up and down from where he's standing. His eyes trace my figure from head to toe like he's burning me into his memory. "Where's your mask?" he asks with a smile.

"I forgot it at home." I stand up and brush any leftover snow off my yellow raincoat.

We start walking down the snow covered pathway slowly.

326

"So, is this usually covered with snow or is there more to it?" I kick some off my sneaker and swipe my hand across a snowy ledge.

"Nah, usually there's more greenery or tourists." His warm breath stains the air. He's not even wearing a mask. "That's when it's warmer. Speaking of which, aren't you cold? It's *snowing*." He gestures to my skirt, tights, and rain jacket.

"The cold never bothered me anyway," I sing off-tune. "And that's how you make someone's ears bleed," I say happily. I take some of the gathered snow in my hand and pack it into a little sphere. I could make hundreds of these at a time if I was using the power. I raise it into the air and hurl it at Tonnerre's face. It hits his target head on and swipes the hat off his head and the grin off his face.

"Hey! What was that for?" he yells. "You know I've got super strength, right?" He grabs an armful up snow and continues to pack it into the size of a human head. I proceed to take a few steps back and then a full-out run. I leap onto a planter and flip off it. I am such a show-off.

The cannonball of snow hits me square in the back and sends me skidding against the floor of snow and ice. "Aie," I groan. I can taste the snow in my mouth. It tastes like defeat.

"Are you alright? I think I threw that little harder than I meant." He walks up to me and pulls me off the snow.

"I feel pain."

He laughs a little and wraps his arm around my stomach and carries me. "Well, maybe you shouldn't have started this mess."

I slip over his arm and stand up tall (I only measure up to his shoulder on my best days). "Well, *I* didn't use lethal force. Oh but no. You just *had* to throw a ball of ice at me," I sigh.

"It's a good thing I didn't damage that tongue of yours." He smirks down at me. "So, how about some coffee?"

"Not Starbucks. There's only so much I can stand in one lifetime," I groan.

"Fine. Where else did you have in mind?"

"I don't know! This is my first time in New York."

Andrew

She sits down at the table first. I didn't know her hair was that short. She must have just cut it. I bring over our coffees and sit down with her. She sits up and looks at me.

"What?" I ask her.

"Nothing." She looks away and grabs her coffee. "It is just so weird seeing you like this. I mean, you've got a life too. It's not just me." She takes a sip and cringes. Brown liquid drips down her chin.

"What?" I take a sip of mine and do the same. "Oh, that's terrible."

"Give it here," she sputters and reaches for mine. I give it to her happily. She takes it and takes a long sip. "Oh, that's much better." She smiles widely and relaxes into her chair.

I grab her old one and drink it. "How can you drink that? It was practically all java."

"Do you know how many hours of sleep I get? I practically exist on Red Bison and java." She takes an impossibly long sip without a pause to breathe. "And Wi-Fi." She adds.

"That doesn't sound like a very healthy lifestyle."

"This was before I became a superhero."

"Well, when you put it that way." I roll my eyes at her. She's insane.

"So," She takes a sip of coffee in the middle of her sentence. "Why did you want to meet, Mr. Smithe?"

"Mainly just to talk things over and to see whether you're still alive or not."

"And what else?" she sighs. She knows me too well. "Are you going to make me explain everything, again?"

"It's just- there's so many good things happening for you right now. Why can't you just continue being a superhero?" I blurt out. "You've worked so hard for this. You can't quit now! I won't let you!" I grab her arm.

She twists her wrist away from mine. "I've explained this one too many times already, Tonnerre. I can quit and I am. And if you think there's been 'so many good things' happening for me, you do not know me at all. My birthday is coming. Not even I can stop it. I can't keep pretending like nothing is wrong and neither can you." She gets up with her coffee and walks out of the store. The door slams behind her.

Rikki

That idiot just makes me so angry. His idiot head is so, so dense! How many times am I going to have to explain this to him?

I look behind myself to make sure that he's not following me then I look up. He could be anywhere.

I smear the crappy makeup off my face and put on some black shades I had from San Fransisco.

My coffee tastes tainted all of a sudden. I drop the rest in a nearby trash can (the whole city kind of is one) and make my way back to the hotel.

Stupid, stupid, stupid. I tap my foot on the elevator ride up to my room. I barely even notice my phone beep in my pocket.

I huff and stick my tongue out at it. If it's from Tonnerre, I'm personally sending it through a trash compressor. My finger taps the green button quickly. Oh. It's from Penny. I guess I don't have to spend another two thousand dollars on buying another useless fruit object.

'Where are you??? We have lab!!!!'

I frown at the message. I don't. It says right here on my schedule. I've still got... No, I don't! I have a lab session! Why is my schedule this confusing?

The elevator stutters to a stop at my floor and I sprint out to change into something else.

By the time I make it to the lab that's practically across town, everyone's already started. I know we're not working on Achelium currently but that doesn't mean that they aren't storing it here.

Aaron's eyes bite at me from the front of the room. I let out my breath and smile lopsidedly back. He stomps right over to me until we're practically touching.

"Where have you been?" he hisses.

"I was at the... laundromat! Doing my laundry. It took a while and by the time I realised what time it was, I was very late already. And then it took me-"

"Okay, okay," he sighs and holds his fingers to his forehead for a second then drops them. "It's fine. You're here. You're not dead. Yet."

"Yes, yet," I breathe and smile.

I rush over to the only open spot, the one beside William, and drum my fingers on the table. "What are we doing?" I whisper to him.

"I have no idea," he murmurs back. "They told us to make ourselves comfortable and that was it."

"Then how does everyone look so busy?"

"It's difficult for nerds like us to get 'comfortable'. Too many traps have happened in our pasts."

"True. Very true." I drop my backpack on the seat and pull out my laptop. I launch my chemistry program and check my formula. *My baby.*

"What's that?" He peers over my shoulder. "Some kind of code?"

"No, it is a magic recipe for growing things magically." I wipe my hand across the keyboard as a grand gesture to display my beautiful masterpiece.

"You're the one who made the growth formula?"

"Uh, yes?"

"That's incredible!" He walks up to my computer and looks at it more closely. "I would have never thought of this. Then again, my fortes lie in technology, not chemistry."

"Science." I wave my hands in the air like a rainbow.

***

A new lady wearing a snow white lab coat walks in through the open door in the back. She nods at Aaron. He scoffs back and taps his watch.

"Alright students. I don't like you and you won't like me but we're going to have to work together if we don't this thing to go to hell." Her voice seems to be so full of excitement and happiness and then you listen to her words. "I'm the head scientist at Smithe Industries and I've been sent here by the boss to try and teach you kids some real science. You may address me as 'Head Scientist', 'Queen of Knowledge', or my personal favorite, 'The Chemistry Master'. Anyway, you're going to listen to me or I'll give you such a beating-"

"Actually, corporal punishment got banned a long time ago. You're not allowed to use any physical violence against our students," Aaron coughs.

"Fine," she grunts but mouths 'yes' at us and makes a punch movement.

"I saw that you know. Elizabeth, if you use any force, you could get us and yourself sued." Aaron walks up to her an taps his clipboard impatiently.

She grunts in response and continues. "You are going to listen to me, or else." She drags her finger across her neck when she's sure Aaron's not looking. "Anyway, at the beginning, we'll have each of you work in groups or whatever." She flicks on some spectacles asif they were sunglasses and grabs a clipboard on the side of the glass benchr. "And then we're going to split you into groups depending on your specialty. You chemists will be working for me and- Whoa! Who made a Growth Formula? Now that's impressive." She smoothes down her dirty blonde hair with her hand.

William tries to speak but I slap him on the cheek before he can yell *'Rikki did!'*

"Anyway, the chemists in this group will work for me in decoding and altering Achelium."

William opens his mouth to ask what it is. "What is-"

"Those of you who don't know what that is are not chemists and will be asked kindly to keep their little mouths shut. Thank you," she responds quickly like the pop of a balloon. "Anyway," She flips through the clipboards pages again. "This is useless," she mumbles under Aaron's radar. "Just get into groups of what you generally do. Chemists over here." She points to her table. "Techies over there." She points to mine and William's bench. "And the rest can go wherever. I don't really care."

Everyone shuffles into their assigned groups including me. I pick up my computer, lift it over my head, and place it gingerly on the bench at the front. The rest of the chemists surround the table as well. Elizabeth looks at every one of us and judges us separately.

332

"So, which one of you made this growth formula?" She slams her hand on the table and asks.

A boy with long and loose brown hair speaks up. "There's no way anything like that's possible, I mean, really? They've *got* to be kidding," he laughs. "But my explosion recipe *is* the real deal." He looks to Elizabeth for approval but she frowns at him sighs.

"Uh, what's it made of? Alkali metals?" I ask him.

"What?"

"I mean, are your bombs made of condensed and/or powdered Alkali powders? Oh, wait, no. that would only work with water. Never mind." I smile my usual lopsided smile awkwardly.

"No, that's exactly what they're made of." He nods and smiles at me. "What'd you make to get into the program?"

"Oh, I made a growth formula." I smile widely at his disbelief.

"Really? Then why did you enter it here instead of using it to really help people?" Elizabeth smiles at me evilly like I'm cornered.

"Actually, I haven't made it to animal testing yet due to a lack of rats and mice and I would prefer not to cause any catastrophic events with something that should save millions." I tap my finger on the table.

She nods with an approving smile and writes something on her clipboard. "Very good, Ms. Dubois, very good."

***

So, that was *fun*. Elizabeth pretty much just judged us the entire time and wrote down who was 'scientific' and who wasn't (I checked and I was under scientific).

I dive into my bed and lie down. I pull the pillow over my face and scream into it. "Mon Dieu! Pourquoi ça continue?" I kick my legs into the mattress and stand on my knees. I smooth down my short-ish hair and breathe in the hotel air. I look out the window and watch the snow fall. I sigh and click my phone open. No new messages. I lie down on my bed again and sigh.

We're supposed to work with Achelium tomorrow. I'm working for Tonnerre's mom. I scream into my pillow again. Why is my life so awkward?

The hotel door clicks open and Penny wheels in.

"There are some real crazies at this hotel," she mutters and looks at the closed door. "You could hear the screams from the hallway. Sounded like a tortured cat."

"That was me." I groan, still covered with the pillow.

"Well, you've certainly got Rikki's awkwardness." She leans on the edge of my bed and pulls the pillow away from my grasp. She's smiling sweetly at my pain.

I frown and grab at the pillow.

"Is this about the date you had earlier today because it can't be that bad or is it about arriving late and making a fool of yourself? Or is it because everything's just going downhill and there's this unspeakable event coming up and you have no idea what to do about it." She looks right into my soul and tears out every truth. This could be my chance to finally talk about how I *really* feel.

"You don't know anything about me!" I yell in French, ripping the pillow from her hands and throw it over my face.

"So, you're working on Achelium tomorrow, huh?"

"Yes," I mumble, switching back to English. "And that wasn't a date. It was just a casual meetup. A *rendezvous*, as we say in French."

"The way you say it, it sounds like you were there for drugs," she snickers.

"What? I would never! I hate alcohol, do you think I can stomach drugs?" I exclaim in horror.

"So, innocent," she whispers as she wheels over to her bed and lies down on it.

I sigh and close my eyes. The world really sucks.

***

The sun's light shines right on my eyes for once. I grunt and get up slowly and look around my room.

"Pourquoi suis-je encore là?" I yell and lie back down in a huff. Penny's not in her bed and her wheelchair's gone. Lucky her. I sigh and roll off my bed into some other clothes. Today: a tank top, the dark blue skirt, tights, and the heels.

The only thing I've got today is lab which isn't for another half hour. I sigh for a longer time and open my messages. Nothing. I sigh angrily and throw my phone on my bed with such a force it bounces off the sheets.

I trudge grumpily to the bathroom and look in the mirror. I blink my eyes once before sticking the brown contacts into my eyes. Does Penny have any makeup that can fix my ugly? I look down at her black bag and pick up a tube of lipstick. Nah. My ugly is mine. I drop it back in. I smooth out my hair and flip it around for the perfect angle. I pucker up my lips and pat them with my fingers. The cut I had a few weeks ago is nearly gone. I'm glad it didn't scar. I've got enough of those.

I walk out of the bathroom and stuff all my things into my suitcase. I already know I'm not going to leave yet, but it calms my nerves a little. I sit on top of it and watch the clock fold from nine-twelve to nine-fifteen. I sigh and stand up. This skirt's a little short.

I walk around my room for a solid five minutes and ponder breaking my leg so I can go home. I've already come this far so it would be stupid to turn down an opportunity like this. I know my formula has peaked Coleen Smithe's attention so there's a chance she'll steal it to finally perfect her Achelium. But Tonnerre's Achelium is perfected so she must already know how. And that means that she's just choosing not to give the victims the thing that won't degrade their body to a disabled state. That is just messed up. But then again, why would she want my formula?

'Make the better parts bigger' That's what Kai said, right?
Maybe Achelium isn't powerful enough for her. Maybe she wants it more concentrated. Wait no, all she does is work with Achelium. She's just looking for a cure. It's not like she's Vaccine. Vaccine's dead.
Tonnerre killed him.

***

Achelium is a chemical that's relatively new in chemical standards. It was first found somewhere in Central Africa by an archeologist who died because of it about a week later. The rest of the expedition who's main focus was actually looking for diamonds, recognized its volatile actions and took the necessary precautions. The shipped it to New York to be analyzed by a lab. The lab confirmed that it was a new substance and rightfully dubbed it 'Achelium' from the archeologist's name which was Achan Leroy. Achelium is used commonly used around the world by labs but is known best by the events in San Francisco. Or that's what Wikipedia says, at least.

I sigh and close my computer. I look over at the three empty tubs of ice cream. I ate all of them in under fifteen minutes and that's not even my record.

I throw my computer into my bag and walk out of the hotel room. C'mon Rikki, you can do this. All you have to do is pretend to acknowledge whatever they're saying and you're golden. I walk into the lab one minute early and open my formula.

"Good morning, Ms. Dubois. How are you on this excellent morning? Are you working on your formula?" Elizabeth asks with a coffee pressed up to her lips.

"Uh, yeah," I mumble. There are a lot of ways to say 'yes' in English. Yeah, sure, yep, yes, and so on. In French, there are like two: *ouais*, and *oui*.

"You said you haven't moved on to living things yet, right?"

"Well, I have tested on plants and I thought that that is what is really necessary because-"

"Okay, you make a good point." She waves her hand in front of me to cut me off. "But you don't need to drone on."

"Yes, you're right," I mumble again and shut the lid of my laptop. The rest of the kids are starting to fill the room.

"Kyle!" Elizabeth breathes. "Is that a dog?" she yells at the brown-haired boy from yesterday who's holding a little fur ball of joy.

"Aww, it's so cute!" I moon in French and walk up to it. It's a little golden corgi-dog. "Mon Dieu, you are adorable," I tell it as I stroke its hair. It smiles up at me with its little tongue waving. "I think I'm in love," I whisper in French.

"His name's Weber," Kyle says with a smile. Elizabeth just frowns at the dog. Weber barks happily.

Aaron walks up to our bench. "Kyle, is that a dog?" He points his pen at Weber.

"Yes, he's a corgi," Kyle responds. "His name is Weber, like the barbeque."

336

"Kyle, I have no idea how you snuck that dog into New York, let alone the lab, but I'm going to have to ask you to leave it in your hotel room or at a dog sitters club," Aaron responds with Elizabeth smiling.

"But Aaron," I look up at him and instantly regret my decision. "Please? He's just a dog. Just this once? Please?" I ask him and do my best impression of 'puppy dog eyes' instead of freaking out. Weber backs me up.

Aaron's face seems to explode with color before he turns away. "Fine. But only for today," he mutters sheepishly and walks away quickly.

"Merci beaucoup!" I yell at him with a smile. He flinches and continues walking towards the next bench. "So fluffy," I whisper as I puff up Weber's hair.

"Do you want to hold him?" Kyle asks and holds him down to my chest.

"Yes," I breathe and hold the dog like a little baby-child. "Who's a good little boy?" I tickle his belly. "You are," I coo.

Elizabeth grimaces as she looks at me. "Those things are filthy little creatures, you know. They're no better than coyotes or foxes."

"Well, I think he's adorable," I tell her as I scratch him behind his ears. I hold him up to her face and he sticks his tongue out like dogs usually do. "Just scratch his belly."

"If that will make you stop," she moans.

"Sure." I nod at her and press Weber further to her face. She holds up two fingers and scratches him between his two front legs. He barks happily.

"There. Are you happy?" she asks as she wipes her fingers on her lab coat.

"Very happy."

***

All we really did today in the lab was just brief what Achelium does and its dangers and the safety precautions. It was pretty basic. After that, we finally introduced ourselves to each other. Kyle, Rina, and Paul are in my group not including Elizabeth. We all pressured Elizabeth to take us to the Empire State Building during our break.

That's why we're wandering aimlessly through New York's massive and loud streets.

"I don't know how you kids get me in these situations," she grumbles from the head of the group.

"It's just because you love us!" Rina chirps. Weber barks happily.

"Remind me why we brought that stupid animal again." Elizabeth glares at Weber's green collar which I hold firmly. He keeps chasing after birds and squirrels. He may seem like he can fit in a dryer but he has the strength and power of ten.

"We don't him crapping all over the lab, do we?" Kyle asks her. "Besides, he needs to stretch his legs and so do we."

"He can go wherever he wants. This whole city is a trash can." I smile. Weber sniffs at some ice and barks at it.

"New York isn't that bad." Rena looks at me. She says she's lived here all her life. "You just need to get used to it first. In a way, it's truly beautiful or it isn't. It's all about perspective."

"Preach," Paul says. Their arms are linked at the elbows. It's only been a day but they're already a couple.

Weber sees a pigeon and throws me towards a vent on the sidewalk covered with feather-rats.

"Weber, no!" Kyle yells but its too late.

My head slams into someone's coat and Weber skids to a stop.

"Aie." I take a step back and rub my forehead.

"Rikki?" Aaron asks. "Are you alright?"

"Oh, I'm fine." I smile up at him. "I've been through worse, really," I reassure him. "Not that you're bad or anything. I mean you're really good. It's just this is nothing compared to some injuries I've had." Oh god. Why is my life this awkward? Personally, I blame the universe.

"Oh, okay then. That's good." He smiles then frowns quickly. "Not that it's good that you got hurt, that's pretty terrible. I mean that-"

"Is this what romance has come to?" Elizabeth towers over us. "You two? The world really has been going to hell, hasn't it?" Weber barks in agreement and scampers over to her side. "Finally, something we agree on. Even if you are a dog." She tickles him between the ears. "Come on." She grabs me by the wrist and drags me forwards. "Don't say goodbye to him," she whispers in my ear. "Guys like that don't come around every lifetime."

"Uh, Aaron, would you like to come to the Empire State Building with us?" I ask him.

"Sure!" He chases after us and walks beside me happily.

Elizabeth lets go of me and takes Weber's collar.

***

"Well, here it is. Can we go back now?" Elizabeth grumbles.

"What? No!" Rina exclaims. "We need to go to the top! otherwise, you guys will never have the full New York experience!"

"Yeah," Paul mutters. "We should go to the top."

"Sounds good to me." Aaron smiles. He's a lot different without his clipboard. "Let's go."

We walk up to the building's front entrance on fifth avenue. We walk through the spinning doors as a group and look at the piles of people waiting to get to the top.

"Wow. That's a lot of people," Kyle says.

I nod and walk over to a wall.

"Rikki, what are you doing?" Rina asks.

I high-five the wall and walk back to the group. "Nailed it!" I yell in French.

"Good job!" someone in the line responds, also, in French.

"Merci!" I yell back at them and do a little bow before running back to the group.

"What was that?" Aaron smiles.

"Well, I thought since we would most likely not be going to the top of the tower, I may as well touch the wall of the tower that five people died in the making of." I shrug. "It was on my, how you Americans say, 'bucket list'."

"You wanted to touch the wall of the Empire State Building?" He asks me.

"It's only fifty-seven meters higher than the Eiffel Tower." I shrug. "Which is much better than this building, by the way. When you come to Paris call me up and I'll give you a tour."

"How do you know I'll come to Paris?"

"You can't live a good life without visiting France at least once. It's science." I smile.

"Of course, it is," he laughs. His watch beeps. "Oh, crap. We need to get back to the lab, everyone."

We all stumble our way through the snow, with a few snowball fights in between, back to the lab.

Aaron stops unbeknownst to the piece of dried mistletoe above him.

"Stay. There." Penny wheels up behind us.

"What?" He asks and looks up. "Oh."

Penny grabs my jacket. "Hey, what are you-" She shoves me right at Aaron. "Aah!" I yell.

"So, do you have this tradition in France?" He asks, his warm breath wafting down on my face.

"Yes, on New Years, you kiss your friends and family," I blurt out.

"Here, it's bad luck if you don't kiss someone under the mistletoe."

"I know." I think my brain has stopped working. "You told me in San Francisco."

"Oh yeah, that." He smiles awkwardly. "That was weird."

"Oh my god, just kiss already!" Penny yells at us from her wheelchair.

***

After that, we kind of left for the lab in a hurry. That little circumstance was awkward and 'adorable' (Penny put it that way) but it won't do anything when Mrs. Smithe has our heads.

I grabbed Weber's leash and stayed my distance from Aaron who also was still pretty red in the face. Once we got to the lab, we stayed in our respective groups and stayed relatively quiet. Or at least I did.

My mind won't stop repeating that same scene in my head. I hide my face with my hand and focus on my computer while Elizabeth talks about safety measures for the three hundred time. I spin my cursor around to enbiggen it.

"Rikki, do you have anything to add?" Elizabeth asks, turning everyone's attention on my face.

"Have fun?" I'm a mess right now. Literally. My hair's everywhere and so is Weber's. Plus, my face has quite noticeably changed from a dark brown to a deep red like that of a raspberry.

"Sure, have fun," Elizabeth says and rolls her eyes. "Anything else?"

"Don't expose your skin to Achelium?" I remark but she still frowns at me. "Don't drink it? I know your country has a thing for drinking bleach but you should not drink Achelium. It is very dangerous."

"Close enough." She shrugs and continues rambling about safety procedures. I sigh and continue to play online chess.

A loud bang goes off in the hallway and both me and Weber perk up. "What was that?"

"Rikki, if you're going to ignore the lesson, at least do it quietly." Elizabeth glares at me.

"No, I thought I heard fireworks or something. Didn't you guys hear that?" Another two go off except closer. Weber and I twitch. "Did you at least hear that one?"

"Those were gunshots," Elizabeth mutters under her breath. "Everyone!" She addresses the entire lab. "Get under the benches! Something's going on!"

"But there should be security stationed everywhere outside the lab. We should be safe." Aaron flips through his clipboard at the front of the room. He's closest to the doors.

"There have been three shots already! How many security guards are there?" I ask him. He flips through the clipboard again and just looks at me with fear placed evenly all over his face. I grab a ring stand (google it) from our bench and jam it between the knobs of the door. "I hope this *handles* it," I mumble in French.

Something slams against the door but the ring stand holds.

"Merci," I whisper to the higher powers at work here.

"Boss, there's something blocking the door here!" Someone shouts in English from the other side of the door. Their voice is muffled so they've got to be wearing a mask.

"Did you try kicking it open?" Another one yells. There's more than one gunner.

"Yeah, I kicked them right in the middle like you said!" That's not how you kick open a door! These guys are *idiots*. Obviously, you need to kick the door at the weakest point which is right below the door's handle.

Aaron tugs at my arm and drags me to the nearest bench.

"I can't trust you guys to do anything right," someone new grumbles. "When I said I wanted cheap henchmen, I didn't mean *this* cheap," he mutters harshly and knocks on the door. "Hello? Anyone home?"

"Sorry," someone whimpers. They're also a new voice. "I just thought that- "

"You can't do anything right." The harsh dude grumbles again.

"It's a miracle I have Sergio and Tess to help out when you continuously screw up." Two even newer people grunt in response.

That means at least six people plus guns. And two of them are especially large. Only strong, muscly people grunt. It's science.

***

The harsh dude knocks carefully on the door again. "Are you sure no one's in here?" You can hear the smile in his voice. "We're not going to hurt you, I promise." He's a practiced liar.

"Then why do we have the guns?" Tweedle-dee asks.

"Yeah, didn't you say we were going to shoot them all if they didn't give us the power juice or whatever?" Tweedle-dum asks.

"Or even if they did," Spineless whispers.

"Ugh, why can't you idiots be more like Tess and Sergio? They're quiet and they don't ruin everything."

"That's because you ripped out Sergio's tongue," Someone with a deep, gruff tone mumbles. Someone else grunts as an addition.

Harsh dude sighs. "Can you all just shut up? I'm trying to rob a laboratory here," he groans. He knocks on the doors again. "Hello? Little people, I know you're in here. Come talk to me. If you give me what I want, I can assure you that no harm will come to any of you." He seems to turn around and glare at his band of misfits because he whispers something like a *"Shut up or I'll rip all your tongues out and turn them into an eighties hairstyle."*

You know villains are serious when they bring the eighties up.

Everyone in the room stays dead silent.

"Now, I know at least someone's in here because this door does not lock from the outside. My patience is running a tad thin today if you haven't noticed so it would be incredible if someone could just open this door and hand me that Achelium, it would make everyone's life easier. Not to mention, it would save someone's life," Harsh dude says in a sickly sweet tone.

Once again, no one in the room makes a sound. William pops his head out but someone from his table grabs him before he can say a word.

"Fine," Harsh dude continues. "Sergio, break the door." Sergio grunts in response and the door splinters open. The ring stand clatters to the floor leaving six massive bodies exposed.

"Alright, alright, alright," Tweedle-dum smirks. "Now, we get to business."

"You!" Tweedle-dee yells. Is he pointing to me? I can't see. Oh crap. Oh crap. Oh crap. "Yeah, you!"

"Hey!" William yells. "Let me go!"

"Who else is here? I know there can't be just one of you, kids." Harsh dude says with a smile.

"Don't do it! No one come out! They're not going to touch me! Well, aside from collar I guess which they're grabbing and- "

Someone fires another gunshot and William goes silent.

"William?" I squeal as I spring up from my bench.

Aaron

Someone booms up to our bench and tries to grab Chaos. Her feet leave the ground and kick the person in the face.

"Anyone else?" she laughs in her heavy French accent. Dammit, Chaos, they have guns. You're not invincible. "William, are you alright?"

William grunts from the floor. He's not dead yet. That saves me a lot of paperwork.

"Boss, she's doing karate! What do we do?" One of the dumber ones ask. "She just kicked Tony in the face!"

"You idiots have guns! Use them!" The ringleader yells.

A few gunshots go off and silence rings through the air. No French accent, no karate moves. Just silence.

"Rikki!" I spring up from behind the desk. Yellow cuts through the air around Rikki. She's using her power. "Oh, thank god. She's come to her senses," I mumble.

She looks at her hands in shock and looks around the room. A black shape roughly Rikki's size hits the gunner on the back of the head.

"What." Rikki looks at the person, her eyes as wide as the moon itself.

"Oh, sorry, I don't think I have introduced myself, I'm Corbelle. You're from France, right?" Corbelle holds her hand out to Rikki who's still holding up the power shield. What the hell? I thought Rikki was Corbelle. I even checked underneath her mask.

"Que se passe-t-il," she mutters and shakes Corbelle's hand with nothing less of a face filled with confusion.

"Faites-moi confiance."

"Pourquoi?"

"Are we interrupting something or...?" The head of the gang asks. He's wearing bulletproof armour, ammo, and a black ski-mask. "Because, if you don't mind, I'd like to get back to my heist, please." He cocks a gun at them.

"Oh, allow me to handle this," Corbelle says underneath her dark grey scarf. She's obviously smiling. She spins and kicks the guy in the stomach. His armour doesn't do a lot to protect him from her foot.

"Now you and the Dreamer?" he huffs. "You've got to be kidding."

"Well, often I do kid," Corbelle snaps her fingers. "But I have yet to make a terrible pun today."

"Maintenant, je suis vraiment confus. Que se passe-t-il." Rikki turns to Corbelle. Corbelle just shrugs. Rikki throws her arms into the air and groans. "Pourquoi moi?"

The ringleader coughs. "Start shooting." He nods to his gang who fire a few rounds at the wall behind us. "Who here has access to the chemical vault?" He turns back to the benches. "Do you?" He points at me and I shake my head and duck back down. "Now, I'm starting to get mad." He grumbles. "Whoever you are, if you stand up now, you'll be saving a lot of lives."

"I have clearance," Elizabeth says and stands up. "If you stop firing, you can help yourself to as much Achelium as you want."

"What's Achelium?" one of the stupider gang members ask.

"Finally!" the gang leader says joyously. "Someone who can get me what I want!" He fires his gun up at the ceiling.

"Elizabeth, don't do it!" Rikki yells. "Il est définitivement américain," she adds.

"Yes, she's right, Elizabeth." Everyone seems to aim their guns at Corbelle. "There's no telling what they'll do when they get what they want." Yellow flows through the room again. "So, I'll just be taking this."

"Follow her!" The ringleader yells and several heavy footsteps leave the building.

"Qu'est-ce qui vient de se passer. Sérieusement, qu'est-ce qui vient de se passer?" Rikki says.

Rikki

So, a refresher: William got shot in the foot and sort of passed out, a bogus 'belle showed up (a Bellegus, if you will), and a gang broke into the lab. They tried to fire a few shots at me but failed. The Bellegus couldn't do anything to save me before the power did. It created a shield to protect me from the shots seconds before they hit me. This makes my situation even grimmer. The power reacted without me telling it to which means the Prophecy is even stronger than I could have imagined. It has a will to live which means it's not going to let me die which means I've got immortality for a while. I'll have fun playing in traffic.

The gang that I am currently following through the hallways of the Lab lead by a fake Corbelle (Bellegus). Of course, they don't know I'm following them because I'm amazingly stealthy unlike them. The silent alarm is already ringing which gives them like, what? Fifteen minutes?

"The lab's this way gentlemen," Bellegus says and waves her hands out in front of her. The three muscular and masked bros. How much do they have to work out to get abs like that? "If you look to your right, out the window, you can see the many police cars speeding towards this very lab to arrest you." She smiles.

The harsh dude grabs her by the neck and pins her against the wall.

"Aie," I whisper and wince. That looks like it hurt a lot. It's like what Tonnerre does when he's had more than enough.

"Stop playing games," He hisses in her face. "Where is the vault? Tell me now before-" He taps a walkie-talkie on his side. "-I tell my henches to start shooting. I don't want to commit mass homicide and you don't want it to happen. How'd you like to keep it that way?"

"Fine," she huffs and he lets her down. The continue you their merry way down the hallway with me skittering behind them in the ceiling panels. Just call me *The Rat*.

Their footsteps pause again and I slide another panel back and peer down.

"Which way?" Harsh dude asks. They're at a fork in the hallway. They can go straight or to the right and veer off the hallway.

"Uhm, I'm not sure. This was about buying time, actually." She balances the walkie-talkie on her finger and throws it against the wall.

Harsh dude looks like he's about to blow a fuse. "Do you know who you're talking to?" He takes a step towards her.

"Some second-rate villain? You can't even afford a decent gang," she laughs at him. "Did you really think you could get away with this? I mean, really?" She lifts her arm and traps him and the three other muscle peoples in a yellow bubble. So, she has my power too. Maybe it really was her who created the shield, not me. I don't if this frightens or reassures me. Or maybe it does a little bit of both. What emotion is that? Did I just create a new emotion?

"Let me out!" He pounds on the yellow.

"Uh, no." She starts to walk away and looks straight up at me into my eyes. She smiles. "Bonjour, mon ami. Voulez-vous descendre?" I shake my head violently and slowly close the panel slowly. I do not like this.

I creep away until I get a few doors away from the room in which two idiots hold guns and point them at teenagers. Yellow surrounds the air behind me.

"Pensiez-vous que vous pourrez vous débarrasser de moi si facilement?"

I freeze. "...Oui," I mutter.

***

The fake Corbelle settles in behind me. "Shouldn't you be saving the people?" I ask her in French. There are two gunners in the room and both of them are idiots to a certifiable degree.

"They're not in much danger." She grins. "Their guns are on safety. They're not very useful unless armed."

"Why are you here, I mean, I thought you were me or I'm you? What is this? My brain is extremely confused and this is basically like hydrogen peroxide."

"Don't go that far." She grabs me by the shoulders and shakes me.

"What are you?" I grab her by the shoulders and start shaking her. "What is even happening? You're a me but you can't be me because I'm me and-"

She pulls off her mask and it's me looking back at myself.

"This doesn't help!" I groan. "It only makes me more confused! You can't be me because I'm me and-"

"I'm you and you're also you and-"

"That logic doesn't check out!" I yell at her. "Are you a clone? A twin I never knew I had? A me from a different universe? My mother?"

"Please, you know none of those are possible. Besides, our mother still has no idea where we are."

"Then what are you?" I throw my arms up.

"I thought you would be able to tell!" She throws her arms up.

"And why would you think that? I'm an *idiot*!" I bring my hands down to her and gesture at her face.

She slaps my face. "No, you aren't. If you were, how'd you get into this program?"

"Plagiarism is a serious problem affecting this world's youth-"

She slaps my face again. "Rikki, I swear to god," she warns me with a finger as she draws her hand back. "What do you think I really am?"

"Someone who likes to slap people in the face." I frown and rub my cheek.

She slaps me on the other side of the face. "Rikki," she warns me again with a finger.

"Fine. Obviously, you're a copy or a double. Otherwise, I've got no idea what you are. Unless..."

"Yes?" She leans closer.

"Unless you're a fangirl," I mumble.

She slaps me again. "Try again," she hisses.

"You're an illusion." I sigh and rub both my cheeks carefully. "That hurt, by the way."

"Wow, you got it right." She sounds genuinely surprised. "I was starting to think you were just a clown."

"Wait, then who's controlling you?"

***

"Oh, you can meet him later. Now, I need to stop a wannabe robbery." The fake Corbelle smirks at my confused frown.

"Why didn't you do that ten minutes ago? Or maybe right before William got shot in the foot!" I yell at her.

"Oh, excuse me, do you have any idea how difficult it is do this? I mean, never mind being an illusion-" I cover her mouth with both my hands.

"You don't have to explain to me. I know. Just go and stop the idiots with the guns, please," I groan.

She nods and flies through the panels onto one of their faces. She's totally stealing my moves, by the way. No one else does that except for me. It's one of my signature moves. I mean, I'm cool if she borrows it, I just want to point out that I invented it.

The second idiot tries to fire his gun at her but, thanks to the safety, only proceeds to pretend to fire.

"Oh no, your gun isn't working. What a shame that is." She kicks it out of his hands. It skids across the floor to where William lies. I'm pretty sure he's either in shock or in a pain-induced sleep. Neither of those are fun. Don't ask me how I know that.

Tweedle-dum looks at the gun, then at the fake Corbelle, then at the door. I drop down just as he makes a run for it and land straight on his back.

"Whoops. I'm sorry, I'm such a klutz," I laugh in English.

He groans under my weight. Corbelle runs out and looks at the dude then at me.

"Good job," she says in French.

"Thank you, and you too. Also, I was wondering, since you're me and I'm you, does that mean you can read my thoughts?"

"That's not how it works."

"Are you sure?"

"Honestly, I didn't think it was possible to annoy myself but I guess you've just accomplished it. Congratulations, Rikki."

"Thank you. I'd like to dedicate this award to my good friend Maya and also to Tweedle-dum. Because of your idiocy, Tweedle, I

349

wouldn't have had the chance to show off my skills." I stand up and use his body as a pedestal. I press my arms at my heart and have a moment of silence.

"Seriously, stop."

"Fine." I shrug. "But you can never silence my speech, no matter how aggravating and annoying it is!" I throw one arm into the sky and look firmly at her.

"Just go, the police are coming," she sighs and grips her forehead.

"Alright, toodle-oo." I smile and walk off the dude. He tries to get up and reaches weakly for the fake Corbelle's ankle. I frown and punch him down. "And stay down."

I dash down the hallway and throw the door of the women's bathroom and spin in. I run up the side of a brick wall and flip off of it for no real reason.

She was pretty much telling me to go and search the city for whoever was controlling her, right? I'm pretty sure she was.

***

New York isn't that different from Paris if you get over the fact on how much it sucks and the other dozen cons. When it's dark, it still lights up, it still has muggers.

I leap off a building and chase the traces of light. If I created a perfect image of myself, where would I hide? I pull my scarf tighter and dig my cold fingers into the deep pockets of my black zip-up sweater. I look down at the flashing lights and moving people in Time's Square and try not to get dizzy from the height.

It's started snowing again. On the other side of the skyscrapers, a moving beige shadow dashes across the roofs at an equal speed.

"Hey, you!" I yell at them. "Yeah, you!" I grab a flashlight from my pocket and shine it on them. They stop and stare at me. They seem to be confused but run over on what looks to just be plain air.

"Were you just calling me?" he asks and looks me over, blue sneakers and all. "You don't seem like the type to climb a building in the middle of the night."

"So, there's a type?" I look him over with his long, golden curls and white getup without a mask. Is he wearing a built-in headband?

He sighs. "You're the Carmen girl, right? the 'ultimate destroyer'?"

"Hey, I'm not going to become Chaos! I found a loophole! Why does everyone keep bringing it up?" I yell and throw my arms up.

"There's no way of avoiding something as big as the Prophecy, you should know that." He crosses his arms. "They told me so."

"They? Oh no, don't tell me you're insane. I cannot stand any more insane people, I tell you." I groan and pull my face.

"What? No! It's the- yes, I can tell her! I know her, besides, what could you have against her?"

I take a step back and stealthily drop down to a lower awning of the massive building.

"Hey, where'd she go?"

I run away as fast as I can without making a sound (I can go pretty fast while also being perfectly silent). He catches up with me and drops down from his invisible walkway of crazy.

"It's probably not the smartest thing to hide from a guy who can see the future." He smiles and taps a weird wristwatch on his wrist. I twist in the air, kick him in the face, and yank the bracelet from his arm. I hope this is what controls his crazy powers.

I run away and jump off the roof to another. He stops where he is and looks kind of regular. His white costume's gone, replaced with blue jeans and a black shirt. His golden locks have also been cut down to a few measly brown stubs.

"Come back! I need that!" he yells at me from his ledge.

"As a famous man once said: 'If you're nothing without it, you shouldn't have it!'" I yell back and happily skip away. I wait until I'm out of eyesight before sliding the little bracelet of quartz onto my wrist. Lights explode around me like white fireworks and the world spins like a carousel. I fall but still feel the ground underneath me. I suffocate but still breath the air in my lungs.

"Welcome to The Infinity, Chaos," three voices say warmly at once. "We are the Fates."

"Okay, okay, okay," I mumble in French. "Can I be the first to ask what the hell is going on?"

"What is there to question? We are all that is and all of what will ever be." They say at once, matching my French.

They each have six arms, clear skin, and wide, gaping, circular eyes. Their wide mouths are drawn into wide smiles spilling with a clear, blue light. They almost look like really fancy fountains.

"First of all, you're all speaking simultaneously which is completely creepy. Second of all, the three Fates don't exist! You're all just myths!"

Their clear, blue eyes flare a deep, scarlet shade of red. Almost like blood. Their long arms curl and their even longer fingers curl into tighter fists.

"Third of all, I'm not Chaos. I found a loophole," I insist.

"Oh. Is that what you think?" They ask me with devilish grins, releasing all signs of anger from their bodies.

"Well, yeah. There's a loophole, right?" I take a step back and land on something squishy. The whole ground is basically a pillow. "Where am I?"

They all cackle wildly at me. "When the Hurly Burly is done-"

"No, Macbeth is dead, don't you remember? We told that to the Shakespeare fellow," they argue passively with each other.

"Then, he made a play off of it. Don't you remember?"

"Oh, yes. That fellow. His name was Shakespeare, wasn't it?"

"Yes, I believe it was. Hasn't passed away in your world?" They turn to me in a single moment. "Yes, he did." They answer their own question.

"What other world is there?" I ask them.

"The trillions of other planets in the multiverse." They nod and agree with each other. "The same ones that you will ravage."

"What do you mean? I'm *not* becoming Chaos." I make an X with my arms and cross out the idea. "Wait... did you say ravage?"

"Oh, yes," They say cheerily. "Did you really think that what you knew was the real truth?" They cackle again. "Of course not. Chaos represents everything *bad* in everything. Not the good."

"But the book says-"

"Did you really think an ancient book could know as much as us? We are the Fates. We know all."

"Wait, you know *all*? Like, the future and so on?"

"Yes! Exactly! You catch on rather quickly, Chaos."

"Stop calling me that! I'm not Chaos!" I scream at them.

"Chaos, you are Chaos. We know that. It is the future. You cannot change it. It is your fate." They tell me with wide smiles, yellow light spilling out of their mouths and eyes.

"No, it isn't!" I scream at them. Why can't they understand?! I am *not* Chaos! I will *not* become Chaos!

They look me over slowly. "You are alive, therefore, you do not belong here. Yet. Your life will end soon, though."

"What does that mean? What do you mean it will end soon? Are you telling me that I'm going to die? There's no way that that's happening. I mean, I'm sixteen, what could possibly kill me?"

"Those closest to you can betray you at a moment's notice." They point at me.

"What are you talking about? *None* of my friends would betray me." I laugh. "They're my *friends*."

They sigh, annoyed, and look at me. "A Smithe is going to kill you, alright?" they groan in French. "We've already given up too much. We must get rid of her."

"Agreed," they talk amongst themselves. "How did she get here in the first place?"

"She stole our champion's armour, correct?"

"Yes, he's still stuck on the rooftops. Will he be alright?"

"He will be just fine. How shall we send her back? Our world is starting to stake claim to her. Look at her skin."

"What's wrong with my skin?" I look down at my arm only to see the skin fading into bones which are decorated with coloured etching. "Oh my god! What's going on?" I turn to the Fates who link their arms and start spinning through the air. Wind starts pushing me back from their spinning circle. I hit something solid and start folding through it. It stretches behind me and rips open to let me fall on some cold hard concrete behind me. "Aie," I mumble on the cold roof.

Penny

Rikki came back to the hotel room in a huff. She went straight to the bathroom, had a shower and lied down in bed for an hour. After that, she grabbed her phone, walked outside to the balcony, and made phone call for over half an hour. The only words I made out were 'die', 'Smithe', and 'Maya'. Not in that order.

I casually asked her what was wrong and what the phone call was about but she didn't want to talk about it. She's been extra jumpy since then. I tried to hand her a blueberry muffin for breakfast but she threw it out the window as soon as I tapped her on the back. She looks she's seen a ghost. Perhaps of the real Rikki.

She's been walking back and forth through the hallways, bleary-eyed. I don't think she got any sleep last night.

"Rikki?" I ask her. She doesn't respond and just mumbles to herself. "I have coffee." I shake a cup of dirt-black coffee in her face. "You know, this is probably why you're so short."

She grabs it quickly and frantically drowns herself in it. I mixed some Red Bison in it for an extra boost. She mumbles something in French and nods at me. "Thank you. This makes everything better."

"No problem. You looked like you needed a coffee."

"I just heard some very weird news last night and so I stayed up all night contemplating it," she tells me. "It's pretty much impossible but it still is possible."

"What are you talking about? Can you make some sense, please? Is this about hiding Rikki's body?"

"How many times do I have to tell you? I am Rikki! The only way I could have killed Rikki was suicide!" She throws her arms up and walks off. "Stupid Fates," she mumbles as she leaves. What is she talking about? That girl is insane.

Rikki

It took them a few extra hours to make sure the room was still safe and also to fix the doors and anything else that got broken from yesterday. We got let in late but that's probably a good thing. Today we start really using Achelium.

"Hey, is it just me or does Rikki have a frighteningly high amount of energy?" Elizabeth asks the group.

"What are you talking about?" I laugh. "All I had this morning was a coffee."

"What? Rikki, what are you saying? No one can hear you. You're speaking way too fast," Kyle tells me. He didn't bring Weber this morning.

I dash over to another table and say hi to William. Penny follows me back in her wheelchair.

"Sorry, guys," she starts. "Rikki was *really* wiped this morning so I put some Red Bison in her coffee this morning."

"Define 'some'," Elizabeth asks her.

"I put two cans in her coffee."

"What!" Kyle yells. "What were you thinking? She's going to be bouncing off the walls all day!"

"Uh, what's going on?" Aaron walks up and asks us.

"Penny gave Rikki two cans of straight energy plus a coffee," Elizabeth tells him.

He looks down at me. "Rikki, are you okay? You look a little cross-eyed and a really spacey."

"Oh, I'm fine." I wave him away and smile.

"Elizabeth, do you think she's good to work on Achelium today? This probably isn't the ideal situation if one of our star chemists-"

"Not to mention, your girlfriend!" Rina smiles.

"Yeah, didn't we kiss yesterday-" Penny covers my mouth with her hand and shuts me up.

"Sorry, she's not exactly herself right now. It'll probably take her a few hours to get all this out of her system." Penny laughs at his blush.

He walks away quickly and turns to another table. "You two are such dorks." She smiles.

"Did you know that the number centillion has three-hundred-and-three zeros?" I tell everyone. They all groan.

"It's alright, she's making progress," Kyle reassures everyone. "She's already on the fact stage."

"And that about one-hundred-and-fifty people are killed each year by a falling coconut."

"Okay, she knows way too many facts. We need a gag." Elizabeth decides for the group.

"Also, in thirteen-thirty-six, a pig in France was executed for the murder of a child? And, that there is no actual name for a fear of octopi and squids."

"Okay, that last one was a little random," Penny says. "Rikki, are you sure you're alright?"

"Oh, I'm completely chill. Nothing's wrong." I smile. "Everything's good."

"Okay, now I'm really worried." Penny looks up at me. Even in her wheelchair, she's almost as tall as me. "Rikki never says she's alright. She always just mumbles in French or drinks her coffee."

"Who votes on sitting Rikki down until the Red Bison wears off?" Elizabeth asks the table. everyone puts their hands up quickly except for me. "And those opposed?" I raise my hand quickly.

"Hey, that's not fair," I tell them and frown.

"Obviously, Rikki's going to be sitting out until she at least calms down a few thousand notches and until her speech has slowed down enough so we can decipher what she's saying." Elizabeth nods. "Rikki, you can observe but you're not going to be testing today due to your... major difficulties in keeping your hands still."

"I do not!" I yell and grab my hands. They twitch quickly and slightly in my fingers and then it spreads to my arms. "Fine. Maybe I'm having a *little* bit of trouble keeping my hands still, but that doesn't mean I can't handle Achelium."

"Rikki, sit down and just watch." Elizabeth insists and sits me down on a bench. She turns back to the rest of the group. "Alright, I'll be right back with the Achelium, kids. You guys stay right here and make sure she doesn't move or destroy anything." They nod with her as she leaves.

I sigh and tap the counter to the beat of a French pop song. "I'm bored," I groan after what seems like an eternity.

"It's been five minutes."

"Elizabeth should be back by now! What if she gets murdered on the way there and we're the only ones who could know?"

"Rikki, that's highly unlikely."

"But still!"

"Hey, everyone! Was Rikki being good?" Elizabeth pinches my cheek.

"I think the worst of it is over," Kyle says.

"Anyway, I got the juice." She gingerly places a box filled with vials of light blue liquid on the table as everyone puts on gloves and goggles and lab coats. "Is everyone ready?" She pops open a vial.

Penny

Elizabeth pours the liquid into another vial which is more cylinder with a flat bottom and a wider opening. Rikki is practically buzzing with anticipation.

"The worst is over?" I ask Kyle critically.

"At least I wasn't the one who gave her two full cans plus a coffee. What were you thinking?"

"She was really tired and I mean beyond the standards of tired."

"And now, she's as high as kite!"

"I take the blame for that but at least she hasn't spilled any acid all over herself."

"Yet," Elizabeth remarks.

"Come on! Aren't we going to experiment with it already? What about its effects on living creatures and plants and also non-living things?" Rikki practically yells as she bounces up and down.

"Once again, I'm telling you, that was a bad call. I mean, two whole cans? Even I can't drink that much!" Kyle tells me.

"I know, I know. It seemed like a good idea at the time."

"So did giant air balloons filled with helium! Those exploded and so will Rikki!"

"Would the both of you shut up? I'm trying to run an educational program here. It's educational!" Elizabeth yells at us as she concentrates on pouring the blurry, clear liquid that gave me my powers. "Penny, you should get away from here. Achelium has been known to have magnetic probabilities."

"Okay," I say as I wheel away about a meter or so. Elizabeth does some more things with the liquid and makes it explode in a puff of smoke.

"Wow!" Rikki yells. "Do it again! Do it again!" She claps happily.

"Okay, Rikki, calm the heck down," Rina tries to assure her.

"Wait, wait! Combine it with some Alkali powder!" she yells crazily.

"Rikki, that's a terrible idea. Do you want to kill us all?" Kyle asks her.

"But we'd die a fabulous death! What's more fabulous than dying in an explosion?"

"Rikki, I think you've got your adjectives messed up. It's not fabulous, it would be gruesome," Kyle tries to correct her.

"Okay, then we'd die a gruesome death! What's more gruesome than dying in an explosion?" she corrects herself with a smile. She has no idea what gruesome means.

"This was a mistake."

"What time is it? I can't deal with this child for much longer," Elizabeth moans at the group.

"It's about one," Paul checks his watch.

"Wonderful, we can take a lunch break before exploding the lab," Elizabeth smiles. "Just perfect."

"Can we have waffles?" Rikki jumps up on Elizabeth. "With whipped cream?"

"Well, you can have waffles, I was thinking something a little more lunch like, but sure. You can have waffles."

"Yes," Rikki hisses excitedly before running off to cause more havoc elsewhere. It probably wasn't the best decision to give her that coffee.

"Does anyone know how to use a child harness and do they have one?" Elizabeth asks as I wheel closer to the table. She looks at Kyle who only shakes his head sadly.

"How are we going to drag her through New York with her acting like this?" I ask Elizabeth.

"I don't know! Maybe we can bribe her with waffles. She seemed to be interested in that."

"Sounds like a plan."

"Alright." Elizabeth nods her head. "Rikki! We're getting waffles! Are you coming or not?" Elizabeth yells over the crowd of people who are also leaving the room at the same time.

"Coming!" Rikki yells as she runs up to the table in a yellow rain jacket.

"What are you wearing?" Kyle asks her.

"It is my jacket." Rikki smiles innocently. "I stole it."

360

"Okay, waffles," Elizabeth mumbles. "Where do we get waffles in New York?"

"From a waffle store!" Rikki says and jumps in the air. She can jump pretty high for how short she is.

"Let's go," I mumble as I grab her by the yellow sleeve follow her group. "Yo, Aaron! Are you coming or not?"

Rikki

Finally, it's the weekend. After drowning myself in waffles and whipped cream (I actually got most of it in my hair apparently) I was twice as sugared up so they just sent me back to my room to try and sleep it off. Penny told me that that mostly worked but it took a while to force me underneath the covers. About three hours later, I woke up in the middle of the night, brutally confused. I honestly thought that I was having a hangover. But no. Penny accidentally gave me two cans of pure energy and a coffee. This is just great.

Now, it's about nine in the morning and she decided to take me out for breakfast to make up for spiking my coffee.

"Really, Rikki, I'm sorry! How many times do I have to tell you?" Elizabeth asks me from the other side of the wooden table covered with cheeseburgers. I couldn't stand any more waffles. Penny said I packed down about seven full waffles plus whipped cream and toppings before running off to go and pet a dog.

We're sitting at a crappy American burger brand.

"Why did you give me two cans? Would one not be enough?" I ask her, annoyed.

"I know, I know, it's just you seemed really jumpy and tired and I thought you could use an extra kick. Besides, what could have scared you so bad to stay up for an entire night and then some?"

"An 'extra kick' does not qualify as two complete cans of energy drink," I mutter angrily as I stuff my face with fries. Another one of the very few things I've missed about America.

"You're not answering my question. You're avoiding it."

"So what? Maybe it was something so terrifying that it would make your skin crawl. That is an American saying, no?" I stick fries in my teeth to make them look like fangs and wag my fingers in her face.

"Is it something I should be worried about or did you just go out to watch a scary movie?" she asks me and bites the end of her burger.

"Yes, it was just a very scary movie." I nod.

"Hmm," she says thoughtfully and chews even more so. "You know, I think I like my guys the same way I like my fries."

"Oh?" I ask, not really paying any mind and letting my attention rush out the window to chase the yellow taxis and bustling people.

"Tall and blonde like Andrew Smithe."

I spit out my food and look at her in a snap. "W-what did you say?"

"Wait, do you know him personally?" she laughs and puts down her burger. "Tell me everything."

"No! What are you talking about?" I laugh as awkwardly as physically possible. "Why would I know someone like him?" My phone buzzes in my pocket.

"What's he like? I heard he's kind of a jerk." She smiles and takes a sip of her root beer or whatever poison she's filling herself with.

"I think I have to take this." I point to my buzzing phone and stand up from my seat. It's from Maya.

"Sure, you do." Penny grins.

I sigh and step out of the greasy, tacky shop. I press the green button and lean against the glass. "What is it, Maya?" I ask in French with a sigh.

"Corbelle?" Tonnerre asks in clear English. "Is this you?"

"Tu plaisantes," I groan and grit my teeth like he does. "C'est *bien,*" I mumble, sarcasm dripping from my lips like thick blood.

Andrew

This is bad, really bad. There's no way I would be calling her if things weren't as bad as this. Paris is being torn apart from the inside.

"Look, I know you don't want to hear from me or anything but-"

"A large emphasis on anything," she seethes from somewhere across the world. "I thought I made that very clear, Mr. Smithe," she says my last name like it's a curse.

"Corbelle. Stop it," I tell her. "This isn't about me. I know you haven't heard about what's going down in Paris but you need to get over here now. Every one of the Warriors has fallen except for me." I look down at the city which is nothing more than a stain of black against the green of France. "Everything's gone bad."

"I told you, Tonnerre, I'm not a hero. I'm *done*." Her words still echo through my head from our last chat.

"Damn it, Corbelle! Would you listen to me already? Paris is covered in a dark magical fog. Anyone who touches it instantly becomes her slave. I saw it happen personally. All your friends, probably your family, everyone. Reine Blanche is back and she came back with a bang."

"It can't be that bad," she tries to reassure herself.

"No, it's worse. You need to get here *now*. I'm going to do the best I can but I know it's not going to be enough." I press the red button and break the phone's glass. "Dammit," I hiss and drop the phone into the clouds.

Stage two of the plan is a go.

Rikki

This can't be happening, right? I mean, it's practically impossible he's telling the truth, right? He's like the mother of a child star. He'll do anything for attention. Besides, wouldn't I have heard about it if things were this bad in Paris?

I sigh and open my computer. I type 'Paris flights' into my browser, press enter, and spin around in my chair.

"Night flight to Paaaaaaaaaris," I screech in a sing-song voice and turn back to my computer. All flights to Paris are either closed or cancelled. That's more than a little worrisome. It means that Tonnerre wasn't lying. That's *terrible*!

What am I going to do? Clearly, if the airports are closed, that means something is going down in Paris and that no one's getting in that city without having superpowers of some sort. I look down at my hands.

It can't be that bad, right? I mean, Tonnerre's probably just exaggerating again, right? Besides, even if the Warriors can't handle it, I'm sure the army will come and save the day, right? I smile for a second and pretend that everything's alright.

No, it isn't. Paris could be falling apart right now and I'm just standing by.

I sigh, stand up, and walk to the door. I put the deadlock on the door handle and walk over to the centre of the room. I drag every piece of black clothing on, grab my backpack, and sigh. Do I have to do this? I don't want to be a hero... but I have to be one.

I sigh and lift my hands. The power stretches out of my hands and wraps around me. The wind rushes through my hair and I'm falling into Paris.

Tonnerre wasn't kidding at all. The city's covered in a thick, black fog and falling right for it.

***

I sit on a circle of my power and stare down at the cloud of black fog enveloping the city. If I wasn't already terrified of the black smoke, I think I'd probably be crapping my pants thanks to the height.

It looks like whatever the smoke is doing is controlling anyone who walks into it or touches it. So, I'm guessing that if it comes to any immediate contact with your skin, you get infected with Reine Blanche-itis.

I rip some duct tape out of my backpack and wrap it around my waist, wrists, ankles, and anywhere my scarf overlaps. I close all the flaps of my makeshift costume (It's pretty bad). It makes it a little harder to breathe and I can barely see but that means it'll work for a little while. This isn't a permanent solution but it should work long enough to punch Reine Blanche at least twice. Isn't science great when it restricts the functioning of your respiratory system? It really puts the 'fun' in function!

The power swells as I explode into my apartment. Willow isn't here so there's no sense in staying. I breathe in deep and close my eyes for a few seconds. Nope. No weird, dark, mystical fog taking control over me. That's a relief.

I prop open the window and jump out of it. I land on the awning of a coffee shop and look down at the people in the streets. They're just standing there. They're barely moving. Their chests occasionally rise or they start swaying for a second but that's it. They remind me of zombies.

Instantly, all their heads snap and turn right to me.

"Aah!" I squeal and jump back.

"Corbelle," A massive hiss engulfs all of Paris, "It's wonderful to have you join us here," they say in French.

"Oh, crap," I mumble quietly, also, in French.

A mess of blonde hair and blue leather smashes into the concrete in front of me.

"You're kidding, I really hope you're kidding," I hiss and vault up a wall, away from him. "Crap in a hat."

He flies into the space of wall under me and makes the building shake. It throws me off and I land on my back on the cold, hard concrete. I can barely see anything through this scarf but I know that I'm being grabbed.

"Aie!" I yell and jump up onto a yellow platform. "Didn't anyone tell you to keep your hands to yourself?" Tonnerre flies into my back and tears me off the yellow floor.

He throws me into a building. I crash through a window and land in a heap. Pain shoots through my wrist but my makeshift containment suit's holding. For now.

"Okay, that's probably not very good," I groan as I get up.

He smashes through the concrete wall and just hovers there, glaring straight at me.

"What? Didn't you pay the doorman enough?" I ask him in English and use my scarf to wipe the blood away from my lip.

He grabs a chunk of rubble from the building and throws it at my head. I jump up and nearly avoid it before another piece grazes my side and bites at my shoulder.

"I don't want to fight you, Tonnerre. Seriously, don't make me do this."

"I'm afraid Tonnerre isn't here right now, hero," Paris hums.

I lean against the wrong wrist and fall backwards. I must have sprained it while being thrown through a window. Whoops.

I kick another window and flit through it. I run above the streets on my platforms and desperately try to get away from him. Yellow circles around me as a force field just as Tonnerre rams into it. He recovers quickly and grabs it. He flies up and shakes it with me in it. He flies up higher with me in the bubble in his arms. We're at Eiffel Tower height right now. I can see it in the distance.

"Tonnerre, I just want to tell you-" I look down frantically and take a breath. "-that whatever mind control this is, I forgive you, I really do."

"You dumb idiot," Paris laughs. "If this were really mind control, why isn't anyone else in the air helping him?"

"But you're controlling his voice!"

"Yeah, his voice, not his actions," Reine Blanche cackles as Tonnerre drops me. Great. They're both liars.

I break the bubble and open a portal into the Seine. I fall through it and land in brisk, cold water. If it was hard to breath before, this is going to be murder.

I burst through the surface gasping for air and splashing berserkly underneath the weight of my wet clothes and inability to swim.

Another blue flash (This time with red hair) throws me underneath the surface and pushes me farther underneath the water. I can actually touch the bottom of the river now. At least if I die, it'll be at the hands of Maya. Yay. Feminism.

***

Isn't this fun? I just love me some underwater-mortal-combat with my best friend who's being mind controlled to kill me. So much fun. Also, our oxygen is rapidly depleting.

She uses her flight power and tries to torpedo into my stomach. The power opens a portal in front of her and she flies right in. My lungs are about to burst. I try to move my legs and arms to climb up to the surface and to grab some air but my miniature knowledge of swimming is failing me. I struggle to touch the air at the lips of the river. Yellow explodes around me and I draw in the longest breathe I have ever taken. I sit up and take another and look down at the river.

"Merci," I thank the power taking me out of the river and dropping me on the dry concrete. I lie there for a moment and appreciate how non-drowning the air is. I sit up after two seconds and check my suit for any leaks. I'm good. Probably.

I stand up only to get thrown down again by Kai and Kaden.

"Once again," I start in French. "I'm not fighting you guys. I just want to stop whatever she's doing to you."

"It's not mind-control!" Paris shouts at me.

"Well, now it's just obvious," I shrug from the ground.

Tonnerre lands down on my ankle. I hear the snap before I start feeling any pain. I start screaming at the sound and I forget about the power. Before I can do anything, I explode. Everyone who was standing on the river bank flies back as the ground falls apart in a seizure-creating storm of the brightest yellow. My body shoots into the sky as I collapse into a second sun among the dark air and atmosphere. The windless city is neither comforting or settling.

I drop back down into the Seine water which is now only a few feet deep thanks to the nest of submerged rubble and debris. I take a deep breath and look down at my left leg. It's bent the wrong way in a few different spots. I don't think it's supposed to look like that but I'm not a doctor.

I try to edge myself out but flinch when I put any pressure on my wrist.

"Are you kidding?" I scream through a heavy breath. I let out a groan and a few swears of exasperation before rolling onto the dry concrete. I balance on the wall of the Seine that tries to prevent floods from taking over the city like they did before (Read a history book, what are you? Ten?). I hobble up the steps only to see Tonnerre, unconscious and in a heap at the top of them. "You are kidding." I lift up my sprained wrist and put him in a bubble. Maybe if he wakes up he won't be all mind controlled.

I hop along the sidewalks trying to avoid people. Thankfully, I'm not the most distracting thing at the moment so, I'm only being attacked repeatedly by crowds of little children and the elderly. My good hand balances on light gold ovals of my power to keep me from falling on my shattered leg. I groan and shift my attention from the zombies to the top of the Eiffel Tower. A scarlet red floats down from its peak and blends into that solid black that's engulfing the city. That's where she's hiding. Damn, I feel like an idiot, now. Of course, I could never measure up to Tonnerre's ignorance.

I let the power flow through me and take me to the base of the tower. I lean against the metal and regain my footing and breathe. I never knew that having your leg smashed (literally) and your wrist sprained was this tiring. Some of the pain is starting to hit me slowly and benevolently. Look at me using big words. My mom would be so proud.

My stomach isn't feeling too good. I really, really hope I don't have any internal bleeding. That would be *really* bad.

I draw in a heavy breath and shake Tonnerre's bubble.

"Wake up, sleeping beauty!" I yell at him.

He groans and slowly gets up. "I had the weirdest dream," he mumbles, "I thought I was killing you and- it was terrible. I'm so glad it-" He opens his eyes and looks at me. "It was real."

"*Is* real. You still may succeed. The Fates warned me," I mutter and watch the people around us. They're still zombies. I look at the giant clay golems. Are they supposed to be looking out for me? They're not doing a very good job of it. It's like making a chihuahua a guard dog.

"A-are you alright? Your leg is-"

"Shattered. That was you. You landed right on it," I sigh and look up at the red flaring out of the massive tower. There's no way I can climb this but there's no way I can teleport without her noticing. If I want this to stop I'll have to grab her wand which will require the element of surprise in my sorry condition.

"And your costume- "

"Andrew, it is fine. Once this is all over, I will be put into healthcare and they will pump so much anesthesia through me I forget all about the pain and I will feel like a plane. I look forward to it." I take a deep breath and let the power do its thing. Is it wishful thinking to believe that we've bonded over this whole experience? I still hate it but, you know, I think we've bonded at least a little.

I start falling over the tower's needle with Tonnerre in his bubble closely following me. I start screaming. So much for the element of surprise.

***

I flail through the air as I scream. My leg curves in ways I didn't think were possible in the wind. My misplaced body barely misses the gap between more height and the top of the tower. I fall on the fence (More injuries to add to the pile, yay!) and roll over only to fall off and land on the top viewing section of the tower. I land on something like a pile of bones and spandex.

"Aie," I groan wearily and look up. I'm getting way to bruised to keep on doing this. At least Tonnerre's safe in his bubble. I sigh and struggle to get up. Reine Blanche had better be up here or I swear I'm just going to explode something.

I balance on my one good leg and look at the pile of white fabric and blonde hair I landed on. Oops.

"Please don't be dead. Please don't be dead. Please don't be dead." I reach down and grab her wand. It fades into dust in my hands and drifts down onto the rusted metal.

"That's not supposed to happen," Tonnerre says blatantly and looks down at the crumple of Reine Blanche.

"What are you talking about?" I ask him in English. "What wasn't supposed to happen?"

"Alright, you've officially annoyed me," A clearly feminine voice says in French as walks up. The *real* Reine Blanche crosses her arms over her chest and looks me over.

"I get that a lot."

"Aren't you a sight for sore eyes?" she laughs as she walks around my attempted fight-ready stance. "Wow, he really did a number on you, didn't he?" She smiles and looks up at Tonnerre who practically whimpers. So much for chivalry.

My fists flare up with a yellow energy that sharpens into an épée. I've been itching for an excuse to use my wondrous expertise in fencing. What I lack in swimming I make up for in sword-fighting.

"Whoa, calm down, Corbelle. I am not here to fight you quite the opposite, actually. I have a proposition." She smirks and waves her wand through the black air.

My bright yellow épée dissipates back into the presence around me. So much for that plan.

"Go on, I'm listening." I tighten my fists and loop the power around my wrists just in case.

"I'll do away with all this miasma and darkness and evil if you do one little favour for me," she taps her wand against her finger.

"And that would be what? Washing your laundry for a year? Mowing your lawn for six months? I'm on the edge of my seat here."

"No, I want your power. If you let me funnel all of this-" She circles her wand through the air. "-into you, I won't expand its borders. I'll give Paris back its freedom and this will be the last the world will hear of me. That's all you have to do for me," she says happily and continues to tap her wand against her finger. She knows I don't have a choice either way.

"And if I refuse? You'll level Paris and then the world?"

"Wow, you do catch on quickly. That's right but don't worry, it's really only a small thing, right? Just be my slave and I won't hurt anyone ever again. Think of what a hero you'll be! No one would dare think of you as a thief or as a villain! Corbelle! The greatest hero of the world!" She grabs my shoulder like Willow does.

I think about it for a second and shake my head.

"What would you do with it? The power, I mean," I ask her.

"That shouldn't worry you. I said I wouldn't hurt anyone, didn't I?" she says sweetly. "Besides, it's not like you have any other options." She starts to dig her nails into the skin of my costume.

"You're right," I sigh. "You are."

"Of course, I am." She smiles sickeningly sweetly. "Now take a few steps back, dear." I do as she says and hang my head. Her wand flares as she waves it in the air. Its tip shivers a dark red like that of the shade spilling out of the top of the tower. In turn, I release my control over the bubble I'm holding Tonnerre in.

"There. Do it."

The blood-red fire shoots out of her wand like loud fireworks and flies into the sky like them too. The black fog pours into my mouth and seeps into my skin. Tonnerre makes it just in time to throw her out of the way and the black fog snaps at the wand.

"Merci, Dieu," I mutter as I breath in the fresh air.

Andrew

Corbelle grabs Reine Blanche's wand and throws it over the side of the tower.

"Oops," she laughs and covers her mouth like she just started a nuclear war. "I am *such* a klutz, yes?" She watches Reine Blanche's horrified expression.

"What have you done?" Reine Blanche screams as the darkness fades from the air and the blue sky reappears from hiding. She breaks free from my grip and lunges at Corbelle. Reine Blanche grabs Corbelle by the collar and pins her up against the chain fence.

"Aie! What are you doing?" Corbelle yells.

Reine Blanche punches Corbelle on the face and then again in the stomach before I can grab her. She scratches me and pulls my head closer to her mouth.

"I thought you were with us," she hisses in my ear. "Your family." She breaks away from me as Corbelle watches. Reine Blanche climbs up the fence and jumps off. A company hovercraft flies underneath her and catches her feet.

"Non!" Corbelle yells and looks over the edge. "Why didn't you grab her?"

"I-" I try to stammer.

"Wait, you're not being affected by the air, are you? I think her spell has stopped working! Yes! we saved the day!" She throws her arms up in the air and falls over. "Oh, right. I am injured."

"We need to get you to a hospital, Corbelle." I try to pick her up but she refuses.

"No. Get Sage. She'll take me. She knows my name and it helps that we are the same gender." She leans against the fence surrounding us and sighs. "Aie. That hurt a lot."

"So, does this mean you're going back to being a superhero?"

"What? Of course not! This was a chance encounter, I had no choice. All the other heroes were missing in action. It will not happen again," she breathes and leans her head against the fence. "This was a one-time sort of thing. It will not happen again," she repeats herself and shovels through her bag. Her fingers pull out a rectangular shaped object. She taps phone and sighs. "I hope I don't have any internal bleeding."

"What exactly happened?" I ask her.

"I came to Paris and then you threw me into a building then Sage tried to drown me then you broke my leg and now, I have a black eye. It has been a very eventful day," she sighs. "I just want to sleep forever."

I walk over and sit beside her.

"So, the loophole for the Prophecy?" I ask her.

"I don't know what to think anymore. It has a will to survive. It created a shield to protect me from bullets without my asking so. It's clearly sentient." She stares at her hand.

Sage flies up behind us and says something in French before taking Corbelle away in her arms.

"Adieu, Tonnerre. May we never meet again," Corbelle mutters as Sage flies away.

Maya

Rikki has seen better days. I've never seen her this broken. I took her straight to the hospital after putting her and I in some respectable clothes. The nurses told me to wait for her outside of the room until she was conscious again. I don't know what surgeries they did but I know it helped her somehow.

I walk into the room and immediately get hit by its plainness. I throw the curtains open and sunlight spills onto Rikki's hospital bed.

"What are you doing?" Rikki groans and shields her eyes from the sudden light that looks just like hers. Her leg is propped up over the sheets and put in a cast.

"You've been asleep for two days. What were you thinking?" I try to take a deep breath and think but I can't. This idiot risked her life for something I could have handled. "You could have died! You almost did, Rikki!"

She blinks at me and sighs. "Maya, I'm fine. See? I'm as high as a plane now, I don't feel anything!"

"That doesn't change anything! You had internal bleeding! They had to cut you open, Rikki! How do you think that makes me feel? You're my best friend. I can't lose you."

"You didn't lose me, I'm right here," She giggles drowsily. She's too high to have a serious conversation.

"You are such an idiot," I groan and hold my elbows. "Does anyone else know you're here?"

"I don't know." She smiles like an idiot that just got beaten to a pulp. "I don't really care."

Rikki

I'm doomed to spend the next few days in the hospital until my stitches heal. After that, I'll have to wait another two weeks before they can take off my cast. It's already been two weeks. Merry Christmas everyone. Happy holidays. Of course, since my real mother has no idea where I am for good reason, and I don't know any other members of my family, I'm alone.

It's snowing out the window and most of the doctors and nurses are hanging out in the children's ward with the kids who have some sort of belief. There's no crime, no monsters, no heroes. They all have families. I'm the curly haired orphan of the group.

I sigh and close my eyes.

Jingle bells ring through the hallway as something solid hits the edge of my bed.

"If this is some sort of Christmas thing, I don't want to be part of it!" I yell and open my eyes. A tiny, porcelain white box wrapped with red ribbon and finished with a golden bell sits lopsidedly by my feet.

I look around carefully and pick it up. This is just weird. Santa can't be real, right?

My fingers grab the ribbon and tug it off. I open the lid carefully and peer inside just to make sure there's not a bomb in it. There isn't. I let go of the breath I was holding and fully open the package. There's a silver croissant necklace in it.

"What?" I look around the room again and pull the necklace out. It's actually a tiny little croissant attached to a silver chain. Who in their right mind would get me this?

I sigh and tie it against my neck. I look back in the box for anything else. I look in the lid for a note. Scrawled in the white paper opposite to the bow are a few recognizable characters.

'I hope our paths croissant again.' That's actually a decent pun. I could really go for a croissant right now.

***

All that's changed since yesterday is that a nurse came in and put on an English movie for me before rushing off for more Christmas stuff. It stars a giant furry green guy who hates Christmas and terrorizes a village of smaller furry beings. It's a little confusing but it reminds me of high school for some reason.

Anyway, the green dude tries to ruin Christmas for all the mini-furries and then he almost does but then the true spirit happens in the village and makes his heart grow. Then, he celebrates Christmas with them. At the beginning, when the dude hated Christmas I was actually really touched that there was finally a character in a Christmas movie that doesn't actually like Christmas. Of course, they just couldn't have a character like that so at the end, he was all like 'Yay! Christmas, everyone!'

I groan and look out the window and the fresh snow. I can't wait to leave this place tomorrow. Everything is suspiciously white and in the middle of the night there are always noises. I swear, it's like they're trying to cover up a zombie outbreak.

Maya said she was going to try and see me today and give me some Warriors of the World gossip. I could really use a pick me up. They took me off most of the medication so I'm stuck in this hospital cot with paper thin blankets.

Someone knocks on the wooden door to my room.

"Come in!" I yell as I try to drown myself in a pillow.

Maya walks in and looks around. "Ugh, this place is so bland." She drops her bags filled with designer clothes and drops down onto the black seat beside my bed.

"Good morning," I mutter and drop the pillow.

"It's three o'clock in the afternoon."

"Oh. Well, good afternoon, then." I try to sit up and look at the clock on the bureau opposite to my bed.

"What are you doing? You need to stay down and heal." She grabs me and forces me back down onto my bed.

"I'm fine."

"Rikki, you had two surgeries and a cast. You are not fine," she hisses at me. "You almost died like, seven times. I could have killed you."

"But you didn't. I'm right here and I'm alive, see?" I wriggle my fingers at her frowning makeup.

"I found you in a pool of blood. You fell unconscious in my arms. Do you have any idea how scary that was?" Tears start to fall down Maya's cheeks thickly.

"I'm sorry, really, Maya, I'm sorry. I thought I could save everyone but I couldn't and I got really hurt, as you can see," I groan, frustrated. "I'm just really sorry, I never meant for it to go that far. I thought it would be easy like just punching her and solving the problem."

"But it wasn't."

"Yeah, you got me there. She did do most of the punching, she's got a pretty strong hit," I sigh. "But hey! Look on the bright side, aside from my leg, I'm completely healed! Even my stiches are gone."

Maya laughs and wipes away her tears. "Are you ready to get out of this terrible place since you're completely healed?"

"I don't get released until tomorrow," I sigh. "I think they plan on keeping me her forever."

"Don't be so sure about that. It wasn't hard to bribe the receptionist to let me in so it won't be extremely hard for them to let me take you a day early. Besides, it's not like you're immediately dying, right?"

"I sure hope not."

"Good, change into some of these and I'll wheel you out."

***

Maya wheels me out of the hospital in a wheelchair.

"Uh, excuse me?" One of the nurses chases after us. "You can't actually take a wheelchair. It's only a temporary thing. We've got crutches for you, though." He passes me two metal sticks and shivers underneath Maya's stone cold glare.

"Fine," she mutters as she picks me up from the chair and grabs the crutches. After the guy leaves hurriedly away with the wheelchair, she puts me back down and hands me the crutches.

"Aw, for me? You're so sweet." I fit my armpits onto them and awkwardly try to balance.

378

"It's so surreal to see you as both Corbelle and Rikki Dubois. I don't think I'll ever get used to it."

"Just imagine how it feels to be me. I feel like screaming all the time."

"And don't forget the puns. Those things are truly terrible."

"What? I thought I was really punny!" I frown at her excessively.

"Please, do everyone a favour and keep your massive mouth shut," she tells me and pulls me into a coffee shop. The bell on the door rings as we walk in. Maya pushes me down into a seat at a table and props my cast up on another chair. After that, she walks up to the barista and brings us two drinks.

"Don't think this is an excuse to do everything for me because once this cast is off, I'm going to use my awesome puns non-stop and I'll do anything I want."

"Rikki, your leg is broken. The cast isn't coming off for another few weeks even with all the special treatments and antibiotics or whatever they're giving you, your leg will still be broken. You can't do anything to change it."

I take a long gulp of my coffee and frown.

"How can you drink that? It's like drinking liquid dirt." She winces and looks away. "It's disgusting."

"Actually, it's called mud and it's delicious." I take an even longer sip and rub it in her face. She sticks her tongue out and grimaces.

"Whatever. It's still disgusting."

"If that's what you want to believe." I smile. "So, what's the scoop on the Warriors of the World? It's been a while since I've really pissed Maverick off."

"Oh no, she's steaming about how you singlehandedly beat Reine Blanche. The break room is practically destroyed," Maya laughs as she drinks some more of her coffee. "Everyone's angry at you except for me, really."

"That's good."

"Yeah, and it turns out we'll be staying here for a while since everyone thinks you're staying in Paris!"

"I *am* staying in Paris."

"Rikki, you can't be serious." She drops her drink and looks at me seriously. "You almost died here. Reine Blache and a dozen other villains including the Warriors of the World are out to spill your guts and you think you can stay here?"

"It's not like they'll expect me, my leg is broken. I can't do any parkour for a few more weeks."

"A few weeks is not enough. Do you really think they'll just stop after what? Two weeks?"

"Three weeks. The treatments aren't that fast."

"Speaking of which, it's not like you're made of money. How can you afford that?"

"Willow thought it was her fault I 'fell off a building' so she decided to pay for my expensive, advanced healthcare."

"You went with that? Did she really think you fell of a building?"

"Well, technically I did. Plus, I quickly changed the subject."

"Why did she think it was her fault?"

"That's exactly what I thought. I asked her and she gave me the whole speech about how she should have been looking out for me and everything. Honestly, I think she's up to something. After I found out who Tonnerre was-"

"You know who Tonnerre is?"

"Maya, shut up! This is a public area!" I yell at her before switching to a whisper. "Yes, I know who he is. Didn't you guys have that 'initiation' where you all took your masks off?"

"Yeah, but not tall, blonde, and brooding. He just stood in the corner and contemplated his little rich boy problems. Wait, is he rich?"

"Oh yeah, very rich." I nod vigorously.

"And handsome?"

***

Happy New Year, everyone. It's already time for me to go back to school. It's pretty underwhelming. I sigh and struggle to mount the stairs on my crutches.

Once I make it to class and sit down, I shut my eyes tightly.

"It's good to have you back." Kai smiles at me from the desk beside me. "Despite your current situation." He points at my cast with a frown.

"It was a rather unfortunate accident. I fell off a wild moose in New York while riding it through the streets in style."

"But how else would one ride a moose through the many streets of New York?"

"That's exactly what I said after they told me I was no longer allowed to ride them. It's a shame those Americans don't understand our culture." I look at the front of the classroom with a faraway look before breaking down in a fit of laughter with him.

"And how have you been aside from the obvious?"

"It was a little difficult and then I shattered my leg so I can't say I've been doing very well. How has it been trying to avoid your brother?"

"He won't stop being dramatic about it! It's killing me," he groans. "Whenever he walks into a classroom after me he just stands there and says 'Oh. You're here.' like he doesn't remember we have the same classes!"

"That seems like a special hell."

"Oh, it is."

Kaden walks in and looks right at both of us for a second like we should say something. I look over at Kai for a response but he only groans.

"Oh. You're here," Kaden mutters just loud enough for everyone in the classroom to stop and stare at us with him.

"Really? Which TV drama did you get that from?" I start laughing wildly and knock my crutches over. Kai looks at me for a second then joins my fit of laughter.

Kaden just stands there for second and takes his place at the front of the classroom.

"Don't think for a second I'm not angry at you two for using Achelium though," I mutter gravelly in Kai's ear so only he can hear.

I drop his ear and return back to my desk and twiddle my thumbs. Maya walks up to my desk herself and blabbers a bit about this and that (mainly about fashion so I sort of tuned out).

The teacher walks in and sends Maya flying to her seat. She nods at me and focuses on the rest of the class.

"Everyone, settle down!" she yells at the class. "Now, we have some special announcements today. First of all, let's all welcome Rikki back from New York." The class just groans and accepts me again as a background character.

Andrew

I step into the dimly lit warehouse to find they've been waiting for me.

"You're late," Willow hisses as she slides her white mask off.

"Well, sorry, it just takes a while to fly here to the outskirts from the center of Paris," I mutter.

"Perhaps it'd be easier if you lived closer to us and maybe, just once in a while, stuck to our plans!" She takes a step closer and starts to lurch towards me.

"Maybe if your plans didn't-"

"Ugh, both of you, shut up!" Mom groans angrily and massages her forehead. "Listening to you two is like scraping nails against a chalkboard."

We both shut up flawlessly.

"Thank god, now, Andrew, would you like to tell us exactly why you couldn't follow through with our mind-numbingly easy plan I made with you in mind," Mom says as she looks at me harshly, her voice full of disappointment.

"I-I couldn't stand just using her like that. Couldn't we have just, I don't know, just taken blood from her while she was sleeping?"

"Oh, I'm sorry, Andrew, that is *such* a great plan! Now, why didn't we think of that? Wrong, idiot. How would we know where she sleeps?" Willow spits. She's always tried too hard to be the favourite child.

"Both of you, shut your insolent mouths! Willow, I didn't ask you for your opinion. I asked your brother's. So, Andrew why exactly could you not follow our plan? The one in which we'd show her what I could do which would make her realise how powerful I was and how I could take over the planet with or without her help."

"But we can't anymore because-" Willow stammers and looks at me to take the fall for her.

"Because you lost the wand. If you hadn't and if your brother had followed through with the plan, we could have taken control of her and used her blood and convert it into pure power."

"Well, with the tests the Warriors of the World did, they were able to turn some of the samples into energy but not all of them-" I try to lead them away from the concept of draining all her blood since when I did it with the Warriors, not all of it worked. If none of it works, we would have killed her for nothing.

"Are you comparing me to the Warriors? Those guys are total idiots!" Willow whines at me.

"Shut up! Would you two let me finish?" Mom snaps. "Finally. Anyway, because of your stupidity, I'm looking at both you now." Willow gapes at Mom's words. "We lost that chance to peacefully take her and now we have to go through with plan B which is significantly more gruesome. Andrew, if you had stuck to our plan, she would have died thinking she was a hero which now, she won't. She'll think of you as a traitor. Don't get angry at me for this, after all, it's your fault." She smooths down her suit and walks out of the warehouse with Willow trailing behind closely.

I look over at the wide glass tank. That's where she's going to be kept.

Rikki

Well, I survived my first day back at school. You know what the worst pain I've actually suffered is? Worse than breaking all my bones, being beaten, and bleeding out? Stubbing my toe. That is the worst pain anyone could possibly feel. Forget giving birth and being burnt alive, stubbing your toe is by far the worst suffering one can experience. The reason I bring that up because somehow, I managed to do just that with my other foot.

I sigh and sit in my chair which I've angled to look out my window. Now that I'm finally back in Paris, it's so weird adjusting to the regular time. There's also the trouble with trying to ignore the sudden urges to jump out my window and race across the rooftops in the dark. To make sure I wouldn't escape prematurely, Maya actually locked my window from the outside. She knew I'd find a way to pick it from the inside so she flew up to my window and deadbolted the outside of it. I even tried to pick it from the inside but my needle flew out the window into the dark streets. I'm almost at the point in which I just take a rock to it. Then I'm reminded I'm wearing a massive cast and that the only way I can walk is with two giant metal sticks. I have never been this bored.

I rattle my window as a last-ditch effort to pop it open but it just shivers smugly. I yell a few French swears at it before collapsing back into my chair. I pick up my phone and stare at it blankly until it buzzes in my open palm. My finger presses the green messages button. Tonnerre tried to send me another message through Maya. I groan and drop my phone on my bed.

"Why doesn't that idiot understand?" I sigh and look at my phone like it's the source of all my problems. "It's *so* simple." He wants me to meet with me to talk about my 'situation'. What is this? The fifth time? The fourth? Obviously, it's been about four times too many but it's not like I've been following what I've been preaching. I went out as a hero and saved all of Paris and what do I have to show for it? A white cast. I even asked them to print dogs on it or something instead, they gave me a boring white one.

The power buzzes through my finger and explodes at its tip. It's so strange. I've been trying so hard to suppress it but it keeps rising through my barriers. It's like the poppies on Flander's field. From what I've read about and picked apart from the Prophecy and the Book is that I'll be in control of this power when I turn seventeen which is basically the magic number. There's a lot of weird things I've found out from the Book. Like apparently, humans were too busy fighting with each other to actually agree on a system of time so the Ancients, a now extinct group of super powerful aliens, came to Earth and made a deal with the populace. They offered peace between the planets and universes and ours if we joined their evil and good thing. It's universally known as good and evil or chaos and harmony. Our Earth's deal was that, when our time came, two people would take the mantle of Chaos and Harmony and balance out the universe. Me, being chaos and evil and Harmony being well... harmony and good.

Speaking of the book, I sort of stole it from the Monastery on my last visit. I've filled my new sketchbook with all sorts of summarised info about it. I can't say it's been extremely helpful, though. It hasn't given me any information on the power and why it's been surging. Now, all it takes is a sudden movement for it to explode out of my fingertips.

I sigh and stand up slowly and carefully. I hobble over to my desk and throw all the books to the side other than the book of Chaos and Harmony and my own rendition of it. I flip it open and read one of my summarised paragraphs out loud.

"Chaos is the evil in everything and Harmony is the good. They fight a lot and Harmony usually always wins aside from those two times when it didn't. Also, they both can open up portals between dimensions and universes and also into the Infinity." I'm a villain who always loses. I sigh and slam the book shut. I've been to the Infinity. There's not a lot to see there. Just three crazy ladies with six arms each.

***

Tonnerre's been sending me hundreds of messages once again through Maya. At some point, I started to wonder whether he had killed her just for her phone. It's not completely unheard of. Hopefully, Maya gave up a pretty good fight before passing on.

Every time he tries to call me or message me I press the red button and eat some of the chips out of the bag I've piled on my desk. I've made a game up. I call it 'How long can I ignore Tonnerre?' I'm winning so far though I have read a few of his texts.

'We need to talk now'

"About what?" I want to yell in his ear and into his small brain. "What is there left to talk about? Haven't I made my situation crystal clear?"

I cram a few more chips in my mouth while my phone buzzes (every time it buzzes, I eat more chips and it goes like that for what is going to be an eternity). I continue to watch the movie playing on my laptop and try to ignore my phone.

"Hey, Rikki," Willow walks into my room, still oblivious to the common courtesy of knocking.

"What's up, Willow?" I ask her in English. I don't even bother to glance at her. My movie is at its climax. The clown is about to murder the gang of little kids.

"I was wondering if you had that redhead's number." She walks around my room and looks for my phone. It buzzes on my bed and she picks it up quickly.

"Maya?"

"Is that her name? Also, what's your password?"

"It's two-two-five-five-three-eight."

"Who keeps texting you? Your phone's buzzing like every three seconds." She nearly drops it as it vibrates in her palms.

"Just someone who cannot take a hint for some reason."

"Can't. Not cannot."

"He can't take a hint for some reason."

"Good. Hey, is this Maya texting you?"

"Something like that. It's annoyingly complicated. Are you going to ask her on a date?" I press the spacebar on my laptop and spin around in my chair to face her.

"Yeah, she's pretty cute even though I can't speak French."

"Please don't bring me along as a translator. In the presence of love, I break out in dangerous amounts of sarcasm."

"Please? I'll owe you a massive favour!"

"Willow, I am not a third-wheel. Please, don't make me go on a date that's not even mine."

"Please, Rikki! I promise I'll make it up to you! I'll get you a date with my brother!"

"What? No! Do not! I do *not* want that. If you make sure I'll *never* have to see your brother again, I'll do the date thing!" I drop my bag of chips and press my hands together like a prayer.

"Sure! That shouldn't be a problem! Now, can you show me how to text Maya in French? I'm kind of in a rush. It's a family emergency."

***

Maya walks over to me as I mount the steps of our school on my crutches.

"You know, I can just carry you all the way to class, right?" Maya offers and she nudges me.

"Oh, I know. You can if you want, too. Of course, I'll just start kicking, screaming, and making puns so it might benefit you not to carry me to class. You should probably just *carry* on."

"Once your leg heals, I'm going to break it again."

"Sure! I'll add you to the list," I chirp happily. "I've already got one as long as Santa's!"

"I believe that." She looks around the schoolyard as she holds the door open wide for me. She pulls her fingers through her caramel hair and loosens the expensive scarf digging into her neck.

"Thank you, my dear lady. We're going on a date soon, aren't we? Well, you and Willow. I'm just the translator. I can picture the next bestselling romance novel." I spread my elbows out in a rainbow carefully to make sure I don't fall on the linoleum again. "*One speaks French, the other, English. They overcame their barriers and finally came together.*"

"Tonnerre keeps asking about you."

I stop in my crutches. "Not this again," I sigh. "He keeps trying to text me."

"Yeah, I know. He keeps grabbing my phone and flying into the sky. I'm surprised he can even get service up there."

"What does he want, now? To talk? Can't he understand that I don't want to be a superhero anymore? I mean, you do. How hard is it for him?"

"From what he's been saying it's pretty serious."

"How serious? Did he forget the periodic table and he needs it to disable a chemical triggered bomb planted in the centre of the Earth that could extinguish all life on Earth?" I ask her with a sigh.

"Nothing that serious but it's got something to do with his secret identity apparently."

"What? What do you mean?" I ask her as she holds the door to the Science room open for me.

"His real name. He didn't say much but he said it involved his name. Knowing you, I thought you would classify that as serious. He said he needed your help because you know his already."

"Not to mention I have an unlimited superpower."

"I guess there's that." Maya rolls her eyes. "So, are you going to help him?"

"Do you think I'm in any condition to run around in the middle of the night?" I balance on one leg and use my crutches to point at my cast with a frown. "Do you have any idea how difficult it is to change a sleep schedule once you've gotten used to having more than four hours of sleep each night?"

"Come on, Rikki. Are you seriously just going stick up your nose and ignore the fact that everything of his is at stake?"

"I didn't say I wouldn't do anything though it's not like you'll let me run around. I'll investigate, obviously. Did you think that all I had was a pretty face?"

"I wouldn't say it could be considered pretty, yet." She grabs my chin and looks me in the eyes. "What are you actually going to do?"

"I'm going to respond to his texts which he sent using your phone and then I'll see if it's really serious." I sit down in my bench and

Maya sits in hers and brushes her hair behind her shoulder. Kaden moved to Lilith's bench to get away from me.

"And if it is?"

"Maya, there's not a ton I can do while wearing a cast."

"It's getting taken off next week. After that, you'll be fine. You can go and play Romeo and Juliet with him and see what's the matter. Problem solved."

"He's not my Romeo," I sigh, annoyed.

***

I frown as I text him using Maya's number. After I send it, I groan and throw it on my bed. I recline in my chair and sigh long and terribly. It buzzes a few seconds later with his response. I pick up my phone begrudgingly and look at it.

"A supervillain found out my identity and is threatening to sell it the world's governments." I read out loud as my phone buzzes again. "I really need your help. Can I trust you?" I sigh and type my response in right before I flip open my laptop. I type the keyboard slowly at first as I open my internet browser and then launch some of my hacking programs and codes. I launch my 'invisi-mode' so my IP address can't be traced back to my Wi-Fi address. I crack open the darknet and check for any superhero identity listings. There are some B-list heroes' names so I cut them out quickly and send a rather nasty virus to the dude who posted them. I crunch on some old chips and put some more keywords into my search. There's nothing on Tonnerre. No one knows his real name aside from me. I check 'Andrew Smithe' one last time before shutting the lid of my laptop. He was lying to me.

I sigh angrily and type a rather nasty message to Tonnerre and throw my phone on my bed. He responds seconds later with a hearty *What are you talking about?'*

I don't bother typing or picking up my phone. I start shouting French swears at my phone and lie on my bed in a heap.

"Why does this always happen to me?" I sigh. My phone buzzes by my open hand with his response. I mumble a few more swears and pick my phone back up.

'Can we meet? I feel more comfortable talking to you in person.'

I throw my hands up and then throw them down at my white cast now dotted with signatures and then grab my phone. I click my tongue and send him a very strong *no*. I hop over to my window and start beating the shutters with my fists. I just want to have some fresh air to clear my thought. Or maybe I'll just jump out the window. That could work too.

My fingers pull the handle of the scissors on my desk and I arm myself with them against the window. I stab the lock from the inside until I hear a satisfying thunk as the lock falls to the bottom of the dumpster. I throw my window open a take a deep breath of the night air.

"That feels so much better," I hum to the wind and balance my torso out of the window. "Now I can think." I grab my phone and tell him to just tell what the matter is. My cast is coming off in a few days. After that, I can meet with him if it's really this serious.

"So, I see you've beaten my lock," Maya mumbles as she sticks her masked head in my window and looks around my room. "That was a good lock, you know."

"It was nothing compared to my mighty scissors. Your lock just didn't make the *cut*."

"Your room decor is really terrible, you know. My eyes are burning just looking at it. I thought with Willow around, she would help improve your terrible lifestyle."

"Well, having a super-rich, super girly roommate is surprisingly difficult. Especially when balancing a double life."

"I thought you said you were done with that which brings me to why I came here, what's going to go down with the whole 'Chaos' thing?" Maya asks patiently from outside and just below my window.

If my life were an anime, the background behind me would crack in half.

Maya

Rikki stutters uncomfortably and teeters around in her distasteful bedroom. It reminds me of a public bathroom.

"So, does Tonnerre have your phone because my phone is still buzzing with messages from you," Rikki laughs awkwardly.

"I let him borrow it because he was being really whiny about texting you and- Hey!" I stop and look her right in her yellow eyes. "Are you avoiding my question?"

"Maya, I don't want to talk about that right now or, come to think about it, ever." She presses her lips tightly together.

"Didn't you say you had a loophole? Is it working?"

"I've already got Tonnerre asking about it. I don't need you trying to find out my secrets too."

"But Rikki, when are you going to talk about it? I barely know anything about you!"

"So, is this about not knowing me very well because if it is, I can tell you things about me so long as they don't have anything to do with the Prophecy." Yellow energy swirls around her tightly closed fists and sprints up her arms all the way up to her elbows.

"I'm worried, all right? When I first met you I just thought you a were an average kid. Poor parents, greasy hair, ugly clothes. Now, that I know you a little more, *none* of that is true. You have the most powerful energy running through your veins, your mom is in jail, and you can flip off of walls without even using powers! I think I'd like to know a little bit about you like, I don't know, what jail is your mom in?"

"Jail? My mom's not in jail." Rikki scrunches her nose up but maintains a frown.

"You told me that your mom was in jail. That she was an international thief and you turned her in."

"What? I didn't- I mean, yes, I did! She was a terrible mother. Really terrible. Left my father and took me away from the rest of my happy family and then she turned me into a little thief so, I turned her in. Ha-ha mother, you lose again!"

"I'm not as stupid as you think I am."

"Okay, fine. My mom's still out there probably robbing some rich guy. Is that what you wanted?"

"That's not all, is it? Rikki, I'm not going to force you to tell me. If you don't want to tell me anything, you don't have to. I just want to make sure you're safe."

"I'm safe. I know to knockout someone in like, fifteen different ways plus, like you said, I have the most powerful energy running through my veins. Trust me, I know how to use it."

"Yeah, I've seen you use it. It's kind terrifying but in a good way. I think."

"Oh no, terrifying is a perfect way to describe it," she laughs as the bright yellow clouds disappear from her arms. I laugh with her while carefully eyeing the power as it floats beside her.

"Just let me know if you want to talk about anything surrounding your power. I'm all ears to whatever you have to say about your prophecy." Her power seems to hazily take the loose shape of a yellow, hissing fox before moulding back into a yellow cloud at her shoulder.

"No, it's alright. I'll be fine."

I look at the power which seems to grin smugly at me from its post on her bare shoulder. "No. It isn't. You're not 'fine' are you?" The power watches me closely as I speak.

"Why does it matter to you?" She turns to me gravely. "You're not my mother. Why should you care?"

"Rikki, I don't care if I'm your mother or not. The fact is that you're not taking care of yourself and someone needs to do it for you. Willow doesn't. Tonnerre doesn't. Your own mother doesn't. *I* do."

"Why do people keep telling me I need to be taken care of? I'm sixteen! I don't need to be spoken to like a toddler! I know what I can do and what I can't. Please, stop asking me about this! Tonnerre peppers me with questions all the time and I hate it! I don't need two people always following me around wondering about a stupid prophecy!" She grabs her head and starts messing up her hair.

"*Everything* is going wrong and no one understands!" Something cracks in her room.

"What was that?" I fly in and look around for some broken glass or something.

"Oh no," Rikki breathes quietly. "I broke my cast."

Rikki

My cast broke off and my leg is fine. Better than fine actually. It's perfectly healed. Whatever magic science Willow bought for me really worked. It still feels a little funny when I stand on it but it's not like I've been vaulting off of it for a few weeks so it's a little weak. Maya made me promise to go to the doctor in the morning but she didn't say anything about not scurrying around the Parisian rooftops. I've even been slowly building up its strength at school by jumping off various heights and jumping up walls. I'll have to stay out of her patrol because if she finds me running around in my costume she'll definitely do whatever she can to keep me indoors and I don't want her to go and break it again.

My smoke grey scarf curls around my neck and the collar of my costume and the silver croissant necklace. I pull my mask on and throw myself out my window. I fall into the wind like a rock before grabbing onto the metal roof of a smaller building and bouncing onto solid ground. That hurt but it was a good pain.

I promised myself I wouldn't do this but I also promised myself I wouldn't use the power. I knew I couldn't stop the prophecy. The Fates knew I couldn't. The power has a mind of its own. It doesn't want to be suppressed and how can I try to stop something like it? It's the most powerful thing ever and I'm in charge of it. I can't help but relate this to being Corbelle. It's part of me. How can I try to hide who I am?

I check my phone to make sure I'm going in the right direction. I agreed to talk with Tonnerre tonight. He keeps on insisting on how important it is that we talk about whatever's going on with him. He asked me to meet him at a warehouse on the edge of town, a little farther even. I've never been so there's no chance I can teleport. I'm pretty sure it's near where I saw Reine Blanche that time before she mind-controlled all of Paris and broke my leg and gave me a now healed black eye.

A light blue blur whizzes past me and practically leaves me spinning around on my toes.

"And here I thought birds flew in the sky." Kai grins from behind his thin mask.

"I thought idiots kept to the names strictly in their vocabulary."

"What? Velocity is an English name! What's the big deal?"

"It's a pretty stupid name, even in English."

"It's a reference to an American comic! There's a guy with super-speed and he saves his city and his name's Velocity."

"And that's where you got your name?"

"Uh, yeah."

"What? You got to choose your name? I didn't get to choose my name! How is that fair!" I yell as I run off towards the old warehouses. He stares at the back of my head as I run away. I get to the edge of the roof before screeching to the stop. "How do you even get on the roofs?" He already left. I guess that's one of the perks of super-speed. I wish I had super-speed. It seems pretty cool to be able to beat someone at a race.

I flip off the roof and latch onto a balcony. I spring off its fencing and repeat it until I get to the top of the building. Probably an apartment complex. My little pager/phone beeps at the side of me. I throw my Diamond up and catch it to see what's wrong. It doesn't usually beep, it makes more of a 'blep' sound. The tracker I put on Maya (don't you judge me) is moving this way *very* quickly. I look behind me at Maya as he flies at me. I Jump over her head and launch off her back and land safely on the roof.

"What are you doing out here? And why are you wearing that?" she yells at me as she turns around and skids across the metallic roofing until she stops.

"I can explain!" I throw my arms up between us. "But you need to calm down first."

"You're out in the middle of the night meeting Tonnerre at a warehouse on the outskirts of town wearing a completely black costume. Am I missing anything?"

"... Actually, that's pretty accurate. Did you check your messages?"

"I checked my messages." She holds up her phone in my face.

I snap my fingers together and grin. "Well, I guess that explains that." I start walking towards the next roof but she grabs me by the collar and holds me up to her eye level.

"You're going back home, now," she insists.

"But, Sage-"

"Don't you 'but, Sage' me! You're going home right now!"

"I can't! It's really important! It's about his secret identity and he needs my help!"

"So? You're going in the middle of the night, alone! How am I supposed to allow you to do that?"

"Maya, I can handle myself!" I kick her chest and handspring over to the edge of the roof. "I'm a superhero." I fall through a portal and land closer to the border of Paris.

Andrew

Corbelle gasps for air as she mounts the side of the old warehouse.

"That was quite the workout," she breathes out as she keels over and tries to catch her breath. "Why was it so important that we met here? Couldn't we have met at our usual spot? I would even have gone to San Francisco. Or maybe not."

"It's important."

"I really hope it is. I mean, it's got to be if you wanted to meet this far away from Paris. Do you have any idea how hard it is to jump from tree to tree?"

I look at her in response and she continues.

"Neither did I until I did. It is very, very difficult to jump from tree to tree." She looks at me for the littlest response but I don't move. "Is something wrong?"

"Don't mess this up," Mom hisses through the communicator she made me put in my ear. "You've worked so hard for this. You can't turn back now."

"No, nothing's wrong. I'm fine. How are you?" I wipe the monotone look off my face and try to put on a smile.

"If nothing's wrong, then why are we meeting here?"

"No, yeah, there's something wrong. A-"

"An international terrorist has found out your identity and plans on auctioning it off to the highest bidder," Mom whispers in my ear.

"An international terrorist has found out my identity and plans on auctioning it off to the highest bidder," I stammer at her annoyance clearly displayed by her black mask, hood and scarf.

"Yes, you said that over the messages. I checked the darknet and there wasn't anything regarding you or your real name. However," She looks me right in the eyes. "There was an add posted for 'people who have no life purpose' who were offered the chance to become 'superheroes'. I tracked the link back to your family's website. Would you like to explain that?"

"She's good," Mom remarks. "Tell her this: I don't know what my father's trying to do but with your help, we can beat him together."

"I don't know what my father's trying to do but with your help, we can beat him together," I say obediently and offer Corbelle my hand. She looks at it silently and brings her arm up to her chin thoughtfully.

"Fine." She grabs it and shakes my hand.

"Now, take her to the trapdoor," Mom orders.

"Quickly, you need to follow me. Someone could be listening." I latch onto her wrist and drag her over the hidden wooden panel the warehouse's roof that would drop her into the tank of formaldehyde and water.

"What are you doing? I don't need you leading me around like a dog," she mutters and snaps her wrist away from my hand and walks off the trap door.

"Don't let her escape! Hit her if you need to!" Mom yells in my ear nearly making me go deaf.

"Corbelle, stop! It's dangerous!"

"It's dangerous? Every waking moment of my life is danger. I think I can handle a few wild cats. In fact, I'd prefer spending time with them instead of you when you're like this."

"I'm not moody!" I yell as I smash my foot down on the roof. It breaks the old wood but not the new metal underneath.

"Wait..." She walks up to me and looks at the dented metal. "This is supposed to be an empty warehouse. There shouldn't be any metal in it." She looks at me critically for a second before realising why we're here.

"You idiot!" Mom screams in my ear. "You've ruined everything! I knew I should have left this to your sister!"

"The Fates were right." Corbelle breathes as she falls to the ground. "They said I was going to die at the hands of a Smithe."

"Corbelle, I'm not going to hurt you," I try to falsely reassure her. She stands up quickly as I take a step towards her. She lifts her fists up between us as they fire up with yellow energy.

"Stay away from me!" she shouts. Tears start streaming down her cheeks. "I don't want to die! I can't!"

"Hit her!" Mom yells. "Prove to me you're not a disappointment like your father!"

I grab a rock on the roof before I can think. I don't need my thoughts to tell me not to when Mom says I should.

"Please, Andrew!" She creates a shield as I fly up into the air. I collide against it with my legs and her concentration is broken as easily as I broke her leg. The rock in my hand collides with the top of her head and she falls to the ground, blood streaming down her face.

"Stop fooling around! Put her in the tank!" Mom shrieks. "Drown her!"

I grab her by the neck and bring her to the trap door which opens with an aged creak. Her tears and blood drip down my arm as I throw her in the vat of water and poison. It's going to be her watery coffin.

Her body splashes in and sinks to the bottom elegantly. She doesn't even look up at me as the doors slowly close.

Rikki

A new light appears just as the one above me disappears. I'm drowning quickly and painfully. I try to hold my breath and swim to the surface but the water is spinning and spinning so even if I knew how to swim, I'd still drown. This can't be how it ends. I can't drown. I can't die. I'm only sixteen.

I look over at the other light which illuminates a stainless steel lab like the white hospital except ten times scarier. Willow and her mother along with a dozen scientists watch me flail about in the whirlpool. I pound against the glass and try to scream. Mrs. Smithe nods at a few scientists and all the white lab coats walk away leaving just Willow and herself. Andrew walks up to them solemnly and it hits me. They're all in this together. This was their plan from the start.

I watch my air bubbles spin upwards and upwards until their shapes mould into the faces of the Fates. They grin at me.

"We told you so," they say eerily together. "Welcome to The Infinity, Carmen Dubois."

My world turns black and it finally sets in. I'm dying. But I'm not going to become-

Andrew

The light in her eyes fades quickly and the horror on her face relaxes softly. She's gone now. The thing bobbing around in the water with its blood staining the water is nothing but an empty husk that used to be human.

"It was fun playing with it while it lasted," Willow hums as she watches the tank with her arms crossed. "It's a shame we had to kill her. She was a real powerhouse"

"I had to kill her. You sat around and did nothing," I hiss at her as I rip my mask off my face.

"There's no 'her' after all, you killed her and I sat around and did nothing," Willow chirps happily.

"You-"

"Shut up, both of you." And that's that. Not another word under mother's watch. "Come, Willow. There's still work *we* need to do." She drags Willow to the lab to convert Corbelle's power into a *real* weapon.

I want to be left alone. I can't tell if this is a nightmare or if it's real. My hands won't stop shaking. The hands that killed an orphan. The hands that killed the girl I loved. The most terrifying thing about it is that I don't even feel sad. I don't feel anything. I'm just... here and she's... in there. Dead. It's over. It's really over.

Water springs from my eyes as I watch its blood spin through the water.